INTO *the* STORM

MELANIE MORELAND

All characters and events in this publication, other than those clearly in the public domain, are fictitious and any resemblance to real persons, living or dead, is purely coincidental.

Cover Design: Mayhem Cover Creations

Interior Formatting: Mayhem Cover Creations

Editing : Emma Stephen

ISBN : 978-0-9936198-0-9

DEDICATION

This book is dedicated to Kate.

For her friendship, her encouragement and her belief this had to happen. Without her, my dream would have remained where it was ... a whisper I was too scared to listen to. She screamed it for me.

Thank you my friend. You mean so much.

⇒TABLE OF CONTENTS⇐

⇒ACKNOWLEDGMENTS⇐

To Liz, Sally and Trina. Thank you for your wisdom, support and eyes. You have read, encouraged, and been great friends and this would not have happened without you.

Deb – what started out as a common interest, blossomed into a friendship which is a great gift to my life. Your support is always there. Thank you for being you.

My online readers who asked for this – here you are. Thank you.

Holly—you stepped in and made this come alive. Your talent amazes me. Thank you.

And finally. To My Matthew.

My giver of love and the strong, safe place I call home. Nothing is complete until I share it with you – so here you are, my darling husband. I love you. Always.

⇒PROLOGUE⇐

The snow swirled around wildly in the fierce wind. I could hardly see in front of the car. I knew it wasn't safe and that I should pull over, but I had to get away. I needed to get as far away from there as possible. I shifted in the driver's seat trying to find some relief. The ache in my side, from being hit repeatedly, flared painfully again, the burn intense. The slight shift in my concentration made the car swerve on the icy road and I struggled to regain control.

I could feel the tears running down my face. My head ached. Everything ached. I was so tired; yet I had to keep going as I'd only been driving for a few hours. Was it three? Four? I had no idea at this point, but I hadn't gone nearly far enough. He would be able to find me with no trouble. I reached up and wiped away the moisture from my cheeks and winced as my hand came into direct contact with the bruised flesh.

So angry. He'd been so angry over something so utterly inconsequential. This time he'd lost control and hadn't stopped. Unlike the other times, these bruises would be visible for people to notice.

I shivered, remembering the one thing that had saved me from a worse beating; his iPhone had rung with his assistant's ringtone. That had snapped him out of his rage and he walked away, leaving me gasping in pain on the floor. When he returned, I was curled up in a ball with my knees sheltering my chest, trying to find the strength to stand up.

He grabbed my hair hard and pulled me up, causing short bursts of pain to resonate through my head. "I'll be back in a few hours and we'll finish this," he snarled, and then released me with a jerk. I heard him storm out the door, slamming it behind him, and I knew when he came back he would pick up right where he left off. Somehow, I found the strength to grab a few things and get to my car.

I knew I had to get away from him.

The storm that had been threatening all day hit when I was about half an hour outside the city. I had no idea where I was headed; just away. Now that the snow and wind had gotten so intense, I was one of the only cars on the highway. I wasn't sure how much longer I would be able to keep driving. My windshield wipers could barely keep the window cleaned off anymore, and I heard a harsh sob escape my lips in frustration. I slowed the car down but kept driving, needing as much distance between me and him as possible. I wondered if any distance would be far enough. I kept my eyes trained on the road, turning up the radio to help keep me awake.

The snow became increasingly heavy and I knew I would soon have to find a place to stay until it relented. With a heavy heart I knew I had driven as far as I could for now and I had to find a motel and pay cash. If I used my credit card, which was on his account, he would be able to trace it. I strained my eyes, trying to see if there was any place coming up ahead where I could pull off. I had stopped in a small town a short while back to fill up with gas and briefly I wondered if I should turn around and seek shelter there for the night.

Just then, I hit a patch of ice and the car swerved from side to side. I fought to gain control and finally came to a sudden stop in the middle of the road. After taking a few deep breaths, I looked around and had no idea which direction I was facing. After a few moments, I chose to keep heading in the direction I was pointed and prayed it was taking me away from, and not back to, the hell I was fleeing. I drove as quickly as I felt I could, considering the treacherous conditions. I came to what I thought was a fork in the road and followed it to the right. The road seemed to have gotten narrower and I hadn't seen a directional sign for a while, either. *Had I somehow strayed off the highway onto a smaller road when I spun out?*

Suddenly, the road took a sharp turn and I felt the car shudder as I tried to make the curve and stay on the slippery surface. But I was driving too fast and the back of the car fishtailed. I tried overcompensating, only to find myself in a complete skid heading swiftly for a tree. Desperately, I cranked the wheel but the car veered out of control and continued sliding. I felt the hard impact and a sudden sharp pain in my head, and then the world went black.

My eyes fluttered open; I wasn't behind the wheel anymore. I could hear movement, which meant I wasn't alone, either. I was so cold; so very, very cold, and I hurt…*everywhere*. I heard myself groan and my eyes shut again. Suddenly, there was a low, rugged voice somewhere close to my ear. "I've got you; you're okay." Although spoken quietly, the voice sounded displeased. I tried to speak, but all that came out was another small groan. Something wet was on my cheek. The sensation was rough, warm and wet. Something was licking me? I raised my hand and felt soft fur.

"Leave her alone, Bear!" the voice said in a sharp tone, now openly angry.

There was a funny hummphing noise and the licking stopped, but the fur came closer and I felt it settle beside my head, its warmth comforting. I tried raising my head, but the pain was too intense. There were more noises and the car felt like it had started to move at a slow pace, but I was unsure. Then the movement ceased and I felt arms come around me, lifting me. I gasped at the onslaught of pain, my eyes flying open as it tore through me. The last thing I saw before I passed out was a pair of intense ice-blue eyes staring at me, filled with confusion and resentment.

⇒Chapter One⇐

Joshua

Shutting the door behind me, I looked around. The wind was still fierce and now the heavy snow had joined in and I knew it was going to be an ugly night. Judging from what they said on the news, more ugly nights would follow. I slowly made my way to the barn to check on the generators, aware of the fact I would most likely lose power soon. Earlier, when the storm had started, I had opened the gates so I would be able to plow down the driveway to the road when the storm passed. Once I had built enough courage up, I would also plow out the road, so deliveries could get in. Then I would immediately shut the gates again. I was grateful I had a full delivery of groceries: supplies and liquor arrived only yesterday, so I wouldn't have to worry about anything while the rest of the world coped with the aftermath of the huge storm. I was good for a few weeks. I'd been through this before and knew what to expect and how to be prepared.

Bear ran ahead of me, rolling in the snow and chuffing away as he chased the swirling flakes. I had to smile. Damn dog could find delight in anything around him. Entering the barn, I made sure the generators were ready to be fired up. My large 4x4 truck was already equipped with its plow and everything was prepared. A strange noise suddenly caught my attention and I saw Bear's ears perk up as well. I walked to the door, recognizing the noise.

A car. On my property.

How the hell had someone found my driveway in this weather? Just as I was wondering, I heard a loud crash; and then there was silence. All of a sudden, Bear took off barking in the direction of the noise and I followed, yelling at him to return. He disappeared from sight, and I cursed as I followed as quickly as I was able. Last thing I needed was him getting lost in this fucking storm. I rounded the bend and froze in my tracks, looking in disbelief at the car that had crashed into the large oak tree by one of the trickier bends in the drive. I felt the stirrings of panic at the thought of who might be in the car. There were only a few I allowed on my property and it wasn't a car I recognized. Part of me wanted to turn around and go lock myself in the house until whoever it was went away, but Bear was pawing and barking madly at the passenger door, which was swinging open in the wind. Taking in a deep, cold breath, I realized the driver must be hurt, and I knew I couldn't walk away.

I made my way to the car and did a quick inspection of the situation. The engine was still running, and the extensive damage was on the passenger side where it had slammed into the tree. I could see a figure slumped over the wheel. The passenger door was hanging open from the impact, and I bent down and leaned into the car with nervous reluctance.

Behind the wheel was a woman. She was unconscious, and I could see her head was bleeding. I looked around, feeling helpless, unsure what to do next. Obviously, the only person around to help her was me. Bear was pushing and shoving me from behind, trying to get into the car, and I fell forward, tripping over something beside the door. Ignoring it, I pushed him back and crawled into the car.

Unsure of the injuries I was dealing with, I slowly pulled the woman away from the steering wheel. I could see a lot of blood and there were already bruises on her face. She was very pale and felt cold to my touch. I quickly undid her seatbelt and carefully tugged her over to the passenger side. I struggled, but managed to get the door shut before I moved around to the driver's side and slid in, after getting Bear into the back. I wasted a few seconds trying to figure out how to move the seat back so I could attempt to drive the vehicle up to the house.

I heard a groan beside me and leaned over to assure the woman she was okay. Bear's enormous head appeared over the back seat and I watched in shock as he licked her cheek, as if giving her comfort. He never went near anyone but me. I growled at him to get down and he surprised me by ignoring me once again and settled his head onto her shoulder. I saw her hand reach out and touch his fur before dropping back into her lap. Bear stayed where he was and I shook my head.

I was surprised but grateful when the car actually moved. I could hear the tire protesting as the dented metal from the car rubbed loudly where it was crushed into the wheel well and I hoped it wouldn't go flat before we made it closer to the house. I maneuvered the car up to the barn and parked it in the empty space beside the truck. I moved around to the passenger side and opened the door. I gathered up the injured woman and heard a sudden gasp of intense pain as I straightened up. Startled, I looked down to see her staring back up at me, confused. Her tear-filled eyes were wide with pain. For a few seconds our eyes locked and then she went limp. But not before I also saw another emotion flit through her eyes.

Terror.

I laid the unconscious woman down on my bed and stood back, uncertain of what to do next. Bear sat down beside me and looked up at me with one of his chuffs.

"What?" I snarled at him.

His answer was one of his usual looks that said, 'Duh, stupid human.' He raised himself up on his enormous paws and pushed at the form on my bed and looked back at me.

I nodded. Right. I needed to look after her and check out her injuries. I went and got some cloths, bandages and warm water. I should probably clean her up a little so I could see what I was dealing with. When I came back, Bear was stretched out beside her on the bed.

"Yeah, get comfy. That helps a lot," I snarked at him.

He ignored me and proceeded to lay his head down beside her. I saw a shiver go through her body.

Fuck, she was probably freezing.

Damned dog actually knew what he was doing, trying to warm her up.

I put down my supplies and got to work. I undid her wet, rather useless, coat and pulled it off her, gently lifting her to do so. Even unconscious, she let out a low groan of pain. I grabbed a blanket and draped it over her as I tried to clean up the blood on her face so I could tell if she was still bleeding or not. As I gently wiped away the blood, I frowned. The lump and bruise that were forming on her head were obviously from hitting the steering wheel. But another, even darker bruise was too low to have happened when she hit the wheel and there was a shape to the bruise. A definite outline. I bent lower, trying to discern the shape. My investigation stopped when she shivered again and I could see her shirt was wet from the snow and blood.

Taking a deep breath and hoping she didn't wake while I was undressing her and begin screaming, I pulled off her shirt to change her into dry clothes and was horrified at what I saw: bruises covered her torso and arms. I lifted one arm and examined it. The dark impression of a large hand was wrapped around her small bicep, as if someone had used an ink roller then pressed their hand into her skin. It had taken a lot of force to make the clear imprints. Her right side was also deeply bruised, red and swollen. I shook my head. These injuries were not from hitting a tree. Suddenly furious, I removed her pants and found more bruising on her legs. Sickened, I realized I could actually make out the outline of a shoe print and, when I looked again, saw it matched one of the marks on her side.

I felt the bile rise up in my throat. Someone had hurt this little woman and unless I was mistaken, she was trying to escape from whoever did this. There was no other explanation as to why she would be out in this hellish storm. She had to be running. The anger I had been feeling at the unwelcome intrusion melted away as I stood looking at her bruised and battered body. Unpleasant memories of waking up in the hospital, beaten beyond recognition, swam through my mind. It had happened years ago, but I could still remember the pain I had been in.

Cursing under my breath, I cleaned her up as best I could, before dressing her in a set of my own shorts and shirt to cover her body. Not only was she a great deal shorter than I was, she was thin, and my clothes were huge on her but would at least warm her up. I added a couple of blankets and watched as Bear climbed back up on the bed and settled back down beside her. This time I didn't protest.

The lights began to flicker and I knew I need to start up the generators and close up the barn. It had been impossible to do so with the unconscious woman in my arms. Leaving Bear with the woman, I grabbed the flashlight and I made my way outside, slower than ever. The efforts I had put forth had added a huge strain on my leg, and I was now limping worse than usual.

Just as I got to the barn, I was plunged into darkness as the power finally gave out. I turned on the flashlight and powered up the generators that would keep the house going for a while. Then, struggling against the fierce wind, I closed the barn doors and made my way back to the safety of the house. Inside, I stripped out of my wet clothes and changed into dry ones from the laundry room. I lit some candles and lanterns, and then made my way back to the bedroom to check on the woman.

Bear was still beside her and chuffed happily at me when I entered. I stroked his massive head as I looked down at her unconscious form. What if she didn't wake up? What if she had internal injuries? I shook my head sadly. No one could get here even if I could call for help.

And I couldn't leave to get help.

It had only been the last few years, after I got Bear, that I was able to leave the house. Still, at times, I felt the surge of overwhelming panic when I did.

I hadn't left the property for five years.

We were stuck here.

I could only hope she woke up soon. As soon as the storm was over, I could plow the driveway and take her to the gate. Someone could come get her and take her away.

She could be their problem. Not mine.

I already had enough problems of my own. I had no idea how I could help anyone else when I couldn't even help myself.

⇛Chapter Two⇚

Joshua

The wind howled ferociously and the heavy snow beat against the sides of the house all night. I sat in the chair beside the bed, occasionally checking on the woman to be sure she was still breathing, as well as adding logs to the fireplaces to keep the house warm.

Bear stayed beside her all night, seemingly guarding her. Aside from the occasional groan or whimper that escaped her lips, she remained still. Once, her hands fluttered upward and what sounded like scared little gasps came out of her mouth. Unsure what to do, I made some hushing noises like my mother used to make to soothe me as a child, and I gently clasped her hands in mine and tried to tuck them back under the covers. Both of her small hands grabbed onto one of mine and gripped it fiercely. I could see bruises forming on the back of both her hands, more evidence of the cruel beating she must have endured. Her gasps stopped and she became silent again, but her grip on my hand didn't lessen. I leaned back in the chair, allowing her hands to stay resting on top of mine. Surprisingly, I didn't feel the normal anxiety or panic I would at being touched by a stranger. I only felt the need to allow her this small comfort, and in turn, felt like I was being offered the same.

I studied her face in the dim light. The paleness of her skin was emphasized by the darkness of her hair that was spread across the pillow. I glanced down the bed and back up guessing she was at least a foot shorter than me. Her hands were small and well-manicured, so I doubted she did any sort of manual labor. Her face wasn't classically beautiful, but rather attractive in a soft, lovely way. I imagined she was infinitely appealing when she smiled.

I shook my head. Why was I wondering what she looked like when she smiled?

I closed my eyes wearily, listening to the storm continue its destruction of the world outside the windows. Briefly, I wondered how long it would last. Last year we had one that went on for three solid days. It had taken two weeks before I was able to get my driveway plowed. A sudden sense of foreboding filled me and I opened my eyes again, staring at the woman lying in my bed.

What if I was stuck here with her for two weeks?

A strange gasping noise woke me with a start. I had fallen asleep in the chair, my hand still being held by the woman and the storm raging around us. Three things struck me as my eyes snapped open.

The storm was still blowing, the wind and snow beating against the house in their fury.

My hand was no longer being held in a death grip.

The woman was awake, pressed against the headboard and staring at me with terror-filled eyes of the bluest cornflower shade I had ever seen. Her body was shaking with fright and I felt the urgent need to calm and reassure her.

I stood up and she whimpered, trying to back herself even farther away. I saw her glance between me and Bear, who was sitting on the bed, head cocked, looking at her, and I knew she wasn't sure who she should be more afraid of.

I held up my hands in what I hoped was an innocuous gesture and smiled kindly. "He," I nodded toward Bear, "won't hurt you. He's a gentle giant. He's been watching over you all night."

She continued to stare at me, frightened.

"I won't hurt you, either. You're safe. I promise." For some reason, I wanted to tell her I'd been watching her too, but I kept that part to myself.

Her voice was shaky and raw when she finally spoke. "Who are you?"

"Josh. I'm Joshua. The huge beast sitting there is Bear," I explained. "He's my dog," I added unnecessarily.

She nodded slowly. "Where am I?"

I sat down, thinking maybe she would relax a little if she thought I wasn't about to pounce on her. I gave Bear the hand signal to lay down and this time he actually did what I instructed him to do.

"You're in my house. You, ah, got caught in the snowstorm and crashed your car on my property. Bear and I found you."

"You... you found me?"

I nodded. "I think you took a wrong turn and ended up on the road leading to my place rather than the main road. The storm is really bad." I frowned. "You shouldn't have been out driving in it."

I paused, watching her. She was still tense and shaking, but didn't seem as frightened as she had been.

"You must have lost control of your car and hit a tree. You hit your head on the steering wheel pretty hard. You were out cold when I found you."

Her hand came up and gingerly touched her head. I saw her wince as her fingers made contact with the bruised skin. Then her hand drifted down to her cheek and paused. "I hit my face as well?" she whispered.

I paused, not sure what to say now. "You, um, seem to have several sets of bruises on you," I said quietly, indicating she should look at her hands.

She stared down at them, examining the bruising, but saying nothing. She looked at the massively large shirt she was wearing and glanced back up me. "This isn't mine?" she questioned, her voice hesitant.

I shook my head. "The passenger side door had flown open with the impact of the crash. You were wet from the snow being blown in. I took off your wet clothes."

Her eyes opened wide in fear again. "You took off my clothes?" I could hear the panic in her voice.

"I only did that to put dry ones on you while I check your injuries. I swear. I didn't remove your underwear," I hastened to assure her. "I only wanted to help you." I wanted her to believe me. I wanted her to stop looking at me with so much fear in those huge, blue eyes.

"I saw other bruises," I added gently.

"Where?"

"Your, ah, your legs and your arms."

I watched as she pulled the covers back and rolled up the shorts I had put on her. In the dim light of the overcast day the bruises looked even darker, and I could clearly see the imprint of a shoe. She traced over the bruises again, not saying a word.

Then she glanced back up. "I don't know you. How do I know you didn't do this?"

I sat back, shocked, and felt a ripple of anger go through me. She thought I had done this? I took in a deep calming breath and stood up, approaching the bed. Instantly she shrank away.

"It's okay. I'm not going to hurt you. I promise. I just want to show you something that will prove I didn't do this to you."

"How?" she questioned me, her voice trembling.

"Do you see the imprint on your leg?" I asked, pointing to the large bruise.

Looking down she nodded. "Someone *kicked* me?"

"Not me. It was *not* me. Can I show you?" I kept my voice soft and calm, feeling the desperate need, for some reason, to show her it was not me who inflicted those injuries.

She regarded me for a moment, and then nodded. I grabbed the back of the chair, knowing I wouldn't be able to keep steady, and slowly raised my foot and laid it beside her thigh. We could both see my foot was easily two sizes larger than the imprint on her leg. I saw her shoulders relax a little and heard her breath release.

"I'm going to sit beside you now, okay?"

Again, she nodded.

"Roll up your shirt sleeve. Just the sleeve. Hold your arm out. Please. I *won't* hurt you."

She regarded me silently for a moment, then I watched her wince as she lifted her arm and rolled up one sleeve and held it out slightly, trembling in fear.

"I'm going to touch your arm now, all right? I'm just going to show you something, I won't hurt you. I promise."

She nodded warily and I lifted her arm higher, the loose shirt falling away even more, revealing the deep bruising on the upper part of her flesh. She gasped when she saw it, and then watched as I silently placed my hand over the imprints that the bastard, who *had* done this, left behind. My long fingers and large palm easily encompassed the mark showing both of us there was no way my hand could have left them. "I didn't hurt you. I found you like this. I swear. I would never, ever strike a woman," I spoke slowly and with conviction.

"I... I believe you. Thank you for showing me," she whispered as her eyes drifted up and met mine. I was relieved to feel a little more of her tension ease away. I removed my hand and helped her lower her arm back down.

"The question is; who did do this to you? Who were you running from last night?" I asked quietly.

I watched a multitude of emotions play out across her face.

"I don't know," she whispered, her voice quivering.

I sighed. She was hiding something.

"What is your name?"

Her mouth opened, and then her brow furrowed in concentration.

"I don't know." Her voice was filled with confusion.

"You don't know?" I repeated, dubiously.

 Her expressive eyes widened and filled with tears.

"I can't remember how I got here and I can't remember my name."

⇒CHAPTER THREE⇐

Joshua

I stared at her, watching the tears fall down her cheeks. I was wrong, she *wasn't* hiding anything; I could see from the fear and confusion in her eyes that she couldn't remember. Wanting to comfort her somehow, I reached down and stroked her hands gently. "You hit your head pretty hard. No doubt things are fuzzy. I'm sure when you feel better, you'll remember."

She continued to stare at me, frightened and upset. "I'm going to make some coffee and something to eat. Do you feel up to joining me in the kitchen?" I asked, keeping my voice quiet.

I saw her glance down dubiously at the shorts she was wearing. I stood up and grabbed a pair of sweats and a heavier shirt out of the drawer, along with a pair of socks, and handed them all to her. "I know they'll be far too big, but they'll keep you warm. The only heat sources we have are the fireplaces. The storm has knocked out the power and I need to make the generators last as long as possible. So we'll have to stick to the rooms with the fireplaces, okay?"

She nodded silently.

"The kitchen is in the front of the house; it's sort of one big room, so you'll find it easily. Come join me when you're ready." I indicated the door behind me. "There's a bathroom right there. Help yourself to whatever you need. There's hot water if you want a shower. Just keep it as short as possible, please?"

Again, she nodded silently. I watched her wince as she tried to move from her defensive position against the headboard. For a brief moment, she sat on the edge of the bed and then stood up. As she went to step forward, she gasped in pain and stumbled. Instantly, I lunged forward, catching her before she hit the floor. Instead of falling, she ended up pressed against me, a shaking mass of raw sobs. Unsure what to do, I held her loosely, not wanting to press what were obviously very painful injuries. Surprisingly, she allowed me to hold her and soothe her. I stood, feeling her resting against me and found myself noticing how well she seemed to mould into me, her head fitting right under my chin as she sobbed. Tentatively, I raised my hand and lightly stroked her back, trying to calm her.

Why did she feel so right in my arms?

Slowly her sobs eased off, and I pulled away. Leaning down, I tilted her chin up with my finger so I could see her eyes. The pain and fear I saw in them tore directly into my heart and I found I wanted to erase both. Gently, I eased her back down on the mattress, handed her some Kleenex and went into the bathroom. I found the painkillers that I used when the agony was too much to handle, and filled a glass with water. Returning to her, I showed her the bottle so she wouldn't add the fear of me trying to drug her to the mix, and gave her two of the pills. I sat beside her as Bear came up to rest his head on her knee, adoration in his eyes as he stared up at her. I shook my head at his actions.

"What?" she asked; her voice raw and broken.

"He doesn't go to anyone but me. He is as leery of strangers as I am. But he seems to have taken a liking to you."

"Where did you get him?"

I told her about rescuing him not long after I had moved here. He was just a puppy and it seemed to be the right fit. Both of us were abused and needed to heal; we helped each other. He was a great companion for me, and Bear had a good life here. I made sure he was treated well and would never be hurt again. I spoke quietly and gave the medication time to start easing the pain before she moved again. As I talked, I watched the pain fade a little from her eyes.

"Ready to try again?" I asked.

She nodded and this time I helped her up. She still winced and moved slowly but she was able to stay upright.

"Do you want me to bring you something to eat in here?"

She shook her head no.

"Do you feel up to coming to the kitchen?"

She nodded, so I helped her into the bathroom. She promised to call if she needed me; I told her I would leave her alone but I wanted the door open so I could hear her. Again, she nodded, but didn't say anything.

"I won't leave the kitchen unless you call. Okay?"

Her eyes looked up at me for a minute, unblinking. "Okay," she whispered.

Calling Bear to come with me, I left.

I made my way to the kitchen slowly; I was stiff from sleeping in the chair and my leg was aching with the strain from yesterday. I stood at the counter for a minute, thinking about what had just happened. I had no idea why it was so important that I comfort her. I shook my head at my own odd behavior. My mind seemed to have a will of its own at the moment and I couldn't stop the reactions. I started the coffee and grabbed some eggs from the refrigerator. All the appliances were working, thanks to the generators. I heard the water start-up and was pleased to know the woman was able to get into the shower. I stopped for a minute again, thinking. I couldn't keep calling her 'the woman.' How should I address her? I puzzled briefly, and then decided I would figure it out later. Earlier, I had hoped she wouldn't be here long enough for me to have to address her at all. But looking out at the storm, still pounding away outside, I knew that probably wasn't going to be the case.

Just as I was finishing up the scrambled eggs, I heard a noise behind me and turned. She was swimming in my grey sweatshirt and pants with the arms and legs rolled up; staring at me with those huge blue eyes, filled with trepidation, and looking totally lost. Her hair was wet and hung down past her shoulders. Her face was so pale, and the bruises stood out vividly against the white of her skin. She was clutching my socks in one hand. Again, I felt the need to comfort her, and without thinking, held out my hand in a gesture of welcome. I watched her look from my face to my hand, then her arm raised and she moved forward, painfully slowly, placing her hand in mine. I smiled at her and squeezed her hand softly; mindful of how sore it must be with the bruises on it. "Need help with those socks?" I asked gently.

She nodded. "It, um, really hurts to bend over. I couldn't get them on."

I felt my anger flare. Of course it hurt; no doubt her ribs were badly bruised if not cracked. I tamped down my anger and knelt down, quickly tucking her feet into my socks. I grimaced. Even her feet had bruises on them.

Fucking bastard, whoever he was.

I stood up. "Rather large, but they'll keep your feet warm." I smiled at her and was rewarded with a shaky little smile in return. I guided her to the table and then set down a plate of eggs and toast in front of her. I took a seat beside her and held up the coffee pot in silent invitation. She nodded and I filled her cup, watching as she added cream and a tiny amount of sugar before stirring it and taking a sip.

"Thank you," she breathed quietly. "I love coffee." She smiled, and then froze, staring at her cup.

"What is it?" I asked, startled. Did she think I had added something to the coffee? Was she in more pain?

She looked up at me, confused. "How can I not know my name, yet I know I love coffee? Or, how I take it? I didn't even think before adding the cream and sugar. That doesn't make sense!" I saw her chin begin to quiver again.

I looked at her, perplexed, unsure how to respond. Then I shrugged my shoulders. "I have no idea. Maybe after we eat, we can try to figure it out. Okay?"

"Okay."

I smiled. "Eat your breakfast then and we'll see what we can find." I pushed her plate towards her. She could use some food. She was far too thin, in my opinion.

I smiled as I watched her pick up her fork and take a bite.

"It's good. Thank you."

I picked up my own fork, satisfied she would eat. "You're welcome."

After breakfast, I took her upstairs to the huge loft, where my office was located. It was the only thing on the second floor. The walls were lined with books and my desk was at the front, overlooking the entire main floor. When I was seated, I could look out and see the surrounding woods and the large lake that spread out in front of the property. The ever-changing landscape often provided me great comfort or inspiration while I worked. Watching the trees dance in the wind or the snow swirl in the air was a welcome distraction at times. I watched as she walked around slowly, looking at all the books. On the shelves were different awards I had won, but she didn't pay much attention to them. There was a large chair where I often sat and went through notes, or just sat and read, Bear usually asleep at my feet. I directed her to the chair and made sure she was okay before I perused the shelves. I found the medical books I kept on hand for research and handed one of them to her.

"What am I looking for?" she asked.

"Any information on head trauma, memory loss, that sort of thing," I instructed as I sat down at my desk with a large volume.

Silence filled the room, except for the turning of pages, for the next few minutes. Not finding anything of help in the book I had, I stood up to go get another one and looked over towards the chair. She was asleep, the book hanging loosely from her fingers, and Bear sitting right beside her, again standing guard. She looked so vulnerable and small. She reminded me of ... something. I searched my brain, and then realized what it was. A frightened rabbit. One of the little grey ones I saw from the woods all the time. I smiled at the comparison. She had also looked at me the way they did, all frightened and confused as I threw out feed for them, not sure what I was doing. Strangely enough, she also looked so right, dressed in my too-big clothes, curled into my chair with Bear beside her. I felt a sudden rush of tenderness as I studied her. I shook my head.

Where the hell were all these feelings coming from? I didn't know her, or what her story was or her situation.

And I certainly wasn't in the position to feel anything towards anyone.

I made my way over and gently placed a blanket on her.

Because I didn't want her to get cold and then be sick and require extra care.

That was the only reason.

At least, that was what I tried to convince myself was the only reason.

―――――――⋅•⋅●⋅•⋅―――――――

I made my way through a few books until I was satisfied that I understood what I thought was happening. Turning around, I saw she was still asleep and had burrowed under the blanket I had placed on her. I observed her for a moment when inspiration struck. Her car. No doubt her purse would be in the car. All of the books seem to indicate that temporary amnesia was common after a head trauma and, often, some small detail allowed the person to regain their memory quickly. No doubt if I knew her name and she saw items that belonged to her it would stir something.

I looked out at the still-falling snow. I could make it to the barn and get in the side door. I had one large snow blower right by the front porch and I could plow my way through. It would be worth it if she could remember her name. Maybe she would relax a little. She jumped a little every time I moved or spoke. I didn't want her afraid of me. I didn't like it.

I made my way downstairs and added a couple of logs to the fire. I left a couple more pain pills on the table in case she woke up and came downstairs. Then I dressed warmly and went outside in the storm. It took a while to even get to the snow blower and by the time I made it to the barn it had been well over an hour. I was panting as I finally opened the side door and got inside, and my leg was now throbbing painfully. I stood for a few minutes, catching my breath. I lit one of the gas lights and checked on the generators, making sure the gas level was good. I had a large supply of full gas containers, having learned the hard way how long these storms could keep me isolated.

I made my way over to her car. The back passenger side was heavily damaged. Obviously, she had hit the tree very hard. The back tire was now completely flat. I shuddered thinking what the results would have been had she hit it head on. I went around and opened the driver's side back door and saw a bag on the floor. Leaning in, I grabbed it. It didn't look like a purse to me; more an overnight-type bag.

I looked around the car but that was all I could see. I had another thought, and leaning in, opened the glove box, searching for a registration slip. There was nothing in the glove box at all. I looked in the small console but it too was empty. I noticed the dust on the dashboard and the slight musty odor in the car. Obviously, it hadn't been driven very much. I felt around under the seats and then checked the trunk, but aside from a snow scraper, the car was empty. I shook my head as a shiver ran through me and knew I needed to get back to the warmth of the house. The mystery of the car would have to wait. I grabbed the small bag I had found and blew out the light before stepping back into the swirling snow. The path I had cleared was already filling in and I started the snow blower back up and made my way towards the house as quickly as possible.

I entered through the side door, dropped the bag on the bench, and then pulled off my snow-laden clothes. I hung them up on the line, threw on a pair of sweats that were there, padded into the kitchen intent on heading for a shower, and stopped short.

Standing in front of the stove, stirring something that smelled delicious was ... Rabbit. I smiled internally at her new nickname. She, meanwhile, looked up at me, startled.

"What are you doing?" I asked as I walked toward the stove. She shouldn't be moving around. She should be resting.

She stepped back quickly away from me. "I ... I woke up and heard the snow blower. I thought you'd be cold and ... hungry when you were done, so I made some soup. You had lots of vegetables and things in the fridge. I didn't think you'd mind. I'm sorry... I shouldn't have ..." her voice trailed off, trembling.

Fuck. She was afraid again.

I raised my hand and smiled at her. "No ... no, that's great. It smells wonderful. I had hoped you would still be sleeping. I wanted you to rest. I'm sorry the noise woke you."

I watched her shoulders relax a little. "I'm happy to do it. I think ... I think I like to cook. And I thought if I moved around a little the pain would ease up."

I grinned at her. "You like to cook? Good to know. Because I hate it. And my repertoire is highly limited. But please, don't overdo it. I'm just gonna go shower and change, and then we can eat, okay?"

She smiled shyly and nodded.

I was right.

Rabbit had a lovely smile.

It was indeed very appealing.

⇒CHAPTER FOUR⇐

Joshua

Twenty minutes later, I looked up from my bowl. "Seriously, all of this was in my kitchen?"

Rabbit smiled shyly. "I just rummaged around and threw in stuff until it tasted good. I thought it would warm you up. You were out there so long."

I nodded. I hadn't shown her the bag yet. I thought I would wait until after we had eaten. I dug back into my bowl. "So, you don't have a name for this?"

She shook her head. "Um ... just soup?"

I smiled. "Well, its great 'just soup'. Thank you."

We were both quiet as we ate. I wondered how she would react when I gave her the bag. Would she remember everything?

A sudden gust of wind rattled the windows. Rabbit jumped slightly with the unexpected noise.

"It's okay, Rabbit. It's just the wind. You're safe, I promise." I spoke without thinking.

Her head tilted to the side as she regarded me. "Rabbit?"

I shrugged sheepishly. "I have to call you something. 'Hey you' doesn't seem right. And you remind me of the little grey rabbits that are around here."

"I don't understand. I'm furry?"

I laughed. "No, you're small, kinda jumpy and, dressed the way you are right now, you're all grey. And they look at me apprehensively when

I approach them, just like you do."

She regarded me quietly for a moment, her eyes locking me in their gaze. "Are you hunting or feeding them when you approach?" she asked.

I smiled soothingly. "I'm a sucker. I feed them. I don't hunt. At all."

Her shoulders relaxed a little. "Rabbit's okay then."

I grinned. "Rabbit it is."

After we were done, Rabbit moved back into the chair upstairs, Bear hot on her heels. I was pleased to see she wasn't as unsteady on her feet as she had been. She did, however, take some more painkillers when I offered them to her and she didn't argue about not cleaning up after we ate. After I tidied, I went back to the mudroom and grabbed her bag. I threw more logs on the fire and went upstairs. I approached her slowly and stood in front of her

"What's that?" she asked quietly.

I knelt down, gingerly, on the floor in front of the ottoman and placed the bag on top. She looked at the bag with no recognition. I pushed it towards her. "I think it's yours. I got it out of your car. I'm hoping your ID will be in it."

"You didn't look in it?" she asked surprised.

I shook my head. "No. It's yours. Not mine."

She stared at me briefly then reached for the bag. I watched as she pulled out various pieces of clothing, the store tags all intact, a few toiletries and then pulled out an envelope and opened it up. Inside was a large pile of cash. She looked up at me, confused. "That's it. Just some clothes and this money."

"Does any of it look familiar?" I asked.

She held up a few of the clothes, studying them, and then set them down, looking discouraged. "No. Not at all."

She looked at me with a sudden burst of hope. "What about the glove box? Maybe there's a registration card? Or insurance papers?"

I shook my head. "I looked everywhere. This is all there was."

"I don't understand. Why don't I have any ID? And why do I have all this money?"

"I don't know, Rabbit."

She looked down at the clothing and money again. "I don't even know if this is mine."

Abruptly, she dumped the money out of the envelope and slowly sorted it. I watched her silently as she counted it and then looked up at me. "Eighteen hundred and fifty dollars, Joshua. Why would I be traveling with a few pieces of clothing and eighteen hundred and fifty dollars in cash?"

"Maybe you were running from something, Rabbit."

She looked at me. "You think that because of the bruises, don't you?"

I glanced down to her bruised hands, which were now tightly clutching the edge of the blanket. The overriding need to comfort her hit me again and I leaned forward and loosened her hands and wrapped mine around them. I spoke gently. "*Something* happened to you. *Something* put you on that road in the middle of a storm."

Her voice was unsteady. "Why don't I remember?"

"You hit your head. Hard. There is a very good chance you'll remember everything in a few days. You need to rest and let yourself heal."

She sighed shakily and was quiet for a few minutes. I sat with my hands still wrapped around hers, gently rubbing them in comfort. Suddenly, she looked at me with fresh trepidation in her eyes. "What if ..." her voice trailed off.

"What if what?" I prompted

Her voice was quiet. "What if I'm a bad person? What if I stole those clothes and that money? Maybe the car isn't even mine. Maybe I'm running because of something I've done. Maybe ..." she hesitated. "Maybe I ... knocked up a store? Over a store? Knocked over a store?"

I snorted. "What, like a career criminal, Rabbit? You think you're a thief?"

She looked at me. She was serious. The woman who had just made me soup and who my dog had taken instant ownership of, thought she had to be a bad person.

I shook my head. "Then you're a bad criminal, Rabbit." I gestured to the small pile on the ottoman. "If your haul is a few items of clothing, less than a couple grand, and a five-year-old Escort, I suggest you give it up," I smiled at her and winked. "Plus, your inability to come up with the right lingo suggests that perhaps you aren't so inclined."

I saw the corners of her lips twitch. "Maybe I was having an off night."

I threw back my head and laughed. I was pleased to hear a small giggle escape her lips.

I smiled over at her and squeezed her hands gently. "I highly doubt it, Rabbit. You don't strike me as a hardened criminal. Or any kind of criminal. I'm sure there is another explanation. You could have lost your purse. Or left it behind, if you were in a hurry."

A sudden searing cramp in my leg reminded me of the awkward position I was currently in. I groaned, releasing Rabbit's hands and grabbing for the top of my right leg.

She moved, kneeling beside me. "What is it, Joshua? What's

wrong?"

I gritted my teeth against the pain. "Need to stand," I managed to get out.

Rabbit wrapped one of my arms around her shoulder and helped me to stand. I didn't fail to notice her grimace of pain from the effort of helping me.

"What can I do? Tell me, please."

I took a deep breath in, the pain abating a little. "I need to go get in the hot tub; that will help ease it."

"You're limping worse than before. It's because of doing all this for me, isn't it? The extra snow blowing and the work of waiting on me? Oh God, you carried me yesterday as well. Tell me what to do, Joshua, please."

I looked down at her earnest face, touched by her concern and even more so from her lack of prying questions. I smiled reassuringly at her. "I had to get to the barn anyway, Rabbit. And since you weigh about two pounds, carrying you was not an issue. This happens. Please don't worry."

"I'll go run a tub for you," she said as she tried to duck out from under my arm. I held her against me, shaking my head.

"I have a hot tub in the basement. I hate using the electricity right now, but I need it."

She hesitated. "What can I do?"

"Nothing. Really, this happens a lot. The heat helps a great deal. Then I'll stretch it out and give myself a rub down. I'm an old pro at this." Reluctantly, I let her go. I liked the feeling of her tucked under my arm.

I made my way to the stairs and gingerly began the descent. I stopped part-way down. Turning around, I looked back at her. She had moved to the top of the stairs and was watching me. "I wear my shorts in the hot tub. You're welcome to join me," I offered. "It's big."

Her eyes widened.

I stumbled over my next words. "The hot tub that is. The hot tub is big. You'd be perfectly safe. It may feel good on your injuries as well. Especially on your back and legs."

She glanced down.

"Grab one of my t-shirts." She still didn't look up and I softened my voice. "You don't have to, Rabbit. Only if you want to, okay?"

She nodded, not saying anything.

"The stairs to the basement are beside the mudroom door." I turned and kept going. "Please be careful going down the stairs," I added.

I shook my head when I got to the basement.

What was going on with me?
Rabbit; in the hot tub with me.
A little voice in my head snickered at my stupidity.
What had I just done?

⇶CHAPTER FIVE⇷

Joshua

I relaxed into the bubbling hot water with a deep sigh of relief. The burning pain in my leg began to ease quickly. I leaned my head back and tried to relax. Part of me was listening to see if Rabbit would join me. What was it that made me feel so protective of her? I had never had this kind of response to another person. Normally I didn't like strangers. Yet she didn't feel like a stranger to me. The couple of smiles I had seen flit across her face made me want to see more of them. Every time she grimaced in pain or fear, I wanted to immediately make both go away. I found my reactions highly disconcerting.

The basement room felt chilly outside of the tub. The walls and floors were all tiled due to the moisture from the tub and the exercise pool and, with no heat the air was cold. I sunk down further into the water. A few minutes passed before I heard soft footsteps coming down the steps.

Opening my eyes, I saw Rabbit standing at the bottom of the steps looking very conflicted. Smiling, I held out my hand. "Don't stand there too long. The room is way colder than in here." Still she hesitated. "You're perfectly safe, Rabbit. I promise. Nothing will hurt you here."

Slowly, she came forward. She had removed my sweatshirt and pants and was back in the t-shirt she had woken up in. I could see the bruising that ran down her leg. My mind was also quick to notice how shapely her legs were. Shaking my head to clear the unwelcome thoughts, I held out my hand once again. "It will feel good on your back

26

and legs," I said quietly. "I *won't* hurt you. I promise."

Her head tilted and she regarded me briefly. "I know that," she whispered. "I'm not sure why, but I feel safe with you." I smiled at her soft confession, feeling pleased. I wanted her to feel safe with me. I wanted to make her safe. I watched as she made her decision and, grasping the railing with one hand, she placed her other in mine. I was amazed how well her tiny hand fit within mine as I helped guide her down the steps into the hot water.

Where were these thoughts coming from?

Slowly she sank beneath the water and closed her eyes. I heard a small hiss escape her mouth as the hot water hit her body and then I saw her relax. I pointed out where the jet adjustments were and moved away from her. We both were quiet for some time as the water bubbled and flowed around us, its soothing heat working its magic on painful limbs and muscles. Opening my eyes, I saw her looking around the room. "It's usually much warmer down here," I spoke up, startling her.

"You use all this equipment a lot?" she asked indicating to the various pieces of exercise equipment.

I nodded. "I have to try and keep the strength up in my leg and I have a program I follow. The exercise pool helps a lot. The hot tub was really just a want more than anything. I found when I was in therapy it was a welcome relief."

Internally, I groaned.

Nice word vomit. I could simply have said yes.

She nodded, not saying anything else for a bit. "How long ago did you hurt your leg?" she asked softly.

"Six years," I replied shortly.

She nodded, but didn't ask any other questions. I closed my eyes again and allowed the heat of the water to continue to help ease the pain. Using one hand, I attempted to imitate the rhythmic hand movements my therapist in the hospital used when working on my leg after a session. My attempts were, as usual, rather pathetic, but it was all I could do. I looked down into the water wishing I could do a better job and noticed Rabbit watching me intently. I smiled sheepishly. "My therapist used to rub it while in the water, said it worked best that way." I shrugged. "I don't do quite as good a job as she did." Rabbit's face twisted slightly as if in thought, but didn't say anything. I shut my eyes, not wanting her to think I was staring at her.

After a few minutes, I felt the movement of the water and opened my eyes, surprised to see Rabbit was beside me, looking at my hand as it kneaded the muscle in my leg. My hand stopped and her eyes flew up to meet mine. We stared at each other for a moment. Even in the dim light, I could see the various emotions in her expressive eyes. Trepidation, caution and, finally, a look of determination passed through her amazing pools of blue as she looked at me. Unsure of what she was thinking, I smiled warmly at her, once again wanting her to feel safe.

"I could ... do that for you. If you want?" Her words rushed out quickly, as if she needed to say them before she changed her mind.

I stared at her dumbfounded. "What?"

"I'm sure it would be more effective with two hands, and I want to help. Please. I could try."

I wasn't sure how I would handle my reaction of feeling her hands on me. "I think your hands are probably too sore for that, Rabbit," I said quietly, not wanting to seem ungrateful. "I know you're in a lot of pain."

She shook her head. "No, I think it would be good for them. They need to move and flex. Please, Joshua, let me try."

I regarded her quietly for a moment. "If it hurts you, or you are uncomfortable, then you need to stop. Okay?"

She nodded. "Show me where it hurts."

I took in a deep breath and placed her hand on the area that ached the most. Again, I was surprised at the warmth and comfort I found in her touch. Normally, I would be tense if touched by a stranger; even a handshake, but with her I was very relaxed. I could feel her gentle fingers move as she seemed to examine the area and then she started kneading the muscles. I was surprised at the strength in her small hands and immediately felt some relief. I tried to bite back the groan that threatened to escape my lips at her touch, but a small one escaped.

She stopped. "Good groan or bad groan? Is it okay?" she whispered.

"Yes, it's okay. It's ... good. So good. Please don't stop."

Her hands continued to knead and massage. My eyes shut partially out of pleasure and partially out of embarrassment. My reply had been uttered in a low tone and sounded oddly... intimate. Peeking out of one eye, I could see Rabbit seemed only to be concentrating on the task at hand and either didn't notice the odd tone of my voice or chose to ignore it.

For that I was grateful.

———————————◆◆◆●◆◆◆———————————

"Don't be ridiculous, Joshua."

I shook my head. We were having a stand-off in my bedroom. After the hot tub and Rabbit's surprisingly well-done massage, my leg felt much better. I was holding a pillow and a blanket, getting ready to go sleep on the couch. Rabbit was being stubborn and insisting she would sleep there.

"You need your rest, Rabbit. I've slept on the couch many times."

She shook her head. "No. This is your bed. Your leg needs a good rest. I am way smaller. I would fit on the couch better. Or, I can sleep in one of the others rooms; if I'm covered up, I'll be fine. "

I rolled my eyes and snorted. "The other rooms are closed off and have zero heat. You would freeze all night, so that's *not* happening. Nor are you sleeping on the couch. This discussion is over. Get in bed." I lifted the covers indicating she needed to crawl in. She looked at me, walked forward and, in a move I wasn't expecting, pushed me so I stumbled forward onto the bed. Before I could react, she grabbed the blankets and covered me. Bear immediately jumped up and lay down right beside me as I struggled to sit upright.

Rabbit's triumphant grin was infectious and I found myself chuckling along with her. "Think you're pretty clever, do you?" I asked her.

She nodded. "You're in bed now. I'll just take this blanket ..."

My hand covered hers, stilling the words she was about to speak. "I can't let you sleep on the couch, Rabbit. I can't. It's just not ... right."

She smiled sweetly. "Well, I can't let you either, Joshua. So what do you propose? We both sit up all night?"

I looked at the empty side of the bed and before I could reconsider it, I spoke up. "We share."

Her eyes widened in doubt.

"Rabbit, it's a king size bed. I'll stay on my side. Bear will be in the middle and you'll be on your side. You're perfectly safe. Then neither of us will be on the couch or trying to sleep in a freezing cold room."

I watched her face as she mulled it over. She bit her lip as she processed the idea and then sighed in relief as she nodded in agreement. Leaning over Bear, I ignored his chuffs of disapproval of being disturbed as I pulled the covers back in silent invitation. She crawled in bed wordlessly, although I noticed the winces of pain as she tried to make herself comfortable. "Do you want some painkillers?"

She hesitated before saying yes. I got her a couple of tablets and some water and watched her take them. After she settled down, I made sure she was warm enough, and then I returned to my side of the bed and blew out the gas light. The reflections of the flames from the fireplace danced on the darkened walls and the soothing crackle of the wood popping was the only sound in the room. Outside, the snow and wind was still pounding against the house.

"How long do you think the storm will last?" Her voice was a quiet whisper in the dark.

"Another day, maybe more." I shrugged in the darkness. "I don't know."

Quiet filled the room and I lay there listening to the fire, feeling remarkably calm considering I hadn't shared a bed with another person in years.

"I'm sorry." Her quiet words startled me. I leaned up on my elbow and looked across Bear at her. She was curled into a ball, her back to me, hugging her pillow and I found myself wanting to reach across and touch her, comfort her. Instead, I simply asked, "Sorry for what, Rabbit?"

"For causing you so much trouble. For disrupting your life."

I could hear the emotion in her voice. I stared at her in the dark. I was shocked at the words that I spoke.

"I'm not sorry, Rabbit. You're here and you're safe. That's all that matters."

I lay back down, surprised at what I had just said.

When she had appeared twenty-four hours ago, I *was* angry she had disrupted my life.

Now, I meant exactly what I said.

She was safe. That was *all* that did matter.

For the first time she had arrived, both my mind and I were in agreement.

⇒CHAPTER SIX⇐

Joshua

I woke up slowly, knowing something was different. My senses picked up that the storm was still blowing outside. I felt the weight and warmth of Bear as he slept, stretched out across my feet, as usual. I buried my head deeper into the pillow and my arms tightened around the warm body that was curved into mine. Smiling, I leaned down and nuzzled the soft hair … and my eyes flew open as my body suddenly realized what was different.

Rabbit.

Rabbit was sound asleep, burrowed into my chest, my arms around her. The large body that had separated us last night was now snoring away at the foot of the bed, draped across our legs which were tangled up together under the blankets.

I blinked in confusion. I remember falling asleep. Bear was between us. A protective wall for Rabbit. When had that changed? I searched my brain and remembered. Rabbit had cried out in the night having a nightmare, and Bear had jumped up, growling, ready to attack whatever was frightening her. I had pushed him out of the way and reached over to wake her, only to have her roll into my chest and burrow herself into me, shaking and sobbing. I had held her and whispered soothingly into her ear, stroking her hair until she stilled and slept again. Not wanting to disturb her, I had laid there trying to figure out how to separate myself from her without waking her, yet not really wanting to separate myself from her.

Obviously, I fell asleep. Now, I was faced with the same dilemma. I didn't think she would be very happy waking up to find herself this close to me. Looking down on her face, I paused. Her long dark lashes were resting on her pale cheeks as she slumbered. Her hands were both clasped against my chest holding onto my shirt and her dark hair was spread across the pillows and down her back. I couldn't help but raise my hand and gently stroke away the few wisps that were lying across her face. The bruises were out in full color today and looked dark and angry against her skin. I frowned looking at them, wondering again how and why anyone would strike this small person with that much maliciousness. I was tracing over one bruise on her cheek with a fingertip, fighting the sudden intense desire to follow its trail with my lips, when her eyes suddenly opened. She stared at me for a moment and I waited with baited breath for the screaming and accusations to begin.

Instead, she smiled a shy, tremulous smile. I smiled back at her warily.

She spoke, her voice quiet in the dim light. "I had a nightmare."

I nodded. "Yes."

"You comforted me."

"Yes."

"You've held me all night?"

"Um, yes. You, ah, seemed to sleep better when I held you."

She didn't say anything for a minute. Then, she closed the space between us and gently pressed her lips to mine. Instinctively, my one hand reached up and held her face to mine, enjoying the feel of her warm lips before she pulled away.

"Thank you." She whispered, then untangled herself and grabbed her clothes. I watched as she slowly went to the bathroom, favoring one side of her body.

I lay there stunned and completely aroused.

Sitting up, I glanced at the bathroom door, and then down at Bear, who regarded me knowingly for a moment before huffing and laying his huge head back down on the bed. I was pretty sure he just rolled his eyes at me.

I had no idea what just happened. All I knew was I liked how Rabbit felt curled up against me. And I really liked how it felt when she kissed me.

I shook my head.

This was so not part of the plan.

After Rabbit had disappeared into the bathroom, I quickly got dressed and then plowed my way out to the barn to check on the generators again, needing some distance and space between us before I faced her again. After adding gas to the generators and checking that everything was okay, I sat down heavily on one of the benches, trying to clear my head.

She kissed me. She didn't scream or accuse me of taking advantage of the situation. She had kissed me. And I had responded. *Every part of me had responded.* What did that mean? I mulled it over for a while, and decided it meant exactly nothing. She thanked me. Just as I had responded to her need to be comforted in the night, she responded this morning and thanked me. A sweet kiss. And given the close proximity we had been in, and the fact that I was a man, my body had reacted as well. That was all it was. Nothing else came of it and nothing else would. We didn't know each other. Given her current state of memory loss and the secluded life I lived, we couldn't know each other.

I nodded. It was good. It was nothing. A spur of the moment thing. I doubted it would happen again. I resolved to watch my reactions to her. She was vulnerable and I couldn't let myself take advantage of that. No matter how appealing I found her.

I needed a new plan. I had to stop the impulsive need to touch her when I felt she was upset. Or any other time. I needed to distance myself more. I could be friendly and supportive. But that was where it ended. I couldn't think in terms of caring for the woman currently residing in my house. Or a relationship with her ... of any sorts.

Finally, having no further excuses, I decided I needed to return to the house soon. Going to the door, I whistled for Bear, who came running from the mounds of snow he was frolicking in. I looked up at the sky. It was lightening up and the wind was dying down some, but the snow continued to fall, albeit lighter. I hope that meant the storm would soon be over. Suddenly, I shook my head. I had a satellite radio in the house. I had never even thought to turn it on. Rabbit had totally taken over all my thoughts. Maybe there would be some news of a missing person on it and we could get some answers today.

I made my way back to the house and entered via the mudroom. Both Bear and I shook ourselves off and I hung up my coat, leaving my clothes on. I would change after a hot shower. Entering the house, Bear padded his way over to Rabbit, who was standing by the stove again. I watched as she greeted him affectionately and grabbed a towel to help dry him off. I shook my head at how the sight of her in my kitchen, tending to my dog, looked so right. Stepping forward, I laughed. "Now *someone* is getting spoiled with all that attention."

She looked up shyly. "What does he normally do?"

"Lies by the fire." I smiled as I went over to add some logs to the fireplace.

"Ah. I guess that makes sense."

"Do I smell coffee?" I asked hopefully as I came closer to the kitchen again.

Rabbit nodded and handed me a cup. I sat down at the table and took a deep drink of the hot liquid.

"Wow. This is delicious. Did you put something in it?"

"Um ... cinnamon."

I took another sip. "It's great. I'm gonna have a quick shower and get out of these wet clothes."

"I'll have breakfast ready when you're done."

I stood up, shaking my head. "You don't have to do that, Rabbit. I don't want you pushing yourself."

"I know. I want to. Please? I feel like I'm contributing. Not just being ... in the way."

Something in her voice made me stop. I looked at her, but she was looking anywhere but at me.

I stood in front of her, hesitating, then lifted her chin, and looked at her. Her eyes, once again, told me exactly what she was thinking. I could see the worry and apprehension in them. The new plan went right out the window and I found myself wanting to take those feelings away. This time it was me that leaned down and gently pressed my lips to hers. "Not in the way, Rabbit," I whispered quietly. "Not even remotely in the way."

I pulled away and made my way down the hall. Pausing, I turned around. She was sitting at the table with her fingers on her lips, staring at me. For a minute, we just stared. Then we both smiled and I went to have my shower, cursing my weakness when it came to her, yet remembering the softness of her lips on mine the whole time.

------•••◦◉◦•••------

Omelettes and toast were waiting when I went back to the kitchen. Sitting down, I smiled as I looked at my plate.

"I hope you like omelettes?"

"Absolutely. Mine never look quite like this though."

"Sorry?"

I laughed. "Mine tend to look more like scrambled eggs with lumps. Never quite figured out the turning and folding trick."

I dug in and smiled at her again. "They certainly never taste like this either."

"What do they taste like?"

"Um ... well, scrambled eggs with lumps, I suppose," I chuckled.

She smiled and began eating. I was amazed at how comfortable it was to sit and share a meal with her. I was used to the silence surrounding me, and although I didn't feel the need to fill the quiet with conversation, I did want to try and draw her out some more. I loved hearing the sweet timbre of her voice.

Rabbit spoke up before I could think of anything to say. "Do you think the next time you go to the barn I could go with you?"

I looked at her as I chewed another delicious mouthful. "Why?"

"I thought maybe if I saw the car, I might remember something."

I nodded. "That's a good idea. We'll go out later. I remembered I have a satellite radio in the cupboard. We'll turn it on after breakfast and see if we can get the local station. See what's happening out in the world."

"Okay."

Nothing. There was nothing on the radio except warnings to stay off the roads and how extensive the storm was. It was expected to rage for at least another day, maybe longer. People were stranded at airports, train stations, all over the place. There were massive power outages and abandoned cars on the highways. But there was no announcement about a missing woman. Sitting beside her on the couch, I looked over at Rabbit, but I wasn't sure what she was thinking. Her troubled eyes lifted to me.

"Sorry," she whispered, before lowering her eyes again.

"Hey." I leaned over and lifted her chin. "We covered this last night, okay? You're safe here. You aren't disrupting anything."

Her eyes remained troubled. Wanting to see her smile, I winked at her. "Besides, if you keep cooking like you have been? Maybe I'll just keep you."

Her quiet giggle made me smile and I watched her relax a little. Without any thought, my fingers stroked her soft cheek. Our eyes locked again and I could feel myself being drawn into the depths of her gaze. Slowly, I leaned forward, Rabbit meeting me halfway. Our mouths met sweetly, lips pressing and moving together. My hand wound itself into her hair, holding her close. Before we could get carried away, I pulled back, resting my forehead against hers. Neither of us said anything for a minute. I moved away and looked at her. Her gaze was questioning, but still warm.

I shook my head. I had no idea what there was about this woman that was causing the reactions I was having to her. But I needed to stop the responses. I reminded myself that nothing was going to happen between us.

I stood up abruptly. "Let's go have a look in the garage, okay? See if that shakes anything in your memory."

She stood up and accepted my proffered hand. But, I saw the flicker of sadness and confusion that passed across her face.

Knowing it was me that put it there, I hated it.

⇒CHAPTER SEVEN⇐

Joshua

I watched silently as Rabbit walked awkwardly around the car. I saw her study the license plate, her brow furrowed in concentration, but no sign of recognition passed over her features. I opened the driver's side door and she gingerly sat down and again looked around slowly. A soft sigh escaped her lips as she struggled to get out. Leaning down, I helped her stand, then immediately dropped her hand. I had to stop touching her.

"Nothing?" I asked.

"No."

We both stood looking at the car. "There are snow tires on it," she observed.

"Yeah, I noticed that. That probably helped you stay on the road longer than you would have been able to."

"Would the reading on the odometer help?"

I was impressed with her logical thinking. "No, the tank is pretty full and I think it was reset when you filled up. The mileage is about right for the distance from the closest town."

"Oh. No receipt?"

I shook my head. "You probably paid cash. You know, from your last heist."

Her lips twitched and I heard her sweet giggle. I smiled; glad the tension that had sat between us since we kissed had eased a little.

Realizing there was nothing to be achieved here, I pulled up my hood. "Come on; let's head back to the house."

I walked over and opened the door and waited for her to catch up. She was walking slower than ever, thanks to the huge boots and my coat, which I had insisted she put on. I had tightened the boots as tight as I could make them, but she was an amusing sight as she attempted to walk, lifting her feet in clumsy-looking steps. As she drew near, I flicked up her hood. "Stay close," I instructed.

The wind had picked up again and the swirling snow was almost blinding at times. I walked in front of her, trying to block the wind, checking over my shoulder every few feet to make sure she was still behind me. We were close to the house when I heard a gasp behind me and I spun around to see Rabbit lying face down in the snow, her shoulders shaking. Thinking she had somehow hurt herself, I quickly kneeled down and gently turned her over. "What? Are you hurt?" I asked anxiously, my eyes scanning her for fresh injuries.

She shook her head but her shoulders continued to shake. I realized she was laughing.

"What is so fucking funny you had to lie down in the snow?" I asked, annoyed at her for scaring me.

Still grasping my hand, she pointed wordlessly at her feet. Unable to help myself, I joined in her laughter. She had obviously stumbled into the deeper snow where the boots had gotten stuck. Her feet came out and she was currently lying bootless, her socked feet wriggling in the cold. I stared down at her pink cheeks, her eyes lit up with mirth as she lay like a mummy in a coat I could have wrapped around her twice, unable to get up.

Her laughter died and silently we regarded each other. I could feel my body responding to her again and the overwhelming desire to kiss her, really, truly kiss her, tore through me. I wanted to taste her. I could feel myself bending forward, closer, my one hand now cupping her cold cheek, watching her breath escape from her lips in tiny puffs of steam. I wanted those lips on mine; I wanted that steam in my mouth. As I bent over her, so close to where I wanted to be, Bear suddenly appeared, pushing his face between us and dousing both of us from his cold wet fur, barking excitedly at whatever game we were playing, wanting to join in. Startled, I sat back, reality hitting me in the face.

Fuck, I needed to stop this.

Cursing and pushing Bear out of the way, I leaned down. "Arms," I instructed.

"What?"

"Put your arms around my neck, Rabbit. Now."

Rabbit lifted her arms around my neck the best she could in the bulky coat. I picked her up easily and carried her inside and let her down on the mudroom floor, not looking at her. I went back out and grabbed the boots and came back in. She had already left the mudroom and I stood silently cursing myself. I had little doubt what would have happened if Bear had not interrupted us. All it took was one touch from her and I lost all common sense. The need to be closer to her drove all normal thought out of my head.

It was simple. I would just not touch her. At all. I could talk to her, laugh with her, but not touch her.

And tonight, I was sleeping on the couch.

I welcomed the scent of coffee brewing when I entered the kitchen. Rabbit was sitting on the couch and Bear was tucked up right against her legs as she stroked him. I turned away, grabbing a couple of mugs with more force than necessary, cringing a little as they slammed down on the counter.

Lucky fucking dog got to have her touch him.

I turned to grab the coffee and saw Rabbit staring at me. I purposefully relaxed my posture and smiled at her. "Oops. Cold hands," I laughed, shrugging my shoulders as if in jest. Then, to buy myself some more time, I dug in the freezer and pulled out some steaks to grill later. An idea occurred to me and I opened a drawer for a pad of paper and a pen. I took a couple of calming breaths and poured both of us some coffee. I went and sat on the other end of the couch from Rabbit after handing her a mug.

"What's the paper for?" she asked, her brow furrowed as she regarded me warily.

"I thought I could ask you some questions. Maybe we could trigger a memory or something …" my voice trailed off.

Liar, that little voice in my mind was taunting me.

You just need to stay busy and not think about touching her.

My mind was right.

She turned and faced me, drawing her legs up against her chest. "Okay. Ask away."

Two hours later, I knew that Rabbit was sure she hated liver and brussel sprouts. That she thought blue was her favorite color and lilies were the prettiest flower. She liked music of all kinds although she did wrinkle her nose at rap. She loved to read and did so voraciously. She hated the smell of cigarette smoke and intensely disliked the colors navy, brown and black. I found her reaction to that question interesting since she had been dressed in a navy shirt and dark pants with a black coat when I found her. But she was adamant in her dislike.

She could not, however, tell me where she had gone to school, the names of any friends, and no matter what female name I threw at her, none struck a spark or made her even pause. She couldn't recall the name of a boyfriend or husband. Part of me was relieved at that piece of information. We talked about different careers, but nothing seemed to break through to her memory. She could rattle off the names of books she had read, movies she had seen, but nothing personal. No information that would give me a clue where to start looking for her identity.

I looked down at the paper I had been scribbling furiously on. I just kept throwing out questions and jotting down notes. It was both an exercise in trying to help her jog a memory as well as a way not to look at her too often and keep my hands busy. I would glance at her as she would close her eyes at times and seem to try and search her mind for an answer but would avert my gaze when I would see her eyes start to flutter open. Her eyes saw too much. I couldn't let her see how I was struggling right now.

We were both quiet as I looked over the various things I had written down. I was trying to find something, *anything,* that could tell me who she was but nothing leapt out at me. Sighing, I put the pad and pen on the table in front of me. I stood up and went to the window looking out at the snow that was still falling. It was hard to tell how heavy it was with the strong wind blowing it around.

"How long have you lived here?"

I started at the sudden question and turned to face her. "Five years."

"What do you do … for a living?"

"I'm a writer."

She sat up. "What do you write?"

I grinned, teasing her. "Books."

I was rewarded with one of her shy smiles.

"What kind of books? Would I have read any of them?"

"My last one might actually help you," I said thoughtfully.

"Really? What was it?"

I turned back to the window. "How to be a better career criminal for dummies," I said, biting my lip to stop from laughing.

I never saw the cushion coming, but certainly felt it hit me squarely in the back of the head.

Laughing, I turned around. "I'll add possible pitcher to your list of maybes, Rabbit."

"Just for that, I'm on strike," Rabbit sniffed, crossing her arms. "I'm not cooking again today."

I continued to laugh as I placed the cushion back on the sofa. "Not a problem. Dinner's on me tonight."

"Better be good," she mumbled.

Grateful I had diverted her questions, I retreated to the kitchen to make dinner. I turned the radio on to see if there were any updates on the storm, and of course, any updates on a missing woman. I was strangely relieved not to hear any news on that front. My mind laughed at me. When she showed up, I could hardly wait to get her off my property and now I was dreading news of a way for her to leave.

Rabbit wandered in and, without asking, began to assemble the salad. She set the table and soon we were ready to eat. She looked down at her plate in disbelief as I sat down beside her. "What?" I asked.

"You don't really expect me to eat all this meat do you?" she asked skeptically.

"You don't eat enough. You leave more food on your plate than you eat," I said firmly. "You need your strength."

She looked down for a minute and then back at me. Her eyes were sad. "I feel like that is what I'm supposed to do. I don't think I eat very much." She shrugged self-consciously. "I get the feeling ..." her voice trailed off.

"What? Tell me."

"I don't think I'm ... allowed to. Like it's a rule."

I felt the anger building again. Something or someone had ingrained that so deeply in her mind that she could follow *that* rule but not remember who she was or why she was doing it.

"New rule, Rabbit. You eat what you want and however much you want. Don't stop because you think you *have* to; stop when *you* want to. I don't want you hungry. Understand?" My voice was firm, and I looked at her, my gaze direct and serious. She nodded, looking down at her plate nervously. I softened my voice. "However much or little *you* want, Rabbit. But your choice, okay?" Her eyes met mine and she nodded. I hated the nervous look in her eyes and I desperately fought the need to stroke her cheek or hold her hand. Instead, I got up and went over to the cupboard and grabbed a bottle of red wine and a couple glasses. Sitting back down, I poured a glass and offered it to her. Then I poured myself one. I needed the alcohol.

We ate in silence for a few minutes when she suddenly looked down at her plate and I heard a muffled giggle.

I looked up at her. "Something funny about your dinner?"

She shook her head, letting out a snicker, her head still bowed.

I looked at my plate, mystified. What was I missing?

I looked up and met with her vivid blue eyes dancing with mirth. "Share. Please."

"I was just thinking ..." another giggle burst forth, making my lips twitch with the desire to join her.

"What?"

"I hope I'm not a vegetarian ..." her voice trailed off as she burst into laughter.

I had to join in her merriment. Lifting up my glass, I toasted her. "Here's hoping you're not an alcoholic either."

She clapped a hand over her mouth but the amusement spilled over. Unable to help myself, I found myself roaring with laughter with her.

Rabbit had a great sense of humor.

I liked it.

Fuck. Of course I did.

⇒Chapter Eight⇐

Joshua

Rabbit moved yet again. We were sitting by the fire, neither of us talking much. The silence wasn't uncomfortable. Since our shared laughter at dinner, we had slipped back into a more companionable state. Using one of the gas lights, I was scanning some notes I had printed before the storm had hit. Rabbit was sitting across from me, closer to the fire, but seemed to be shifting a lot. I watched her for a few minutes and noticed the constant winces of pain as she moved.

"Did you hurt yourself when you fell this afternoon?" I asked, breaking the silence.

She looked over, startled. "I'm not sure, but my side aches."

I thought about it for a moment, remembering the huge patchwork of bruising she had on her side. What if she had caused further damage today? I took in a deep breath. "Your side was really bruised and swollen. I was worried about how bad it looked. Would you let me look at it? Just to make sure it's okay?"

She hesitated and then nodded. She got up slowly and came over to me. I switched on a light, using precious power, but needing it to see clearly.

"I'm just going to lift the shirt so I can see, okay?"

"Okay." The one word was spoken so faintly I could barely hear her.

I lifted the edge of the shirt and saw a large mass of bruising. Once again, I fought back the wave of fury I felt at seeing the evidence of her beating. The area was still swollen and red and the imprint of the top of a shoe, which was more vivid than ever, told me whoever had done this, had stomped on her. Hard. I felt my stomach lurch at the thought of what she had endured.

"Is it okay if I touch you?"

All I got was a nod. Gingerly, I traced over the bruises. The area was warm but not overly hot. I couldn't see any additional bruising but I noticed how she suddenly flinched and heard the small gasp as my fingers traced the shoe imprint. "Sorry," I whispered, hating the thought of causing her additional pain. The desire to press my lips over the bruises and heal her with my touch hit me and I pulled back quickly before I followed through on my impulse. I dropped the shirt and hesitated before asking her if I could look at her leg as well. She nodded and I pulled back the sweats she was wearing, checking the dark angry bruises there, as well. "I think they're just tender. You probably hit them when you fell, so you are feeling it more tonight," I assured her. A thought occurred to me. I sat back unsure how she would take my idea.

"I think we should take some pictures of your bruising," I said quietly.

She stiffened. "Why?"

"When you remember who you are, you may need evidence of what happened to you. I'll use my camera and put the pictures on a flash drive for you. I'll erase them after. I promise."

I heard another soft okay.

I got up and grabbed my camera and a ruler, and then took some pictures. Each bruise I looked at made me nauseous again. I used the ruler against the hand and foot prints to show their approximate size, in case Rabbit needed that information. I could feel the anger building at the faceless person who did this and I wanted nothing more than to give them a taste of their own punishment. When I finished, I stood up. My voice was tense. "All done."

I helped her straighten up from where she had been leaning on the sofa, holding onto her until I felt she could stand on her own again. She stood; her eyes downcast and I could see the tears falling down her cheeks. I knew exactly how vulnerable she was feeling at the moment. But I wasn't ready to share that with her. Instead, I leaned forward and brushed my lips gently against her forehead.

"You were very brave to let me do that," I whispered quietly against her skin, wanting to praise her for her courage. She didn't say anything, but I felt a deep shuddering sigh flow through her. Before I could even acknowledge the need to do so, I wrapped my arms around her and stood holding her. She burrowed into my chest and my arms tightened, holding her closer, still mindful of her injuries. We stood silently for a few minutes, both taking comfort in our closeness. Regretfully, I pulled away and sat her on the sofa. I got some pain pills and gave them to her. "Don't let it get so bad. Stay ahead of the pain," I scolded her gently.

"I don't want to use all your medication," she replied quietly. "You obviously need it as well."

I nodded as I sat beside her. "I do. But I have enough. I don't require them that often anymore."

Rabbit was silent; I looked at her and saw her staring at me, her forehead furrowed in concentration.

"What?"

"You know a lot about pain," she said simply.

I tensed slightly, but nodded.

"Your leg, was it an accident?"

"No."

"What happened?"

I shook my head. "I don't want to talk about it."

"Why?"

I pulled my hand through my hair. I was already struggling to remain calm after seeing all her injuries again. I couldn't handle this conversation right now. "Because I just don't, Rabbit. I don't owe you any explanation."

"I know that," she murmured, her voice gentle. "I just thought ..."

"What? You thought what?" I snapped.

"I thought maybe you'd like to talk about it."

"Well, you thought wrong. Drop it." I could hear the tightness in my voice.

"Sorry, I just thought since you didn't have a lot of people to talk to ..." her voice trailed off.

I stood up, my anger reaching its boiling point. "Why would you say that? You don't know anything about my life. Fuck, at this point, you don't know anything about your *own* life," I hissed at her.

She stood up, tears glistening in her eyes. "That was unnecessarily cruel," she whispered. "I just wanted to help."

I stepped forward, my hands clenched tightly at my sides. "Well, there's the point. I didn't ask for your help. I don't need *your* help. Unlike you, I'm not the one imposing on a stranger to take care of me." I could feel the glare on my face as I spoke to her.

She backed away from me, shaking her head. The expression on her face had turned from confused and hurt to fearful. She turned suddenly and left the room, moving as quickly as she was able to. I heard the bedroom door close.

I spun on my heels and caught sight of my reflection in the window and stopped, aghast at what I saw. No wonder she backed away. I looked menacing even to my own eyes. My hands were clenched in fists and my face was a blank mask of anger. She probably thought I was ... *oh, fuck.*

I sat down and dropped my head into my hands. I scared her. She thought I was going to hit her. I was sure of it. I was angry, but I would never do that. I shook my head as I pulled on my hair. She didn't know that for sure though, did she? All she saw was someone towering over her in anger.

I groaned. She had finally relaxed enough at dinner to joke with me and actually eat. And now I had fucked it up by acting defensive and stupid. Just because she had asked me about my leg at the wrong moment. I stood and went into the hall, approaching the bedroom door. I listened, but didn't hear any sounds on the other side. Bear was lying outside the door, eyeing me with distaste.

I put my hand on the door and knocked lightly. Not surprisingly, there was no answer.

"Rabbit? I'm sorry. I lost my temper. You're safe, I promise. I wouldn't hurt you."

Nothing. There was no response.

"I'm going downstairs. I'll leave you alone. Bear is out here. You can open the door and let him in if you want, after I go."

I waited, but there was only silence.

I patted Bear's head. "Look after her, boy," I said quietly. His answering snort let me know exactly what he thought about what had just transpired.

I came upstairs a couple hours later, having exhausted my anger by throwing myself into my workout. Bear was gone from the hall, so I assumed he was in the bedroom with Rabbit. I added some logs to the fire and lay down on the couch, trying to get comfortable. My mind would not let me rest though. I kept tossing and turning and worrying about Rabbit. Was she okay? Was she still scared? The whole time I was downstairs, I kept hoping she would appear. As I did my exercises and worked out in the pool, I kept an ear open, listening for her soft steps. When I sat in the hot tub, rubbing the sore muscles, I remembered her soothing massage and how good it felt when she worked on my leg. The leg she had simply asked about, wanting to give me the chance to talk about it. I had plied her with questions all afternoon but as soon as she asked one of me, I had become angry. I groaned, thinking about my behavior. What a complete ass.

Finally, I sat up. I needed to check on her, and then I could go to sleep. Once I was sure she was okay, I would relax. Quietly, I made my way down the hall. I tried the door; grateful it wasn't locked, and slipped into the room. It was far colder in the bedroom and I immediately went over to the fireplace and added some logs to get the fire going again. After it was blazing, I went over to the bed where Bear was watching me from his usual place at the bottom. His expressive eyes told me he agreed with my assessment that I was an ass. Rabbit's eyes were shut, but I could see the dampness still on her cheeks from crying. Wordlessly, I got another blanket and tucked it around her. I stood looking at her sadly for a moment, and then turned away. The sudden feeling of her little hand clutching mine stopped me. I turned back around and saw her eyes were open, looking at me. I knelt down beside the bed. "I'm sorry I frightened you. I was already ... angry and your question just caught me off guard."

"Why were you angry?"

"Because someone hurt you. I hate seeing that."

She stared at me for a moment.

"Still, I shouldn't have pushed you. You're right. It's none of my business," she replied quietly. "I am sorry ... for imposing. I'll stay out of your way."

The look in her eyes was heartbreaking. I drew in a deep breath. "You're not imposing, Rabbit. I was an ass. I didn't mean it. You're not in the way."

She didn't say anything. I leaned forward and pressed a kiss to her forehead. "Sleep. We'll talk in the morning."

I began to walk away when she whispered, "Wait."

I looked back and saw her moving. I watched as the covers lifted in silent invitation. Even as my mind was screaming at me to walk away, I crawled under the covers and pulled Rabbit into my arms, sighing with soft relief at having her there.

"Why do I feel so safe here in your arms?"

"Because you are. I would *never* hurt you."

She looked up at me. I couldn't stop myself from stroking her warm cheek. "I'm sorry, Rabbit. I know I scared you. I might get angry and say stupid things but I would never, ever, touch you in anger."

My hand cupped her cheek, "And, you are not imposing. I'm so sorry I said that."

Her eyes gazed into mine. "What am I doing then?"

The words were out before I could stop them. "Saving me from my loneliness," I whispered.

Her eyes widened. "Joshua ..."

Then my lips were on hers. She opened her mouth and my tongue slipped in, tenderly exploring. I groaned at the sweetness of her and her low moan spurred me on. Her hands slipped up into my hair, holding me close. I tilted her head and deepened the kiss, needing to be closer to her.

Her velvet tongue, which seemed hesitant at first, grew bolder and soon our tongues danced together, swirling, hot, and wet.

Stroking. Savoring.

Deeper and deeper.

I felt like I was drowning in her. I wanted more. I wanted her. Hot pulsating desire tore through me. I pulled her even closer, needing to feel her, but the gasp that came out of her mouth this time was not one of pleasure but rather of pain. I pulled back in horror. I had forgotten about her injuries.

"Baby, I'm sorry. I hurt you. Oh, God ..." I ran my hands frantically over her torso.

"Joshua. Stop. I'm fine. It was just a little too ... tight."

I gazed at her, her lips swollen from mine; her hair mussed up from my fingers and leaned forward, kissing her again, this time tenderly. I nuzzled her cheek and then I lay down on my side and pulled her close to me, stroking her hair while our breathing calmed. The quiet of the night and the soft pulse of her breath were so peaceful as we lay together. It was as if the events of the evening which had opened up something inside me and, suddenly, I wanted to answer her question from earlier.

"I was attacked."

Her hands tightened on my shirt as she reacted to my sudden words. "Where?"

"Outside my apartment building in Toronto. I was walking home from dinner one night. I was jumped and dragged into an alley ... and beaten. Badly."

Her hands released my shirt and wound around my waist, holding me. "When I woke up, I was in the hospital. I had been in a coma for two weeks."

"Oh, Joshua," she breathed.

"I was pretty much a mess. My face was beaten, my nose broken, two broken ribs, a ruptured spleen ... and my leg ..." I drew in a deep breath. "It was literally in pieces. They had already operated on it and it took more surgeries and months of physiotherapy before I could begin to walk again." I shuddered, remembering the pain when I had first woken up.

"Are you in pain a lot?"

"Some days. There was so much damage and not all of it could be repaired. Add in the pins, screws and whatever else they pieced it back together with, I feel it every day."

"Why?"

"Wrong place, wrong time. They were high and wanted to get higher. I didn't have enough cash on me and they were angry. So, they punished me for it." I was quiet for a minute.

"It wasn't until I was partway through my recovery that I was given the news I would probably never be able to father a child. They had taken that away from me as well. There was… a lot of damage."

Rabbit's hand came up and pulled my head down to her chest. I was surprised to find my face wet with tears. Her hand stroked my head gently and she whispered soothing words, allowing me the comfort of her embrace. With her warmth and softness around me, I felt myself let go and I acknowledged the pain I carried with me without even realizing it. After a few minutes, I looked up at her. "Sorry," I whispered.

Her hand wiped away the remnants of my tears. "Don't be sorry. I understand." She smiled and warmly grazed her lips on my forehead. I tightened my arms around her in a silent thank you.

"Did they … did they arrest the people who did this?"

I shook my head. "No. They were gone when I was found and I never got a good look at them. They've never been discovered."

Her arms tensed. "That must be a frightening thought?"

I nodded. "Sometimes more than others."

We were quiet for a few minutes.

"How long were you in the hospital?"

"Six months."

"You moved here after that?"

"Yes. I couldn't stay in the city. I had bought this property a year before it happened and had the house built. I had come up for a weekend and I loved the area and the scenery and one day I was out driving around and stumbled across this piece of land and I had to buy it. So, when I needed to escape the memories of the city, I came here to recover and … I have never left." I drew in a deep breath and looked at her directly. "I have *never* left, Rabbit."

She nodded in quiet understanding, her eyes sad. "Agoraphobia?"

"Yes."

"You can leave your house though?"

I nodded. "It took a long time before I could. Lots of counseling. And Bear. He helped me. He needed to go out and I didn't want him lost, so I had to go with him. But I never leave the property. I'm not sure I ever will."

Rabbit was quiet. "I … I know who you are."

I pulled back and looked at her. "What?"

"I saw the awards on your shelves while you were making dinner and I was putting away the medical books you left out. I saw your books on the bottom shelf. I've read all of them, Joshua. I know you're a mystery writer. A very good one."

I looked at her. Her gaze was soft and accepting.

I shrugged. "I suppose it was only a matter of time before you figured it out. I wasn't trying to hide it. It's just … well; J.B. Bennett is my professional persona. *He* doesn't live here. Joshua does."

She nodded. "I understand, Joshua. I won't say anything. When I leave. Your secret is safe."

My stomach tightened at her declaration.

When she left.

Because she would. Even she acknowledged that. The storm would end, the road would be plowed and she would leave. And, I would stay here and continue with my life. She would figure out her past, pick up the pieces of her life and move on. Those were the facts.

Suddenly, the room was too warm, and Rabbit was too close.

I pulled away and got out of bed.

"Joshua? What's wrong? What did I say?"

I shook my head. "Nothing. I'm thirsty and need a drink. Go back to sleep."

"Are you coming back?" her voice was sad.

"No."

I didn't look back before I walked away.

⇶CHAPTER NINE⇷

Joshua

The rest of the night passed slowly. I didn't even bother trying to sleep, as my mind went back and forth. In the early hours of the morning, the storm finally broke and the wind died down. I stood at the window watching the sun break, gazing at the vast amount of snow that had fallen. The world was white as far as the eye could see. Tree branches were weighed down heavily and ice was visible on the electric wires that I could see towards the one end of the property. I knew I would probably be without communication or power for at least a couple of weeks, maybe more. Mentally, I was going through the gas supply I had left compared to how long I thought it would be before I could get any delivered, when I heard a noise behind me.

I turned to see Rabbit hesitating in the kitchen, unsure if she should come any closer. She looked as exhausted as I felt. Bear stood beside her, eyeing me with utter disdain.

Traitorous dog.

I was exhausted and not in the mood for any kind of confrontation, even though I knew one was about to happen. "I made coffee," I said, turning back to the window.

She nodded and retreated into the kitchen. I sighed and looked out into the vast white world again. I had to talk to her. I needed to stay away from her. And to do that, I had to get her to want to stay away from me.

A mug of coffee appeared before me. I thanked Rabbit and took a sip of the hot liquid, casually stepping away from her. "Storm is over." I pointed out the window. "I'll start plowing in a while."

"Can I help somehow?"

I shook my head. "No. I don't like Bear out when I am driving the plow so he can stay inside with you."

"Joshua?"

"Hmm?"

"What did I do last night? Why did you leave?" she asked nervously.

I sighed. I sat down on the chair and indicated she should sit on the sofa. I couldn't sit beside her. Already, I could feel myself wanting to reach out and touch her. Make her smile. If I was close, I wasn't sure I could resist.

"You didn't do anything, Rabbit," I assured her. "I did."

"I don't understand."

"I crossed the line last night. I shouldn't have done that."

"Talking to me? Telling me about your attack?"

I shook my head sadly. "No, I don't regret telling you that. Kissing you."

"You regret kissing me?"

I couldn't look her in the eye and lie, so I stared at the floor. "I shouldn't have done that."

She looked at me for a minute, puzzled. "I wanted you to kiss me, Joshua. We kissed each other."

My heart clenched a little, hearing her say that. But I had to continue.

"Rabbit, you don't know what you want. You're confused and lost. You have no idea who you are." I drew in a deep breath. "I have no idea who you are."

Her voice was quiet. "What are you saying?"

"You could be married, Rabbit. There could be someone out there looking for you. You have a whole life you don't know anything about. Right now, you're struggling and I took advantage of that."

Her eyes narrowed. "And I might not have anyone in my life." She pulled the sleeve of her shirt up exposing the bruises staining her skin, "Or maybe the person in it did this."

I averted my eyes. "That's the problem, Rabbit. We don't know. I have no right to add to the problem."

"*The problem*? I'm a problem again?"

I stood up, walking over to the window. "No, Rabbit, you're not a problem. My … attraction … to you is, and acting on it only complicates an already confusing situation." I turned around and looked at her. "You need to rest and recover. I need to work. I think it's best if we just try and stay away from each other as much as possible."

"What if that isn't what *I* want?"

"What do you think you want, Rabbit?"

"To be close to you. To get to know you."

"To what end?"

"I … I'm attracted to you as well, Joshua. You make me feel safe. I thought about this all night. I don't feel like there is anyone. I don't have a wedding ring; I don't have any longings for someone like I am missing them. If I had someone, wouldn't I feel something? Some sense of someone?"

I wanted to tell her she was right. I wanted to tell her she was safe. But I couldn't.

"You don't know what you're feeling. And I make you feel safe because, right now I'm the only person you have to depend on. That's all."

"Don't tell me what I'm feeling," she snapped at me.

"I'm trying to stop a huge mistake from happening, Rabbit. One that neither of us could take back," I snapped back.

"And, you're so sure it'd be a mistake?"

"Yes."

"Why?"

I ran my hand through my hair in vexation. She wasn't going to let this go. I straightened my shoulders and stared at her steadily.

"Because you want a relationship."

"And you don't?"

"No."

"What do you want?"

I kept my voice flat. "I just want to fuck someone."

She stepped back in shock.

"But last night you said …"

I laughed humorlessly. "Don't you get it, Rabbit? I'm a man I've been alone for a long time. I'm attracted to you because you're a woman. Nothing more. And last night? Words. I'm good with words. I'm a writer, remember? It worked didn't it? I could have had you so easily …" I sneered at her.

Her hand flew to her mouth. I watched her eyes fill with tears of hurt. I went in for the kill.

"Is that what you want, Rabbit? A couple of weeks of mindless, meaningless sex with a stranger? Then you can go back to your life and pretend it didn't happen? Will you be able to look your husband or boyfriend in the eye when they tell you how much they love you and how happy they are you're back? I'm happy to accommodate if that's what you're after."

She shook her head, the tears coursing down her cheeks.

I turned my back before I broke down in front of her.

"Just stay out of my way. I won't take advantage of you anymore. As soon as the roads are clear, I'll make sure you get to a hospital or police station."

I heard the sound of her feet as she ran from the room.

My shoulders sagged.

She'd stay away from me now, for sure.

I came in from clearing the front of the house. I'd been at it for a couple of hours and I needed a break. The house was utterly silent. I hung up my wet clothes and went into the kitchen, passing the closed bedroom door. Nothing had changed or moved. Obviously, she hadn't come out. I made a sandwich and hesitated. Should I offer her one? I looked over at Bear who was by the hearth and continuing to ignore me. I sat and ate, not even tasting what I was chewing. Not caring how it tasted, I just heated up some of the leftover coffee. Now that the snow had stopped, the temperature had dropped and it was cold out. I just needed the warmth. I added some logs to the fire and sat looking at the flames. I glanced towards the hall. Would Rabbit think to add logs and not let the fire go out?

I shook my head. Fuck. I didn't want her cold or hungry. I just needed to stay away from her before I allowed something to happen that she might regret. If we acted on our impulses and it turned out she was married, she would regret it. I knew she would torture herself for it. I would rather she hate me, than carry that kind of guilt around.

I stood up and made another sandwich. Then, I went down the hall and knocked on the door. There was no answer but I opened it and went in. Rabbit was sitting in the chair by the window, with a blanket and a book. She stared at me wordlessly as I walked in. I placed the sandwich on the table beside her and went over to the fireplace, adding logs. "Don't let the fire go out, Rabbit. We need it."

She said nothing. I stood up and went over to my closet and grabbed some more dry clothes. "I don't expect you to stay holed up in here. You can go anywhere you want it the house. And eat. You need to keep up your strength."

Still nothing. I sighed and looked over at her. She was staring down at her book. She was incredibly pale and drawn-looking. My heart lurched at the sight of her suffering. I softened my voice. "I'll be in and out all day, and probably tomorrow, working on the snow. You don't have to stay in here." I paused, but there was no response. "Are you in pain? Do you need some pills?"

She shook her head but still didn't say anything. "I'll be in later to add more logs to the fire. Eat your sandwich, Rabbit."

I walked towards the door.

"Joshua."

Her voice stopped me and I turned.

She looked at me with pain-filled eyes.

Her voice was tight. "Don't call me that again."

I nodded and pulled the door closed behind me.

It worked.

She hated me.

⇾CHAPTER TEN⇽

Joshua

I sat in the hot tub, the water moving around me; my leg throbbing painfully. The front part of the house leading to the barn and the drive was plowed, but it had taken most of the day. Tomorrow, I would start the process of the long, winding drive, but at least I would be inside the truck where it would be warmer. After a while, the jets shut off and I lay there in the hot water just letting the warmth seep into my cold body. I had heard some footfalls moving overhead earlier and knew Rabbit had gone back into the bedroom now that I was back in the house. A couple of times when I stopped to take a break, I had caught a glimpse of her at the window looking out. The urge to wave at her had been so great, and yet I resisted. I wasn't sure if she knew I saw her and I didn't want her staying in the bedroom all the time to avoid me seeing her. I was dreading the long evening that stretched out in front of me. Normally, I would read or work, but neither appealed to me. What did appeal to me was some great-tasting dinner and the quiet company of a tiny stranger. I grimaced as I stood up. I wouldn't be having either of those again. I winced as I recalled the tone in her voice when she told me not to call her Rabbit anymore.

I dried off and dressed, climbing the stairs slowly. I needed some pain meds. I hesitated outside the bedroom door, then straightened my shoulders and knocked before walking in. The room was darker now and Rabbit was curled up on the bed, her back to the door. I added logs to the fire, noting that she had brought some in from the front room. I went and got some pills, also noticing they were in the exact place I had left them, meaning she hadn't taken any. I knew she had to still be hurting and I closed my eyes and took a calming breath as I felt a ripple of anger go through me. I swallowed a couple of tablets and shook two more into my hand and refilled the water glass.

I strode over to the bed and set the tablets and water on the table. "If you think not taking any pain medication is somehow getting even with me, then you're acting stupid, Rabbit. The only one suffering because you're being stubborn is you. Take the pills," I said coldly.

"Just leave me alone, Joshua," she said faintly.

"If you don't look after yourself, you can't heal. If you can't heal, you can't remember. You need to eat, rest, and take the pain medication. Give your body the chance to recover. Stop being so bloody stubborn," I snapped.

Her head shifted and she regarded me in the dim light. "I ate the sandwich, I am resting and I didn't take the pills because they make me sleepy. I was saving them for later. I took some regular Tylenol. Don't worry, Joshua. I'm doing everything you want me to do, including staying out of your way. I even brought in some wood so you don't have to come in here and stoke the fire. I am quite capable of doing so myself."

I stood looking down at her. "Do you want to come and have some supper with me, Rabbit?"

She sat up. "I told you to stop calling me Rabbit. Why would you want to have supper with me? You're the one who said to stay out of your way. So, I'm doing that. Or, since you can't fuck my body, you thought you'd just fuck with my mind instead?" she snapped at me. "At least have a little fun that way?"

I stepped back at the venom in her voice. "I just want to make sure you eat. If I don't call you Rabbit, what would you like me to call you?"

She stared at me. "Just don't call me anything. Leave me alone. You're hurting me, Joshua. You just keep hurting me." She lay back down and closed her eyes. I could see her chest rising and falling in distressed little gasps of air.

My hand hovered in the air, desperate to touch and soothe her. I pulled it back. I walked to the door and hesitated. "I'm leaving the door open so the air can circulate. It's really cold outside and I want the house to stay warm. I won't bother you. Okay?"

"This is your house, Joshua. I'm just the person making you uncomfortable in your own home. Do whatever you want," she whispered tiredly.

"Call me if you need something, Ra ... I'm just down the hall," I said quietly, my voice sad.

There was no response.

I knew she wouldn't call.

The silence in the house screamed around me.

I pulled the plow into the barn and got out, slamming the door. I stood looking towards the driveway. It was almost done. The drifts in some places were massive and I had to use not only the plow but the snow blower to clear some of them. I figured I had about another three hundred feet to go before I got to the gate. Then I would start on the dirt road. I sighed, exhausted and in pain again. I glanced towards the house, wondering for the hundredth time what Rabbit was doing. Not a word had been spoken between us in the last two days. When I went into the house for breaks, I would see a washed plate or glass in the drainer. I knew she left them so I would know she was eating. I would hear her moving around when I was downstairs, so I knew she was making sure to only come out of the bedroom when she was sure not to bump into me. I also knew she was sleeping about as little as I was, as I saw the dim light from the lantern burn long into the night as I lay on the sofa. Once she crept out of the bedroom to get a drink and I pretended to be asleep. She stood over the back of the sofa and I felt the blanket being pulled up and around me. I wanted to reach out and capture her hand in mine and talk to her, but she turned away quickly with a soft sigh and walked away. When she did sleep, she often cried out in fright, and more than once, I had snuck in and stroked her hair until she settled, often sighing my name. It took everything I had not to crawl in beside her and pull her into my arms. Bear was her ever-present guard, only sitting with me for short periods and looking as sad as I felt as he walked around the invisible mine fields in the house.

I pulled my hand through my sweat-soaked hair as I made my way back to the house. From the news on the radio about the large disaster area around me, I knew we had at least two weeks before any communication or aid from outside would get through. I wasn't sure how either of us was going to survive two more weeks.

I looked at my watch. It was just after three. I needed a shower, a soak in the hot tub and something to eat; in that order. I had taken a casserole out of the freezer that Cecilia had left for me. I was going to heat it up and make Rabbit eat some of it. I was sure she was existing on toast or sandwiches.

Inside, I hung up my coat, went into the bathroom in the hall and, shivering in the cold, I stripped and hopped into the shower quickly. I grabbed some clean clothes in the mudroom and went downstairs. Almost immediately, I heard footsteps above me. I sank into the tub, letting the heat ease my muscles. The footsteps ceased, so I assumed Rabbit was now back in the bedroom. I heard Bear bark sharply and frowned. He rarely barked. Rabbit must have closed the bedroom door and he wanted in. The ache was so bad in my leg that I reset the timer for another twenty minutes when it went off, needing the extra cycle today. I rubbed the muscles ineffectually, thinking once again of Rabbit's well-done massage. The timer shut off and I got out and dried off.

Bear was barking again and I could hear his paws beating across the floor. I went upstairs and found him waiting for me, pacing. I remembered I hadn't fed him and walked slowly to the kitchen. I noticed the bedroom door wasn't shut, just pulled to. I knew his reason for the barking and pacing now. He was hungry. He continued to pace back and forth to the front window and I sat his food down and called him. He came over, looking at me, a low whine in the back of his throat. I looked at him, leaning down and patting his head. "What's up, Bear?" I asked, confused at his stance. He was acting rather strange. He padded down the hall towards the bedroom and stood whining by the door. My stomach clenched and suddenly I was nervous. Was Rabbit okay? I followed him and pushed the door open. The room was empty. The bathroom door was open and she wasn't there either. I made my way to the living area and made sure she wasn't lying on the couch. My heart began to beat faster. Where was she? I called her name but only silence greeted me. I quickly checked the closed-off rooms but they, too, were empty. I made my way upstairs, praying she had fallen asleep and hadn't heard me but there was nothing but another empty room staring at me.

She wasn't downstairs.

She wasn't in the basement.

She wasn't in the house.

Anywhere.

Rabbit was gone.

⇒Chapter Eleven⇐

Joshua

I took in a calming breath. She probably went outside to get some fresh air and I was panicking over nothing. I went downstairs, opened the door and looked around. I called her name but heard nothing. A thought occurred to me and I went back into the bedroom, searching. The bag I had found in the car was gone.

She was running. But to where? What was she thinking? Where the fuck was she going? I roared out in frustration and panic as I grabbed my coat and boots and hurried to the barn with Bear hot on my heels. I had to find her.

The truck thundered to life and I tore down the driveway, the tires spinning on the snow-covered surface. As I rounded the last bend, I saw her, trudging slowly through the still-unplowed snow about a hundred feet ahead of me. Her head was bowed and she was struggling to keep moving forward. I threw the truck in park and climbed out of the cab. Bear jumped out behind me barking and running through the thick snow.

"Rabbit!" I yelled, following Bear. She kept going. I pushed forward closing the distance. Bear had reached her and was in front of her, dancing around, barking and jumping. She ignored him and kept plodding forward. "Rabbit! Stop walking right fucking now!" I snarled loudly in anger. I closed the last few feet and grabbed her arm, spinning her around. "What the fuck are you doing? Where are you going?"

She barely looked at me, pushing my hand off her arm, as she turned back away from me. "Away from you."

"Exactly how far do you think you're going to get before you fucking freeze to death?" I demanded, grabbing her once again.

"I don't really care," she muttered.

"Well, I do," I shouted. "You're coming back to the house. Now!"

She looked at me and my heart lurched at the sight of the frozen tears on her face. "I'm not your problem, Joshua. Just forget I was even here. I'll just get to the main road and someone will pick me up there."

I stared at her in horror. She really thought she'd just walk to the road? That it was that simple?

"Rabbit, the road is at least a mile away—probably more. And, it won't have any cars on it. It won't even be plowed yet! Even if I let you go, you'll never make it!"

She gazed at me for a minute, and then turned her head towards the road and shrugged. She pushed my hands off her shoulders and turned around, beginning to move forward again.

What the fuck? Obviously, she wasn't thinking clearly; if she was thinking at all. Without another thought, I lunged forward and, in one motion, spun her around and flung her over my shoulder. I heard her gasp of shock and pain as she hit my shoulder, but I was past caring. She wasn't going anywhere; she was coming back to the house with me. I strode through the snow holding Rabbit closely so I didn't jostle her any more than I had to. The entire time we closed the distance back to the truck, I berated her. What the fuck was she thinking? There was no way in hell I would let her just … leave. Did she really think I could act as if I didn't care and stand here and watch her walk away? Did she not realize she would die before she reached the main road? It was fucking freezing out and she wasn't even dressed properly! Where the fuck was her common sense? By the time we got to the truck, I had finished my tirade, Rabbit not once interrupting me. I opened the truck door and literally flung her on the seat, slamming the door behind her. I went around the truck and let Bear into the back. I began to climb in the driver's seat, only to see her scramble out of the truck and begin walking back towards the house. "What the fuck are you doing?" I bellowed, chasing after her. "Get back in the fucking truck, Rabbit! Now!"

She kept moving. I caught up to her and spun her around. Tears were pouring down her face. "Leave me alone, Joshua," she pleaded. "Just leave me alone. I can't … I can't …" her voice trailed off into deep chest-ripping sobs. My anger drained away. Intense longing tore through me. The need to comfort, to care and to claim the sobbing woman in front of me overwhelmed my senses and I dragged her into my arms. I rained kisses over her wet face, struggling to keep her close. She twisted and pulled, trying to get away from me. I refused to let her out of the cage of my embrace and eventually she fell forward, burrowed into my chest, her body shaking with emotion and cold. I picked her up, gently this time, and carried her to the truck. I kept her trembling form in my arms, across my lap as I drove the truck back to the house. My lips never left her skin. They brushed soft kisses and gentle caresses over her cheeks, forehead, and the crown of her head; anywhere they could reach. I could feel the deep cold in her body as she shook in my arms, not saying a word, her sobs tearing at my heart.

Once inside the house, I moved as quickly as I could. I carried her to the basement and sat her down on the stool. Bear sat beside her, whining deep in his throat, sensing her distress. She was shaking violently and I knew I had to warm her up, albeit slowly. I hastily removed my clothes, leaving my boxers on and then knelt in front of her, removing her frozen shoes and socks. Her feet were like ice. I rubbed them, trying to stimulate circulation and then reached up and pulled off her jacket. The entire time I bit my tongue to stop myself from screaming at her again. I doubted she would have even made it to the end of the drive, she was so cold. The thoughts of what could have happened kept playing over and over in my head. Gently, I stood her up and lifted her chin. "I'm taking off your clothes, Rabbit. I need to warm you up, okay?" I spoke calmly and kept eye contact with her, making sure she understood what I was saying. She continued to stare at me and I quickly pulled her shirt off, followed by her sodden pants, leaving her in just her underwear. Her skin was freezing cold to the touch, with a slight bluish tinge to it. I braced myself for the next part. Lifting her up, I walked over to the exercise pool. I looked down at her. "Hold tight, Rabbit. This isn't going to feel good at first, but we need to do this." I stepped into the lukewarm water and submerged us both quickly. Rabbit gasped at the shock and struggled in my arms. I held her tightly.

"I know it feels like you're burning, Rabbit. Your body needs to warm up slowly. It's okay. It will pass." I whispered quietly into her ear, continuing to hold her as the chills raced through her body. She whimpered but stopped struggling and I sat down on the ledge in the pool and loosened my hold. I ran one hand up and down her legs and arms, trying to add more warmth to her body. I stroked her hair, grazed her cheeks with my lips and hummed lovingly into her ear to distract her. I have no idea how long we were sitting before I was satisfied she was back to a more normal temperature, and her sobs had silenced. Then I stood up and carried her over to the hot tub and, once again lowered us both into the water. This time she simply sighed and relaxed in my arms, welcoming the heat. Her head fell against my shoulder and I stroked her hair as I leaned back and allowed myself to relax.

Minutes passed, the only sound in the room that of the bubbling water. Rabbit's unexpected apology was spoken softly.

"Why?" I asked back just as softly. "Did you think I wouldn't notice you were gone?"

"I thought I'd be long gone before you did," she admitted, not looking me in the eye. "I didn't realize how far away the road was."

I sighed. "If I didn't find you, Rabbit, you could have died from exposure." I lifted her chin up and made her look at me. "Do you think I could have lived with myself if that happened?"

Her chin quivered. "I didn't think you cared. That you would just be happy I was gone. I didn't really think you'd come look for me."

My heart clenched at her words. "No, Rabbit, the problem is that I care too much," I confessed. My hands moved and cupped her cheeks, stroking the downy skin. "And, it scared me, so I said some dreadful things to push you away. But I didn't mean them. I'm so sorry I ever said them."

Silently, we regarded each other. Slowly, I brought my hand around her neck and pulled her closer, my eyes never leaving hers. "Tell me you believe me, Rabbit. Tell me you forgive me," I pleaded.

Her whispered 'yes' escaped just as I crashed my mouth onto hers, pulling her against me. I poured everything I was feeling into that kiss.

My relief.

My apology.

My need.

My want.

My desire.

All for her.

Her arms wound around my neck, pulling herself closer. I shifted her body and soon she was straddling my lap, our chests pressed together, hands roaming, stroking and caressing each other gently. Eventually, I pulled back and gazed down at her. My thumb traced over her bottom lip as we both struggled to catch our breath. "What about what you said? What if there is someone …?" her voice trailed off.

I shook my head. "Later, Rabbit. We'll deal with that later. You're here. With me. And while you're here, you're mine," I replied, my voice low. "You belong to me. Right now, you belong to me. Understand?"

"Yours, Joshua. Yes."

I claimed her lips again.

Mine.

⇒Chapter Twelve⇐

Joshua

Warmth. Sweet-smelling, delicious warmth. My arms tightened around the soft form pressed into my chest and I settled deeper into the covers. Gentle lips brushed against my chest, up my neck and across my jaw. Slowly, I opened my eyes and smiled into the vivid blue eyes of Rabbit, who was gazing up at me nervously. "Hi," she whispered.

"Hi, yourself," I whispered back, leaning down to kiss her. "Why are you looking at me like that?"

"I ... umm ... I wasn't sure if I was awake or if this was just a good dream." Her voice was shy and hesitant.

I quirked my eyebrow at her. "Just a *good* dream, Rabbit? Well, that's just not ... acceptable." Grinning, I quickly rolled us, making sure not to hurt her and slowly lowered my head. "Let's see if I can't make that an amazing dream ..." my voice trailed off, sounding low and husky. I lightly grazed my lips on hers, and then drew her bottom lip into mine. Gently, I nibbled on the plump flesh, before slowly drawing my tongue along the top, teasing her. The quiet whimper at the back of her throat made me smile, and I covered her mouth with mine, groaning as I felt her tongue reach out to twine with mine. My senses exploded and I gathered her to me carefully, deepening the kiss. Her hands reached up, curling into my hair, pulling me closer and responding so sweetly that another groan broke from my throat. Shifting my weight, I rolled us again to the side and my hands found their way under the t-shirt she was wearing and began a circuit, slowly caressing her skin, needing to feel her warmth.

Desire raged through me and I drew back, panting as I looked down at her. Her wide eyes gazed back pleading. "Don't stop, Joshua ... please."

"Rabbit, I'm afraid I'll hurt you. I *can't* do that ..." I whispered, pleadingly, needing her to understand why I had stopped downstairs, why I was stopping now.

She shook her head. "You won't." Her hands pulled me down closer. "You won't ..." she breathed, her tongue flicking out, touching my mouth, gently trailing its sweet moisture across my lips. "Please, Joshua."

I groaned deeply and gave in to the need I had been fighting since I carried her up from the hot tub and placed her back where she belonged. With me; in my bed, in my arms.

The need to make her mine filled me. Completely. My mouth hungered for her taste, my hands were desperate for the feel of her skin under them and my body wanted to possess and claim her. I needed to hear her calling my name as she came. I needed it now. She was right, I *would* have her now, and I wouldn't hurt her.

I rolled us yet again so she was on top of me. I sat up, drawing her close as I captured her mouth with mine, delving, tasting her sweetness. My hands removed her t-shirt and explored her curves, learning the spots that made her whimper with need into my mouth as she clutched my arms, trembling.

"Touch me, Rabbit," I begged, breaking away from her mouth and running my lips down her neck. Her hands drifted down my arms and ran up my chest, delicately stroking and exploring, her lips following their path as she shifted. My head dropped back as I felt the warmth of her mouth on my skin. Her hands slipped down, finding me hard and wanting and I hissed in pleasure as I felt her wrap her hands around my throbbing erection, stroking gently. Leaning forward, I claimed her mouth again and felt her rise up to greet me, I reached down and my hand found her slick and ready for me. Slowly, I explored and touched as she moaned into my mouth. Smoothly pulling her up, I positioned her and watched the expression on her face as I slowly lowered her onto my cock, her warmth engulfing me inch by inch. For a minute, we both stilled at the intense feeling of being joined and my eyes drifted shut at the extreme pleasure. I began to move, slowly at first, and as Rabbit began pleading, faster and harder; still keeping in mind not to hold her too tightly and hurt her. She clung to me as my thrusts began to become more powerful and I buried my face in her neck as I felt my orgasm begin to build, its tendrils curling their way hot and desperate through my body.

"So close, baby," I whispered, against her ear. "Let go, Rabbit, come for me," I begged, feeling her body starting to shake and quiver. Her head fell back and she gasped out my name as her orgasm raced through her and her muscles tightened around me. Then, like a dam breaking, my body responded and my release tore through me like molten lava; hot, burning fire racing through my veins as I roared out her name, thrusting until I was spent.

My head fell forward, resting on top of Rabbit's, which was burrowed into my chest. Neither of us spoke, the only sound in the room was our deep intakes of air as we both calmed. Slowly, I sat back, raising her chin and looking at her. Her eyes stared back at me, mirroring the sweetness of the moment. Leaning down, I brushed her lips tenderly and then gently moved us so we were again lying side by side. I kept my arms around her, holding her closely, not yet ready to let her go. Her hands were tucked between us and I felt the movement of her fingers as she ran them in lazy circles over my chest, one hand over my rapidly-pounding heart. My eyes closed as I relaxed, enjoying the soothing rhythm of her touch, only to fly open in panic as I felt dampness on my chest. Releasing one arm, I cupped her cheek, feeling the tears that were running down her warm skin. "Rabbit, what is it?" I whispered.

Silently, she shook her head, burrowing into me even deeper. I moved my hand and lifted her chin, hating to see the tears filling her eyes. "Did I hurt you?" My voice shook.

"No, Joshua … it's …" her voice trailed off.

"Do you regret it?" I asked, already feeling the pain of her of answer.

"No! I don't know how to explain this properly, Joshua … it's …" she paused and her voice became so soft, I had to strain to hear it. "It's as if my body can't handle what just happened. Like I am so full of bliss it can't be contained. It's like I've been waiting for something and I finally found it." Her eyes looked up at me. "I guess that sounds crazy, doesn't it?"

I leaned down and kissed her lovingly. Then again. And again. Each time a little deeper. Each time a little longer. Until I was once again drowning in the taste of her and still needing more. Finally, I broke away and buried my head into her neck, shaking my head as I tried to hold in the feelings that tore through me as she whispered her confession.

"I feel it, too, Rabbit. I finally found it as well."

"What is it?"

I lifted my head and locked my gaze on hers.

"Home, my beautiful girl. I finally found my home."

⇒Chapter Thirteen⇐

Joshua

The fire was crackling in the hearth, Bear stretched out contently in front of it. When we had emerged from the bedroom, he looked at us as if to say 'finally' then had chuffed and walked away as if his job was done and laid down. Rabbit and I were on the sofa, the remnants of the casserole between us, two forks lying in the dish, not even bothering with plates. One glass of wine was passed back and forth, tasting all the better for sharing it with her. Our hands were entwined on the back of the sofa, neither of us willing to be without that connection, even to eat. We were quiet, both of us lost in our thoughts, weary from the emotion of the day, but peaceful with the feelings we had shared and that permeated the atmosphere of the room.

Rabbit stood up and took the dishes into the kitchen, coming back with the bottle of wine to fill our glass. I pulled her down beside me, wanting her closer, and she leaned into me, her head resting on my shoulder. Affectionately, I nuzzled the top of her head, amazed, once again, how well she fit into my side. My hand gently stroked her arm while her hand rested on my knee. I closed my eyes, enjoying a tranquillity I had never experienced before. It was as if everything I needed was in this very room and the sense of emptiness I always felt had vanished.

I heard Bear get up and walk around and then felt the sudden impact of his large body jumping on the sofa. I cracked open one eye and saw he was now sitting beside Rabbit, his huge head in her lap as she stroked him. He sighed deeply and rested his head on his paws, soaking up the attention. I grinned as I leaned over, scratching his neck. "Spoiled dog," I muttered as I glanced at her. She smiled at me and flexed her hand on my knee.

"How long have you had him?"

"Just over three years."

"And he has, um, helped you?"

I sighed. "Yeah, he has. Leaving the house before he came was almost impossible. When I got him, I realized he would have to go outside and be walked and the only one who could do it was me. We learned to go outside together. He hated it as much as I did at first."

"He's been your only … resource?" she asked timidly.

I leaned over and stroked her cheek. "Ask me your questions, Rabbit. I won't get angry."

"You said you had some counseling. How did that work … exactly … if you couldn't leave the house?"

"Ah. The same way I conduct a lot of things in my life. Via webcam."

She looked at me incredulously. "Really? I didn't know that sort of counseling … existed."

"I don't know how common it is. When I was finally able to leave the hospital and I came here, it was just going to be for a while. I didn't plan on staying here. Maggie had been my doctor at the hospital and I kept in contact with her. I'd been here for a couple of months when one day I realized I hadn't been outside for weeks. When I tried I found it wasn't just that I didn't *want* to go outside. *I couldn't.* I knew I was in trouble."

"What did you do?"

I laughed humorlessly. "Nothing. I figured it was just a delayed reaction to the attack and I kept quiet. I just found more and more excuses to stay here. I didn't have to go anywhere. One click of the mouse brought almost everything I needed to me. For a while it was so bad I didn't even go to the door. Whatever was delivered was dropped off in the mudroom and I would get it after they left."

"What changed?"

"My assistant, Cecilia. She acted as a liaison between me and my publishers, brought me things I didn't want to order online, checked up on me, and so many other things, I don't think I could list them all. I thought I was fooling her. I thought I was fooling everyone. But she showed up on one of her bi-weekly trips with Maggie, and it all came out. The next week the webcam was installed and I started sessions with Maggie again. She also sent a local person in that I talked to and who could monitor my medications and work with me in person. Actually, it was his idea to get Bear."

Rabbit looked at me quietly for a moment, and then squeezed my hand. "And things got better?"

"Not right away. It was all baby steps. But, eventually, I was able to leave the house and move around the property. I got to know the delivery people and was able to go out and greet them without a panic attack. I could walk Bear around freely. Work in the barn. Mow the grass. Simple things I couldn't do before."

"But you still can't leave?"

I sighed and shook my head. "Every attempt has failed. Badly." I stood up and began to walk around. "Maggie died a couple years ago. I tried other therapists but none of them were right. Dave still comes to see me and we talk but nothing else has changed. After all this time I don't think it ever will for me."

"What about ... doctors, vet visits, that sort of thing?"

"Cecilia takes Bear for his checkups. I get house calls from the local doctor and even the dentist. Unorthodox, yes. But, at the risk of sounding like a snob, you can do anything when you have the money to pay for it. And, I have the money."

She was quiet for a moment, and then looked at me, her brow furrowed.

"Don't you get ... lonely, Joshua?"

I sat back down and picked up her hand. "I do, occasionally. Really though, I was never much of a social person, Rabbit. I was always a loner. Even my chosen vocation, before this happened was done alone for the most part. And, really, when things are up and running around here, I see and talk to people all day on the computer. I talk with my publishers, editor, Cecilia, other people. I write and edit. Occasionally, a friend comes to visit. Cecilia is still here every couple of weeks. At night I read, listen to music, watch TV, sometimes play a game on the computer; do what most people do with their downtime. I just don't leave my property. This is my life, Rabbit. I've come to accept it and I'm okay with it ... most of the time."

For a few minutes, there was silence. Her voice was husky when she spoke up again. "Do you have any family?"

"No. I was an only child. My parents died when I was in university. There's ... just me."

"Ah," was her quiet reply.

She stood up suddenly, causing Bear to huff in displeasure at being disturbed. "I'll be right back," she murmured, as she left the room. I looked down at Bear, who was staring directly at me.

"She's not going to the bathroom is she, boy?" I asked. His great head shook as he snorted at me before jumping down and moving closer to the fire.

I got up and followed Rabbit. As I suspected, she was in the bedroom, standing in the dark, crying. I pulled her into my arms. "Don't, Rabbit. Don't feel sorry for me. Please."

She shook her head against my chest. "I don't. I just … I can't stand the thought of you alone. I'm sorry about your parents. About losing Maggie. For what those bastards took away from you."

Stunned, I held her closely, rocking us. Her simple words sank in. She didn't start to lecture me on trying to overcome my phobia again. She didn't tell me to try harder. She just offered me her quiet comfort and acceptance. She could no more stand the thought of my being alone as I could the thought of someone hurting her.

I sighed.

We were both in over our heads.

But neither of us was willing to stop.

⇒Chapter Fourteen⇐

Joshua

"This won't work if you don't relax, Joshua."

"I'm trying, Rabbit. It's just … not working."

"It worked before. You enjoyed it, in fact. You groaned … loudly."

I sighed. "I know, Rabbit, but it was different then."

"Different? How?"

"I didn't really … know you as well."

Rabbit's hands stilled. "So 'knowing' me more means you can't relax and let me massage your leg?"

I shifted a little in the deep water. "'Knowing' you makes me, ah, keep thinking of somewhere else I would rather your hands … massage me. It's hard to, um, relax."

Rabbit looked down, her cheeks pink. I watched her bite her lip and then glance up at me from under her lashes. I held my breath as she leaned in closer to my face, her hands slowly drifting higher on my leg. "Are you saying you're aching elsewhere, Joshua?" she breathed softly into my ear. "That there is somewhere else you'd rather my hands … stroke?"

My head fell backwards at the huskiness of her voice. I felt her lips gently caressing my earlobe and her hands gradually, painfully slowly, inched their way to my now rigid, throbbing cock. A growl escaped my lips as her hands finally reached their destination and wrapped around me.

"Here, Joshua? Is this where your ache is?" she whispered, her hands moving and stroking in the hot water.

"Fuck. Yes. Right there, Rabbit … just like that … yes …" I moaned.

Her lips made their way over from my ear, her tongue sweetly dancing along my lips. Groaning, I pulled her mouth to mine, winding my hand in her hair, holding her closely as our tongues stroked and tasted each other. Her hands continued to play with me, stroking, teasing, fondling, as the moans in the back of my throat grew louder. She pulled back from my lips, watching me. She leaned forward again, whispering in my ear again. "Is this how you handled your *aches* on your own, Joshua? With your hand?"

I grunted my acquiescence, not able to form words at this point. I tried to pull her lips back to mine. She resisted me. "Maybe … I should show you a … different way of easing your … ache," she growled softly, her hand stilling. I stared at her as her meaning became clear. My eyes widened as a surge of pure desire shot through me. I knew I should tell her no … that she didn't have to … that I didn't want her to … but the thought of her mouth on me suddenly became an urgent, pounding need. One I couldn't survive without having.

She backed away, pulling me with her. "Stand up, Joshua," she instructed quietly. Shuddering with desire, I did what she asked. "Sit on the edge of the tub and lean back." Keeping eye contact with her, I sat down, the air outside the hot tub cold on my skin. But that wasn't the reason for the shivers I felt run through my body. It was the thought of her … and then it was there. Her mouth, wrapped around me, warm and wet. Her tongue stroking, tasting, swirling. My head fell back against the wall. "Fuck … Rabbit, yes … baby … yes …" I gasped lowly. Pleasure I hadn't experienced in years tore through me as she worked me with her mouth. The intimacy of the moment was overwhelming. And all too soon, I could feel my orgasm start to build. My hands pushed on the hard tiles beside me, my hips thrusting up, my cock needing, yearning for more of her mouth, her swirling tongue. I wanted to be deeper, desperately craving her warmth.

"I'm close, baby, so close … stop … you need to …" I groaned, my voice trailing off. But she didn't. Instead her hands gripped my hips tightly, the gentle sucking becoming rhythmic. I stiffened, my body caught in a stretched arch, shouting loudly as I came, my body shaking with intensity. I sat breathless, shocked at the power of my release when I felt a pulling on my hips. Opening my eyes, I looked down at Rabbit, smiling shyly up at me as she silently urged me back into the water of the hot tub. I lowered myself back into the hot water and instantly reached for her, gathering her into my arms. I lifted her chin and kissed her deeply, tasting myself on her tongue. I groaned at the taste mingled with hers and then buried my face into her neck, trying to calm my racing heart and gasping breaths. Her arms came around me, holding me to her as her hands stroked the back of my neck.

I pulled away and looked at her tenderly. "That was … incredible. Thank you," I whispered. I watched her cheeks turned pink as the vixen that had suddenly taken charge melted away, and, she once again became the shy, endearing woman I was captivated with. I stroked her warm cheek, smiling. I adored every side of her that I discovered. Leaning forward, I nuzzled her neck, slowly trailing my lips up to her ear. I felt her subtle shiver as I nipped softly at her lobe. I was surprised when she pulled away and drifted back into the corner of the tub. "Can I massage your leg now?"

I blinked. "What?"

"You must be relaxed now…?" her voice trailed off.

I moved through the water, resting in front of her. "I am. *Totally relaxed*. Maybe I could do the same for you, Rabbit?" I suggested, smiling as I raised my eyebrow at her suggestively.

"No," she shook her head. "I want to make your leg feel better."

"My leg is good. Promise," I whispered as I wrapped my arms around her, drawing her closer. "What's wrong?"

She shook her head. "Nothing."

My lips rained small kisses on her neck, feeling the tension she was holding. "You're a terrible liar, Rabbit. Almost as bad as you are at being a criminal. Tell me."

"Nothing. That was … just for you. Today is just for you."

I shook my head. The last two days had been 'just for me'. Every time I came in from clearing the snow, there was hot coffee, something ready to eat and the sweetest of kisses waiting. Today, when she had noticed how bad my limp was, she insisted the hot tub was needed and she would massage my leg.

"Rabbit?"

She fixed me with a stern glance. At least, I think it was supposed to be stern. "Your leg, Joshua. Now." Her voice was firm. I gave in for the moment and sat back in the lounger and lifted my leg onto her lap. Her hands began their magical kneading and soon I could feel the ache begin to disperse. I closed my eyes and gave in to the quiet pleasure of her gentle ministrations. Every so often, I would steal a peek and watch her face as she worked on the muscles. I enjoyed watching the myriad of emotions play across her expressive face. Her brow would furrow when she would find a tight spot and then she would frown as she worked on it. Often, she would look at me, biting her lip as if to make sure I was okay. The times when our eyes would meet I would smile at her and she would return it with my favorite of all her smiles, her shy one.

Looking down in the water, I could see her hands moving as she worked, kneading and stroking the muscles. The pain was almost totally gone and all I was feeling were the ripples of pleasure of her hands on me. I found myself staring at her hands, silently willing them to move higher, suddenly wanting to feel her hands stroking me again. I could feel myself start to stir as my body, once again, grew taut with desire for her. Her hands stilled and she glanced up at me in question. Our eyes locked as I stared silently at her, my eyes darkening with longing.

"Again?" she whispered incredulously.

I grinned to myself. I wanted her all the time. Leaning forward, I pulled her to me, kissing her deeply. "Again."

This time she didn't push me away. Her arms wrapped around my neck as she pulled me closer, settling herself onto my lap. Our mouths met again in a frenzy of wet, deep kisses, tongues entwining, exploring; our teeth nipping and teasing. My hands traced over her curves again and again, reaching around to cup her breasts, stroking and teasing her nipples as they grew hard and tight beneath my fingers. Her head fell back as I began caressing her neck with my tongue, soft, fluttering touches that had her moaning constantly. My lips reached her ear and I pulled on the lobe gently with my teeth.

"Are you ready for me, Rabbit? Can I have you *now*?" I growled lowly into her ear.

"Yes … please …" her voice was plaintive and full of want.

Pleased, I captured her lips again and thrust up into her. She broke away from my mouth, gasping as I filled her. I wrapped one arm around her waist and the other around her neck as I moved in her, keeping her anchored to me. My body surged into her again and again as my lips claimed her, kissing and nipping at her wet skin anywhere they could reach. Her body arched into me, meeting my thrusts as her hands gripped my biceps, her soft moans of pleasure becoming louder and deeper as we both reveled in the pleasure. Her head snapped back suddenly as she cried my name, her body stilling with the intensity of her orgasm. I continued to move until the rush of her pleasure had abated and finally let myself go, her name tumbling from my lips as I emptied myself deep inside her.

Rabbit slumped forward, her head resting on my shoulder. I wrapped my arms around her, once again sinking into the deeper water, my hands caressing the skin of her bare back as we both regained our senses. My lips ran an endless loop of small caresses on the top of her head. Her head tilted up, her ever-expressive eyes gazing up at me, warm and content. Groaning quietly, I kissed her, needing the feel of her lips against mine again. "We'd better get out soon, or we'll both be prunes," I whispered regretfully. I could stay here, inside her, for an eternity.

She nodded silently. We made our way out of the tub, and I wrapped her in a huge towel, pulling her to me after draping one around my own waist. Her eyes were heavy and I couldn't help the grin that tugged at my lips. "Did I tire you out, my girl?" I whispered against her lips.

She nodded while trying to stifle a yawn, "Working on your various ... aches ... was rather ... exhausting," she admitted with an indulgent smile.

Bending down, I scooped her up and, over her protests, carried her upstairs to the bedroom. "Hush, the rest of the day is about *you*. Now, let me show you just how well you worked out all my aches."

She hummed in contentment.

I smiled in triumph.

Mine.

⇛Chapter Fifteen⇚

Joshua

I pulled the truck into the barn. The driveway was done, and I had cleared one path down to the main road. That took the longest time since as soon as I lost sight of the gates the panic would set in. Having Bear in the truck with me helped but it was still a slow process. I could only go so far then I had to come back to gather up the courage to go even further next trip. Emotionally, it was exhausting.

I climbed out of the truck with Bear clamoring past me, pushing his way through, obviously in a hurry to see Rabbit. The sudden sound of her voice greeting Bear startled me, and I turned to see her standing in the doorway.

Immediately, I was worried. "What's wrong?" I asked as I stepped towards her.

Her smile eased my worries as she came forward. "Nothing, Joshua. I knew you'd be back soon and I just thought I'd come out for some air and bring you your coffee." It was only then I noticed the thermos in her hands. I smiled and reached out, wrapping my arms around her. I nuzzled her cheek fondly. "Hmm ... cold."

She laughed. "Yes, it is rather, isn't it?" She pulled away looking at me. "Are you okay, Joshua?"

Ah. The real reason came out. I smiled and tucked her back under my chin. "I am now," I admitted quietly.

"Would it help at all if I came with you next trip?" she asked gently.

I thought about it and nodded. "It might." Having her beside me might ease the panic.

Wanting to keep things light, I grinned and squeezed her quickly. "Although you are gonna have to fight Bear for shotgun. He called it long ago, you know."

"Pfffth," she giggled. "I can take him. He's putty in my hands."

I pulled away and looked down at her. Her vivid blue eyes gazing up at me, cheeks pink from the cold, the bruises finally starting to fade. "We both are," I smiled and kissed her warmly. The thermos hit the ground as she wound her hands into my hair, pulling my head back down to her lips. I went willingly and lost myself in her, savoring her taste. All too soon Bear distracted us, pushing the thermos around with his nose, thinking it was some sort of new game. After the third time of knocking into us and almost sending us both onto the floor, Rabbit broke away laughing. She bent down and grabbed the thermos. "Not yours, Bear," she scolded sweetly. Then she dug into the pocket of my hoodie that she was wearing, and handed him a biscuit. "This is for you." I watched smiling as he gently took the biscuit out of her small hand, set it down on the floor, and rubbed his head up against her in thanks before picking it back up and trotting away.

Rabbit opened the thermos and poured me a cup of the steaming liquid. I took it gratefully and drank it swiftly, holding it back for more. Rabbit's eyebrow arched but she silently poured me another cup. This time I sipped it, offering to share. She took a sip and handed it back to me, and started wandering around the space. I watched her stop by the car and look at it, studying it, only to shake her head and move away. "You can't force the memories," I reminded her.

She shrugged. "I know. I'm not trying to. I just keep thinking something will bring my head back into focus."

I watched her, feeling worried. She'd had some nasty headaches the past couple days and I was worried it was because she was trying to push the memory loss issue too hard. I hated seeing her in pain.

Her eyes moved around and, for the first time, she noticed the staircase. "What's up there?"

Grateful for the distraction, I held out my hand. "I'll show you."

Feeling rather self-conscious, I took her upstairs and showed her my art studio. I sat on the bench, watching her take it in.

She was silent as she walked around, stopping to gaze at a canvas or one of the charcoal drawings that were tacked on the wall. "Joshua, these are marvellous!"

I shrugged. "It was part of my therapy with Maggie while I was in the hospital. I was surprised how much I enjoyed it, and when I built the barn, I added this space."

"Do you sell your work?"

"I have sold some, yes. It's more a hobby than anything."

"Watercolors and charcoal; are those your favourite mediums?"

I nodded. "I tend to do more between the spring and fall. But sometimes I fire up the heaters and work in here in the winter. The views from up here are amazing."

She came and stood in front of me. "They are beautiful, Joshua. Thank you for showing me."

She shivered and I stood up from the bench. "Let's go back to the house. I don't want you cold." Hand in hand, we trudged slowly back, Bear running ahead only to stop and come barrelling back towards us playfully barking and circling around us. Rabbit laughed in delight at his antics and I grinned at her reaction. I loved seeing her relaxed and carefree no matter how briefly. Once in the house we made our way into the main room and I smelled the aroma of something sweet.

"What do I smell?"

"I … umm ... baked some pies. Apple. You have so many and I didn't want them going bad so I thought I'd try."

I walked over and examined the pies sitting on the counter cooling. I grinned widely. I couldn't remember the last time I'd had homemade pie. Or pie of any sort. "When can we eat them?"

Rabbit laughed. "Don't get too excited, Joshua. I did them without a recipe, just from an idea in my head. And we both know that my head isn't very reliable these days. They might not be very good."

I shook my head. "Impossible. They smell fucking amazing and I want a piece. Now." I looked at her pleadingly. "Please?"

She laughed and went to the cupboard to get me a plate, and then cut me a generous slice. She watched anxiously as I cut into it and chewed. "I used butter in the pastry since you didn't have lard. Is it okay?"

I shook my head. "No, it isn't actually."

Her face fell. I leaned forward and kissed her. "It is beyond okay, Rabbit. It's the best pie I've ever tasted. Thank you."

The relief was evident in her voice. "Really?"

I nodded and kept eating. The rich, buttery pastry melted in my mouth and the filling was sweet, dense and well-laced with cinnamon. Looking down, I realized I had eaten the entire slice, except for one bite. Embarrassed, I glanced up to see Rabbit watching me with a grin. I returned her grin, and then silently offered her the last bite off my fork. She leaned forward and covered my hand with hers, guiding the fork to her mouth. I watched as her lips wrapped around it and she slowly drew back, keeping her eyes on me as her tongue darted out, flicking the tiny crumbs of pastry off her mouth as she chewed. She closed her eyes and moaned quietly.

I shivered.

Fuck, that was hot.

Her eyes opened and looked at me steadily … and the vixen was back.

I narrowed my eyes at her. "Rabbit …" I warned subtly.

She looked at me, smiling innocently, her eyes dancing. Her head tilted to one side teasingly. "Joshua?"

I stepped forward.

"Did you want me to … fork … another piece for you?" she giggled suggestively.

My lips twitched in amusement at her word play. "I *would* like to … fork … a piece …" I grinned at her, stepping forward again.

Rabbit backed up, hitting the counter. I stepped forward until I was right in front of her. Slowly, I reached beside her and set my empty plate down. Then I leaned on my arms, creating a cage around her. Her eyes gazed up at me, suddenly wide with longing, her chest rising rapidly in short breaths. Smiling, I leaned forward, my lips grazing up her neck to her ear, nipping on the lobe. I felt the rippling shudder flow through her body. "If I wanted that … *fork* … right here and right now Rabbit, would you have a … problem … with that?" I whispered huskily into her ear.

Her whimper was all I needed and I pressed myself flush against her and covered her mouth with mine. Her mouth opened and instantly our tongues began their sweet dance. I groaned and wrapped my arms around her, lifting her to the counter. Her legs draped around my waist, drawing me closer and I felt myself swell further and begin to throb with desire. My hips began thrusting slowly, rubbing my sheathed cock against her warmth as my mouth devoured hers.

Her hands stole under my shirt, stroking my back, pressing me closer. Her feet were moving and shifting and then I felt my sweatpants and boxers being pulled down. I pulled back, gasping, as the cool air hit my skin. I quirked my eyebrow at her. "Very dexterous trick, Rabbit," I growled.

In a quick move of my own, I wrapped one arm around her waist and lifted her, grabbing the waistband of her pants and dragged them down her legs. Then I sat her down on the counter with a grin. "Touché," I grinned as she gasped in surprise when her skin met the cold granite.

I leaned forward, my teeth nipping and licking at her neck. I made my way up to her ear. "Don't worry, Rabbit, I'll warm you up."

Her hands pulled at the hem of my shirt and I lifted my arms to accommodate her. I did the same for her and then crushed her against me, my hands stroking and caressing her warm skin while hers wandered over my arms and back, finally settling on my buttocks urging me forward.

"*Now, Joshua. I need you. Please.*"

I pulled her forward and drove into her slick warmth in one thrust. Her legs tightened around me, holding me close, meeting my rapid thrusts with a series of small whimpers and moans. Her head fell back and I buried my face in her arched chest, my tongue laving, swirling; tasting the softness of her skin and teasing the hardness of her peaks. I could feel myself losing control and began thrusting harder, erratically, as I chased the overwhelming sensation that was spiralling through my body. Her sudden shudder of ecstasy was what I needed to let go and I held her tightly as I came deeply inside her, moaning her name.

Finally, I stilled, holding Rabbit tightly, one hand fisted in her thick hair. I pulled back slightly and captured her lips and kissed her over and over again. Gentle, sweet touches of my lips to hers. Small loving caresses that whispered of feelings we hadn't expressed yet but we both felt. "Arms, Rabbit," I whispered.

Her arms lifted and wrapped around my neck. I picked her up, still buried inside her and carried her into the shower.

The warm water rushed over us and we took turns lathering up and gently washing each other. I grabbed the towels and wrapped her up in one before wrapping one around my waist. I lazily ran a towel over her damp skin, nuzzling her shoulder. She giggled softly and padded ahead of me into the bedroom. I watched her as she pulled on a pair of her pants, but grabbed my grey hoodie, pulling it over her head. "I'm going to have to charge you rent on that." I grinned, coming up behind her. "I never get to wear it anymore." She wrinkled her nose at me in the mirror as she struggled to get the comb through her hair. Leaning over, I plucked the comb from her hand and carefully worked it through the snarls. "I'll get you some conditioner as soon as I can get a delivery to us," I said, frowning. "This must hurt, Rabbit." I met her eyes in the mirror. She was smiling sweetly at me.

"What?"

"You never hurt me, Joshua." Her voice was confident.

I smiled and continued to work the knots out of her hair. Once I was satisfied, I put down the comb and grabbed some clothes. I sat on the side of the bed and pulled some socks on my feet. Lifting my head, I saw Rabbit was in front of me. She held up the comb. "My turn."

I snorted. "Knock yourself out. It won't help much." But I let her run the comb then her hands through my hair, enjoying the feeling of being cared for.

Holding her hand, I escorted her to the sofa, making sure she was comfortable before sitting beside her.

The sound of Bear's giant paws descending from upstairs made me turn my head. He walked over to the fireplace and stood looking at us. There was no mistaking the expression on his furry face. "Uh oh," Rabbit giggled, the sound muffled behind her hand. "I don't think he approved of the kitchen … forking."

I laughed as he turned his back to both of us with a huff and lay down, ignoring us. I pulled her to me, settling her into my side. "Too bad, because that is definitely gonna happen again."

Her eyes looked up at me. "Is that a fact?"

I leaned down and grazed my lips on hers. "Trust me, I have many, many plans of things I want to do to you, Rabbit," I growled roughly.

She giggled. "All this because of apple pie?"

"No," I shook my head, stroking her cheek with my hand. "All of *this*, because of you."

With a contented sigh she leaned forward, pressing her forehead to mine. I pulled her close and leaned back on the sofa, nestling her into my chest. We sat gazing at the fire, our bodies close, limbs entwined, and happy to just be close and quiet.

⇉CHAPTER SIXTEEN⇇

Joshua

I sat behind the wheel with the engine rumbling and looked at the gate which seemed to loom large and ominously at me. I drew in a breath and hit the remote, watching as the gate swung open. I glanced up and met Rabbit's eyes in the rear-view mirror. She had determined it was better for her to be behind me so I could see her easily. She nodded, not saying anything.

Still, I hesitated.

Slowly, I felt arms encircle my shoulders from behind, and Rabbit's head rested against my neck. "I'm right here, Joshua," her tender voice whispered into my ear. "It's still your property. You're still safe."

I sighed and shifted into drive. I lowered the plow and began clearing a path further from the gate. The entire time Rabbit's arms stayed around me, her voice in my ear as the distance from the gate lengthened. Every day we had gone farther and we were almost to the road now. When she felt the tenseness and shaking start, she leaned forward, laying her hand over mine at the wheel. "Just stop, Joshua."

I did as she said. "Breathe. Just breathe with me." I nodded silently and concentrated on pulling the air into my lungs. "Good, that's good," she encouraged gently after a few minutes. "Why don't you just clear a wider path for now? We've gone quite far today."

I shifted and slowly worked my way back up the drive, cutting another swath through the deep snow. Over and over, I repeated the pattern until a large clear area was in front of me. Then I raised the plow and drove back up the road, through the gate, hitting the button to shut it behind me, even though I knew no one could get as far as the gate since the last stretch of the road was still impassable.

I pulled the truck up to the front of the house so I could clean it off before pulling it inside the barn later. I jumped out of the truck and, opening the back door, reached in for Rabbit, dragging her across the seat and out of the truck. I stood holding her closely, feeling the panic finally beginning to subdue and my body ease. Her arms were wound around me tightly as she stood locked in my embrace, wordlessly offering me the comfort I needed.

"You did so well," she praised, pulling back slightly, her head tilted up. I shrugged self-consciously. "What?" she questioned.

I looked over her shoulder. "It should be easy after all this time. I should be able to do this."

"Joshua …"

I pushed away from her, pacing, suddenly angry. "Why, Rabbit? Why is it so fucking hard? I walked out my door and into the world for fucking years without even thinking about it. And now, I can't make it a few hundred fucking feet from my gate without acting like a …"

"Like a what, Joshua?"

I spun around.

"Like a fucking helpless child!" I shouted. "I'm so weak. I disgust myself! I don't how you can stand there and tell me how well I did. I *know* the driveway is blocked and there is no one there. I *know* there is nothing out there that's going to hurt me. But I can't fucking get past this. I just … can't …" I shook my head, my voice trailing off.

I looked at her as she stood gazing at me. I kept shouting. "I can't ever be the man you need, Rabbit. I can't give you a life outside these gates. I can't take you to dinner. Hell, I can't even take you to the grocery store. Or on a vacation. I can't give you a family. I have nothing to offer you."

For a minute, she said nothing. Then she strode forward and pushed me. Again and again until I was pushed into the side of the truck, staring down at her in surprise.

"Listen to me, Joshua. I have no idea what brought that little speech on, but stop it. You are not weak. You have pushed and fought your way back to being able to get out to the gate and beyond. And you keep pushing yourself. You will beat this someday, I know you will. Something will finally be reason enough for you to overcome what those bastards did to you," she spit out angrily. "But if you didn't? If you were never able to leave this place? It makes you no less a man in my eyes. What you do with your life is what makes you a man."

"And what have I done that makes me a man, Rabbit?" I asked wearily.

Her eyes narrowed. "You have persevered. You found a way to keep going. You kept writing. You found a way to still be a part of the world even if it means NOT going out that gate," she insisted, pointing behind me. Then her voice softened. "You didn't stop being able to love. To show love, Joshua. You heard about Bear and you rescued him. You care and look after him" Her hands came up and cupped my face. "You care and look after *me,* Joshua. I was a total stranger and you helped me. You tended to my bruises, held me when I was upset, and showed me it was okay to trust." Her voice became filled with emotion. "You showed me it was okay to love someone. How to love someone. And I do. *I love you,* Joshua."

My eyes were locked on hers and I couldn't look away.

"There is so much you would miss being here with me." I whispered.

She shook her head. "I wouldn't miss anything, Joshua. Not being here is what I would miss. Because then, I wouldn't be with *you*. I don't care about dinners or vacations. *You* are all I *need*."

I swept her into my arms. My lips lovingly kissed her sweet mouth. Small, soft, little caresses. Her hand crept around my head, pulling me to her. My tongue traced the edge of her lips gently, tasting her sweetness. She parted her mouth and my tongue slipped in, teasing hers. Her quiet whimper had me gathering her closer, tilting her head, deepening the kiss. My tongue explored her sweetness, swirling, tasting, stroking, tenderly at first, and then becoming greedier. I couldn't stop tasting her, savouring her warmth. All the emotion I had been feeling, the panic, the anger and the love swirled and spun into a mass of hot, pulsating need. I broke away, gasping for air, planning on pulling her into the truck and having her right there. I looked down at Rabbit and stilled. Her breath was coming out in small gasps, her chest rising and falling quickly. Her hair was a mass of waves, rippling in the sun, begging for my hands to wind themselves into it. Her lips were swollen and damp from my mouth. Reaching down, I traced a finger over her soft, pink flesh, shuddering as she reached her velvet tongue out, teasing my finger. Her eyes opened and I saw the burning desire in her depths. Her gaze was warm and filled with a love I had never seen directed my way before. My heart began beating faster. "Why did you stop, Joshua?" she breathed.

My urgent, hot desire faded, instead replaced with an overwhelming tenderness. I didn't want her any less, but *how* I wanted her changed. "I love you, Rabbit. So much." I kissed her tenderly again, lips moving and moulding to each other. "I love you. I love you." My voice was urgent, needing her to understand the depth of what I was feeling for her. "I want you, Rabbit." My voice trailed off with a groan as I felt her hand reach inside my coat, stroking me.

"Take me," she whispered.

I shook my head. "Not out here. It's too cold and I want to take my time. I want you to *feel* how much I love you."

She whimpered in desire and I smiled down at her. "Arms, Rabbit," I instructed lovingly. Her arms reached up around my neck and I lifted her up and carried into the house. I walked directly to the fireplace, disturbing Bear from his warm spot. His eyes regarded us with utter distain for a moment, and then with a deep huff, he headed down the hall to the bedroom. I slowly lowered Rabbit to her feet and we stood regarding each other. Her hand drifted up, cupping my cheek, stroking slowly. "Love me, Joshua," she whispered.

There were simply too many clothes between us and our hands moved with indulgent caresses as clothing was shed and soft skin was exposed. I lowered us both onto the plush rug making sure she was surrounded by cushions. I kissed every inch of her delicate body as it was exposed, worshipping her with my lips and tongue until she was trembling and undulating under me. Reaching up, I captured her mouth with mine, kissing her deeply over and over again. I teased her, withdrawing my tongue from her mouth and drawing hers into mine, gently sucking and stroking it, drawing out her soft whimpers and moans. Her hands wandered restlessly over my back, pulling me closer, her leg hitching over my hip. "Please, Joshua … *please,*" she begged, her eyes pleading.

I hovered over her, staring down into her wide, loved-filled gaze. Slowly, I entered her slick warmth, closing my eyes as the pleasure of being inside her rolled through me. My head fell into the crook of her neck, inhaling her scent as I began moving in long, slow strokes, wanting to be buried in her as long as possible. Her hips rose, meeting me, her legs tightening around my hips, pulling me in as deeply as she could. I could feel my orgasm building like a rapidly moving storm, gathering in strength with each thrust as I moved in her. Her muscles fluttered and clenched and her arms tensed as she gasped out my name, coming apart around me. I continued to move and felt the intense burst of heat as I came intensely, not even able to make a sound as I finally stilled.

We were both quiet, the silence broken only by our shuddering, panting breaths as we slowly came down to earth. I pulled away and looked down at her. Rabbit's hand came up, affectionately stroking the back of my neck. She smiled her shy smile and wordlessly pulled my head down to her chest, her hand continuing her gentle caresses.

"You wanted me to feel how much you loved me? Mission accomplished, Joshua," she said quietly.

I couldn't help the smug smile I felt pull on my lips.

⇒CHAPTER SEVENTEEN⇐

Joshua

Bear pushed on my arm, and I moved to allow his great body access to see what I was doing under the hood of the truck. I sighed as his shadow blocked the light. I tried moving around him, but he continued leaning against me. Impatiently, I pushed him away. "Down, Bear!" I snapped. He sat looking at me with a huff, but I ignored him and went back to my inspection.

I had just finished the last of the private drive that led to the main road. Even with Rabbit and Bear with me in the truck it had been a panicky, tense exercise and I only cleared a wide enough path to allow a vehicle through. At one point, I had thought I would pass out from my hyperventilating. The gate was just too far away. Rabbit again sat behind me and it was only her voice in my ear and her tight embrace that helped me get through it.

I had noticed a strange noise in the engine and the thought of the truck breaking down that far away was overwhelming. Then when I raised the plow it seemed to seize and that was the last straw. I turned the truck around and headed back to the gate as quickly as possible. After dropping Rabbit at the front of the house and telling her where I would be, I decided to work on the truck in front of the barn. I needed to be alone for a short time and calm down.

The sun was out in full force today and it was warm on my back as I bent over the hood. I was checking out the source of the noise, and then I would move on to the plow.

I leaned forward, checking on the timing belt, when Rabbit appeared. She snuck up under my arm, and once again my light was blocked. "How's it going?" she asked sweetly.

"It's not," I said through gritted teeth.

She turned her head and regarded me. "How come?"

"I keep getting interrupted."

"Oh." Her voice was soft. "I brought you some coffee."

I nodded. "Thanks."

But she didn't move. "Can I help?"

The emotion of the morning was still running through me and my patience was highly insufficient. When she fell heavily into my side I saw that Bear had heaved himself up beside her, joining the party. She stroked his head lovingly as she chuckled. "Wanting to see what Daddy is doing, Bear?"

I pulled up and away from the engine. "I am NOT his daddy. He's my dog. And I'm never going to get anything done if the two of you don't go away and stop blocking my fucking light!" I snarled.

She regarded me quietly. "I'll take that as a no. Your coffee is in the thermos. Come on, Bear, your *master* is busy." She leaned down and grabbed his collar, then walked away.

Finally.

I went back to work; I tightened the belt and continued checking. Except, now that I had all the space and light I needed, I couldn't concentrate. All I could see was the soft hurt that had appeared on Rabbit's face when I had yelled at her.

And what had she done? Made me coffee and asked if she could help.

Yeah. That so deserved my anger.

Instead of telling her how tense I was still feeling from pushing my boundary limits when plowing and the fact that the road was once again open which made me anxious, I yelled at her and sent her away.

Fuck.

I threw down my tools and grabbed the thermos. I didn't even bother pouring it into the lid. I just drank it from the thermos directly. The hot liquid's aromatic steam drifted upwards and I closed my eyes briefly, enjoying the cinnamon-laced beverage. I went to place the thermos down and noticed the slice of pie sitting on the tool chest as well. And lying across the top was a fork. I felt my lips twitch in memory of the kitchen events of a few days ago, and then I groaned.

I was such an asshole.

She *knew* without me telling her how distressed I was and had come to offer me her quiet comfort with both her company and her treats.

Instead of accepting either graciously, I snapped and hurt her feelings.

Suddenly, the truck didn't seem as important as finding Rabbit and apologizing. I'd go get her and she could hand me my tools and talk to me while I worked. We'd both feel better.

If I could get her to listen to me.

I trudged up the path to the house and had just rounded the bend when the first one hit me.

THWACK!

I stopped walking and raised my hand to my head. It came away wet and covered in snow.

What the fuck? A snowball?

Before I could even figure out what happened …

THWACK!

This time the snowball hit me right in my chest.

I looked down, mouth agape, and made the mistake of raising my head to scan the area around me.

THWACK!

Right. In. The. Face.

Blinking, I stood there speechless and was suddenly hit with a barrage of snowballs. Very few missed.

I hit the ground. I heard a mischievous giggle and then there was silence.

"Rabbit!"

Nothing.

"Rabbit, where the hell are you?"

Nothing.

I crawled back around the bend and then poked my head back to see. The large piles of snow were excellent hiding places. Especially when you were tiny. I focused my gaze on the direction I thought the snowballs had come from. As I was doing this, my hands were busy getting some of my own ammunition ready.

"Rabbit! I'm coming out now. No more snowballs. I'm warning you!"

I stood up and poked my head around the bend. Sure enough, I watched a snowball come flying my way, but this time I ducked.

And thanks to Bear's tail sticking up in the air, I knew exactly where she was. Right behind the clump of bushes ahead and to my right. I chuckled to myself. If I went back towards the barn, I could sneak around and come up right behind her. Just to throw her off, I yelled out one more time. "I'm soaked, Rabbit! And the last one got me in the eye! Come out!"

My only answer was another snowball that flew past me. I stood up and threw one widely, wanting her to think I had no idea where she was.

"Fine! I'm going back to the barn!" I yelled, trying not to laugh. I crouched down and quickly made my way back towards the barn, and once I got to the other path, I quietly made my way around behind her. And there she was, huddled behind the row of bushes with an impressive pile of snowballs sitting beside her, ready to do battle. I could see her peering through the bushes trying to see where I was, while Bear sat beside her, chewing on one of the snowballs. He glanced at me and I gave him the hand signal for silence. He stared at me briefly, and then looked over to Rabbit. Finally, he gave a huff as if to say 'I'm out,' and then went back to chewing on the snowball. I quietly crept through the snow until I was about five feet behind Rabbit. "Where are you, you grumpy man?" she muttered. "Come back and I'll show you an interruption."

My lips twitched at her angry mutterings. Pulling two snowballs out of my pockets, I steadied myself.

"Right here, pretty girl," I growled.

She whirled around, gasping just as I threw the first snowball. It hit her square in the chest. Instantly, she retaliated with one that barely missed my head. I threw the next one while reaching into my pocket for more. My arsenal was soon depleted and I stood looking at Rabbit. Her cheeks were flushed with cold and laughter and her hair gleamed in the sunlight as she danced around trying to avoid being hit. My earlier anger now forgotten, I grinned as I watched her. I pulled the last snowball from my pocket and dropped it on the ground. "I surrender," I laughed. "Do with the grumpy man what you will."

I wasn't prepared for what happened next. One moment I was standing and the next Rabbit came barrelling at me, hitting me square in the chest, knocking us both into the snow. My breath left me in a large gasp as I stared at her, wide-eyed in shock. Then I rolled her over and, grinning, whispered "Gotcha," as I pushed a handful on snow down her neck. Her squeals and laughter made me chuckle and I gazed down at her. As her laughter died away, I leaned down. "Forgive me, Rabbit," I whispered quietly into her ear. "I'm such an asshole."

I pulled back and was startled to see tears in her eyes. Had I hurt her somehow? Her healing injuries were always foremost in my mind, but maybe I accidently held her too tightly?

"Baby, are you okay? Did I hurt you?"

She shook her head. "I know you were upset, Joshua. I know you only see the failure, but I see the victory. And these last few days, as hard as it was, you won." Her quiet words of praise rolled through me and I gazed at her, feeling my own emotions suddenly shift.

Groaning, I lifted her head out of the snow and crashed my lips to hers. My tongue pressed decisively onto her bottom lip, demanding entrance, and when her lips parted I delved inside impatiently, wanting her taste. I wound my hand into her hair and tilted her head, wanting more. Deeper. Wetter. Hotter. Over and over, I tasted her, my tongue stroking, dipping, and pressing. Hot, blistering need filled me. The need to feel her wrapped around me. Now.

Her hands wrapped around my neck, keeping me tightly pressed to her face, while soft whimpers came from the back of her throat. My free hand found the zipper to the bulky parka she was wrapped in and pulled it down hastily, my hand diving inside and up under her shirt to the warm skin. It still wasn't enough and, abruptly, I sat up pulling her with me. I leaned back, gasping. "Tell me to stop, Rabbit. Tell me to stop now, or I won't be able to," I pleaded, my body already trembling with the effort of staying back from her.

She shook her head. "Don't stop," she whispered, her voice ragged with desire.

Leaning forward, I pulled the parka off her, grinning when I saw she had my hoodie on underneath and I shrugged out of my coat. Both were tossed to the snow and I immediately lifted her on top of them. I hesitated, and then pulled off my heavy cable knit sweater leaving my skin bare to the sun.

"Joshua, you'll get cold!" she gasped

I shook my head.

"No. I won't, Rabbit. Right now I'm so fucking hot for you, *that* would be impossible," I growled.

I pulled down the zipper of my hoodie she was wearing, exposing her to the cold and quickly laid her back, covering her skin with my own. I loved that there was nothing under the hoodie to stop me from feeling all of her skin. Again, I tilted her head and ravaged her mouth deeply. Every nerve ending in my body was screaming for her. I felt her arms wrap around me and her hands caressing my bare back in long slow strokes. Her legs wrapped around my hips and I pressed my throbbing erection into her warm centre.

My hand roamed over her upper torso and arm and then down to the waistband of the sweats she was wearing. I pulled on the elastic and plunged my hand inside. I groaned when I felt her soft slick centre.

"So wet, Rabbit … always so wet for me." I moaned lowly, breaking away from her mouth.

Her hips arched into my touch and I stroked and teased her, my lips never leaving her skin. I licked and nipped at her neck and ears, kissed my way across her collarbone and down to her chest, teasing her cold nipples with my tongue. I could feel her shivers and prayed it was from lust and not the cold. She shifted and then I felt her hand wrap around my rigid cock, stroking, gently at first, then more firmly. My hips thrust forward into her hand.

"Rabbit ... I need to be inside you."

Wordlessly, she lifted her hips and I pulled the sweats down over her feet and mine followed suit. We both gasped at the cold air, and then again when I plunged inside of her in one stroke. My head fell forward, the sensations of the heat of her engulfing me and the cold air that surrounded us creating an intense experience. I began to move and closed my eyes. "I'm not going to last long, Rabbit," I gasped out.

"More, Joshua ... *oh God* ... please ..."

Another long shiver rolled through her and this time I couldn't ignore it. Leaning down, I gathered her up, parka and all, and pulled her up to straddle my lap. I leaned back on my knees, ignoring the pain, and we both moaned at the angle. I started thrusting deeply, holding her tightly against my chest to keep her warm. I couldn't stop taking her now if I tried. Her arms were wrapped tightly around my neck, her face buried in my chest.

"Oh ... oh ... *oh ... Joshua ...*"

Her body stiffened as she came around me and I followed quickly.

"*Fuck ... Rabbit ...*"

I stilled and held her tightly. I could feel the cold penetrating me as the heat of my sweat rose off me, evaporating. I stood up, taking Rabbit with me. I set her on her feet and pulled up our sweats. I wrapped the parka around her and pulled on my jacket quickly. I grabbed my sweater, shoving it in her arms and scooped her up.

"Put me down, Joshua," she mumbled against my chest. "You're not carrying me to the house."

I kissed the top of her forehead. "Yes, I am, Rabbit."

She fidgeted a little and I pulled her closer as I walked toward the house. "Hush. I like carrying you."

Bear was waiting on the steps and went ahead of us, disappearing to the living room. No doubt he wasn't any more impressed with our outdoor activities than he had been with the indoor ones the past few days.

Inside, I went straight to the basement ... and the hot tub. Tenderly, we helped each other discard our clothes. We both sighed when we sank into the heat of the water and I pulled her against me, relaxing as the water bubbled around us.

"I'm sorry," I said regretfully after a while. "I was an asshole."

Her arms tightened over mine in silent acceptance.

"How did you know I would come find you?" I asked. "Or were you planning on lying in wait all afternoon?"

Her head tilted up and she smiled at me.

"No. I knew you would think about it and come find me fairly quickly. I knew you wouldn't be able to stand it if you thought I was upset."

I lifted my hand and stroked her soft cheek. "No, I couldn't." I grinned down at her. "So, you were ready to forgive me, but you thought you'd show off your mad snowballer skills first? Teach me a little lesson?" I teased.

She giggled in response. "I thought it would make you laugh. I, ah … didn't realize it would bring out other … reactions in you. Not that I'm complaining."

I nuzzled the top of her head. "Good to know." I paused. "You bring out reactions in me I have never experienced before, Rabbit. You make me laugh when I least expect it, feel things I have never felt before and, God help me, fill me with a need to make love to you at the most inopportune times." I bent forward and nipped her earlobe. "Not that I'm complaining either."

She looked up and kissed me warmly.

"Good to know."

⇒Chapter Eighteen⇐

Joshua

I sat back, running my hand through my hair. I leaned back in my seat and looked over toward Rabbit who was curled up in the chair behind me. She looked up, smiling softly at me. "How're the edits going?" she asked. Now that the clearing was done, I had been working on edits for my latest book. Rabbit had been a great help, looking over my notes and making suggestions. We worked together quietly, but I found having her close very soothing.

I shrugged. "They go. It's been a couple weeks and I have a lot of notes to discuss with my editor. Once we have contact with the outside world, I can get going properly."

A shadow passed over her face, but she didn't comment. Instead, she leaned down and stroked Bear's head. As usual, he gazed up at her adoringly.

"The world is going to show up, Rabbit. We can't avoid it forever," I said gently.

"I know." Her reply was muffled as she continued to stroke Bear.

I hesitated then decided to try and broach the subject, albeit carefully. There was so much we needed to talk about, so many things we had to figure out, but it had to be done the right way.

"How's the headache?"

"Better."

"You keep having headaches—you've had one every day for the last four days."

She looked up, her brow furrowed. "I know, Joshua."

"You've also had nightmares. Every night."

She sighed. "Your point is?"

I leaned forward, resting my arm on my knees as I regarded her. "You are trying to push yourself to remember, Rabbit. I see it. I've seen you studying the contents of the bag from your car and concentrating. And I think the headaches are your body's way of trying to protect your mind. It's not ready yet."

"The nightmares scare me, and I can't remember much of them," she admitted quietly. "What I can remember doesn't make sense."

"Tell me."

"I don't understand them. It's like glimpses. A hand coming towards me. Loud noises. Bright lights. Feelings."

"What kind of feelings?" I prompted.

"Fear. Pain. Confusion. Running. Struggling."

I looked at her. "Maybe you're actually remembering bits of what happened that night."

She looked away but I saw the glint of tears in her eyes. I got up and went over to her, scooping her up and sitting down in the chair, cradling her on my lap. Bear stretched out on the rug in front of us with a sigh, knowing his attention had just ended.

"I hate hearing you cry at night and not being able to help you. But you're so far under I can't get you to wake up. All I can do is hold you and try to reassure you that you are safe," I acknowledged. I felt her nod against my chest. "And then you have a headache the next day. I think it's related."

I held her tighter. "I know it's hard, Rabbit, but you just have to let it happen. You can't try and force it just because we want to know the answers. And whether you remember or not ...we'll figure it out."

There was so much more to say. I wanted to comfort her more, but how could I when I was dreading the same thing she was? Instead of talking, I slowly stroked her hair, enjoying the softness as my fingers ran through it.

I felt her relax and drift into sleep and I settled deeper in the chair, holding her close. Neither of us had been getting a lot of sleep with the nightmares plaguing her, and I wanted her to rest. Her head was tucked up under my chin and her hands, even in sleep, clutched my shirt as if afraid I would disappear.

My fear was I would have to let her go.

But for now, she was here. With me.

I shut my eyes and relaxed; the quiet of the afternoon restful.

At some point later, my eyes flew open. I looked at the desk and watched as my phone vibrated again.

I sighed. If I was getting a phone signal that meant the power was back.

The world was about to show up.

Looking down, I saw Rabbit's eyes were open and looking at the desk as well.

"I think the power is back," I said quietly, stroking her cheek.

"What happens now?"

"I'll go to the barn and turn off the generators and get things going. Turn on the furnace. That sort of thing."

"And then?"

I sighed. "We'll take it one step at a time, Rabbit. Okay?"

"Okay."

I nuzzled her forehead in comfort. "Make me some of your delicious coffee while I go get things done in the barn?" I mumbled against her soft skin.

She nodded silently, and I tightened my arms around her before we got up from the chair. I went and pulled on my parka, walking slowly out to the barn, painfully aware of the fact that things were about to change.

How exactly, I didn't know. But something was telling me it wouldn't be in a good way.

I came in and went to the kitchen, Bear pushing ahead of me to get to his Rabbit first. She was sitting at the table with a cup of coffee and, wordlessly, she got up and brought one to me. I nuzzled her forehead and took a sip.

"All done?"

I nodded. "I turned off the generators and refilled them in case another storm blows through. I've got everything switched over. The furnace will warm the whole house fairly quickly."

She nodded. "What's next?"

I watched her hands twisting in her lap. I captured them in mine and lifted them to my lips. "I'll sign-in on the computer and check emails and contact a few people. When you're ready, and not before, we'll do some checking. Not until you're ready, Rabbit."

She let out a shaky breath, nodding.

I stood up, holding out my hand. "Come upstairs with me."

Once upstairs, I handed her a notepad and asked her to make lists of things that were needed and I would contact my usual local merchants, making sure they were capable of making deliveries again. She immediately started writing and I returned to the desk and turned on the computer. It took a long time to download all the messages waiting for me. I went through them all, quickly sent some replies, deleted any junk and prioritized the rest. I kept checking on Rabbit behind me and noticed the fearful looks as she would glance toward the computer; like it was going to suddenly jump up and grab her. I stood up and went over to her, kneeling by the chair. Wordlessly, I cupped her face, my thumbs drawing light circles on her skin as I drew her mouth to mine. I kissed her softly, running my tongue over her bottom lip. She sighed and returned my caresses and I tilted her head, deepening the kiss. She flung her arms around my neck, holding me close, and I continued kissing her until we were both breathless. Pulling back I rested my forehead against hers. "Not until you're ready, Rabbit," I insisted quietly.

We both jumped when a shocked voice came from behind me.

"Joshua, what the hell?"

I turned and looked at the stunned face on my computer screen.

Fuck.

I had opened up my Skype window and forgotten to close it after making sure it was operational and now the world just showed up. And her name was Cecilia.

I sat back with a sigh as Rabbit jumped up and ran down the stairs, obviously startled. I looked towards the computer, rolling my eyes.

"Always such good timing, Cecilia," I remarked dryly as I walked over and sat down in front of the screen.

Her eyes narrowed. "Never mind that. You had better start talking, Joshua. Who on earth was that?"

I leaned forward, my voice quiet and began to talk.

"So you're telling me she's been there this whole time? And she has no memory of who she is?"

"Yes, Cecilia, that's exactly what I'm saying," I said again, trying to remain patient. I was pretty sure we had already gone through this enough. I'd given her a brief overview of what had transpired since the storm hit.

"I am *so* getting you a fucking satellite phone."

I smiled grimly. We'd argued about this before. I gave in.

"Okay."

"I think I'm speechless, Joshua."

"Now *that* I never thought I'd see," I chuckled. I heard Rabbit coming back up the stairs and turned to see her walk over and silently place a cup of coffee on the desk, turning immediately to leave. She had literally run away when I got up to address Cecilia's rather blunt greeting earlier. Reaching out, I grabbed her hand and pulled her into my lap.

"Cecilia, this is Rabbit," I said into the webcam, holding Rabbit close.

"Hey, Rabbit! This is a … surprise, but nice to meet you." Cecilia's voice was filled with unasked questions.

"Um, hello, Cecilia," Rabbit said quietly. I could feel how tense she was, her body vibrating with nerves.

"It's okay, Rabbit. I trust Cecilia completely," I murmured into her ear. I kissed her cheek softly. "You're perfectly safe, pretty girl."

I heard Cecilia's gasp of shock, seeing me interact with another person in such an intimate manner. Especially someone I had only known for a short time.

Cecilia cleared her throat. "I'll be up day after tomorrow. Send me a list tonight of anything you want me to bring. Rabbit, I, um, assume there are some items you need?"

Rabbit shook her head. "No, really, I'm okay but thank you." She squirmed away from me. "I'm making dinner. I'll leave you to your … call."

I watched her quickly walk back down the stairs. I turned back to the computer to see Cecilia eyeing me warily.

"We'll talk when you get here, Cecilia," I said wearily. It was far too complex to do via a webcam.

"What have you done, Joshua?"

I looked at her silently for a minute, and then shrugged. "I fell in love."

She just stared at me.

"Send me that list," she said quietly.

I nodded. "Rabbit needs conditioner. Some good stuff; she gets tangles in her hair. You could find that, yes? At a salon or something? I don't want just some cheap stuff off the shelves here."

Her eyes went wide. "I'll get that and anything else you want." She paused. "Joshua?"

"Yeah?"

"You won't be able to avoid my questions when I get there."

Closing my eyes, I nodded. "I know."

<hr />

After I shut down the webcam and checked with the local merchants to find out what I could or could not expect in the next couple of days, I went downstairs.

Rabbit was in the kitchen, once again by the stove, stirring something that smelled delicious. She looked up, smiling timidly, as I approached. Once again, it struck me how right she looked here.

I stood behind her and wrapped my arms around her, drawing her back against me. Leaning down, I nuzzled her neck. "Smells good."

She laughed. "It's stew, Joshua. Just stew. I was trying to use up the last of the veggies and some of the meat you insist on cooking in such vast quantities, so really ... it's just leftovers." She held up the spoon and I leaned over and tasted it.

"How is it that your leftovers taste about a thousand times better than what I usually eat?"

Rabbit laughed, sounding pleased at my compliment.

"Did you finish your list?" I asked

"Yes, I finished *your* list, Joshua. It's on the table."

I planted one more soft kiss behind her ear, grinning when I felt her subtle shudder, and went over to the table. I was surprised to see a bottle of wine open and a glass partially full. An empty glass stood beside it.

"Drinking early, Rabbit?"

"I thought we could use it," she said not turning around.

I sighed and filled my glass, topping hers up, and handing it to her. It *had* been a rather emotional day so far. I scanned the list, adding a few things. I made a separate one for Cecilia.

"What size are your feet?" I asked, not looking up.

"Why?"

"I want to get you a pair of boots and a new pair of sneakers. If it snows again, your feet will need to be warm and you have basically ruined the pair you have running around in the snow. You need a new pair."

"They're fine, Joshua. I don't need them."

I stopped writing and looked up, meeting her troubled eyes. "What size, Rabbit?" I asked again, my voice firm.

She sighed in frustration. "Six and a half."

I moved onto the next item. "What size do you need in shirts and pants?"

She came over to the table. "I don't need Cecilia to get me a wardrobe, Joshua."

I shook my head. "She isn't. You can go online and order yourself some clothes; whatever you want. I just thought I'd get her to pick you up a couple of things. I thought maybe you were tired of drowning in my clothes. And there wasn't a lot in your bag. Maybe your own sweatpants and some tops? Some under ... garment ... things?" I explained.

"I put a load of laundry in, Joshua. The things from the bag you found are fine for me. I have enough."

I narrowed my eyes, looking at her. She was studying some highly interesting spot on the floor. Something told me not to push this right now.

"Okay," I said soothingly.

Wanting to lighten the dark mood I could feel spreading, I looked back over to her list.

"Broccoli, lettuce, carrots, apples? Seriously, Rabbit, I see a lot of fruit and vegetables on this list. What I don't see is chocolate or chips ... or any freaking alcoholic items. And where are the jujubes? What are you trying to do to me?"

I saw her lips twitch.

"And don't we need some lard stuff? Because I really need more of those pies. I don't see that either, Rabbit," I sniffed indignantly. "I'd say your list-making skills are more on par with your criminal abilities rather than your mad snowball skills, frankly."

A soft giggle escaped from her mouth and she looked up at me. I winked at her and was rewarded with another giggle and her beautifully shy smile.

I leaned forward and refilled our glasses.

"We'll work it out together, Rabbit," I assured her soothingly.

She smiled tremulously at me and nodded.

I didn't think either of us believed that.

⇒Chapter Nineteen⇐

Joshua

"You're really sexy, you know that?"

I looked up in surprise. Rabbit was sitting on the other end of the sofa, staring at me reflectively over her wine glass.

"I like that sweater … it looks amazing on you." Her head tilted and I watched fascinated as she drew the wine glass over her bottom lip again and again. I was suddenly envious of the glass.

"Of course, it looked even better when it was lying beside me in the snow the other day," she murmured.

I felt myself stir at the memory. "Rabbit, how much have you had to drink?"

"A bit," she giggled softly. "Actually, quite a bit," she admitted. "But you're still sexy."

I grinned. "Good to know. Any reason you decided to share that?"

Her foot reached out and stroked my leg. "No particular reason."

I arched an eyebrow at her and looked pointedly at her foot. She giggled again and withdrew it. Shaking my head, I looked back down at the pad of paper I was holding. I was sure I had everything listed I wanted to order, but I was checking it over again. Suddenly, a bundle of fabric landed on top of the paper and I stared at it fleetingly. Then I glanced up to make sure I was actually seeing what I thought I was seeing in front of me. Yep. Rabbit was sitting topless and the shirt she had been wearing was now on my lap.

"I'm cold."

I chuckled while I sat back and appreciated the view. "I think you'd find if you kept your clothes on you wouldn't have that problem."

"I like yours better."

"Um, Rabbit this *is* mine," I grinned, holding up the shirt she had discarded.

"Your sweater looks warmer."

I smirked. "Why don't you come and get it then?"

I wasn't entirely prepared for how quickly she pounced. One minute she was on the other end of the sofa, the next moment her entire body was delving under my sweater, her head popping through the loose neckline. She wrapped her arms around my waist with a sigh as she snuggled closer to me.

"You smell so good," she whispered.

Laughing, I wrapped my arms around her, loving the feeling of her skin against mine. "I thought you wanted to *wear* the sweater?"

"I am … I'm sharing."

"Kind of you."

"I know."

I nuzzled the top of her head and let her rest against me. She'd been so tense since the power was restored. I knew why and I felt it as well. If it comforted her to be close to me, I was good with that. It comforted me as well.

"Joshua?"

"Hmm?"

"Why don't you have a girlfriend?"

I was startled at the strange question. "Well, firstly, that would make this position rather *awkward* if I did. Secondly, yeah, I don't get out much, Rabbit. And, thirdly, strangely enough, aside from you, not a lot of women just show up here," I chuckled.

She raised her head. "No. I mean why didn't you have a girlfriend when you came here?"

I looked at her and stroked her cheek. "I was seeing someone before I was attacked, but it ended fairly quickly."

"Why?"

"I was a mess, Rabbit. We hadn't been seeing each other for very long before it happened. She certainly wasn't emotionally invested in us enough to want to stick around while I recovered."

She regarded me for a minute then pulled herself up and kissed me sweetly. "I would have stayed. I would have supported you through that dreadful time. You are too remarkable to give up on, Joshua."

Touched by her words, I smiled and kissed her again. "I know you would have. But you are special, Rabbit. There are very few women out there like you."

She curled back onto my chest, her one hand now softly stroking my skin. "I think you are an amazing man, Joshua Bennett. I don't think I have properly thanked you for taking care of me and being so wonderful. You are ... so incredible."

My throat clenched with sudden understanding.

"Don't, Rabbit. Don't do this."

Her voice was soft. "Do what?"

I pulled her face up to look at me. "Don't start saying goodbye. Don't tell me all the things you think you need to say. Just don't."

We stared intently at each other and I felt her slight nod of acknowledgment. I leaned down and captured her sweet mouth. Our lips moved together softly, languidly, never trying to deepen or push past the soft moment. Eventually, I pulled away and settled her back on my chest.

"I love you, Joshua," she whispered, her voice low.

"I love you as well, Rabbit. So much."

For a while there was nothing but the sound of her soft breathing and the hiss and pop of the logs in the fireplace.

"I still think you're sexy," she said sleepily.

I tightened my arms around her and chuckled. "Good to know, Rabbit. Good to know."

⟫•••◆••••⟪

She was asleep. I smiled as I looked down at her. It had been a tough day for her and she had drunk more than I had ever seen her consume before. Maybe it would help her sleep through the night. After some careful maneuvering, I managed to lift her up and carry her to bed. I did have to leave her in my sweater, ducking out of it awkwardly so I didn't disturb her. She looked so endearingly sweet in the bulky knitted material, now hanging loosely on her, the arms empty. I looked down sadly on her sleeping form, seeing that even in sleep, her face was still tense. But I was feeling the same way she was. We were both frightened of what we would find when we searched for her on the computer. The looming possibilities were terrifying and our emotions had been all over the place for most of the day. Sighing, I tucked the blankets around her and patted Bear's head, as he was already stretched out across her feet.

I went and got my lists and sat in front of the computer. I emailed Cecilia with the items I needed her to get, and then did the same with the local merchants I used. I was grateful for Cecilia. The nearby town was small and although I could get the basics, some of the things I liked had to be brought in from further away. If Cecilia couldn't locate the items, one of us ordered them online and they came via shipping company. But I had missed her regular calls and was looking forward to seeing her again, although I hoped her presence wouldn't frighten Rabbit too much. There were times she was a force unto herself. She had been my assistant and friend for so long; I couldn't even imagine my life without her. Once I was done, I sat and stared at the screen, struggling. Part of me wanted to turn it off and go downstairs and just curl up with Rabbit against me and sleep. The other part of me knew I should be actively looking for answers. That it would be easier if I did this alone, and then shared what I found with Rabbit.

I sighed. I knew what part was the right decision. My hands shaking with nerves, I opened a new search engine and began an investigation my heart didn't want my head to work on.

⊷∙∙•●◉●•∙∙⊶

After about an hour I sat back with a sigh that held both relief and sadness. Each new inquiry I started, my heart would clench and my hands felt like they were weighed down with sand as I typed in new parameters and looked for information. Every time I hit enter my eyes would shut, afraid of the data that was going to appear in front of me. Each time I failed to find something, I would release a deep breath I didn't even realize I was holding, and yet, there seemed to be nothing to find. I could find nothing about a recently missing woman in this area. No reports about a missing Escort that matched the description of the damaged car in the barn. Logistically, I had assumed she had to have come from nowhere further away than about two hours given the severity of the storm she'd been driving in. Coming up with nothing, I expanded the search to larger cities, even as far away as London and Toronto. But still nothing came up.

I even changed the dates, going back further. Maybe she had been missing longer. I searched newspapers and headlines, local newscasts, everything I could think of. An article came up about a kidnapped wife of a wealthy businessman but it occurred *after* Rabbit had shown up, and although the photo was rather blurry, the couple was older looking. I didn't bother looking at the video clip, since she was already here when the kidnapping had taken place according to the date on the article. I checked various sites and headlines but came up with nothing. I even did a cross-country search and went through many articles on missing people. But none of them were Rabbit.

I sat back, perplexed. Nothing?

There wasn't a person looking for Rabbit? Not a single article or newspaper story that remotely matched. Not one person was missing this incredible little woman? I found that hard to believe. Not a spouse or boyfriend. No family member. Not even a friend? Was she that alone in this world?

My heart ached at the thought of her being so alone. It was so wrong. She was so special; loving and giving in ways that constantly astounded me.

Another part of me was relieved. No one was looking for her. She was still mine. She would stay with me.

Neither of us would be alone again.

I leaned forward, my head falling into my hands in exhaustion as I felt a huge weight being lifted from me. I wasn't stupid enough to think it was done, that no one would ever be looking for her or that she wouldn't remember who she was one day. I needed to do some more searching.

But it wasn't today. Today she was still safe here. With me.

A noise made me look up. Rabbit was standing at the top of the stairs, frozen. She still had on my ivory-coloured cable knit sweater, and it hung down past her thighs and the arms were miles too long on her, her hands barely visible through the layers of knitted material. Rumpled from sleep, she looked adorable. Except I didn't like the way her eyes were darting between the computer screen and my face.

"Joshua?" The one word spoke volumes. Fear and anxiety were prevalent in her tone.

I opened my arms. "Come here, Rabbit," I said quietly. I watched her hesitate then make her way over. I pulled her down onto my lap and wrapped my arms around her. She was shaking so badly I became concerned. I pulled her even tighter and felt her head burrow into my chest. "It's okay, Rabbit. I've got you."

Then I quietly explained what I had found, or not found really. As I spoke, her trembling calmed and I got her to look up as I showed her some of the results I had located. I even clicked on the article about the kidnapped wife but she had no reaction other than a murmured 'I hope he finds her.' When I was done, I sat back still holding her.

She raised her head. "Nobody is looking for me?"

"Not that I can find. I'm sorry, Rabbit."

She shook her head. "I'm not."

I was surprised at her reaction. "Why?"

She regarded me steadily. "This is where I want to be."

I smiled at her declaration. "We have to try to find out your identity, Rabbit. Surely, you want to know who you are and what happened to you that night."

She shrugged. "I'm not sure I want to remember that night. And ... I know who I am."

I looked at her in confusion.

"I'm your Rabbit. That's all I need to know," she whispered softly. Her incredibly lovely eyes stared up at me, filled with tenderness and adoration.

"You are," I agreed, relief and lust abruptly coursing through me. I kissed her deeply and stood up, taking her with me.

"What are you doing?"

"Taking you to bed," I growled, walking downstairs quickly. "I'm going to show you just how much you're mine."

She hummed happily. "Good. It's something I need to be reminded of … often."

"Not a problem, Rabbit." I smirked at her as I laid her on the bed.

Almost giddy with relief, however temporary, I playfully arched my eyebrow at her.

"Now, give me back my sweater."

⇒CHAPTER TWENTY⇐

Joshua

I leaned over, laying my hand on top of Rabbit's. She had been nervously fidgeting and playing with her napkin for the last five minutes. "Relax, Rabbit."

Her tired eyes flew to mine. I could see the tension she was holding in, and I could tell from her body language another headache was coming. Her expressive eyes were shadowed with the start of the pain.

"It's just Cecilia, Rabbit. She's one of the people I trust the most. You have nothing to be afraid of."

"What if ... what if she doesn't like me?" she whispered.

I smiled at her. "Not possible, Rabbit. She's gonna love you."

"What if she ..." her voice trailed off.

"What? Recognizes you when she sees you in person?" I asked softly.

She nodded.

"Then we deal with it," I stated firmly. I sat back and looked at her.

I spoke gently. "There is a very good chance it's going to happen, Rabbit. You'll remember your past or one day you'll run into someone who knew you. We can't live in fear of it. I don't want us to live like that."

"Maybe I won't leave the property either," she huffed. "Then I won't run into anyone."

I stood up, annoyed. "Don't even say that. Do you fucking think I chose this? Do you think I want that for you? Never leaving here because you fear what's out there?"

She stood up and came over, wrapping her arms around my tense form. "I'm sorry, Joshua. I shouldn't have said that. I'm just nervous."

I sighed and pulled her closer. "You would start to resent me, Rabbit. Not right away, but eventually. Never leaving gets old really quickly."

"I'm sorry," she repeated gently. "I didn't mean it. I'm just nervous."

I kissed the top of her head. "I know."

We stood together, the closeness comforting. The intercom buzzed.

I looked down into Rabbit's worried gaze.

I grinned encouragingly, wanting her to relax.

"Brace yourself for the whirlwind that is Cecilia."

Rabbit didn't stand a chance.

Cecilia blew in, arms full of bags, issuing orders to help her with the rest. She directed where things went, roughhoused with Bear, pulled Rabbit in for a hug, confiscated my cup of coffee and, after taking a sip, refused to give it back, then informed me I looked great but I needed a haircut; all in the first ten minutes.

Then she pulled Rabbit into the bedroom, showing her the items she had picked up for her, even though Rabbit had insisted she didn't need anything. Luckily, Cecilia was far more practical and had picked Rabbit up other items aside from the shoes and boots I had requested. Things like some socks of her own and some shirts that would actually fit her. I stood rubbing the back of my head, watching them empty the bags. I was glad to see the conditioner I had requested, but I really didn't know shampoo made a difference as well. Or that women liked different lotion for their body as opposed to their face. Good thing Cecilia knew. There were other bottles, jars, and boxes, and I was completely lost. It all seemed so … complicated. I could see Rabbit blushing when Cecilia pulled out some pretty lingerie and I had to leave the room. Seeing Rabbit's pink cheeks and thinking about Rabbit wearing the item she was holding up made me twitch and wish Cecilia was already gone; and I knew that wasn't happening any time soon.

The delivery service I always used arrived, bringing a familiar face as well as the items I had ordered. Jim Unger had been helping me since my first winter here and was well used to the many tasks I needed done. For a while I was busy with restocking the kitchen and bathrooms while Jim drove the truck back into town to fill the tank with gasoline and refill all the empty gas containers so they would be ready for the next emergency. Once everything was complete and he had departed, I trudged back to the house to see how Rabbit was making out with Cecilia.

I was surprised to find Cecilia alone at the table, drinking what was probably her sixth or seventh cup of coffee. "Where's Rabbit?" I asked while helping myself to a cup.

"Lying down. She had a headache."

I sat down, nodding. "She's been getting them a lot."

Cecilia looked at me. "She told me you think she is trying too hard to remember things."

"I think she is pushing herself too hard. I don't think her mind is ready yet," I explained. "I think that's what is causing the headaches, but I want to be sure. I want her to see a doctor. I'm going to contact Daniel and see if he can help. Would you be able to come back and take her? I don't want her to go alone ... and I can't take her."

Cecilia nodded. "Of course, Joshua."

She sat back. "Tell me everything."

I started with hearing the car and kept talking until I had brought her up to date with everything, including the online searching I had done. I left out the intimate details, but was honest about the events that led up to Rabbit trying to leave and my theories on what had happened to her before she got here. She winced when I spoke of the harsh words I had said to Rabbit, but other than a few questions for clarification, let me talk uninterrupted.

Finally, I sat back and looked at her.

"Wow."

I nodded. "I know. Wow is right."

"Sounds like the premise for one of your books."

I chuckled. "Life does tend to imitate art, Cecilia."

Her voice was soft. "You love her, Joshua?"

I sighed. "I do. I have no idea how it happened but I do, Cecilia. Very much so."

Cecilia smiled at me. "She is very endearing, Joshua. There's something about her. I feel like I've known her forever." She looked at me quietly, her eyebrow furrowed in thought. Her voice was quiet when she spoke. "Have you both thought of the implications here, Joshua? Really thought about them?"

"We didn't plan this, Cecilia. We have talked a great deal about it. But right now, she is here, she is safe and this is where she wants to be. As long as she wants that, this is where she is staying."

She regarded me quietly. "You know you could be proactive,

Joshua. I could take her back to Toronto with me and put the press on it. You could find out who she is pretty quickly."

I stared at her in horror. I hadn't even thought about that. Before I could speak up, Rabbit's voice came from behind me.

"This is where I want to stay, Cecilia. I don't want Joshua to be 'proactive.' If no one is looking for me then I'm not sure I want to go looking for them."

Rabbit's arms came around my shoulders and I leaned back into her soft warmth. "As long as Joshua wants me here, this is where I want to be."

I lifted her hand and kissed it tenderly. "Always," I murmured.

I looked over at Cecilia. "She's staying."

Cecilia shrugged. "Okay. Just making sure you guys had thought of all the options."

I pulled Rabbit's arms tightly around me.

"Subject closed, Cecilia."

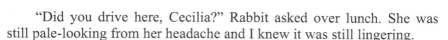

"Did you drive here, Cecilia?" Rabbit asked over lunch. She was still pale-looking from her headache and I knew it was still lingering.

Cecilia shook her head. "I don't usually. The traffic is rather unpredictable on the 400 and sometimes it can take hours and hours. Joshua and my husband, Trevor, co-own a helicopter. I get flown to Gravenhurst from Toronto. I have a car I keep in town and drive out here usually."

Rabbit looked at me. "You own a helicopter?"

I grinned at her. "Co-own. Trevor does a lot of business out of town and it made sense. He can make it home most nights to his wife. I can get Cecilia here fairly quickly and Trevor can use it to come and go when he needs to. Neither of us wants Cecilia driving that distance all the time. It was a sound investment."

Cecilia spoke up. "Sometimes I drive, especially if I am helping Joshua with edits or doing a bunch of things for him and plan on spending longer than a day here. But usually, it's the chopper."

Rabbit wrinkled her nose. "I don't think I've ever been in a helicopter, but of course I can't be sure. It must be an amazing view."

I chuckled. "I'll make sure you get a ride one day."

Her smile was brilliant. "Thank you."

Cecilia and I spent the afternoon going through the edits I had been working on. Rabbit went for a walk with Bear, then came in and lay down with another headache. When I checked on her, I found her curled into a ball, her face buried in the pillow. I could hear her soft sobs from the doorway. I went over and sat down beside her, pulling her into my arms. "Nightmare?" I asked quietly, as I stroked the damp hair away from her face. She nodded. "Tell me."

"It's just images," she whispered. "I keep seeing blue and feeling pain and I can't get away from it. There are lights and flashes of swirling white and a sense of ... being lost. Scared. There are loud angry voices. I can't explain it."

I was convinced she was seeing small glimpses of what happened to her. The images were so consistent now. I sat up, taking her with me. "You're safe, Rabbit. No one will hurt you here."

She nodded silently. "Is Cecilia staying the night?"

I shook my head. "No, she'll head home soon. She is just finishing up a few things for me. She'll be back soon enough with some more work for me. You'll see lots of her."

I stroked her cheeks, wiping away the dampness lingering there. "How about a nice soak in the tub and I'll look after dinner. Cecilia brought some movies I wanted to see. You can pick one to watch and I'll whip up one of my famous pizzas. They're legendary. Sound good?"

She nuzzled her face into my chest, then looked up at me. An indulgent smile was on her face. "I saw the pre-made pizza she brought, Joshua."

I grinned; pleased I could distract her and make her smile with my lameness. She knew that aside from grilling meat or scrambling eggs I wasn't a very good cook. I waggled my eyebrows at her. "I'll even crack open another bottle or two of wine, Rabbit, and let you tell me how sexy I am again."

Her soft giggle made me smile even harder.

"I don't need the wine to see how sexy you are. But the evening sounds perfect, Joshua."

I kissed her, softly stroking my tongue on hers, but didn't deepen it.

I stood up. "Okay, I'll go get rid of Cecilia. I'll tell her I have a hot date for the night and she needs to vamoose. She's cramping my style."

I grinned as Rabbit's laughter followed me down the hall. I made her forget about her nightmare and laugh.

Mission accomplished.

⇒Chapter Twenty-One⇐

Joshua

Two days later, I was surprised to hear the intercom buzz with Cecilia's code. I heard the car pull up outside and, frowning, went to the door before she had a chance to knock. She had sent me a bunch of lists via email yesterday and she wasn't supposed to be back for at least a week.

"What are you doing back, Cecilia?"

"Where is Rabbit?"

Her brusque tone set me on edge. "She's lying down with another headache. How did you get here? Why didn't you call?"

"I flew of course. I was busy tracking down our pilot, who thought he had a few days off, so I could get here quickly. So forgive me for not calling," she snapped.

My stomach tightened at her tone. "What's going on, Cecilia?"

Cecilia grabbed my hand silently and dragged me upstairs. She sat down at the computer and started typing rapidly. She pulled on my hand indicating I needed to be closer and I kneeled down beside her, my stomach clenched in fear.

I watched in dismay as a news story came on and they aired a piece of a press conference. On the screen was a tall man, slightly older than myself. He was begging for the return of his wife who had been missing for a week. I half heard through the buzzing in my ears as he talked in a broken voice about coming home and seeing his wife lying on the floor covered in blood. Of being attacked from behind. Waking up in the hospital two days later to be told his wife was gone. Everything around me faded away as he spoke of how much his wife meant to him, how they were about to start a family. How much he missed her. I watched as he spoke, begging for her safe return. Pleading with whoever had her to contact him. He needed his wife back. His voice broke and he turned away from the camera.

I blinked in disbelief. This was the story I had dismissed. The dates hadn't matched. The couple looked so much older in the blurry picture I had seen. The woman wasn't Rabbit. She couldn't be Rabbit.

Then the news anchor came back with an update. It had been two weeks since the story first aired and still no new information had been discovered, leaving Elizabeth James still missing.

A picture went up and I stared at a clearer image of Rabbit. She was dressed in a black formal gown, standing beside her husband, Brian, at a charity function. She looked ... different. Her hair was swept up and she was looking down, away from the camera, shyly. Her husband's arm was wrapped around her waist possessively.

"When did you find this?" I asked; my voice thick with barely-contained emotion.

"It was on TV last night, Joshua. The original press conference happened weeks ago and this was just an update."

I sat immobilized with numbness.

Rabbit *was* married.

Rabbit had another life.

Rabbit was someone else. She belonged to someone else.

Internally, I shook my head.

No. She *belonged* here. With me.

"I looked," I insisted. "As soon as the power came back, I looked; I searched. I even saw the article that was posted in the paper, but it didn't look like her. That's a different picture of her. And the dates were wrong. It didn't match up!"

"I know, Joshua. That happens sometimes. I read the same article you did, but they had the date listed incorrectly. And although the story made the headlines at first, Joshua, it died off fairly quickly. Brian James is well known in Toronto, but probably not outside of it. He is a wealthy businessman. By the time you looked, it wasn't front page news anymore. I just happened to catch this last night. I hadn't paid any attention before. Since they live outside this community and given the chaos that has been going on here, I'm sure it hardly even registered with the local channels given all the trouble caused by the storm."

Inside my voice was screaming. *No, she doesn't live far away—Rabbit lives here—with me.*

"No one else knows," I whispered, looking at Cecilia desperately.

"No one knows she's here."

Cecilia gasped. "Joshua! You can't keep this from her. She'd never forgive you."

I looked at her and her angry gaze softened as she took in my expression.

"You can't do that to her, Joshua," she insisted gently. "If you care about her, if you really care, you have to tell her."

"Maybe he's lying."

Cecilia looked at me. "Maybe he isn't. He is a respected businessman Joshua. Well-known and esteemed in many prominent social circles. I did some checking last night."

I looked at the picture that was frozen on the screen. I wouldn't have recognized her immediately. "She looks ... older, so serious. And so thin."

"Joshua." Cecilia's voice was patient. "She is the wife of a wealthy businessman. She is no doubt very conscious of her appearance and how she presents herself. I did some checking on her as well. Elizabeth James doesn't work. She volunteers her time. She's on the boards of a few charities. She attends a lot of public dinners and social functions."

"How long?"

"What?"

"How long have they been ... married?"

"Not quite two years."

I stood up and paced around.

"Explain the car, Cecilia? How did she get here? Why did she have new, unworn clothes and cash? Nothing else? Explain that to me," I demanded.

"I don't know, Joshua. I wasn't there! Maybe she escaped from her captors in their car. Maybe she was right when she wondered if the clothes and money were hers. Maybe they were just in the car. I don't know. You have to ask her, Joshua."

I stopped and stared at her.

"I don't know if I can do that, Cecilia. I don't know how to tell her," I whispered. "Or ... if I can take it."

She stood up. "You have to, Joshua. It's the right thing to do. You can't hide this."

I stared at her, knowing she was right. I couldn't lie to Rabbit.

"Do you want me to stay while you talk to her?"

I shook my head. I had to do this alone. "Can you stay ... close?"

"Of course. I packed a bag. I'll go into town. If you need me to come back, call me."

After she left, I sat down heavily in front of the computer. Keeping the sound down, I replayed the news reel again and again. I watched Elizabeth's husband closely. He seemed sincere; filled with worry for his missing wife and struggling. I thought of Rabbit's injuries, her hands in particular; they could have been defensive wounds, trying to fight off an attacker. If so, she had fought hard, thinking of the shoe imprints as well as the dark handprints that had stained her arms. I thought of her nightmares, her feelings of fear and of voices yelling. They could also be memories of being abducted. I shook my head that was beginning to ache from the tension I was feeling. Rolling my shoulders, I sighed.

I pulled up another search engine, hesitated for a moment, then typed in the name Elizabeth James. I looked at the various images of this woman who looked like an older, more sombre version of my Rabbit. Her hair was up in every picture and it was rare if she ever looked straight at the camera. She was always impeccably dressed and looked very ... proper. Sedate. I wouldn't have immediately recognized her unless I saw her eyes. Almost all the pictures had her husband standing beside her. I couldn't tell from her expression if she was happy. Her eyes told me nothing, unlike now when I could read her so easily with one look at her expressive orbs. There was always a small smile on her face, but her eyes were ... vacant? I sighed. Or maybe they were simply cautious. I didn't know. Maybe, I admitted to myself, I didn't want to know.

I was so absorbed in studying the screen that the gasp that came from directly behind me startled me. I spun around to see Rabbit standing behind me, looking at the computer. Her face was pale and her eyes darted rapidly between my face and the screen, not understanding what she was seeing.

Her voice was shaky. "Josh ... Joshua?"

I stood up and went to her, pulling her into my arms. I could feel her trembling. I pressed her face into my shoulder and rocked us, needing just to feel her close for a moment.

I pulled back and looked down at her. Her eyes stared at me with trepidation. I cupped her cheek with my hand in a gentle caress, and then silently led her to the desk, pulling her down onto my lap. She stared at the images on my screen.

"That's me?" she questioned nervously.

"It is."

She stared at the screen for a moment. "I look ... different."

"You're all dressed up, Rabbit. Out on the town."

She looked at me with a frown.

I smiled gently. "You just look different than you're used to seeing yourself right now, that's all."

"I need you to watch something, Rabbit. Watch it carefully, okay?"

She nodded, both her hands clasping one of mine tightly. I hit the button to replay the clip and studied her closely as she watched it. Her brow furrowed as she watched the screen intently. I didn't see any dawning of recognition on her face. The only noise she made was when her picture came up with Brian. She drew back, her hand over her mouth, tears silently coursing down her cheeks. My heart plummeted.

"Do you remember him, Rabbit?"

She stared at the screen in silence. Then she shook her head. "No," she whispered. "Nothing."

She stood up and started pacing. Her hands were wringing together over and over again. "I'm married? That's my ... husband?"

I nodded.

She stared at me for a moment, as if unable to comprehend what was happening.

"But I wasn't wearing a ring," her voice trembled.

"Perhaps you lost it, or it was taken from you," I said patiently.

I held out my hand. "Come back, Rabbit. Look at these pictures." Her head shook silently. "Please, Rabbit."

She approached me slowly and I pulled her back onto my lap. I could feel the tremors flowing through her body with the shock. Even though I was feeling the pain as well, I needed to comfort her.

"It's okay, Rabbit. I'm still right here," I said softly as I held her tightly.

I brought up the images of her again and we were both silent as I flipped through them slowly. I watched her again for reactions, but she remained impassive as she looked at the pictures. It was as if she was looking at images of a complete stranger.

I swallowed the lump forming in my throat. "Does this ... trigger anything for you ..." I drew in a deep breath, "Elizabeth?"

She stood up. "Don't! Don't call me that!" she cried and turned around, fleeing down the stairs.

I looked after her, dumbfounded.

I had to follow her.

I knew that.

But what was I going to say?

How was I going to stop her heart from breaking when mine was breaking right along with it?

⟶ ●●●◐◉◑●●● ⟵

I walked into the bedroom and my heart immediately clenched.

Rabbit was curled up on the floor, her head buried in the chair, sobbing. Bear stood beside her, his head cocked as he observed her pain. One great paw was on the chair beside her head and his stance was protective.

I patted his head and leaned down, scooping Rabbit up. I sat down and held her on my lap while she sobbed. Scrambled thoughts fell out of her mouth between sobs.

"I didn't know... you told me ... I can't ... what to do ... I can't ... how to face him ... how to explain ... don't want to ... *Joshua* ... can't leave ..."

I let her cry and ramble, rocking her, my own thoughts jumbled and chaotic. Slowly she calmed and became limp in my arms with exhaustion. I tilted her chin up with one finger and gazed at her. Her pain and conflict were clearly visible in her eyes. I drew in a painful breath.

"No, you didn't know. Neither of us did. We knew it was a possibility though, Rabbit. And now you do know. You have a life waiting for you. Someone who appears to love you; who is looking for you," I spoke slowly, trying to keep the tremor in my voice from coming through.

Her eyes widened. "What are you saying?"

"If you were mine, Rabbit, and you were taken from me, I wouldn't stop until I found you. It would drive me mental if I couldn't find you. Your husband has to be going through hell."

Her voice was barely a whisper. "I thought I *was* yours."

I had to close my eyes at the pain that hit me. I struggled to keep my voice even. "I only borrowed you, Rabbit. We both know you were never mine to keep."

There was total silence in the room.

Rabbit pulled away and stood up.

"What happens now?" she whispered, choking back sobs.

I stood up. My arms ached to drag her to me and tell her we did nothing. That she could stay here with me and forget about what we had seen. But I knew that was impossible. She had a life waiting. Someone who cared. A chance for a family. For a real life.

Not a life spent stagnating on a piece of property with someone who could never take her anywhere. Who couldn't give her a family or offer her a life outside these walls. Who, over time, she would grow to resent.

"I'll figure it out," I assured her, quietly.

She turned away.

My heart broke.

⇒Chapter Twenty-Two⇐

Joshua

I sat down in the chair, my head in my hands. My mind was full and I longed to be downstairs with Rabbit. I wanted to hold her and keep her close, but I knew I couldn't. She wouldn't even look at me when I left. Bear stayed with her.

My mind raced. Was he telling the truth? Who would make up such an elaborate lie? I watched the newsreel over and over again. If his story was fabricated, it could so easily be torn apart if Rabbit's memory was intact. Why would he risk that? I stood up, pacing and thinking, my mind weary but my body tense and anxious and not able to settle. I found myself, wishing more than ever, that she could remember something. Something that would tell me what I needed to do.

Time passed and I was still in total chaos. I found myself back in front of my computer staring at the pictures of Rabbit. I couldn't think of her as Elizabeth. The difference between the two women was vast. The one on the screen was a stranger to me who lived in a world I no longer belonged in. The one downstairs I knew and loved, but didn't belong in my world.

My mind and my heart were at war. I knew what I should do, what I had to do, what was seemingly the right thing to do. My mind was very clear on that. My heart screamed at the injustice of the decision my mind was making.

It was getting dark when I finally picked up the phone and called Cecilia. She answered on the first ring. "I need your help. And Trevor's," I said without any preliminary greeting.

"He's already here," she informed me. "I thought you might need him. Do you want us to come to the house now?"

My stomach lurched. "Yes."

I hung up.

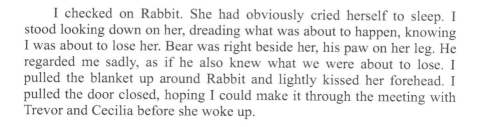

I checked on Rabbit. She had obviously cried herself to sleep. I stood looking down on her, dreading what was about to happen, knowing I was about to lose her. Bear was right beside her, his paw on her leg. He regarded me sadly, as if he also knew what we were about to lose. I pulled the blanket up around Rabbit and lightly kissed her forehead. I pulled the door closed, hoping I could make it through the meeting with Trevor and Cecilia before she woke up.

"Can it be done?" I asked Trevor. "Will it work?"

He looked at me, nodding. "You've thought it all out very well, Joshua. And Daniel has agreed to help."

Cecilia spoke up. "Are you sure, Joshua?"

I shrugged wearily. "What choice do I have, Cecilia? Keep her here; always worrying that she'd be happier *there?* Wondering if one day she will suddenly remember her other life and then leave? I can't even ask *her* to choose because right now she'll choose wrong. She'll choose safe. I have to be the one to make the decision."

"How are you going to tell her?"

"Honestly. She deserves that. And, doing this will make sure she is above question. Nothing will stand in the way of going back to her real life."

"What if it's not what she wants?" Trevor's voice was soft when he spoke up.

I shook my head. "How can I ask her that? She doesn't know what she wants, Trevor. She still can't remember. Right now she only knows me. I think when she is back in familiar surroundings she'll settle into her life and her memory will come back."

I looked down. "Then *I'll* just be the distant memory."

I heard Cecilia's sharp intake of breath.

"What if she remembers and she wants to choose differently?" Trevor asked.

I looked up. "I can't live with that hope, Trevor. Because, when it doesn't happen, it will crush me. I have nothing to offer her here. Just a life of hiding from the world. He has everything. She had a life. What looks like a full, busy life. I can't keep her from that because of how it will affect *me*. There's really no choice here. I'm damned either way. But this … this is the best for her."

I turned to Cecilia. "Can you set up that number? Just as I asked? Fast?"

She nodded.

"How long will it take for you to set up the paperwork trail, Trevor?"

He stood up. "I know this is hard, Joshua, but I agree, it is the right thing to do. I'll call Daniel now. I'm sure it can be done quickly." He went downstairs and I heard the door opening and closing beside him.

Cecilia sat quietly. "I wish I hadn't seen the news last night."

I shook my head. "It was bound to happen eventually. I knew that. Better now than a few more weeks. The longer she was here, the harder it would be to let go."

Her head tilted as she stared pointedly at me. "And it's not hard now, Joshua?"

For one moment I allowed the pain out. My voice was rough.

"It's fucking killing me, Cecilia."

———————◦•◦●◦◉◦●◦•◦———————

I heard Rabbit's soft footsteps coming down the hall. I braced myself for the conversation we were about to have. She came in silently and sat down beside me. I turned to her, wincing at the sight of her ravaged features.

"I made some sandwiches," I offered, not sure where to start.

She shook her head. "I'm not hungry right now."

I nodded. I wasn't either.

"I heard voices earlier. Was Cecilia here?"

I nodded. "And Trevor," I added.

"Why?" she whispered, her voice trembling.

I faced her and reached for her hand. I could feel the tremor in it as she stared at me.

"He is helping me set up some things, so you can go home … Elizabeth."

Her hand tightened in mine.

"Rabbit. I'm Rabbit," she protested.

I shook my head. "No, your name is Elizabeth. And soon, you're going home to your husband."

She pulled her hand away. "What am I going to do—just show up and say 'oh, sorry, I forgot about you and I've been sleeping with someone else. But I'm back so let's carry on?' Is that what I'm supposed to do, Joshua? Pretend you didn't happen? That *we* didn't happen?"

I looked at her. "Exactly. Listen to me, *Elizabeth*. I don't exist. When you leave here, it has to be as if we never happened. Do you understand me? You weren't here."

She stared at me. "Where was I then, Joshua? I'm pretty sure someone is going to ask me that."

"You were found by someone the night of the storm, by a care worker at a small, private care home. They have been looking after you. You've had amnesia, and with the aftermath of the storm, they only just saw the news article about you and contacted the authorities. They were without power or phone lines and were unable to contact the police when they first found you."

She shook her head. "But, I wasn't. I was here."

"It will all be documented. Unquestionably. There will be nothing leading you here."

"I don't understand."

"The care home is privately run by a good friend who is a doctor. Trevor contacted him and he agreed to do this for me … as a personal favor. And, in turn, the care home will get a much needed cash donation."

"And that's it? It's over? Done? I don't get a say?"

"And what would you say? You want to stay here? You don't love your husband or miss your life? You don't *know* that, so you can't say it."

"I know what I feel for you," she whispered.

The pain was like a punch in the gut. "You'll go back to your real life, Elizabeth, and I'll just become a memory you can think of every so often."

She stood up, anger rolling off her.

"Is that what you think, Joshua? That I'll just carry on and everything will be fine? I'll forget about *you* instead of him? That I'll just pick up where I left off? You think my feelings for you aren't real? That's how shallow you think I am?"

I shook my head. "No … Rabbit. I know you feel something for me. I just don't think it's based on reality. You're still confused and grateful. It will fade once you are back where you belong."

"It will *fade*? Where I *belong*? Fuck you, Joshua," she hissed.

I stared at her, my mouth agape. She so rarely swore or expressed anger.

She turned and walked away, slamming the bedroom door behind her. I sat down on the sofa in utter shock. I looked at Bear in astonishment, and then quickly averted my eyes as I saw his expression.

I was pretty sure if he could talk, he'd tell me to fuck off as well.

The sound of Rabbit crying out woke me from my restless sleep on the sofa. Immediately, I ran to the bedroom where she was sobbing in her sleep, twisting restlessly in the blankets. I sat beside her and gathered her in my arms, hushing her, waking her from her nightmare. Once fully awake, her arms tightened around my neck and her sobs started again.

"Don't, Joshua. Don't make me leave you. Please," her shaking voice pleaded, tearing at my already aching heart. "I love you ... I love you ..." her voice trailed off in a deep sob.

I couldn't speak as my own tears finally rolled down my face, soaking into her hair. I kept rocking her, making soft noises until I felt her grow heavy against my chest, pulled back into sleep with exhaustion. I laid her back down but her arms remained locked around me. Sighing, I lay beside her and pulled the blankets up around us, wishing I could make the world go away as easily by hiding under the covers.

◆◆◆◆◆◆

The first things I saw when I woke up in the light of the morning were Rabbit's eyes gazing at me solemnly. The pain I saw in them reflected my own agony back at me. I raised my hand and stroked her cheek gently.

"You're sending me back, aren't you? No matter what I say?" she whispered.

I nodded. "It's the right thing to do. I can't keep you ... no matter how much I want to. If the roles were reversed ..." I shuddered, thinking how I would feel. "We have to do this."

"Do you want to?"

"I love you, Rabbit," I said simply.

Her eyes closed for a few minutes. When they opened, she looked at me with resignation. "I won't fight you, Joshua. You've made your decision. Part of me knows you're right. But I want something."

"What?" I'd give her anything.

"I don't know when I'm leaving. I don't know if it's in two hours or two days, and ... I don't want to know because it will be all I dwell on. But until I do, I'm Rabbit. *Your Rabbit.* Give me that. Please."

My heart hurt so much I was sure it was about to explode. I stared at her precious face, trying to commit it to memory. I knew what she was asking and I would give it to her. I nodded slowly and pulled her to me. I captured her mouth with mine and kissed her deeply, my body already responding to her plea.

"Mine."

The pain we were both feeling was sensed no matter how we tried to ignore it. Rabbit clung to me and I hated even being in a different room than she was. She encouraged every touch, every kiss, to become more and I gave her everything she wanted. I needed her as much as she needed me.

More than once, I found her at the computer studying the pictures of her and Brian. I watched her staring intently at the screen and could see how hard she was trying to recall a memory, but nothing seemed to stimulate her recollection. Her headaches continued but I was now certain they were related to the stress of her memory loss.

She was highly emotional and my own responses simmered just below the surface. Everything was intense. One look could send her into a frenzy of tears, just as a glance from her would have me pulling her onto the nearest surface and taking her in a desperate need to imprint the memory of her skin into mine. Words that should have been exchanged and conversations that should have happened were disregarded. We were both perched precariously on an emotional ledge and neither of us was able to cope with much more. Bear spent most of his time with his head buried in his paws looking sad. He could sense the stress and sadness around us, and although he didn't understand it, it affected him as well. He especially hated it when Rabbit would begin to sob and often his great head would bury itself in her lap in furry comfort, a soft whine coming from his throat.

Two mornings later, I looked over at the clock. It was seven. Cecilia and Trevor would be here soon. Everything was in place. A couple of hours from now, I would once again be alone. But this time I would really know just how alone I was in my secluded world.

I looked down at Rabbit who had only slept fitfully in the night again. Even though we hadn't discussed it, I think she sensed last night was our final night together. Our lovemaking had been stained with a feeling of desperation and she had clung to me afterwards, sobbing. I had lain awake all night watching her, absorbing and memorizing all the little details of her in the light I left burning. I couldn't stand the thought of wasting time sleeping. I would have the rest of my life to do that. I watched her briefly for a few more minutes and then leaned forward and pressed my lips softly against her forehead in a silent farewell, fighting back my emotions. I slid from the bed and grabbed some clothes. I commanded Bear to come with me and I quickly dressed with shaking hands in the kitchen, and then surprised him by snapping a leash on his collar. I stood feeling lost for a minute, then headed out to the barn.

I heard the car pull up and both Cecilia and Trevor entered the barn. Cecilia took one look at me and threw her arms around my neck in a tight hug. I patted her back awkwardly and pulled away.

I looked at Trevor. "It's all set?"

He nodded. "I have the records in my briefcase. The care home has the originals on file. I have the statement of the person who found her and brought her into the care home. No one will question the word of Ellen or Daniel Tate. Everything is covered, Joshua."

I nodded, unable to speak. Bear was sitting at my feet, whining in his throat, unsure as to why he was tied up and why I was so upset. I patted his head. Looking at Cecilia, I handed her a small envelope. "Make sure she gets this. Tell her to guard it carefully. No matter what. Tell her if she needs me ... tell her she'll figure it out."

She nodded.

"Give her my grey hoodie to wear. She likes that one and it will keep her warm." My voice broke and I turned away. "Don't let her come out here, Cecilia. If she asks to stay ... I won't be able to let her go. I can't watch her leave. Please."

"I'll take care of her, I promise, Joshua," she spoke comfortingly.

I nodded and heard her leave.

Trevor came up to me and patted my shoulder in comfort. "I called John and he's on his way with the chopper. I'll make sure they are both okay, Joshua."

I was grateful for that. But I wondered if I would ever be okay again.

<hr/>

I could hear the helicopter approach. It was rare that John flew the chopper onto my property, usually landing at the small airfield in Gravenhurst, and Bear's ears flattened at the strange noise and he buried his head in his paws, whimpering at the loud sound. Unable to help myself, I stood to the side of the door and watched as Cecilia came out, her arm around a sobbing Rabbit. I saw Rabbit struggle to get away from Cecilia and my hand instinctively reached out to her. I began to move forward, every instinct in me telling me to go to her, comfort her and protect her. Trevor grabbed my arm. "Steady there, Joshua. You knew this was going to be the most difficult part."

I allowed him to hold me back and I let the tears drip down my face unheeded as I watched Cecilia push Rabbit into the helicopter that would take her away from me. Bear suddenly stood up, barking madly, desperately trying to get off his leash and to Rabbit. His howls increased as the door shut and the chopper lifted from the ground. I was grateful the sound of the chopper kept her from hearing him and, at the same time, had kept me from hearing her sobs. I wasn't sure I was strong enough for that. Despite being told I was doing the right thing repeatedly, there was a piece of me that was screaming how wrong this was; for me and for Rabbit. My eyes followed the chopper as it lifted and flew away, quickly disappearing from sight. Trevor released my arm and I dropped to my knees beside Bear, wrapping my arms around his great neck. I stayed like that, struggling to calm down, listening to Bear's heavy pants and sad whimpers. I sat up and stared unseeingly at Rabbit's car. In all of this mess, we had never discussed the car. There was so much we had never discussed.

A sudden thought occurred to me and I stood up and crossed over to the car. I looked inside and then went to the work table and grabbed a pen and paper.

"Do you still use Frank?" I asked Trevor.

"Frank the Pit Bull? Yeah, I use him a lot."

I nodded. I had used him a lot as well. The nickname Pit Bull suited him. He never stopped until he had the answers. I handed him the paper. "Hire him again. Tell him it's for me and he's got whatever he needs to take care of this. I want it to be his first priority. I want this VIN traced. I want to know who the owner of the car is. And I want to know everything there is to know about Brian James. And Elizabeth James. Everything."

"Joshua ..."

I held up my hand. "Just do it, Trevor. I did what I *thought* was the right thing. Now I'm going to fucking make sure it was."

"Okay, Joshua. Relax. I'll get him right on it. Now I need to get going so I'm there when Cecilia needs me." He hesitated. "Are you going to be okay here, alone?"

I nodded and walked with him to his car. I stood and watched as it disappeared from view. There was another chopper at the small airfield waiting to take him and Daniel back to Toronto as well. Records would show that helicopter transported all of them back to Toronto together. It was another additional layer to keep Rabbit safe.

I turned around and stared at the house knowing the emptiness that now waited for me when I walked in the door. My knees crumbled as I fell into the snow, my head flung back as I roared my pain into the sky until my voice was hoarse. Bear pushed his head into my chest, whining deeply in his throat. Spent, I sat hunched until I felt the shivers tear through my body from the cold. Rising, I trudged wearily forward and Bear and I entered the house. I stood in the doorway watching Bear run around searching for Rabbit. The silence screamed at me in its intensity. The quiet had always been a welcome reprieve for me, but right now, it was an unbearable torture. I walked to the bedroom and sat on the edge of the bed. I picked up Rabbit's pillow and breathed in the scent of her. A piece of paper caught my eye and I picked it up.

*No matter what— I am **always** yours.*

Rabbit

I fell back on the bed, grasping her note.

My Rabbit was gone.

I buried my head in her pillow and felt the bed shaking with the intensity of my sobs.

The dampness of my clothes soaked into the bedding.

I didn't care.

Nothing mattered now.

⇒Chapter Twenty-Three⇐

Rabbit

I woke up reaching for Joshua, but the bed was empty. Even Bear was gone. I sat up as the door opened, thinking it was Joshua coming in with coffee, only to be greeted quietly by Cecilia.

I stared at her, my stomach instantly in knots. "What are you doing here?" I asked, already knowing the answer.

"It's time, Elizabeth."

"Don't call me that," I whispered, trying not to cry. Not yet. I wasn't ready.

"I need you to get up and get dressed. We're leaving soon," she said kindly but firmly.

"Tell Joshua I need to talk to him ... please."

She shook her head. "He isn't here. Get dressed; I'll meet you in the kitchen." Cecilia turned and quickly left the room pulling the door shut.

Not here?

Joshua wasn't here?

I grabbed a pair of the yoga pants that had come from the bag Joshua found, but added his t-shirt that was lying on the chair. His scent surrounded me and I needed that while I figured something out. I needed to talk to Joshua. I splashed some water on my face and brushed my teeth. I padded out to the kitchen with a pair of his socks in my hand. I stood by the table where Cecilia was sitting. "Where is he, Cecilia?"

"He's in the barn."

I nodded. "I'll go talk to him there then."

Cecilia stood up. "No, Elizabeth. He doesn't want you to."

I stared at her, not understanding. She handed me Joshua's grey hoodie. "He said to make sure you wore this. It will keep you warm."

I shook my head, the enormity of what was about to happen hitting me. "He's not going to say goodbye? He's just letting me leave ... without ... without ..." my voice broke.

No. Joshua wouldn't do that.

I straightened up and pulled on the socks, the tears rolling down my face. I began walking to the door, but Cecilia stepped in front of me. "He can't, Rabbit," she said pleadingly. "This is killing him. Don't make it any harder on him. Please."

I looked at her, my sobs shaking my body. "But I need to see him, Cecilia. I don't know how to get in touch with him! I don't even know where we are!"

"That's what he wants. The less you know the easier it will be to stick to the story he has set up for you. You won't get mixed up."

I looked at her in horror.

"He doesn't want me to know where he lives?"

She shook her head.

His words filled my head; *we never happened.*

I sat down, my legs unable to hold me up. I buried my head in my hands and sobbed.

I heard a strange noise and lifted my head. I looked at Cecilia.

"We had the helicopter come here. We have to leave now," she explained.

I nodded numbly, not even caring enough to ask any questions, and stood up. I went into the bedroom and looked around. I opened the dresser and took some of the money from the envelope. I grabbed a piece of paper and wrote the only thing I could think of on it and placed it on the bed. I left everything else.

I walked back into the kitchen. "Bear is with him?" She nodded, holding out the hoodie again. I pulled it on and stuffed the money into the pocket. I felt the tears welling up again. I wasn't even allowed to say goodbye to my furry protector.

"I don't want this, Cecilia. I want to stay here," I whispered. I looked at her. "I love him. He needs me."

Her eyes glistened with unshed tears. "You have to. Joshua's right. He loves you enough to let you go. He has worked hard to make sure you *can* go back to the life you had, with no repercussions, so respect him for that and do what he is asking you to do. You have to do this … for him." She paused and drew in a breath. "I know you're hurting, Elizabeth. He is as well. This wasn't an easy decision for him."

My heart hurt so much I instinctively lifted my hand, rubbing my chest in comfort. Feeling empty and defeated, I nodded and pulled on my sneakers. We walked out of the house and I felt myself shaking so hard I could barely stand, let alone put one foot in front of the other. I had no idea where I was going, who I was going to. Everything in me screamed this was wrong and here with Joshua was where I belonged. I felt Cecilia's arm come around me and I looked at her through the tears streaming down my face. I could hear my own gasping breath as I struggled to breathe against the onslaught of pain.

Her eyes reflected her understanding of my agony, but still she urged me forward. I struggled to get away, wanting to run to the barn. I could feel him watching me leave. I strained to get a glimpse of him, just the chance to look at him one more time, even from afar, but I was pushed into the helicopter cabin and the door slammed behind me before I could turn my head. Cecilia helped me buckle up, then pulled me into a tight embrace as I wept onto her shoulder as the chopper took off, taking me away from Joshua and Bear.

My saviors.

My protectors.

I turned and watched the house and barn quickly disappear from my view.

Joshua. Bear.

Their love for me.

Mine for them.

My world was gone.

Cecilia looked at me questioningly. "Do you understand, Elizabeth?"

I nodded from my place on the sofa. Dutifully, I repeated everything back. "I woke up in the care home. I have no recollection of how I got there. Nothing they have done has helped me remember. Dr. Tate saw a repeat broadcast of the press conference and recognized me."

She nodded, and I continued. "He contacted his lawyer, Trevor, who brought me here. And you're here …" I trailed off.

"Simply to escort you and to be certain you are comfortable. I came because Trevor asked me."

I stood up and went to the window, restless and unsettled. There was so much noise here. I could hear people and movement and even the traffic from outside. "Isn't that a little convenient, Cecilia? Too close to Joshua? His lawyer and his assistant?" I asked, feeling my hands clench as I thought about Joshua.

"Trevor has a lot of clients, Elizabeth. And, no one knows I'm Joshua's assistant. He only ever refers to me as CC and, legally, my name is Cecilia Jones. Any business I conduct on Joshua's behalf, I go by my maiden name. Josh isn't the only one who likes privacy."

I turned around. "Well, how convenient. He brings mystery and subterfuge into his personal life as well. Aren't I lucky?"

Cecilia looked at me. "I know this isn't easy, Elizabeth. It's not easy for me to see two people I'm fond of hurting either. Can you try and remember that?"

Instantly, I felt terrible. I sat down and reached for her hand, my eyes once again filling with tears. "I'm sorry, Cecilia. I'm just so ... overwhelmed and scared."

She squeezed my hand. "I know."

She smiled sympathetically at me. "Dr. Tate will be here any minute. He is going to do a quick exam and add a few things to your 'records.' Trevor had some things to take care of and then he'll join us. When he gets here, we'll go over everything one more time and then ..." she drew in a breath, "your husband will come and get you."

"He's been contacted?" I asked, my voice trembling.

She nodded. "He has. He thinks you are being brought here later today. Did you want to go shower before Dr. Tate comes? I brought you some things." She leaned over and handed me a small bag.

I nodded and went into the bathroom, more for the quiet and chance to be alone than the desire for a shower. Again, I did as I was told and stripped and stood under the spray. My thoughts were a chaotic symphony in my head. The pain of leaving Joshua, the fear of meeting Brian, the uncertainty of my future. How did I face this man, my husband, after the past weeks with Joshua? Go back to a life with someone I couldn't remember, when the person I loved was somewhere else, living a different life? Could I do that? Would I remember Brian and would Joshua become what he said he would? Just a quiet memory of someone I shared some time with?

I had studied the pictures of myself on Joshua's computer and read snippets about me. From what I had read and seen, my life was very much one social event after another. Fancy dinners and charity events seem to be the mainstay. I was terrified of the kind of person I was before Joshua. I liked the one I was when I was with him. What was I like with

Brian? Was I kind and loving? What was our relationship like? Was he what he portrayed in the news? How could I completely block out someone I was supposedly so in love with?

Wearily, I shut off the water and stepped out of the shower, not feeling any more refreshed. I dried off and changed into the new undergarments and pants Cecilia had thoughtfully provided, but slipped Joshua's shirt and hoodie back on. They were all I had left of him and I wasn't giving them up. I brushed my wet hair and squared my shoulders. I could hear voices in the next room and knew the doctor had arrived. I opened the door and went to find out what was next for me, dreading every single second.

⋙ ●●●◆◗◆●●● ⋘

I sat curled into the corner of the sofa, my stomach in knots and wave after wave of nausea hitting me. Brian would be here any minute. Dr. Tate had been very kind, insisting on me calling him Daniel. He checked me over and used some sort of portable x-ray machine on my head and ribs. He made additional notes on my "chart" and made copies which he had handed to Trevor when he arrived.

Currently, he, Trevor and Cecilia were sitting, quietly talking. I could feel them looking over at me every so often, but they let me remain silent for the most part. I had asked Trevor about Joshua as soon as he arrived and his sad smile told me more than his brief 'it's been a tough day all around' did. He filled me in on the fact that he had contacted Brian's lawyer and told him of my being discovered and between them had made these arrangements. He also told me Brian's lawyer had insisted this be done quietly without any media, as per his client's wishes. I was grateful for that fact since I didn't know what my reaction would be when I saw him.

I shut my eyes as another wave of nausea raced through me. I wasn't a good liar. Joshua teased me about that all the time. How was I supposed to look this man in the eye and pretend to be something I wasn't? Feel something I didn't? Pretend like the last few weeks never happened? Just the thought of being touched by a man other than Joshua made me cringe. How was I supposed to...

My thoughts were interrupted by the sound of a firm knock on the door. I stood up and fled to the bedroom. I wasn't ready. Shaking and desperately trying to stop the tears that were flowing down my face, I sat on the edge of the bed rocking myself. "I need you, Joshua," I whispered brokenly into my hands. I could hear the timbre of a deep voice talking quickly through the door. I listened but nothing stirred in recognition of the voice.

I started when a soft knock came on the door, but relaxed a little when I saw Cecilia slip in. She knelt in front of me. "He's here and wants to see you. You need to come out now, okay? We're all here, Elizabeth."

I wanted to scream no, it wasn't okay. To stop calling me that. To demand she take me back to Joshua. Instead, I wiped my face and stood up. She stood with me and held out her hand. In it was a tiny white envelope, no bigger than a business card.

"Joshua wanted me to give you this. He said to keep it safe. Guard it. And use it if you need to."

I took it carefully. "What is it?"

"I have no idea. He wouldn't tell me. He just said you would figure it out."

Unsure what to do with it, I patted my pockets, then remembered the little one inside the waistband of the pants. No doubt it was there to hold a small item when running but it would do well for this. I slipped it in and pulled the hoodie back down.

"Ready?"

Trembling, scared and feeling ill, I nodded. We stepped out into the living area. There were three men standing to one side of Trevor and Daniel. Two of them were total strangers. I recognized the third as Brian from the pictures I had seen. We stared at each other. He was tall, dark-haired and large, so large he was almost square looking. Bulging muscles were made more evident by his stance. He stood looking at me, his hands on his hips, head tilted to one side. I looked back at him, waiting to feel a rush of recognition. Nothing. I could have walked past him on the street and never known he was my husband. My stomach tightened as he suddenly began walking towards me. He stopped in front of me, still staring, as I fought back the impulse to step back away from him. His hand reached out and I looked down at it. It was out of proportion with the rest of him. Blockish and thickset. Unbecoming. Not like Joshua's long-fingered, beautifully tapered hand. I shuddered at the sight of it extended towards me. His voice speaking to me brought me back from my thoughts. "Elizabeth?" he breathed, his hand flexing, waiting for me to touch him. I drew in a breath and placed my hand in his. His bulky hand closed over mine and this time something stirred.

And, before I could stop it, I vomited all over his shoes. The last thing I heard before everything went black was a muttered string of expletives that I knew were directed at me.

⇒Chapter Twenty-Four⇐

Rabbit

I came to feeling panicked and unsure. My eyes flew open as I remembered why, only to find myself lying on the sofa. Standing at the end of the sofa was Brian and one of the other men that had been in the room. They were quietly conversing. I sat up and looked around, relaxing when I saw Cecilia and Trevor standing a few feet away, looking at me with worried expressions on their faces.

Daniel was leaning over me, his fingers on my wrist. "Are you all right, Elizabeth?" he asked calmly, although the look on his face was intense and questioning.

I stared at him, filled with uncertainty, but I nodded. He handed me a glass of water which I drank gratefully.

Frowning, he stood up, releasing my wrist. "She seems fine now. No doubt a reaction to all the stress," he said to Brian.

Brian came over. "Elizabeth."

"I'm so sorry, I'm just so sorry …" My voice was trembling.

He held up his hand. "Mrs. Jones explained how nervous you have been. No harm done. I over-reacted myself. Are you feeling all right now?" His tone was kind, yet somehow I found no comfort in that fact.

I was puzzled at the formal use of Cecilia's name, but realized quickly I was not supposed to know her, or any of them, very well. I drew in a shaky breath, knowing I needed to remember to act accordingly.

Brian sat down. Again, he reached for my hand and, this time, I steeled myself not to show a reaction, even though just the sight of his wide hands made me cringe. Why, I had no idea.

"I'm sure you're feeling very disconcerted. You have been through so much. I'm anxious to get you home and settled." He drew in a deep breath and studied my face for a minute. "We've much to talk about. No doubt you are eager to be in familiar surroundings as well." His nose wrinkled in distaste. "And, out of those clothes. I suppose that's all the home had to give you."

I looked down. I was in Joshua's shirt and hoodie. I never wanted to take them off. But I looked up and nodded silently. It seemed to be what he was expecting.

He stood up. "I am taking my wife home now. Obviously, she is still recovering and she needs rest. Thank you for your efforts. I will make sure the care home is amply rewarded." His tone brooked no argument.

"You should make sure she goes to her doctor as soon as possible," Daniel spoke up, stepping forward.

Brian's hand shot up, stopping Daniel's motion. "I will make sure my wife is seen to properly. There is no need for you to be concerned any longer," he snapped.

He turned to me. "Come, Elizabeth."

I stood up shakily, nervous at the abrupt change in his demeanor. He turned back to Daniel. "I apologize. I'm simply anxious to get Elizabeth home. And, of course I will make sure she is seen by our doctor. I appreciate the concern for my wife, but it's not necessary."

Daniel nodded silently, his brow furrowed.

Brian turned back to me, holding his coat in his hands. "Wear this Elizabeth. I don't want anyone to see you like that."

Again, I looked down. I was clean and tidy. Did it really matter? But again, I accepted his decree and allowed him to drape the coat over my shoulders. His arm came around me and he escorted me to the door. There was no comfort in his touch, only a sense of being trapped. I felt the stirrings of panic again as I realized what was happening. I was leaving the last piece of Joshua behind. I turned and caught Cecilia's eye silently, desperately wanting her to know what I was saying.

Look after him.

Her nod was barely noticeable.

"Take care, Elizabeth," she murmured.

I smiled tremulously. I couldn't speak. Brian guided me firmly to the elevator. "The car is downstairs and we are well-secured. No one will see us leave."

I nodded, unsure what I was supposed to say to that remark.

The elevator doors closed and, abruptly, it hit me.

I was alone.

The car ride was quiet. Brian's lawyer left in his own car, and other than being introduced briefly to his assistant, Randy, my presence was ignored. I looked out the window watching the bustling city go by. None of it looked familiar to me. Brian spoke at length with Randy, listing off items he wanted done. First apparently was that the shoes he was wearing be thrown out and his suit taken to the cleaners. So much for no harm done, it would seem.

We entered through the gates and pulled up in front of a large, imposing stone house. I gazed at it then turned to Brian. "This is where we live?" I asked quietly.

"Yes," he confirmed. "This is my house."

I didn't fail to notice his emphasis on *my* house.

He helped me out of the car and we entered. I walked in ahead of him and stood looking around the grand entrance. It was so ... austere. There was nothing warm or welcoming about it. I shivered. Or was it just how I was feeling about this strange homecoming? Nothing felt welcoming.

A woman came from the hall. "Mr. James. Mrs. James. Welcome home. Your room is waiting and I will bring up tea when you are settled."

Brian nodded. "Mrs. James will be resting the remainder of the day. No visitors. Take what she is wearing and get rid of it. She doesn't want any reminders of the past few weeks." He turned to Randy. "Wait in the den. I will be down soon." Then he grabbed my elbow and escorted me to the staircase.

I allowed him to lead me upstairs and into a large bedroom. I looked around trying to find something familiar. Brian cleared his throat and I turned to look at him. He stared at me for a minute.

"I didn't think I would ever see you again."

I wasn't sure how to answer him. "You were looking for me though?" I said quietly, knowing I had to try and establish a connection with this man.

He nodded. He made no move toward me. I was unsure if he was waiting for me to move to him or what I should do next. I noticed his hands were clenched at his side and he appeared tense. His stance wasn't helping ease my nerves at all.

He finally spoke. "I'm sure this must all feel very strange to you. I am told you have no recollection of who you are? Or of our life together?"

"No, none," I whispered. "The first thing I recall is waking up in the care home."

He frowned. "Dr. Tate informed me he thinks this is perhaps a permanent condition."

I blinked. I hadn't been told that. Unsure what to say, I murmured, "I'm sorry."

He stood looking at me, a strange expression on his face. "We'll discuss that later. I have matters to attend to downstairs. Mrs. Smith will bring you your tea. You can change into your own clothes and rest. I will come up later and go over the staff and your duties. I'm sure you'll feel better once you understand what is expected of you." With those words, he walked out.

I sat down feeling disoriented after his speech, which felt like a string of orders.

Was he always so formal?

My duties? What was expected of me? Was I his wife or a member of his staff?

Where was the man who had broken down in front of the camera desperate to have me back? I shook my head, my heart heavy and my thoughts chaotic.

What have you sent me back to, Joshua?

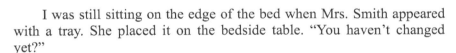

I was still sitting on the edge of the bed when Mrs. Smith appeared with a tray. She placed it on the bedside table. "You haven't changed yet?"

I looked at her blankly. "I, um, I don't know where anything is," I admitted quietly.

Her stern expression softened. "So, it's true. You have no memory?"

I shook my head.

She walked around the room and indicated the bathroom door and then opened a set of double doors. "Here is your closet and dressing room." I followed her and stood looking at the large room. Rows of clothing hung neatly. A large set of drawers was at the end. I glanced at the racks; all blacks, browns, and navy. Suits, skirts, dresses; all organized and tidy. Blouses in white and black and beige hung in an orderly fashion. Shoes and boots were lined up straight. I looked at Mrs. Smith, confused. "Do I have anything, um, less structured?"

She pursed her lips. "Mr. James does not approve of looking casual very much. I would think, for today, it would be all right for you to wear your night clothes since you will not be leaving your room."

I looked at her stunned. He did not *approve* of casual clothes? I was expected to be dressed-up all the time?

She leaned forward confidentially. "You have a few items you wear when he is away and you are alone. But I think, today, you should just use one of your nightdresses." Then she gave me a small squeeze on my arm and a smile. "I will leave you to change and be back to collect your clothes. I have been instructed to dispose of them."

I shook my head. "No, please. I want ... I want to keep them."

She looked at me for a minute then shrugged. "You have to give me something," she said quietly.

"I will. I promise."

She nodded and left the dressing room. I opened the drawers until I found some nightgowns. Luckily, there were some pajamas as well, and even though they were black, they at least would be more comfortable than a suit or a dress. I changed quickly; piling the pants and underwear I was wearing into a ball, being sure to remove the small envelope first. That I tucked into the drawer of undergarments planning on opening it when I was finally alone. I found a white shirt and added it to the ball to make it look bigger. I hid Joshua's hoodie and shirt in an almost empty drawer.

Mrs. Smith was waiting for me, and took the pile from my hands. "Would you like to lie down or sit in the chair?"

I chose the chair and she brought me my tea and a blanket to lie over my knees. "If you want something, the extension is 323," she indicated the phone. "It is only an intercom. Not an outside line," she informed me.

I nodded and she left.

I sat sipping my black tea with a small grimace. Apparently, I didn't use sugar. Joshua always snuck a little extra sugar into my mugs when he thought I wasn't looking. He seemed to think I was too thin and needed the extra calories. I sighed longingly, thinking of his subtle ways of caring for me.

I looked around the room. It was large, with lovely mouldings, but otherwise totally vacant of any personality. No pictures or knickknacks were around. Aside from the bedroom furniture and the chair I was sitting on, the only other piece in the room was a small bookcase which was filled with books, once again in a very neat and orderly fashion. I got up and went to inspect the bookcase. It was mostly novels and my heart clenched when I saw four of Joshua's books on the shelves. I pulled one out and turned it over. I sighed. Of course there was no picture. I looked inside the book jacket in case, desperate to see his face, but there was nothing. His foreword included some general thanks to his editor and his assistant, CC. I smiled a little. I had never noticed that before. He never said her last name. My knees suddenly gave away as my mind tore through every conversation I had ever had with him, Cecilia or Trevor. I didn't know any other information about Cecilia or Trevor. I had no idea where they lived. They were the only connection I had to Joshua and I had no idea how to get a hold of them. I felt my eyes fill with tears. It wasn't like I could just ask Brian.

The envelope. I made my way to the dressing room and my hands shook as I opened the envelope. A small black square fell into my hand and I looked at it. It was a small memory stick. No doubt the photos of my injuries that Joshua took. He promised me he would make sure I had it. I looked inside the envelope and saw a card. I pulled it out, praying it was a message from him.

There were two lines of writing on it, one on the top and one on the bottom. I recognized his large, rather messy script.

WIH 98

AAW193

That was it. I stared at the card. I didn't understand. What did that mean? I held the card up to the light, but there was nothing. Cecilia's words came back to me. 'He said to tell you to guard it. That you would figure it out.' I shook my head, my breath catching on a sob; I didn't understand. I placed both items back in the envelope then put the envelope into a pair of socks where it would not be found. I made my way back to the chair and slumped into it.

My head ached and I was so tired. And confused. I looked around the strange room and buried my head in my hands. I sobbed until I fell asleep.

⟶ •••◑◉◐••• ⟵

"Elizabeth."

The one word woke me instantly. Brian was standing in front of me, holding a tray and looking displeased. "You have been crying."

"I, ah, I get a lot of headaches. Someone … someone said it could be my mind trying to remember things," I whispered, feeling nervous.

"Stop trying then. You're home. That's all that matters."

I was stunned at his attitude. He didn't *want* me to remember?

He sat down on the edge of the bed. "I brought you dinner, but you didn't drink your tea."

I looked at the salad with no appetite and shook my head. "It was rather bitter. I think I would like it better with sugar."

He snorted. "You don't take sugar. In anything. I can see you've gained some weight. Obviously from laying around doing nothing. We'll get you back on your regular diet right away. Maybe even cut back a little so you can lose those extra pounds."

"My regular diet?" I asked, my voice quivering, feeling a bit hurt at his comment, and confused about *that* being the detail he was concentrating on. Not my memory, my meagre weight gain.

"Yes. You follow a very regimented diet. You also work with a trainer to maintain your weight."

I waited but he didn't add anything. I noticed he had a folder in his hand. "What is that?"

"I had Randy prepare this. It's a list of your charitable work. Some information on people we socialize with. Your schedule. Upcoming events. My expectations."

My hand froze in midair while reaching for the folder. "Your ... expectations?"

He regarded me for a minute.

"I hold a very important position within this community, Elizabeth. I expect you to remember that at all times and act accordingly. Your behavior reflects directly on me."

I started to tremble. Something about this conversation felt very familiar, as if I had heard it many times.

"I realize you will not be able to simply pick up where you left off before you were ... taken. But I won't allow you to slack off either. As my wife, you have responsibilities."

Slack off?

Before I could react, he reached into his pocket and pulled out a narrow gold ring. "I noticed your ring was gone. I assume it was taken from you."

I looked down at my hand. I had no idea.

Without warning, he grabbed my hand and forced the ring down on my finger. I gasped at the uncomfortable sensation. "I think it's too small," I whispered.

"Then I don't have to worry about it coming off again," he said curtly, ignoring any discomfort I might be feeling.

I swallowed the lump that was forming in my throat.

"Do I work outside the house?" I asked quietly, sensing not to push him on the ring.

"No. Twice a week you volunteer your time at the local library. Books are a great love of yours so I allow you to donate your time there. You run a reading program. You also donate some time at the children's hospital and are active with other charitable works. It's all in the folder."

He leaned forward, holding out the folder. I reached out again to take it from him, my hand trembling, the light glinting off the unfamiliar ring.

"Are you frightened of me, Elizabeth?" His voice was low, but there was an undercurrent to it. "Is that why you're trembling?"

I looked at him. "I'm nervous because I don't know you, because I don't know what I'm supposed to do," I answered.

His face softened and, for a minute, he looked like the man I had seen on TV.

"I understand. Randy told me downstairs I needed to be more helpful to you. I'm rather out of my element here. You've always been the more ... open of the two of us. I know this is all overwhelming to you, but it's not that easy for me either. I am not sure how to connect with you."

Abruptly, he stood up, taking the tray with him. "If you are not hungry, I will return this to the kitchen. If you need me, my room is across the hall."

I drew back in surprise. "We don't ... ah ... share a room?"

He shook his head. "No. You are a very light sleeper and informed me not long after we were married that I was keeping you up and you preferred to sleep alone. My room is across the hall."

And he left.

I stared after him, feeling sense of relief at his departure. But I was confused; Joshua never said anything about me being a light sleeper. It seemed to me that I slept quite deeply when I was with him. I liked sleeping in his arms. He always made me feel safe.

What kind of relationship did I have with Brian that I would not want him close to me?

I sat alone in the strange, cold room. My thoughts were jumbled and, I felt frightened and lost, my head aching with a constant dull pounding. I wanted Joshua and Bear. I wanted the warmth of the cabin and the feeling of Joshua's arms around me. Trembling, I stood up, and went into the closet and wrapped myself in Joshua's hoodie, breathing in his scent. I spent the rest of the night rocking myself on the floor of the closet, my fingers twisting and turning the ring on my hand that felt so wrong there.

⇒Chapter Twenty-Five⇐

Joshua

A hand was stroking my head. "Joshua."

I sighed in relief. Rabbit was here. It had all been a horrid dream. I reached up for her hand and frowned. This hand was bony and had rings on it—a lot of rings.

I opened my eyes and looked up at Cecilia, the light searing my eyes. I groaned. "Go away, Cecilia."

"No, I won't go away. What the hell have you been doing, Joshua? The place smells like a distillery. Bear has broken into his food bag and there's kibble everywhere! Why is it so fucking cold in here?"

I sat up, my head aching and my stomach rolling.

After I had finally gotten off the bed, I went directly to the cupboard. My writer's imagination had taken over and image after image pounded my brain of a joyous reunion between Elizabeth and Brian. As I laid here holding her Rabbit-scented pillow, he was lying *there* beside her, breathing *her* in, making her his again. I couldn't stop the visions. It was a never ending loop. I grabbed the tequila and started drinking. I didn't stop until the liquor ran out. I vaguely recall stumbling around getting Bear his food and water and, opening the door for him to go outside. I guess I left the door open. I wasn't even sure how long I'd been drinking; it was as if when Rabbit left, time stopped.

Cecilia stomped down the hall and I heard a door slam. I winced. Nope, guess I didn't close the door. She stomped back and I leaned my head back, my arm over my eyes shielding them from the bright light. "Please, Cecilia, not so loud. I'm in pain."

"Which you deserve. God, you stink! And, you look like shit. Go have a shower." She stomped even louder into the kitchen and I heard bottles being banged around.

"What day is it?"

"Monday. You've been wallowing for four days. Now go."

Four days? I'd been drunk for four days?

I went into the bathroom, not wanting to risk anymore of her rage, and stripped, catching sight of myself in the mirror. I grimaced. She was right; I looked like shit. The hot water felt good pounding against my skin and I reached for the shampoo. My fingers touched something and I pulled the object off the bottle. It was a hair tie. Rabbit's. My heart clenched and the pain of her leaving rolled through me again. I lowered myself to the floor as the agony hit me. My stomach tightened and I heaved repeatedly. Finally, I struggled to my feet and cleaned myself up. The last thing I did was wrap her hair tie around my wrist. My watch would cover it. I got dressed and made my way to the kitchen.

Wordlessly, Cecilia sat a mug of coffee in front of me. I looked behind her, wincing. The counter was covered in empty bottles. I had drunk every drop of liquor in the house. I looked at Cecilia who was standing against the counter. Her expression was no longer angry, just sad. I looked away, muttering I was sorry.

"I understand, Joshua. I know you're in pain. I hate to see you going through this." Her hand waved towards the counter. "I do know this isn't the way to handle it. It's not like you, Joshua."

I nodded. She turned to the counter and started gathering up bottles. "Leave it, Cecilia. I'll do it. It's my mess, I'll clean it up."

She stopped what she was doing and grabbed some toast. She set it in front of me silently and sat down. I stared at it for a minute, and then looked at her. "Not really hungry..."

"Too fucking bad. Eat it."

I picked up a piece and chewed, my stomach protesting loudly. It was not gonna stay in long. I took a sip of coffee and grimaced. Cecilia's coffee had always reminded me of tar, and after drinking Rabbit's, it tasted even worse than before. I looked up and saw the expression on her face and wisely kept drinking.

The silence was deafening.

I threw the toast down.

"Just fucking *tell* me, Cecilia."

"What?"

I stood up, pacing rapidly. "Tell me! He walked in and she looked at him and that was it. Right? Her memory came back and now it's happily ever after for them. Right? RIGHT?" The last word was roared loudly.

She stared at me.

"No, Joshua. That's not what happened at all."

I sat back down, exhausted.

"Tell me," I begged. "I need to know, Cecilia."

"She didn't remember him at all. She didn't have exactly the most ... positive reaction to him," she said quietly.

"What happened?"

"She, ah ... she threw up on him."

I stared at her.

"Just like that?"

"Yes. He reached over and took her hand, and she threw up all over his shoes."

I felt my lips quirk.

"Then what?"

"Rab ... Elizabeth passed out."

My humor vanished. "Did she hurt herself?"

Cecilia shook her head. "Daniel moved really quickly and he caught her before she hit the floor."

I stood up, instantly angry again. "*Daniel* caught her? What the fuck was Prince Charming doing while his wife was about to hit the floor?"

"Jumping back and cursing about his shoes," Cecilia looked at me knowingly.

"He cursed her?" I snarled. "He was more upset over his splattered shoes than his wife, the one he begged to be returned to him?"

My mug shattered against the wall where I threw it forcefully, coffee dripping down the walls. The plate of unwanted toast followed, the plate exploding in hundreds of shards as it hit the wall.

"Joshua! Calm down!"

I swung around, my breath laboured. "Don't tell me to calm down, Cecilia! Fuck! I made the wrong fucking decision! I never should have sent her back!"

"Joshua! Maybe he had a thing about being thrown up on! Maybe he was just so shocked, he didn't think. You can't immediately jump to a conclusion like that. He apologized afterwards."

I shook my head and snorted. "He apologized? How ... civil." I looked at Cecilia intently. "She woke up here, bleeding and bruised. Scared out of her wits. She didn't know who she was or who I was, but she allowed me to comfort her. She let me touch her, hold her." I closed my eyes, remembering how she felt tucked up under my chin, shaking and scared. I opened my eyes and stared at Cecilia. "If she had thrown up all over me, I still would have held her and comforted her." I drew in a painful breath. "Her *husband* takes her hand and she throws up and passes out? That's not a nervous reaction, that's her body remembering. That's her body *rejecting* him."

I sat down and grabbed my throbbing head. "I shouldn't have sent her back, Cecilia," I reiterated and my voice broke. "She isn't safe."

She looked at me shrewdly.

Silently, she reached into her bag and pulled out a folder, slamming it down on the table in front of me.

"Then stop wallowing. Do something about it."

<hr />

I sat back, my hand scrubbing my face in exhaustion. I had been through the files Cecilia brought with her again and again. Frank had been busy.

Brian was an only child. His mother having died when he was younger, he was raised by his father. Pictures of them showed their similarity: both tall men, both stern looking. Even in pictures where they were smiling, it looked forced. Brian never married, not even a serious relationship from what Frank had found out, until Rabbit. At thirty-eight, he was twelve years Rabbit's senior; six years older than me. Brian James, on paper, seemed like a stand-up citizen. Well educated, top of his class in everything he had studied. He was active in sports all throughout his school years. He excelled in business and was currently the CEO of James Industries in Toronto. Brian was heavily into charity work, and I noticed with a grimace, heavily into making sure that fact was well-documented. He kept his PR people busy, and Frank had included many of the articles about Brian's generosity. But aside from being a media hog, there wasn't a hint of scandal or as much as a parking ticket in his past. Anyone doing a cursory background check on him would only see a respected, normal person.

But there was a reason Frank had the nickname, the Pit Bull. He was an inexorable Private Investigator; like a dog with a bone, he didn't give up. He had dug deep into sealed records with his hacking skills. Incident after incident of aggressive behavior on Brian's part was recorded, right from grade school into his first year of university, all locked and hidden away in sealed records. Bullying issues, unprovoked attacks on teammates, issues with authority figures seemed to be the pattern, which, when laid out on paper, appeared to grow worse as he grew older.

Suddenly, the first year of attending university, his records showed nothing. I frowned. There was definitely a pattern of anger issues and then suddenly nothing? Obviously, Frank found that strange as well and had dug even further into some financial records. Brian's father had made several huge donations to the university he had attended. And one enormous one to his old high school. The donations smacked of payoffs to keep things completely off the record and to seal other, older records. I felt a shudder of fear go through me at the thought of the kind of person Rabbit was living with now. The control both Brian and his father wielded over her life.

Aggressive behavior, such as Brian displayed, didn't just disappear. And someone like Douglas James didn't just quietly make enormous donations without publicity. He was as much of a media hog as his son. He was hiding Brian's escalating violence with his money. I shook my head. I wondered if he ever considered investing the money in professional help for his son rather than hiding it. Did he think behavior like this would just go away? My gut told me it didn't. It was still there, threatening Rabbit's safety.

I closed my eyes and took in several calming breaths. I had to keep a clear head.

I looked through all the pictures he had included in the file. No wonder I hadn't recognized Elizabeth in the article when I had seen it. The manner in which she was dressed and presented, she looked much older, and always so solemn. In the pictures, Brian's massive size dwarfed Elizabeth, making her look even smaller than she was.

Elizabeth. The name seemed so foreign to me when I thought of her. *Rabbit.*

Yes. *That* was my girl.

Her file was much thinner. She came from a small town in Manitoba, moved to Toronto only a few years ago, not long after her parents, Sandra and Kevin Brady, were killed in a car accident. She married Brian less than a year later. She no longer worked, but volunteered at the same library where she ran a reading program for children and also taught illiterate adults to read. She was active on several charity boards, attended a lot of dinners and functions and was rarely ever seen without Brian beside her. Frank had found some earlier pictures of her and I stared at them with longing. They were more like the Rabbit I knew. She appeared happy, laughing. And looked younger.

I laid out three photos on the table and studied them. The change in Rabbit was dramatic. In one she looked her age, maybe even younger than her twenty-two years and happy, dressed in jeans and a sweatshirt, smiling with her parents. The next was a few years later, she was twenty-five and it was taken not long after she moved to Toronto. In it she still looked younger, but sadder, more solemn, standing beside Brian. The third was a year later. She was far thinner, her hair up, dressed in black and looking older than her years. If I had met her at one of these events, I would easily have put her in her thirties. I studied the last picture again, focusing on her expression. She wasn't just serious. She was … blank. Her face was blank. I shook my head. While she was here her face and eyes were so expressive and I could read her so easily. My finger pushed at the third picture. I didn't know that woman. That was not my Rabbit.

I sighed and pulled the laptop closer. I hit the play button and again watched the press conference Brian held announcing his wife's return. It was brief and to the point and he took no questions; Elizabeth was not in attendance. He simply stated that Elizabeth had been located in a small town many miles away. She had escaped her captors and was recovering. She suffered some aftereffects of her ordeal but he was confident she would recover fully. He asked for their privacy while his wife healed. No interviews or questions would be taken. The search for her abductors was still active.

My eyes narrowed as I watched him over and over again. He played it well. Confident and aggressive, not at all nervous in front of the cameras. Almost smug. I watched the first press conference again as well. I noticed some of his confidence was lacking. Was it guilt or simply worry?

I slammed the laptop shut and stood up. I was so frustrated. My head was filled with so many questions and thoughts; none of them good. All of them led to one conclusion, and I had nothing concrete to prove it other than my instinct.

I had moved too fast. I had made the wrong decision.

He had anger issues. She was beaten. Even without a working memory, her first reaction to him had been negative and his reaction was equally as telling.

I shouldn't have sent her back.

Rabbit wasn't safe and I needed to make her safe.

I needed to get her back here.

Home.

With me.

⇒CHAPTER TWENTY-SIX⇐

Rabbit

The sky was light and I shifted in bed, pulling Joshua's t-shirt a little closer, breathing in its fading scent. Ten days. I had been 'home' for ten days. And, despite the time, I still felt less at home now than I had felt almost immediately with Joshua.

I sighed and got up, realizing I had been lying there longer than I thought. Sleeping-in was not allowed here. Everything was regimented. What I ate, how I ate, how I dressed, where I went in the house. I didn't understand how I was happy here before, and I certainly didn't understand why Brian had wanted me back so badly. It was as if I didn't exist. I was virtually left alone. Brian never had a conversation with me, he simply instructed me as to what he wanted. The staff rarely addressed me, aside from Mrs. Smith and she kept her distance when others were around.

Brian's father came to the house the day after I arrived back, and I was essentially interrogated about where I had been and what I had been doing. There was certainly no welcome home being offered. I kept looking to Brian to say something, to tell his father to leave me alone, but he remained silent. By the time I was dismissed from their company, I was shaking and confused at the open hostility. It was the first time I also admitted to myself that Joshua was right to keep so many details from me. I couldn't accidentally say something I didn't know in the first place.

The only time I had been out in the day was to be taken to a doctor, who barely even addressed me, instead directed all his inquiries to Brian.

He performed a routine and quick exam and studied the x-rays Daniel had provided, and then, with no discussion, I was given a tetanus shot I wasn't sure I needed. He handed a prescription to Brian, and since then a pill appeared beside my plate every morning and I was watched to make sure I took it. Brian informed me it was to help the headaches, but when I mentioned feeling rather groggy when I took it, I was told it was my imagination and there were no side effects. I started to question that, but stopped in sudden dread at the anger building on Brian's face because I was expressing an opinion.

Even more confusing was when we attended one of the innumerable charitable functions together. I had expressed my worries about attending functions when I was still so unsure of myself, but Brian insisted I needed to be at his side, regardless of my concerns. The first night, Brian surprised me by taking my hand when we left the car, and the entire evening he rarely left my side; his arm was always around my waist, keeping me tightly against him. I noticed he rarely allowed me to speak, always stepping in to deflect away any inquiries about my 'ordeal' as it was referred to. I realized none of these people knew I had lost my memory and that was why Brian had grilled me over and over again about the contents of the file I had been given. When someone would approach us, he would quietly remind me who they were so I didn't make any mistakes. To anyone watching, we seemed like a close couple, him at my side, often bending down to whisper in my ear. Only I knew the truth. When the evening was over and we were once again in the car, he always released my hand and the pretense would be over. And again I would internally question why he had ever tried to find me in the first place.

I sighed and got out of bed to get ready for the day. Tonight was yet another dinner. Today, I was meeting with my trainer to restart my exercise routine. I was, it seemed, not as fit as I should be. Monday, I would resume my volunteering duties at both the library and hospital, since Brian felt I had slacked off enough. I was actually looking forward to that, to being out of this oppressive house and with people again.

I stood looking towards my little bookcase. I had read and reread Joshua's books so often I was sure I knew them by heart. They were the only things keeping me sane. I could see his sense of humor in some of the paragraphs and recognized his phrasing so easily now. I felt my eyes begin to burn with unshed tears. I missed him so much. His warmth, his smile and, especially his touch. He always touched me with so much love. His small white card was now a bookmark that I studied every day. I still had no idea what it meant, but I knew it was important. He wouldn't have made sure to have Cecilia give it to me if it wasn't. That I knew for certain.

Once again, I picked up his shirt and held it closely. I inhaled deeply and pretended to be wrapped up in his arms instead of standing here alone. An abrupt knock on the door had me scrambling to hide the shirt that was in my hands. I bent down and stuffed it under the mattress as far as I could.

Brian entered to inform me my trainer was here. I could see he wasn't pleased that I'd not been down to breakfast. He held out my pill and I took it from him wordlessly, turned around and reached over to pick up the water from my bedside table to wash it down with. He watched as I swallowed then instructed me to meet him in the gym downstairs and left.

Once I was sure he was gone, I spat the pill out. I had stuffed it into my cheek while I was turned away getting the water, a trick I had gotten very good at. I tucked it into the drawer meaning to flush it away later, the same way I did with the others I had managed not to take. My head was definitely clearer when I didn't take the pills. I smiled grimly. I now had three objectives for the library. One was to use the computers I would have access to in order to try and figure out what the pills were. Second was to try and find a way to contact Joshua. I didn't belong here. That became clearer to me every day I was here. The other objective was to bring home more of Joshua's books. I needed his words. They were all I had left.

<hr />

My head ached and I was so tired. The evening was filled with yet more of Brian's strange behavior, but for some reason he had been incredibly tense all evening. More so than usual. His hold on my hand had been too tight. His arm around my waist had been uncomfortable and all night he had been terse when speaking to me. At one point, when I was looking around the room, I saw a woman smiling in my direction. Unsure who she was, I looked over at Brian, but he was occupied with his iPhone. Not wanting him to be angry that I couldn't address her easily if she came over, I hesitantly reached over and laid my hand on his arm and leaned closer to get his attention. He reared back as if I had spit on him. Unnerved by his reaction, I pulled back and my elbow hit my water, only to knock it over. His hand closed over my wrist roughly, pulling my hand back from trying to right the glass as I apologized. "Leave it," he hissed. "Stop making matters worse, Elizabeth. You're always making matters worse!"

I sat back, stung, not understanding what I had done except to spill a little water. The glass had been almost empty. I struggled not to show my emotions. Wasn't that what he wanted? For us to seem close when we were in public? Could I do *anything* right in his eyes? Intense longing rushed through me suddenly for the warmth of Joshua's gaze, for his quiet, adoring attention. Suddenly, I felt the tight grip of Brian's hand on my leg. "Remember your place, Elizabeth. Act properly," he spoke lowly into my ear. I felt a shiver go through me at the menacing tone. When I looked up, his face was an icy mask of politeness as he spoke to the woman next to him. I straightened in my chair but I remained quieter than normal the rest of the evening, not wanting to provoke his seemingly growing ire.

Back at the house, I climbed the stairs quietly and headed to my room. I heard Brian walk to his den and the door slam behind him, echoing loudly in the main level. I shuddered as yet another feeling of déjà vu crept up my spine.

I undressed quickly, putting everything back in its proper place. I changed into a pair of pajama pants, and needing it as close to my body as I could get it, I went to the bed and reached in between the mattress and pulled out Joshua's t-shirt. I pulled it on; desperately wishing it was Joshua's arms that were draped around me, not just his shirt. A torn piece of paper fluttered to the floor and I bent down and picked it up. It looked like a torn photograph. I frowned, wondering why there was a picture stuffed between the mattresses. Curious, I reached in between the mattresses and was surprised when my fingers felt something soft. I pulled the item and held it up. Mystified, I stared at a brilliant blue piece of torn cloth. Why was this hidden? I laid it on the bed for a better look. That was when I realized how badly torn it was. It appeared to be a sleeve from a blouse. I leaned forward examining what appeared to be stains all over it. Confused, I took the material into the closet where the light was far brighter than the small lamp on the bedside table. Kneeling down, I spread the piece out on the floor and looked at it. Then I recoiled in horror. The stains were blood.

Time seemed to stop as images started bombarding my brain. I fell forward, my head in my hands, as I tried to process the memories that were, suddenly, vividly alive again in my mind.

It was my blood.

This torn piece of material had been my blouse.

And, it was torn off me by Brian in one of his rages.

As he beat me.

Again.

⇉Chapter Twenty-Seven⇇

Rabbit

I lay huddled on the floor. The automatic lights in the closet had long since turned off. My head was buried deep in Joshua's hoodie, muffling my sobs.

I remembered that day.

Everything.

Brian's fury as he hit me over and over again.

His hands painfully digging into my arms as he shook me, screaming in my face about yet another one of my failures as his wife. How I always ruined things, not made them better.

The impassive, blank look as his foot drove into me repeatedly as I wept helplessly on the floor, the blood from my nose dripping down my face mixing in with my tears.

I shuddered thinking about his face.

Cold.

Angry.

Devoid of any human compassion.

Because I'd worn a colored blouse. Something bright and pretty for a change.

He had almost killed me because I'd worn something not approved by him.

I sat up, still gripping Joshua's hoodie, another wave of terror rolling over me. He had been angry and tense that day, more so than usual. Much like tonight. And, tonight I had failed to be perfect yet again.

My stomach lurched. What would happen now? Would he come up here? Would he hurt me again?

I wrapped Joshua's hoodie around me like a talisman, praying it would protect me. I pushed myself into the corner of the closet and sat rocking, waiting for my answer.

"Get out of those clothes, Rabbit," Joshua's voice hissed in my head. "Get into bed and pretend to be asleep," the voice continued. "Do it, *now*."

I scrambled up on shaky legs and pulled off Joshua's shirt. I stuffed that and his hoodie into the dresser and dragged a nightgown over my head. I made my way to the bed and crawled under the covers, burying my head into the pillow, still weeping, my mind overloaded with images and thoughts.

I heard heavy footsteps on the stairs and I forced myself to be still. I curled into a ball and made sure my face was buried. My heart was thumping so loudly that I pushed my hand over it to muffle the noise. I heard my door open and I felt my body turn into ice with fear. Brian approached the bed and stood beside it. It took every ounce of my strength not to move under his gaze. I could feel the animosity pouring off him in waves.

He spoke in the darkness, his voice low and furious.

"You always ruin everything, Elizabeth. You're always in the way."

And, then he turned and walked out.

Eventually, I crept back into the closet and wrapped Joshua's hoodie back around me. I went back to bed, in case Brian checked on me for some reason, and I lay there shivering in fright as images and memories came crashing back in a chaotic deluge.

I recalled the painful memory of suddenly losing my parents in a car accident. Feeling lost and adrift and needing a change.

The impulsive decision of accepting a job in Toronto, Ontario at one the libraries and moving, thinking a big city and new challenges would help me start to live again. But the move only increased the loneliness I felt instead of giving me a fresh start as I had hoped.

Meeting Brian at the first benefit I attended. Being struck by his confident, almost domineering personality and surprised when he called me a few days later, requesting to see me again.

I shuddered, remembering how I welcomed his sudden appearance in my life. How I unconsciously allowed him to take over my decision-making process, feeling somehow cared for again. His taking control began quietly enough; not liking my outfit and choosing something more 'appropriate' for me, chiding me for being too frivolous in conversations, separating me from what he deemed 'unsuitable friends', insisting my hair be worn a certain way to please him. I attended more and more events with him and he made sure our picture was taken often and seen through many press outlets. Slowly but surely, I was moulded into what he believed was a proper companion for him, and I'd blindly permitted it to happen.

Six months later, we were married in a simple ceremony and that was when the reality of my poor decision-making became apparent.

Always rather domineering and rigid, Brian became a tyrant. I learned very quickly that his word was law. I was the mistress of a large house with no say in how it was run whatsoever. All my personal effects were deemed unworthy of my new status; with the exception of a few of my books. I had a couple of boxes in the closet, the rest were discarded or given away.

I wasn't allowed to change a thing in the house. My ideas of warming it up and making it seem more welcoming were met with unyielding disapproval. My wardrobe was changed entirely to reflect the way someone 'of my status' should represent the James name. I wasn't permitted to work. Brian allowed me to volunteer at the library, but only two days a week. The rest of my time was allotted to the various organizations he felt were worthy of my time and other activities he approved of. With only the people he approved of me being associated with.

I lost myself. I was a symbol. I was Brian James' wife. Taken out and shown off when needed, but otherwise ignored. I was pushed into the limelight as a benefactress of sorts of many charities and reminded of my place by Brian often. I learned rapidly not to let him know the quiet enjoyment I had working with the various groups. My happiness was not a priority with Brian.

Very quickly, I learned the two sides to Brian James. There was the confident, commanding, yet charming, social persona and the cold, angry, dismissive private man. In public, we seemed a perfect couple. I attended every function with him, dressed as he deemed appropriate. We were always close, his arm around my waist, always quietly conversing. No one knew it was usually snide remarks about others being hissed into my ear or remarks about something I was doing to displease him. I learned to keep my eyes downcast and my face blank. His need for validation was obvious in his insistence of documenting all our involvement with the various organizations. I fast became weary of the attention, but he thrived on it. His seemingly doting attention, however, immediately halted when we were away from the cameras and people. In private, I was left alone most of the time.

Our sex life, even from the start, was almost non-existent. While we were dating, I found it romantic that he was holding himself back, that he cared for me enough to wait. After we were married, the few fumbling attempts were disastrous, ending with him cursing and angry and me weeping, unsure of what I was doing wrong. I had very little experience and the blame was laid entirely at my feet. Brian had no problem informing me I was cold and unresponsive and, once again a total disappointment to him. I tried to please him in other ways but to no avail. A week after we returned from our short honeymoon, he informed me the room across the hall was now mine. He would be staying in the master suite. The only time he would enter my room was to inform me of an engagement or to inflict one of his many punishments for an error on my part. Of which there were many.

A noise in the hall startled me out of my thoughts. It was still early, but the house was beginning to stir. Brian's father would be coming for breakfast as he did every Sunday morning. He was the only person I ever saw Brian bow down to. He still controlled the reins at James Enterprises and constantly held a not so silent threat over Brian's head to take the company away from him. I also knew on some level that was one of the things that drove Brian to be so insistent on the appearance of perfection. That on one level, somehow, I was worth something to him, that my presence was needed, but why it was I still didn't know.

I rolled over; cringing at the memory of the first time Brian had used his hands instead of his words to inflict pain. We had only been married a couple of months but I already knew it was a huge mistake on my part. Nothing I did pleased Brian. I was found lacking on every level. He treated me like an object to order around rather than a wife. We didn't even share a bed. And, the control I once found comforting now was oppressive. I had heard him come upstairs and I went to my door asking to speak with him.

Once he was in the room, I told him the truth. Obviously, he didn't love me. I wasn't happy and I didn't think he was either. That perhaps it would be best to divorce and go our separate ways. At first, he stood listening to my halting words, showing no emotion, but the next thing I knew, I was slammed into the wall, his hands gripping my wrists painfully over my head.

"*That* will never happen, Elizabeth. Divorce is *not* an option. You are mine until *I* decide otherwise. This is your life. Get used to it," he snarled in anger. His hands tightened until I was whimpering in pain. I was sure he was about to break both my wrists. "If you so much as step out of line you will pay for it. Do you understand?"

I nodded, unable to speak with the pain he was inflicting. "You will do what I say, when I say it. I own you. And, that is *not* going to change." He pushed down even heavier on my trapped wrists and we both heard the snap.

He pulled away and I sank to the floor, staring up at him in agony and terror.

"Don't bring this subject up again." And, he had walked out of the room slamming the door. I had sat there weeping for the longest time. The next morning he took me to the doctor, who set my wrist and put on a cast without asking me a single question.

It was then I knew how truly alone I was.

Brian was right. He owned me. My parents were gone, and I had only a few acquaintances, but no friends in my life. He had made sure of that. There certainly wasn't anyone I was close enough to that could protect me from Brian. He was too powerful and well-known here. I was viewed as a rich man's wife, living a life most women dreamed of. No one was aware of my nightmare. I had no money of my own, no job and no one to turn to for help. I had blindly allowed Brian to isolate me entirely.

I sat up in bed with a startling thought.

My memory was back. And, while some things were still fuzzy, others were crystal clear.

Now I understood why Brian didn't want me to remember. Why he had wanted to find me.

To make sure I kept quiet.

If he knew I had remembered, I would be in even more danger than I was before.

The stillness of the room was broken by my whispered plea.

"Oh, God, *Joshua,* I need you."

⇒Chapter Twenty-Eight⇐

Rabbit

I checked my reflection in the mirror. I was pale and looked tired. But my hair was perfect and my outfit impeccable. I drew in a deep breath, paused and then took another, desperately trying to calm my nerves. I had to do this. I steeled myself and went downstairs to join Brian and his father for breakfast.

They were both in the dining room and I greeted them quietly before sitting down at my place. "You are pastier than usual, Elizabeth," observed Douglas James with his customary snide bluntness. "As well as tardy."

I shook my head. I was already found lacking, and I had just walked in. "I apologize. I have another headache. It will pass."

"Take your medication," Brian ordered.

I nodded obediently; I knew whatever it was he'd been giving me wouldn't help even if I did have a headache. I leaned forward, picking up the pill as Mrs. Smith came through the door with the breakfast plates and I used the distraction to palm the pill instead of swallowing it. I couldn't afford to be drowsy today.

I listened to the conversation between Brian and his father, only speaking when a question or comment was directed my way, which was not very often. The topics were mainly business. Throughout the entire breakfast I noticed there was a sense of animosity between the two which I could remember feeling before. I had thought that once Brian and I were married I would somehow bring the two of them closer; to be more of a family. I had hoped that one day these breakfasts would include some laughter instead of the veiled resentment Brian showed his father and the cold demeanor he in turn showed towards Brian. It had never happened. I never understood why they insisted on these weekly breakfasts.

I barely touched the bowl of oatmeal in front of me. I disliked oatmeal intensely unless it was covered in brown sugar and cream. I knew, without asking now, that wasn't an option. My bottom lip suddenly trembled as I fought the wave of emotion that ran through me. I didn't want this. I wanted a plate of Joshua's rather lumpy scrambled eggs and his slightly charred toast. I wanted Joshua looking across the table at me shrugging his shoulders, his eyes dancing as he watched me eat his latest attempt at breakfast. I thought of his warmth. How just being in the same room as him made me feel safe and content. I caught my bottom lip in my teeth as the trembling increased.

I was so caught up in my thoughts, I startled when I heard Brian voice my name in annoyance, bringing me back to the present and the cold atmosphere of the dining room. I blinked at him, praying he would blame the behavior on the headache rather than anything else. He frowned at my seeming lack of concentration, but only reminded me of my appointment with the trainer that afternoon. I nodded, picking up my cup of tea to hide my trembling lip. He instructed me that there would be a car waiting for me at 9 a.m. to take me to the library the next day and would return at 3 p.m. to pick me up. I managed to remain calm and acknowledged his statements quietly.

Brian placed his elbows on the table and looked at me. His voice was steady as he informed me a bodyguard would be accompanying me at all times when I left the house in the morning. I wanted to snort with laughter when he stated stiffly that it was for my own protection since the people who had kidnapped me were still at large. Instead, I nodded and thanked him quietly for his concern, the whole time my fingers dug into my leg, fighting the desire to stand up and scream at him that I knew the truth. To tell him I remembered the horrid way he had treated me; that I remembered *everything*. But I remained silent.

After breakfast, I went up to my room, relieved for the brief time I wouldn't have to struggle to hold back my emotions. I sat down on the edge of the bed, trying to relax while my brain raced.

A bodyguard. I felt the growing dread inside my stomach.

He was watching me. Waiting for my memory to return. Waiting for me to run.

I shuddered. What was he going to do when he realized it had returned?

What was I going to do when he knew?

—◆◆◆◆◆●◆◆◆◆—

The next morning, the car pulled up outside the library and I sighed in quiet relief. This was always one place I was fairly free. I began to walk up the steps eagerly when my bodyguard, Bob, appeared beside me.

"You need to wait for me, Mrs. James," he stated gruffly.

I stopped, catching myself. I nodded and continued walking. I had to pretend I didn't know where to go. Or, who anyone was. This was going to be harder than I thought.

An hour later, I was ensconced in my little office at the back of the library. I had been shown around by Kate, who informed me quietly she was sorry to hear of my 'horrible ordeal' and the resulting brain injury and memory problem I was left with. She quietly expressed that she hoped I would settle back in all right. Internally, I grimaced at what Brian was telling people. They were under the impression I was confused and not quite 'with it,' and needed to be treated accordingly. No doubt in case I suddenly accused him of something, he could point out the fact that I was acting irrationally and what I said could not be taken seriously. He was already setting the groundwork to make me look unstable in case my memory returned.

I blinked and realized Kate was looking at me. I had totally missed what she was saying. "Sorry, Kate," I apologized, having just demonstrated exactly the kind of behavior Brian would want to see to prove him right. "I was just ... thinking," I shrugged self-consciously.

She smiled in understanding and patted me on the arm. She then told me they had purposely kept my schedule light for the next couple weeks so I could ease back in. I thanked her and she left me in my office, promising to come back and check on me soon. Bob was down the hall where he had a clear visual on anyone coming or going in the area.

I looked around, soaking in the familiar room. There were piles of books on every surface and pictures that the children I read to had made for me on the walls. I loved the clutter. I knew Brian never came here so I was able to leave it the way I liked it. I could see Bob glancing my way so I made a show of looking around and inspecting the things around me like I didn't recognize them. Then I sat down at my desk and turned on the computer.

My first goal was to try and locate Joshua. Unsure where to start and not wanting to look overly eager, I forced myself to pay attention to other tasks that were waiting on my desk as well. Once I was sure Bob had grown bored with watching me shuffle papers and tap on the keyboard, I took the list of ideas I had out of my pocket and started searching. I kept stealing glances at him, but he was far more absorbed in the contents of his phone than what I was actually doing now that I was at my desk.

Joshua was very good at hiding. There were lots of articles on him, but no recent pictures. There were a couple of grainy ones from when he was much younger and even those images my eyes drank in greedily. All of his interviews were voice or print only and there were very few personal details that I could find. Unable to resist, I plugged in my earphones and listened to a brief interview. Just hearing his warm voice brought tears to my eyes, and I had to blink them away when Kate appeared in my door to see if I wanted coffee. I quickly cleared my browser history, grabbed my mug and joined her. Bob only followed to the end of the hall and watched as we entered the staff lounge. I sighed as I poured a cup of coffee, already feeling the strain of the day.

"You okay, Elizabeth?" Kate asked quietly.

I nodded. "Just trying to find my feet, you know?"

She nodded kindly. "I'm glad you're back."

I forced a smile. "I am as well."

Later that evening, I climbed the stairs slowly. I was so tired. I had spent the day trying to appear to work while also attempting to find a way to contact Joshua. Hitting dead end after dead end, I finally wrote to both his publisher and agent, begging that they contact him with a brief message from me.

Rabbit needs you.

I had no idea if the messages would be forwarded, but I had to try. I sent both via regular mail since I wasn't sure if my email account was being monitored.

Then, I attempted to find both Trevor and Cecilia, but was shocked to find out how many lawyers there were in the general area with the name of Trevor Jones. I didn't even know if he practiced in Toronto or one of the many outlying cities. It was going to take a while. The next time I was back at the library, I planned on trying to figure out the name of the care home and the location I had supposedly stayed in. I didn't have access to a computer at the hospital the way I did here. I had more information at least knowing Dr. Tate's first and last name and the name of the neighbouring town. Surely, there couldn't be many Dr. Tates in Hunstville. But again, it was going to take time and I had to make sure I didn't arouse any suspicion while searching. I didn't want to give Bob any reason to suggest to Brian that I be monitored even closer.

My attempts to figure out what the pills were came up with very little. I needed to get a look at the actual bottle. A general search came up with nothing. I wondered if I dared look in Brian's room for the bottle when he was out. I shuddered, thinking what could happen if I was discovered, and I decided to put off that idea for the time being.

Then I turned to the card. Nothing I tried made sense. I checked maps, atlases, phone numbers, even license plates, but found no answers. I paused briefly and then searched the memory stick but found only the pictures Joshua had taken of my injuries. There was nothing else on it. My stomach clenched as I looked at the pictures and I quickly closed the window. I sat with my head in my hands.

He said I would figure it out. But if I *couldn't* figure it out; how could I let him know how much I needed him?

Oh, Joshua.

I heard Bob approaching and I sat up immediately. He appeared in the door and announced the car was here to take me home. I nodded and picked up my purse. "I just need to stop by the desk," I said quietly. They were holding something there for me.

When I'd left the library I was carrying three of Joshua's books.

I barely managed to make it through another meal with Brian. I kept my head down a lot, faking another headache, and had to force myself to eat the fish and salad on my plate. Other than his banal inquiries as to my day, he was silent, although he did inform me he had a late meeting and left as soon as dinner was done. I was grateful there was no function to attend that evening, and with a sigh of relief, I wearily climbed the stairs to my room.

Sitting on the bed, I stared at Joshua's books. I hadn't even looked at which ones they were. He wrote them and that was all that mattered. They were a piece of him. Apparently, I was lucky that there were any on the shelf as they were very popular, so I was grateful to have gotten them. Two were mysteries and the other was a more of romance/mystery that I had read before and enjoyed, surprised at his slight change of genre. I decided to reread that one. Curling up in the chair, I opened the book and soon lost myself in his mesmerizing words. I must have fallen asleep because when I woke up, the house was silent and the book was on the floor. Bending down to pick it up, I knocked another one off the table and Joshua's card fluttered to the floor. I gazed at it for a moment then my eyes drifted to the cover of the book I was reading. Again and again my eyes darted between the two, understanding dawning in my brain.

WIH98

The book "*When It Hurts*" was laying at my feet.

Trembling, I picked up the book and opened it to page ninety-eight and skimmed through it, my eyes stopping at one line.

"*There are moments you know you have to reach out and ask for help. This was one of them.*"

My heart began pounding. My eyes flew back to the card.

AAW 193

I stumbled over my feet trying to get to the bed and grabbed the book "*An Alternate World*" and flipped to page one hundred and ninety-three.

My eyes widened as I read the passage about a secret message being delivered on a special kind of paper. A type of paper that only showed the writing on it when the paper was wet. I stood shaking, looking down at the card in my hand, wanting to believe I had figured out what Joshua was trying to tell me. Clutching the card, I went to the bathroom as quickly as I could on my trembling legs. I turned on the faucet, praying as I placed the card under the flow until it was soaked.

I set it on the counter and waited. Slowly, I watched in amazement as a set of numbers appeared clearly in between the cryptic messages.

A phone number.

Joshua had given me a phone number.

Terrified the number would disappear; I grabbed a piece of paper and copied it down. Then I sank to the floor, my entire body quaking. I buried my head in my hands and breathed slowly until I calmed down. Ever so slowly and quietly, I made my way downstairs to the kitchen and picked up the phone and dialed the number. When it started to ring, I closed my eyes, praying Joshua would pick up. But there was nothing. After a few rings it stopped; there was a soft sound and then nothing. I stood listening to the silence on the end of the line, my breath coming out in small gasps. Unsure what to do, I hung up.

Unsteadily, I made my way upstairs, trying hard not to sob in disappointment. It was the middle of the night. Joshua must be sleeping, I kept telling myself.

Tomorrow.

Tomorrow, when I went to the hospital, I would call Joshua and he would somehow get me out of here. He would know what to do. He had to.

Then I would go back home to him and Bear.

And I was never leaving them again. Ever.

⇒Chapter Twenty-Nine⇐

Joshua

Cecilia came bustling through the door, arms full. She'd gone into town to get some things while I was looking through the files she had brought. I got up and helped her with the bags and followed her to the kitchen. Silently, we put away the items she had bought and then sat down at the table. She looked over everything I had spread out. "Well?"

I shrugged. "It doesn't add up, Cecilia. Everything a normal investigation would uncover points to an upstanding citizen."

"But?"

I looked at her. "Frank's digging found a pattern of aggression, and it seemed to escalate as he grew older. Then at some point it stopped. Or, at least, stopped being recorded. My gut tells me he never changed."

Cecilia looked at me confused.

"I think his father paid dearly to have all traces of his behavior removed from his records."

"But what about the other people involved?"

I looked at her steadily, my voice quiet. "Money talks, Cecilia. It also buys silence. We both know that."

She nodded in silent agreement.

I opened another folder. "The financial pictures are interesting as well. James is well paid, generous benefits, the whole CEO-type package, yet ..."

"What?" she prompted.

"His house, his cars, all his major possessions are owned by the company." I looked up at her. "It's like his father is still controlling him, and a large portion of his life, with money."

I took in a deep breath. "I think he *does* control him. Maybe he uses the control to try and keep Brian in line. But I think it makes Brian angry ..."

She regarded me fearfully. "And, you think he takes that anger out on Elizabeth."

I closed my eyes as a shudder went through me. "Yes."

"But there are no hospital records? Nothing showing a pattern of abuse?"

I shook my head. "Doctors can be bought off as well, Cecilia. They aren't all like Daniel."

"*Oh*, Joshua." Her hand covered mine briefly. "You could be wrong; she could be fine," her voice was kindly encouraging, but her eyes were troubled.

I looked away. I knew she wasn't fine. I could feel it.

"What are those?" She indicated the three pictures I had of Rabbit in front of me.

"Look at the change, Cecilia." I pushed the pictures towards her. "Look."

She studied them quietly. "Quite the change, I agree." She looked up, frowning. "You do realize the change could simply be her growing up, getting older, and that fact is being reflected in how she acts and appears, right? She is married to a very prominent person and I imagine she takes her role very seriously."

I shook my head. "I'm not talking about the way she dresses. Look at her face. Her eyes. Look at *her*, Cecilia."

Again, she studied the pictures. She nodded, looking at me with solemn eyes. "I see it," she admitted quietly. "She looks ... numb."

I tapped my finger on the last picture. "That is *not* the woman I fell in love with. That person is a stranger."

Cecilia smiled sadly. "What if the person you fell in love with *is* the stranger, Joshua? And the person in the photo is the real one?"

I shook my head. "No. Rabbit was real. I know her."

Cecilia didn't say anything. I didn't know how to explain to her something I felt so strongly; I knew I was right. Rabbit was the real Elizabeth. The person in the picture was just someone who looked like her.

I sighed. "There was nothing in here about the car. I called Frank but only got his voicemail. Do you know anything about the car?"

Cecilia nodded and reached into her bag. "He got the name of the owner. It is a Tracy Allen. She has owned the car for just less than two years. She's out of town but expected back later this week. He'll speak with her when she gets home. I told him to dig into the history of it as well, and into Tracy's background," She shrugged. "It's not a priority, but it could be something or nothing. But at this point, I thought it best to cover all the bases."

She stood up, walking over to the sink and looked out the window. "Joshua," her voice trailed off.

I stood up and went over to her. "What, Cecilia? What is it?"

She paused. "Joshua ... Trevor and I didn't like what we saw at the hotel that day. And ... Daniel tried to contact Brian to check on her. All he got was his assistant telling him she was fine and it was not his concern. That didn't sit well with any of us."

I frowned, my stomach clenching.

"So, Trevor got Frank to have one of his men watch Rabbit. She hasn't been out of the house much. Once to a medical office and a few walks around the grounds. But when he did see her, she appeared to be okay, physically."

I sighed in relief and, reaching out, hugged her. "Fuck. That's good, Cecilia. Thank you for doing that. Make sure you tell Frank, whatever he needs, it's his. More men, more money, whatever. Do we know who the doctor is?"

"Frank is checking it out. It's just going to take time. Our guy couldn't get close enough without being seen. She wasn't in there very long, though."

I frowned. "She should have been checked over carefully. If he was on the up and up he should have had her examined meticulously. It's just another red herring." I shook my head. "What the fuck is he playing at, Cecilia?"

She shrugged. "I don't know, Joshua. I just don't know."

"Well, we need to find out. Now. This thing is all wrong. It's all fucking wrong." I paced in front of her. "I'm anxious to find out about the car; I have a feeling it's one of the keys to this mystery."

I pulled on my hair in frustration. "I want her safe, Cecilia. I *need* her safe. I fucked this up so badly," my voice caught on the last word.

"What are you going to do, Joshua?"

I looked at her. "I was stupid, Cecilia. *Fucking stupid.* I invented an entire story to cover up Rabbit being here with me. He could have done the same thing. In fact, I'm sure he did. I was so overcome with the fact she was married, that I was taking her away from *her life.* I was so sure that I wasn't what she needed; I stopped asking the right questions. Now, I'm going to make sure I know the story. All of it."

"What if you're wrong, Joshua?"

"If I'm wrong, I'll back off and leave her alone. Unless she needs me."

"And, if you're right?"

"Then I'm bringing her home."

———————

Days later, I paced around the house, Bear at my heels constantly. I couldn't relax or concentrate no matter what. He could sense my unsettled feelings and was reacting to them, staying close. I had barely slept the past few nights and my nerves and patience were stretched tightly. I was waiting for Frank to call with news of his meeting with Ms. Allen about her car that was in my barn, now that she was finally back. He kept telling me to be patient; Rabbit was being watched, he was investigating. I knew I had to give him time. I knew he probably wouldn't be calling anytime soon since it was still early, but I was anxious and restless. I had gone through the files again and again, made copious notes and watched the press conferences over and over again. Cecilia had been back and forth bringing me new information to go through and I had also read everything I could find on the James family in general. I didn't like what I found. Under the structured veneer of a wealthy, successful family, I saw a distinctive pattern of aloofness and control. The thought of my Rabbit in an environment like that made me shudder. The only comfort I could find was in knowing she was being watched and was seemingly okay. Physically, anyway. But that wasn't enough. Until I knew she was safe, that she was fine, that she was *here*, I couldn't relax.

Finally, with growing frustration, I grabbed my coat. "C'mon boy," I summoned Bear. We'd take a walk outside and maybe clear my head. I stepped outside into the bright morning sun. I could hear the drips of the water as it splashed on the snow from the melting icicles. The past few days had turned warm and the snow was disappearing at an alarming rate. Soon the piles of snow would be gone if the temperatures stayed where they were hovering today. I shook my head at the drastic change in the weather in such a short span of time. I stepped off the porch and started walking. It felt good to stretch my sore leg, and the fresh air was welcome. Bear ran in front of me, diving into the snow, rolling and chuffing, happy to be outside. I frowned to myself; I had been neglecting him for a while. We hadn't gone for a walk since Rabbit left. I stopped suddenly as the pain hit me, remembering the look I had seen on her face as she struggled to break away from Cecilia to get to me in the barn. It had been ten days ago. Ten of the longest days of my life.

My head was filled with chaotic thoughts.

Was she okay?

Was she scared?

Was I wrong in my assumptions and she was happy to be home?

Was I reading things from the pictures and articles that really didn't exist?

Did she miss me as much as I missed her?

Had she figured out the card yet?

Bear's sudden push on my leg brought me out of my thoughts. I patted his head and looked down at him. "You miss her too, don't you?" I asked as I stroked his head. His answering huff as he shook his large head said it all. "I'll figure out a way to get her back. I promise." His trusting eyes looked up at me and then he turned away, walking down the drive. I followed him slowly, letting him lead the way as usual, although I was surprised when he headed down the driveway and not toward the barn as he usually went, but I let him go.

He continued to trot ahead of me, chasing the occasion snowflake, bounding back to me barking, or running around me in circles, wanting to play. I would scoop up some of the melting snow into a ball and throw it, chuckling when he would chase after it and, of course, not find anything and come charging back wanting another one tossed. The memory of Rabbit's snowball deluge flowed through my head and I smiled, thinking of her that day. How she turned my bad mood into one of laughter with her teasing and playing. How her eyes had looked at me so tenderly while we made love in the snow and how she felt wrapped around me. Again, the pain of loss that accompanied the memory made me pause, and I realized Bear had rounded the corner in front of me. I could hear him in the snow, barking and digging. I hurried forward hoping he hadn't come across some small woodland creature and was scaring it to death while trying to play with it.

Rounding the bend, I saw him digging and pulling on something in the snow. "Bear, stop!" I commanded. He ceased his digging but continued his barking at whatever was in front of him.

Fuck. Probably a real rabbit or a fox.

I didn't want them hurt and in case it was something else, I didn't want Bear attacked either. I yelled for him to heel and he lowered his head, picked something up and reluctantly he came back to my side. I could hear the whines in the back of his throat as he obediently approached me and saw something dark and lifeless hanging from his mouth. I cursed silently. He *had* gotten something. He sat down on his haunches in front of me. "Drop it," I said firmly, dreading what I was about to look at.

He leaned his head down and deposited whatever he was carrying on the snow and sat back up. I crouched down and realized it wasn't an animal, but an odd ball of material. I picked it up and examined the item. Unwinding it, I realized it was a scarf. A woman's scarf. I looked up to where Bear had been digging. It was by the tree where Rabbit's car had hit that night. I could see something dark still sticking out of the snow. My heart started pounding rapidly. Pointing, I looked down at Bear. "Fetch."

He took off and started digging madly again at the snow. I followed him and knelt down, reaching in to where he was digging. The small black piece of leather I could see became larger and, eventually, we worked it out of the snow.

I sat back in shock at what he'd uncovered. Even without opening it, I knew what it was. I had tripped over something trying to get into the car that night, but it had completely slipped my mind with my concern for Rabbit at the time. But this is what I had tripped over.

Rabbit's missing purse.

I made it up to the house as quickly as possible. The purse was heavy and laden with snow. I grabbed a towel and knelt in front of the fire. I spread out the towel and tipped the contents of the purse on it, spreading out the items. I opened the wallet and pulled out the driver's license. Elizabeth James. The same name was on the one credit card in the wallet. There was a library card, a gym membership card, a business card bearing her husband's name, and twenty-five dollars in cash. That was it. I looked at the other items laid out before me. There was a small, sodden package of Kleenex, a compact, a tube of lipstick, a pen and small blank notepad. There was also a small, digital camera which I doubted would work again. And lastly, a sealed Ziploc bag. I opened the bag carefully and pulled out a manila envelope. It was cold, but thanks to the plastic bag, it felt dry. I hesitated a minute, then opened the envelope. Inside was a small journal-type book and when I opened it up, I immediately choked in horror.

Even though her face wasn't in any of them, I knew the person in these dreadful photographs.

They were pictures of Rabbit.

Every page had one taped onto it.

The first one; her hand in a cast.

Then pages of pictures of bruises on her arms, legs, and torso.

Each one noted with a small explanation of why she had received the injury; what the medical treatment had been and the name of the uncaring, careless doctor who patched her up and sent her away, only to be abused again.

And lastly, the name of who had so callously inflicted every single one of her injuries.

I shuddered. My eyes shut in painful realization. I didn't know how long it had been going on, but I now knew without question *who* had caused her injuries.

There were no kidnappers.

He *had* lied. The whole story had been a lie.

Brian James *was* her attacker.

⇒CHAPTER THIRTY⇐

Joshua

I fumbled around and found my phone. I hit speed dial and Cecilia answered quickly. I didn't bother with a greeting. "Get Trevor. Get here. Fast." I didn't even wait for her to respond. I stumbled down the hall into the bathroom and threw up as the images of what the journal showed played through my mind again and again.

The unconfirmed theories and worries were all real. I had proof of my greatest fear.

I sent her back.

I sent Rabbit back to the person who had been abusing her. Repeatedly.

Instead of listening to my gut and keeping her here for a while longer, I reacted to what I *should* do and based it on how I would react if it was me. How I would feel if she had been taken. I did what I *thought*, what I'd been *told*, was the right thing to do. I was so fucking stupid.

I had believed the lies he spoke.

I thought he wanted what was best for her. That was what *I* wanted.

But he wasn't me; he hurt her.

She hadn't been taken; she had run.

And what I'd thought was right, had been the worst possible thing I could do.

My stomach heaved again and I laid my head on the cool porcelain.

She was so far away.

Trapped somewhere alone.

Somewhere I couldn't get to.

Because I was trapped here.

We were both trapped in our own living hell.

———————◆•••◆◗◆◗••◆———————

A few hours later, I stared at the three people sitting with me at the table. Cecilia and Trevor had arrived with Frank. I had heard the helicopter approaching and was surprised but grateful to see Frank with them when the door opened. I was calmer and resolute. Rabbit needed to come home. With Frank here we could figure out how.

"The car is Elizabeth's?" I repeated what Frank just told me.

Frank shook his head. "Ms. Allen, or Tracy, refuses to call her that. She knew her as Lizzy when they were young and they kept in contact after she moved here. I think she is probably one of the only people Elizabeth knew outside her marriage. She says the Lizzy she knew and the Elizabeth James she became are two different people."

I nodded in understanding.

Rabbit.

Lizzy.

Lizzy suited her far more than the formal Elizabeth.

Frank continued. "When she moved to Toronto, Lizzy got in contact with her again and they saw each other quite a bit. Until she started dating Brian. Lizzy came to her not long after she was married and asked if she would accept ownership of the car. Apparently, the car didn't fit the image she was supposed to project and Brian insisted she get rid of it. But it had been her mother's and it held sentimental value to her. Tracy suspected there were other reasons as well for Lizzy wanting to know where the car was and agreed to the transfer. She drove the car occasionally to make sure it ran well and kept it full of gas. She also gave Lizzy the passcode to the garage where it was parked and left a spare set of keys in it at all times.

"Why?"

"She had a bad feeling. She said she met Brian James once and disliked him intensely. 'A wolf in sheep's clothing' she called him. She was hardly surprised when she wasn't invited to the wedding. She was shocked at the difference in Lizzy's appearance and demeanor when she saw her shortly after her marriage." Frank paused, his fingers drumming on the file in front of him.

"She never seemed to be able to get together with Lizzy anymore. There was always an excuse. Lizzy insisted she was just very busy with her new life, but Tracy didn't buy it. She was sure Brian had forbidden

Lizzy to see her any longer." He looked at me. "The last time she saw Lizzy, she didn't like the explanation for the cast on her arm, and she called her on it. After that, their only communication was the occasional email. But Tracy never stopped letting her know her car was there, waiting, if she needed it. That she was there if she ever needed her."

I stood up so abruptly my chair flew back, hitting the floor loudly. I strode over to the sink, trying to remain calm. I could feel the clenching of my chest as the implications of what he said sank in. The first picture in the book was of her arm in a cast. Now I knew how long it had been going on. I looked down trying to concentrate on keeping my breathing even and I saw my hands were clenched so tightly on the edge of the sink that my knuckles were white.

Cecilia came up behind me. "Joshua?" Her hand squeezed my shoulder. "What is it?"

I spun around. "She's been abused for almost two years. She's been frightened for *two years,* Cecilia. And, I sent her back there. I sent her back to that." Angrily, I pushed the small journal over to Cecilia.

She opened it and gasped. Trevor came to her side instantly, and I heard their murmured words of disbelief at what they were seeing. Cecilia set the book back down on the counter. When she spoke, her voice was shaking.

"You did what you thought was right, Joshua. You didn't know. None of us did." She drew in a quivering breath. "We were all wrong, Joshua."

I exploded.

"But it was my decision! It wasn't right! It was never *right!* In my gut, I knew that! I did it for all the wrong reasons. Because I was stupid! I actually *let* myself believe his story. I actually assumed that because I love her like I do, that someone else must as well." I paused, looking at Cecilia, my voice dropping.

"I sent her away because I was trying to protect myself."

"What are you talking about?"

"I thought it would be easier for her to leave on my terms rather than have her wake up three months from now and remember her other life and have to let her go then. I always assumed I would have to give her up eventually. I never had the faith in us that she did."

"But it wasn't easier, was it?" Cecilia asked softly. "Because you love her."

I sighed. "So much, Cecilia." I looked at her and shook my head. "And no, it wasn't any fucking easier. And, now I've put her in danger. I'm terrified it will be too late to get her out of there."

I lowered my head. "This is *all* on me, Cecilia."

Frank stood up. "Stop thinking like that. Get your ass back over here, Joshua. We need to figure out how to get her out of danger. How to get her back here where she belongs."

I looked over at Frank and straightened my shoulders.

He was right.

I needed to do this.

The house was quiet. Everyone had crashed for the night. I sat gazing into the fire, Bear beside me; his huge head nestled against my leg. I didn't even bother trying to go to bed. My mind was too chaotic.

My desire to simply go in and take her was vetoed. So many things could happen. Rabbit could get hurt or even worse. If we failed, we'd never get another chance. Trevor calmly pointed out that even though we had photos, none of them showed Rabbit's face. Going to the police might start an investigation, but we needed Rabbit to be able to verify the claims. If Brian found out what was happening, Rabbit would be in a vulnerable position. Even more so than she was now. I couldn't allow that. I couldn't put her in more danger.

But Trevor and Frank's idea of getting Rabbit out of Brian's hands should work.

I knew the plan would work if everything was handled properly. If everyone played their part and we took it slowly and made sure that we covered all the bases.

Then Rabbit would come home and then we could go after James. But not until she was safe.

I had to believe that was what she wanted. Even if she didn't remember now, I knew it was only a matter of time before she did. But she was still in danger. Something she did or said would push him over the edge and he would go after her. Of that fact I was certain.

Remembering the broken, battered woman I had found, I shuddered.

I had to make her safe. I needed her back with me. I prayed she would forgive me.

I stared into the flames, remembering the words Rabbit had spoken as she stood in front of me, defiant and angry by the truck.

'You will beat this someday, I know you will. Something will finally be reason enough for you to overcome what those bastards did to you.'

She was the reason. For her I had to beat this.

Monday night I was unable to sleep again and paced around the house feeling unsettled and restless. Suddenly, breaking the quiet of the night, the computer speakers upstairs started up with a droning sound indicating a call had come through on the automated, private line I had installed.

The one I had encrypted on Rabbit's card.

I stood listening, my hands gripping the back of the sofa.

She'd figured it out. She needed me. I could hear it from the little sharp intakes of air in the silence of the dark night. I didn't need to hear her voice to know it was her. Her frightened gasps told me she was scared. I wished I could pick up the phone and comfort her. But there was no way to answer the line, only leave messages.

My head fell into my hands. "I'm coming, Rabbit," I promised into the dark.

⟫••••◉••••⟪

The days passed agonizingly slowly. Eating and sleeping were next to impossible. Especially after hearing the messages Rabbit left on the line the following days. Her frightened voice broke my heart and I wanted to go and get her right away. But Frank and Trevor convinced me we had to do this right. We now had people following Rabbit's watchdogs and had even hacked into their email accounts and schedules so we already knew where she was going to be and when. Because of this information, we had the right day, the right time and the right location. She wasn't as closely watched at the hospital. The layout made it impossible for her to walk out without being seen, so her watchdog would be sitting downstairs waiting for her. But we weren't going out through the doors. We were going up. The helipad at the hospital would provide us with a quick way in and out.

I had argued with Trevor over using the helicopter. He thought we should cause a distraction and walk her out of the library's back door and drive away. "The drive will only take a few hours. The helicopter will get noticed, Joshua. We need permission to land and there will be records; traceable records," he had insisted. "You're reacting to your pain. You need to step away, Joshua." He stared at me. "We need to think this through, rationally."

I had stood up, angry and frustrated, sending my chair flying and slamming my hand down on the table. I didn't care that I was yelling now.

"Yeah, I'm reacting to my feelings! I'm fucking done with *thinking*, Trevor! Last time I thought it through I sent her away and that was the fucking wrong decision! My gut is telling me to get her out fast and that's what we're going to do. I won't risk being pulled over and her being taken away from us! The helicopter is the safest, fastest way. I don't fucking care how much money it costs to change the records and get this done. Make them an offer they can't refuse. Arrange for the helicopter to land—just fucking do it!"

Frank had to step in and calm us both down. He agreed with me and, grudgingly, Trevor went upstairs to make the arrangements while Frank and I sat with Cecilia going through the information we had on Rabbit's schedule.

Rabbit's life was very regimented and she was never alone. For weeks ahead, each day was planned out and there didn't seem to be many variances from the daily schedule, aside from the functions they attended. Mondays and Thursdays were to be spent at the library. Tuesday and Wednesday mornings were to be spent with a trainer and the afternoons at the hospital.

Friday mornings were again with her trainer and the afternoon was scheduled as a spa day at a private women's club. Cecilia told me she probably had lunch and spent the afternoon being groomed. I snorted. Like she needed that. She was naturally lovely and didn't need any *grooming* in my opinion. Her evenings and weekends were spent either at Brian's side at a function or alone inside her house. I shook my head. I thought I had sent her back to her *life*, but she simply existed in the environment she had gone back to.

Frank's people even had a few pictures of her, taken at one of the many functions they attended. It hurt seeing how blank she looked again, devoid of emotion, her eyes always downcast. I couldn't see any new marks on her but her clothing covered her completely. And, her glorious hair was once again rolled tightly and hidden away. *She* was hidden away.

I pulled a hand through my hair. The phone calls had stopped. I knew she thought she had been abandoned. I could see it in her defeated stance of the latest photo.

I just had to hold on and know it would be done soon.

I picked up a picture and traced her partially hidden face.

"Hold on just a few more days, Rabbit. We're coming."

⇉CHAPTER THIRTY-ONE⇇

Rabbit

Three days. For the next three days every chance I got at the hospital or library, I called the number on the card. I had to be careful how often I went to the lounge so Bob didn't suspect anything, but he never followed me into the staff room at either place and there was a phone in both lounges. But the number just rang and rang. A few rings each time and then nothing. It just cut off. After the first few attempts, it occurred to me that maybe the soft noise I heard meant there was an answering machine on the other end and, hesitantly, I left a message. Then another, then another…

It's Rabbit. Please. Joshua. I need you.

Please, Joshua. I remember everything. I'm scared …

It was him, Joshua. I don't know how long I have until he knows and I'm being watched …

Joshua … I want to come home.

Joshua … please.

Every time I called, I prayed I would hear Joshua's voice. That he would tell me it was going to be okay. At the end of the first day, I was convinced I had written down the wrong number, but once the card was dry the number disappeared again, and even when I re-wet it nothing came up, so I had no way of checking. But I had been so careful when I wrote it down. So I kept trying. I was desperate. Today was my last day out of the house and the watchful eyes followed me everywhere. By the time Bob came to my door and informed me it was time to leave, I was completely lost and dejected.

Had he changed his mind? Did he just not care anymore?

My head felt too heavy to hold up and I slumped down in the back of the car.

If Joshua didn't care ... then I was truly alone. Nothing meant anything.

And then ... I gave up.

The rest of the week passed by in a haze of sad fogginess. I did everything expected of me and acted the part of the confused, quiet wife well. My behavior was exemplary at all the functions we attended. The weekend passed by in a haze of events and duties. I slept fitfully, waking up frequently, sobbing into my pillow. My appetite was non-existent and my spirit lower than I could ever remember it being.

Monday morning, I woke up feeling un-refreshed and still groggy. I winced as I sat up and looked down at the fresh bruise on my arm. Brian's handprint was visible on my forearm. When I had cancelled the session with the trainer yesterday, pleading exhaustion, he had lost it and berated me for several minutes. I made the mistake of standing up, thinking he was done criticizing me, and he had grabbed me, his hand squeezing painfully down on my arm to stop me from leaving. It was only my gasp of pain that seemed to bring him out of his rage before he flung me away from him and stormed out of the dining room. I had spent the rest of the day in my room, alone and frightened.

I made my way to the shower with a heavy heart, my week stretching out in front of me. It was starting again. I knew that soon enough the grabbing would turn into hitting and the hitting would escalate. I had to figure out an escape plan before he lost control. I wasn't sure I'd survive his rages again. The months it had taken me to escape last time were a luxury I no longer had, and to make things even more difficult, I was now being watched. Somehow, I had to get away and find a way to start over. I needed to figure a way of slipping away from the eyes that followed me and escape. To where and to whom I had no idea. I had already risked Tracy, involving her with my car. I couldn't put her at further risk. I had no one else to turn to. If Joshua didn't want me, I wasn't sure what to do. But I knew I couldn't give up. I knew I had to get away from *him*.

I wondered about going to the police with the pictures I had. Would it be enough? If I told them what had happened, would they believe me? Could they protect me? Brian seemed to control every aspect of my life, and there were no public medical records of my injuries. I knew without a doubt that the doctor he took me to was being paid to stay quiet and not keep records when he treated me. The evidence I had before was lost, buried somewhere in the snow on Joshua's property. Now that my memory was back, I knew my purse had been on the seat beside me before I hit the tree and must have fallen out in the chaos that followed. I wondered if it would ever be found.

I sighed as I felt the tears trickle down my face. Would *anyone* believe me? My head ached with the magnitude of what I was facing and I shut the shower off, dreading the day and the life that seemed to stretch on endlessly in front of me. Joshua had thought I would resent a life with him because of the limitations he lived with. Yet each day I had with him had contained joy and love. The stark reality now was my life here was a prison; one of coldness and obscurity, where I meant nothing. I may not have remembered my name when I was with Joshua, but I knew who I was and what I meant to him.

Brian wasn't at breakfast. Mrs. Smith informed me quietly that he had an early meeting and had already left. I nodded. This often happened after he laid his hands on me. I was grateful for the reprieve. Still, I pushed the oatmeal around my bowl with no appetite, and eventually gave up and waited by the front door for Bob to arrive and escort me to the library. Mrs. Smith appeared wordlessly and slipped a granola bar into my pocket and patted my shoulder before walking away. My eyes followed her gratefully. Although she had always remained reserved, unlike the rest of the staff, she endeavored to be kind to me in small ways.

When I got to the library I forced myself to stay at my desk. There was no point calling the number. I didn't even open a search engine to try and find a link to Joshua. I spent most of the morning working with Kate, planning the next fundraiser for the literacy program. More than once, she asked if I was okay and I smiled and brushed off her concerns.

Just after lunch, my eyes were heavy and tired and I knew I needed a coffee to make it through the rest of the day. Leaning forward, I picked up the mug my favourite little reader had given me, and stopped short as I noticed a small fuzzy object in the bottom. Curious, I turned the mug over and instantly my eyes filled with tears. A tiny, furry, stuffed rabbit, no bigger than a golf ball, sat in the palm of my hand. And, attached to the soft bundle, a small, blank white card. It was identical to the first card Joshua had given me. My heart began pounding and I looked around wondering how it had gotten there. I stood up on trembling legs and walked down to the staff lounge, the items safely in my pocket, my mug hanging loosely from my fingers. Bob remained seated at the other end of the hall. He barely even glanced my way. We both knew there was nowhere else I could go.

Two of the librarians were sitting quietly in the lounge, discussing something, but they were the only other people there. I walked to the bathroom, shut the door and stood in front of the sink. I reached in my pocket with trembling fingers and pulled out the small blank card and rabbit. My hands were shaking as I turned on the faucet and soaked the card, holding tightly to the furry rabbit. I set it on the edge of the sink, watching as Joshua's writing appeared.

I heard you. It's time to come home.

Be careful. Eyes.

Hospital. Tomorrow. 1 p.m.

~J

I sank to the floor, unheeded tears streaming down my face. He hadn't deserted me. He still loved me.

Joshua was sending someone for me. Tomorrow.

Tomorrow, I was going home.

I just had to make it through one more day.

I closed my eyes, praying I could do it.

———— •••••◉••••• ————

I made it back to my desk, looking calmer than I was feeling. I even remembered to take the coffee with me. My mind raced with the implications.

Somehow, Joshua knew I went to the hospital on Tuesdays. He knew I was being watched.

He *hadn't* left me alone.

Would it be Cecilia? Trevor? Someone else? How would they find me? I drew in a deep breath. I needed to trust Joshua and just allow things to happen. Obviously, he had something planned. I couldn't mess it up.

I looked around. I wouldn't be returning here ever again. Casually, I got up and pulled down a few of the drawings and moved a few things around. Kate appeared in my door. "Tidying up?"

I nodded. "It's a little cluttered in here."

She laughed. "You always do this, you know. Tidy it up and then three weeks later it's just as messy. You can't bear to part with any of your drawings."

I smiled because she was right. "At least I try."

"I have a meeting outside. See you Thursday," she laughed.

My breath caught as I smiled back, lying to her. "See you then."

———— •••••◉••••• ————

The evening was a blur. Another dinner, another night of smiling and pretending to be something I wasn't. Inside, I was a mass of nerves. I held myself stiffly all night beside Brian. I couldn't afford to let my guard down or arouse suspicion. After arriving home, I shut my door behind me, sliding down the wall as my legs gave out. I prayed that was the last appearance I would make as Brian James' wife.

The next day, I walked into the hospital with my heart racing, desperately trying to control my emotions. I had made it this far, but I didn't know what would happen next. I hadn't slept all night worrying and wondering. Terrified that I would do something wrong and whatever Joshua had planned, whoever he was sending wouldn't be there. Would I know the person who would come and get me? How would they make contact with me? Bob stopped outside the lounge and I walked in to put my things away. As usual, a janitor was busy sweeping the floors. I hung up my coat and purse and picked up my smock and volunteer tag. Turning around, I ran into the janitor, dropping my tag.

"Excuse me," I apologized.

"No problem, ma'am," he said as he put his hand on my arm to steady me. "Oh, you dropped this," he said as he bent over. He fumbled briefly, and then handed me my tag, winking. Quickly, he turned and walked away, pulling his broom and cart behind him.

Confused, I looked down. In the pouch with my tag was another small blank card. I looked up but he was gone. I drew in a nervous breath as I slid the card in my pocket and put on the tag. Outside Bob waited for me, escorting me to the wing where I volunteered. "I'll be downstairs when you finish," he informed me as the elevator doors shut and the elevator began to climb.

I nodded, my nerves stretched thin. There was one central bank of elevators. Even all the staircases led to the same central lobby. How would I get past Bob sitting there? I could feel the doubts and worries creeping up my spine. I checked my watch. It was 12:45 p.m. When the elevator arrived on my floor, I ducked into the bathroom. Wetting the card, I watched anxiously as Joshua's instructions appeared.

Stairwell. East wing.

Go up.

~J

I took in a deep breath. I had the memory stick, my tiny rabbit, the remains of the bloodied blouse and I had even remembered to add a few of the mystery pills to show Joshua. That was all I dared take with me. Late last night, I had quietly added Joshua's hoodie and shirt as well as the drawings I had taken to one of the boxes in my closet, praying that maybe I would somehow get them back. Brian had never even looked in the boxes and I wasn't sure he was even aware of their existence. They certainly weren't important enough to warrant much of his attention. Maybe I would be able to get in touch with Mrs. Smith and have her send them. She had always been kind to me. Distant due to her position in the household, but kind, none the less.

I made my way to the east wing and stopped outside the stairwell door. There was a janitor's cart, stanchions blocking the door, and a No Entry sign hanging in the centre. There was a large puddle on the floor, seemingly leaking out from under the door. Was that real? Or a diversion? My heart was pounding and my entire body was shaking. I had no idea what I would find on the other side of the door, or who.

Then I straightened my shoulders. If it led me to Joshua, then I was going. I looked around, but the area was deserted. I opened the door and stood listening as it shut behind me. The only sound I could hear was my own breath, coming out in small frightened gasps.

Go up, the card said.

I climbed the steps slowly, listening. My body was shaking harder than ever. For the first time, the thought occurred to me this could be a trick. Perhaps Brian was onto me and was testing me. I stopped for a moment, but then kept climbing. I had nothing left to lose. If it was a trap then he already knew and I was doomed anyway; if it wasn't, then someone would take me to Joshua. I stopped when I got to the sixth floor. The roof was the next stop and the stairway above me was dim. How far was I supposed to go?

There was nothing. No one was there. I looked at my watch and saw is was exactly 1 p.m.

I stood there, unsure what to do. Was I supposed to go on the roof? I could feel the tears gathering in my eyes as I stood trembling, feeling so lost and scared. A small object suddenly landed at my feet from above and I lurched back, startled, with a muffled gasp. I hesitated, and then bent down and picked up the fluffy object at my feet and stared. Another tiny stuffed rabbit lay in my hand. With a choked sob, I looked up. Above me in the hazy light, I could see the distinct silhouette of a man with broad shoulders. I watched anxiously as the shoulders moved and bent forward, then a hand extended over the railing above me.

Even in the dimness I *knew* that hand. I ran up the stairs and flung myself, sobbing wildly, into the arms that were waiting for me.

Joshua's arms.

⇒CHAPTER THIRTY-TWO⇐

Joshua

I pulled Rabbit's shaking, sobbing form closer. Her fists closed around my shirt front, holding the fabric tightly, her head buried in my chest.

I had her. She was safe.

The sheer relief was shocking and intense and I could feel myself shaking from the emotions.

I didn't give a fuck if James suddenly appeared from behind her. Not even the wrath of God was going to pull her away from me.

Nobody was ever going to hurt her again. Especially not James.

The door opened behind me. "We need to move, Joshua." I nodded and leaning down, placing my lips to her ear. "Arms, Rabbit." Immediately, her arms moved to my neck, holding tight. I could feel the soft fur of the little rabbit, still clutched in one hand, against my neck. I scooped her up and ran through the door to the waiting helicopter, Frank leading the way. He opened the door and helped me in, still holding Rabbit. I didn't even try to put her in her own seat. I wasn't letting her go. I strapped us both in and gently pushed her face further into my chest to drown out the loud noise of the blades. Frank sat beside me and spoke into his headpiece, letting our group know Rabbit was safe and to leave the building as quickly and unobtrusively as possible. I knew that the multiple diversions would disappear quickly; unexplained water leaks, stuck doors and a broken-down elevator would all suddenly clear up and the people we had in the building would quietly disappear as per Frank's plans. I felt the immense swell of relief as the chopper lifted off and the hospital quickly disappeared from view. It was then that I was able to draw a deep, relaxed breath. We had done it. She was safe in my arms. My hands kept running small, soothing circles over Rabbit's back and my lips never left her head, kissing, nuzzling, whispering words of comfort I wasn't even sure she could hear. I felt how tightly her hands were clinging to my neck, and how violently her body was trembling. The front of my shirt was soaked with her tears.

Leaning down, I found her ear. "I have you, Rabbit. It's okay, baby. It's over. We're going home now. You're safe." Her entire body shuddered in my arms and I tightened my grip. I couldn't get her close enough. Any space between us was too much. I continued rocking her gently and, gradually, I felt the tremors slow down, although her grip on my neck didn't lessen. I sat watching the landscape fly by, grateful for the miles that were now separating us from *him*. The feeling of contentment that I was able to hold and caress her, and have her close again, was overwhelming.

From the moment I realized that, for certain, she was in danger, I had been in agony. Listening to her broken voice on the incoming-only emergency line I had set up, begging me to bring her home, had torn up my soul in ways I had never experienced. The deep ache I'd felt in my chest was indescribable. Each day that passed had only made the feeling more powerful and today had been especially intense.

I felt one of her hands leave my neck and cup my cheek. I looked down into her beautiful, tear-stained face and imitated her action, my fingers stroking her damp skin. Her other hand pulled on the nape of my neck and I leaned down. "You came for me," her awed voice whispered. "*You* came. You didn't send someone else."

I nodded.

"I knew you could do it, Joshua. I'm so proud of you. You *did* it. For me. Thank you."

I stared down at her, speechless. Her first words spoken out loud were to praise *me*. Shaking my head, I leaned down and kissed her gently. "I found that reason you hoped I would find one day, Rabbit. *You're* that reason."

Her hand reached up and tenderly wiped under my eye. It was only then I realized I was crying as well.

I leaned down again. "I'm never letting you go, Rabbit. Ever."

She smiled up at me, her own eyes brimming with tears. "I don't want you to."

My lips twitched up into my own smile. "Good to know."

⋯•••◉•••⋯

Rabbit fell asleep nestled in my arms and I took the time to study her. She looked so tired, with dark circles under her eyes that I could see even with the makeup she was wearing. She was dressed in a navy-colored suit with a plain white blouse under it. I remembered her dislike of navy, black and brown and hoped Cecilia had kept away from those colors when she picked up some new things for Rabbit. I also noticed she was thinner again; her body felt far too light in my arms. The few pounds she had gained were gone as well as at least another five or so. I could feel my anger building. Her hair was up in a tight knot on the back of her head and my fingers itched to find the pins holding it in place and free it. But I didn't want to disturb her, so I waited. Her little hand was clasped tightly in mine and I softly stroked over her knuckles. My fingers stilled as they brushed over metal and I looked down to see the narrow gold band on her finger. I frowned. That was new. And, it didn't belong there. I wanted it gone as well. I pulled on it but it was tight on her finger. Gently, I held up her hand studying it. Had the bastard purposely made the ring too small so it couldn't be removed easily? Cursing under my breath, I tried to work the ring off but it wouldn't budge. I gritted my teeth and resisted the desire to use my strength to pull it off. But that would frighten her and I didn't want that. Instead, I closed my eyes and concentrated on the welcomed feeling of having her close again, and thinking back on the past couple days.

This morning, after yet another sleepless night, the enormity of what we were about to do had hit me. I was going to get into a helicopter and leave the property. Even the thought caused a sweat to break out on my brow and my hands to shake. The plan could go ahead without me; either Cecilia or Trevor could be the person to meet Rabbit in the stairwell but I knew it should be me. I needed to do this for myself and for Rabbit. I needed her to know she meant more to me than a phobia. That I could overcome it for her. For us.

Frank had joined me at the window, holding a cup of coffee. "It's gonna be fine, Joshua," he grunted. "I've scoped it out, and my people are all in place. It'll be a walk in the park. I'm gonna give her the card and she is going to walk to the stairwell. My people will be on the other floors, cleaning up all the 'spills' and taking care of the problems that have happened to block the stairwells. And since that one can only be accessed after the second floor, it's rarely used so the chances of anyone being in it are slim anyway. I'll join you on the roof and off we'll go."

I drew in a deep breath and shared my troublesome thoughts. "What if something happens to her schedule? Or there is an emergency helicopter landing for the hospital?"

Frank chuckled. "Well, I doubt the first one is gonna happen. That fucker is so anal; he wouldn't think to suddenly change her daily routine.

He has it set in stone for the next two bloody months. We've done everything right, Joshua. We've watched her, we know her schedule. We didn't move too quickly. We've planned this carefully. If he did suddenly change something, well let's just say, I've got some backup plans. If there is an emergency, I already have a backup for that as well. Just like the library. We've thought it all out, Joshua. One way or another, your little lady is going to be home with you tonight."

I nodded and looked at him. "What if I can't do it? What if I can't get in the chopper or, even worse, can't get out on the other end?"

Frank took a deep swig of his coffee and looked back at me steadily. "I know your story, Joshua. Think of it this way. This is the easiest fucking way to make yourself do this. You are gonna walk over there," he indicated the waiting chopper, "and get in. Your pilot is going to fly us out of here and we'll be gone so fast you won't have time to panic. And, on the other end, your girl will be there, needing you. If that isn't enough of an incentive, I'm not sure what is or what could ever be."

I had looked at him. He was right.

"If you can't, I can either sucker-punch you so when you wake up you're already in the air and have no choice, or I'll take your feisty little sidekick with me," he shrugged, chuckling. "Either way, mission accomplished. But if it's you, then there is one more layer for them to try and figure out since you are basically unknown to them. Another way of ensuring your girl's safety."

I nodded grimly. Rabbit. That was the goal. That was what I needed to concentrate on. Not what I couldn't do, but what I could do. What I *needed* to do. Bring her home.

Then he laughed, clapping his hand on my shoulder.

"There it is."

"What?"

"That look of determination I need. I can do this without you, Joshua, but with you it will be so much easier. She needs to see you there. And frankly, you need to be there. Cecilia and Trevor will hold down the fort here. My guy will be on Bob's tail the whole time. He is such an idiot. He has no idea he is being followed or that his accounts have been hacked. For someone in security, he is incredibly lax. Although I suppose for that we should be grateful."

I stared out the window.

For Rabbit. I could do this for Rabbit.

<hr />

Rabbit's eyes suddenly flew open and she struggled in my arms in panic, bringing me back to the present.

I leaned down and spoke in her ear, promising her that she was safe. I stroked her soft cheek and rocked her until she was once again still. "We'll be home soon, Rabbit," I reassured her as I smiled down at her. Her sigh was shaky as she snuggled back into my chest. I tightened my arms around her. I looked over at Frank who had watched our quiet exchange with bemusement. He smiled and shook his head at us then leaned back in his seat. I couldn't help my answering smile. She was in my arms. I had her.

We landed in front of the house and waited until the blades had stopped. Frank got out and I followed, still holding Rabbit. "Let me down, Joshua," she smiled softly. "I can walk to the door." I stood her on her feet, but kept her hand clasped in mine. The door opened and Bear came barrelling out past Cecilia and Trevor, barking and making a beeline for Rabbit. "Brace yourself," I warned, holding out a hand to try and stave off Bear's advance. Rabbit fell to her knees, opening her arms, and within seconds, was smothered by Bear's joyous greeting of welcome. Everyone watching laughed as he alternately licked her face and butted his head into her chest for attention, running around her in circles, barking his happiness at seeing her. Finally, he sat down heavily in front of her, flopping his head on her lap, his large paws on either side of her. She bent over him, lovingly stroking him, giving him his own welcome in return. I bent down and patted his head. "Let her up, Bear." He raised his head and looked at me. "She's not going anywhere," I assured him.

Rabbit smiled as she gave him one last neck rub. "No, I'm not."

I helped her up and she was greeted with hugs from both Cecilia and Trevor. Once inside, we all sat down at the table, Bear huffing and pushing people out of the way to stay close to her, laying his head down on her knees once she sat down. I sat on her other side, my arm still around her, needing the comfort of her touch. She looked across the table at Frank and suddenly smiled. "You're the janitor!"

He laughed and tipped his baseball cap. "Pleased to make your acquaintance, ma'am."

She looked around her in amazement. "I didn't think I would ever be back here," she said softly, looking at me disbelievingly. I could see her bottom lip was beginning to tremble. Cecilia stood up and extended her hand. "Come with me, Rabbit," she said kindly. Then she looked at Trevor. "We need to go as soon as I come back. We all need to be in place tonight. Just in case."

Trevor nodded. Cecilia and Rabbit disappeared down the hall. He stood up. "We're going to lie low for a couple days, Joshua. We'll stick to our normal routine. And, I think you need the time alone with Lizzy.

We'll be back just as we planned. I'll get started on the paperwork we talked about also, and I'll talk to my associate."

I stood up and looked at both him and Frank. "I can't even begin to thank you enough ..." my voice trailed off. Trevor waved me off. "We just made a wrong decision right. It's not over though, Joshua. Getting her back was just the first step. We have to figure out where we go from here."

"I know. But not today."

He nodded. "Not today. Today, enjoy having Lizzy back."

I nodded, too overcome at the moment to speak.

Rabbit was home.

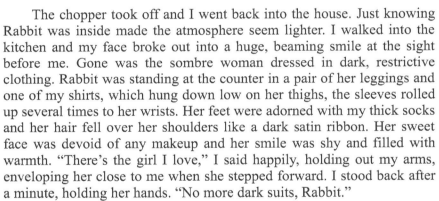

The chopper took off and I went back into the house. Just knowing Rabbit was inside made the atmosphere seem lighter. I walked into the kitchen and my face broke out into a huge, beaming smile at the sight before me. Gone was the sombre woman dressed in dark, restrictive clothing. Rabbit was standing at the counter in a pair of her leggings and one of my shirts, which hung down low on her thighs, the sleeves rolled up several times to her wrists. Her feet were adorned with my thick socks and her hair fell over her shoulders like a dark satin ribbon. Her sweet face was devoid of any makeup and her smile was shy and filled with warmth. "There's the girl I love," I said happily, holding out my arms, enveloping her close to me when she stepped forward. I stood back after a minute, holding her hands. "No more dark suits, Rabbit."

She squeezed my fingers and shook her head. "No."

I looked down and saw the ring was gone. I lifted her hand and stared at the angry red welt that wrapped around her slightly swollen finger. I raised my eyes to her face questioningly. "Rabbit?" I asked quietly.

"It didn't belong there," she whispered, echoing my thought earlier. "Cecilia helped me get it off with cold water and soap."

"Where is it?"

She shrugged, unconcerned. "I tossed the first one out the car window the day I ran, but I hated this one even more so ... um ... I gave it to Cecilia and asked her to drop it out of the helicopter or something. I don't ever want to see it again."

I kissed her swollen finger gently and placed her hands on my chest, stroking her arms. "Okay. Good decision."

I stepped back, squeezing her arms affectionately, and frowned when I saw her wince. I pushed up the sleeves of my shirt and looked up at her, horrified as I saw the dark bruise on her forearm. "He hurt you again. I waited too long," I breathed painfully, my throat tight. "*Rabbit* ..." My hands pushed up the sleeves further, terrified of what other marks I would see.

Her fingers on my mouth stopped me before I could say anything else. "I'm fine, Joshua. He grabbed me once. You got me before it became worse. Please ... don't. Not tonight. I'm home ... tonight is just for being happy ... please."

My hands stilled and I stared into her eyes. They were tired but held so much love and forgiveness in their soft depths. I kissed her fingertips and drew her back to me, cradling her. Leaning down, I kissed her longingly.

"Happy isn't a big enough word, Rabbit."

⇒CHAPTER THIRTY-THREE⇐

Joshua

Rabbit shivered in my arms. I looked down. "Are you all right?" I asked softly, unsure if she was cold, tired or simply overwhelmed.

She nodded. "I haven't been sleeping well. I didn't sleep at all last night. I was so worried about today … so worried I would do something that would ruin whatever you had planned." Her voice caught. "So worried that the one thing I wanted more than anything wouldn't happen."

I leaned down, scooped her up, and headed upstairs. I settled us both in the large chair, throwing the blanket around us. Bear followed closely and lay down by the ottoman. I smiled, knowing he would not be far from Rabbit again for a while.

I looked down into her sweet, tired face, stroking her cheek slowly. I knew we had to have this conversation. I needed her to understand my thoughts and actions.

"I had to keep you in the dark, Rabbit. I know the subterfuge probably seemed overboard but I couldn't risk him figuring it out. I couldn't risk *you*." I grimaced when I looked down at her arm. I picked up her hand, lifting her arm close and delicately tracing the bruise with my lips. Closing my eyes, I took in a deep breath.

"I didn't want to let you go, Rabbit. I didn't. But I *thought* I was doing the right thing." I opened my eyes and looked into her soft gaze, needing her to understand how I felt. "But I was wrong. So fucking wrong. From the moment I knew I was wrong, I have been working on getting you back to me. Praying it was what you wanted as well. That you still wanted me even after what I had done. The night ..." my voice trailed off painfully and I had to swallow before I could continue. "The night the line rang and I knew you had figured out my card ... I could hear you breathing on the other end of the line ... just breathing ... and I knew you were scared and I knew you needed me. Then the next day, when I heard your voice ... *God, Rabbit*, I thought I would go insane not being able to get to you fast enough. I wanted to storm the castle, so to speak. But Trevor and Frank convinced me to do this right. To do it safely and make sure we got you out carefully so you weren't in danger ... and he didn't have a chance to hurt you again." My fingers traced her arm and I looked at her regretfully. I hadn't made it in time.

"I sent that card with you in case you needed me. I told myself I wanted things to work out for you, for you to be happy. But something wasn't right, it just didn't *feel* right, and I needed to know you had something. Something of me that you could use if you *weren't* happy. Some small connection to me if you needed it. I knew you would figure it out. And, once you did, it seemed safest to stay on that path. A piece of blank paper. Even if someone else looked at it, they wouldn't know. But you would know how to find the messages. I was afraid if someone tried to talk to you, that you might not know if they were with me or not. Or, it would be noticed and then he would tighten things up even more, making it so I couldn't get to you." I sighed. "I was just ... so afraid, Rabbit. So afraid I wouldn't get the chance to right my wrong, to make you safe and get you back. So I went overboard."

"What if I hadn't figured out the first card?"

I smiled down at her. "I knew without a doubt that you would figure it out, Rabbit. You read my books, you *know* me. You know how my mind works." I kissed her cheek softly, and my voice became serious. "But if you hadn't, I would have gotten to you anyway. Somehow, I would have found a way, even if I had to kidnap you to get you away from him." I paused. "I found your purse, Rabbit. I saw the journal. I *saw* what he did to you and I was getting you out of there no matter what."

"You found my purse?"

I nodded. "Bear dug it out of the snow. It must have fallen out when the door opened after you hit the tree." My arms tightened around her. "The pictures were the worst thing I've ever seen, Rabbit. It made me physically ill to see what he did to you. What I sent you back to."

"You didn't know," she whispered.

I looked at her and shook my head. "No, I didn't know, but I stopped asking the right questions, Rabbit. I acted rashly and *reacted* instead of thinking." I shook my head. "I put you in so much danger. Seeing those pictures drove that fact home."

She looked away. "You've seen the pictures. So you know it all then."

I lifted her face. "I know what the pictures showed me. I don't know the story. You can tell me when you're ready. You can tell me anything."

She nodded. "I will. But not tonight. Please."

"When you're ready. I'm here," I assured her.

She smiled softly. "I liked the rabbit. How did you get it into my mug?"

I grinned. "Cecilia found the rabbits. She thought it would let you know, without a doubt, that it was me leaving you the messages. That it would give you something to hold onto for the last day. We had someone watching you. Before you got there, they dropped it in your mug. And made sure you saw it."

She looked at me, frowning. "What if I hadn't?"

"Then some nice, older lady would have approached you before you left that day, thanking you for all you had done helping her son to read and would have handed you another one, and another card," I explained. "Today, if anything had gone wrong, you would have been handed another card with a different way to get to me. If all else failed I would have come to you and taken you up those stairs myself. No matter what happened today, you were coming home."

"You must have bought a lot of rabbits."

I smiled and reached into my pocket and pulled out a handful. "I think Cecilia bought out the store. She said she saw them and had a feeling we were going to need them."

Rabbit smiled as she touched the little bundles resting in my palm.

"You thought of everything," she breathed.

I cupped her cheek, stroking her skin gently. "*We* did. Frank, Trevor and Cecilia were all part of this. In some way, they are all responsible for helping me get you home to me."

She covered my hand with hers, her fingers pressing tightly. "You were *so* brave today, Joshua. You overcame so much to come and get me. I know it must have been so difficult for you. But you did it."

"For you," I whispered insistently. "I'd do anything for you, Rabbit."

She sighed and turned her face, nuzzling it into my palm. "I can't tell you how much I love hearing you call me that." She looked up at me. "I've always disliked the name Elizabeth. It seemed too formal, but ... Brian insisted on calling me that."

"You preferred Lizzy?" I asked encouragingly.

She nodded. "It always sounded more … warm and friendly."

I smiled. "I can do that … Lizzy." The name sounded strange on my tongue.

She shook her head. "No. Rabbit. I'm your Rabbit."

Leaning forward, I kissed her. "Always my Rabbit. Always."

<hr />

We were quiet for a while, just sitting close. Reveling in the comfort of being in each other's arms again. Rabbit suddenly spoke up. "Why didn't you pick up the phone when you knew it was me?"

"I didn't have that kind of line installed. It only accepted messages. I did it so fast, Rabbit. All I could think of was a way you could get hold of me. And, in my zealousness to make sure you were safe, I had an untraceable, unanswerable line installed, and I followed it up by encrypting the number on the card. I knew only you would figure out the book references. But if, *somehow*, the card was discovered and someone else called the line … there was no voice on it so no one could accuse you of knowing who the number belonged to." I paused. "Unfortunately, there was also no way of letting you know it was me and that I was hearing you."

"I thought you'd given up on me," she admitted tearfully, averting her eyes. "That you didn't care anymore when all I got was an empty line. I didn't know if I was talking to a machine or to nothing. I so desperately wanted to hear your voice."

I heard the pain in her voice and gathered her closer. "I'm so sorry. I heard you, Rabbit. I cared. God, baby, I cared so much." My lips pressed into her soft hair. "I can't make up for what I did. I should have waited and found out more before I sent you back. Even worse, I should have listened to you and I shouldn't have let you go. I was stupid and arrogant. I don't even know if you can forgive me."

"You never thought I loved you the way you loved me, did you?"

I shook my head. "No, I knew you loved me." I lifted her hand and kissed the warm palm and held it to my cheek. "And, I knew no one would ever love me that way again. You were such a gift to me, Rabbit. An unexpected, wonderful gift. But I thought I didn't have anything to offer you but a half-life, cut-off from the world. Isolated here with me. Nothing outside this place. It wasn't what I wanted for you. *He* seemed to have everything you needed to have a good life. The kind of life you deserved to have."

Her hands came up and cupped my face. "No, Joshua. There is

nothing there for me. You *are* all I need. Life with you is what I want. It's what I need. You have so much more to offer than you think."

"Can you forgive me? For sending you back? For not being what I should have been?" I asked quietly, my voice shaking with repressed emotion.

She looked up at me, eyes awash with unshed tears. "Already forgiven, Joshua. I love you," she whispered, her voice breaking.

I cupped her face, wiping away the tears that were sliding down her cheeks. "I love you, Rabbit. If you let me, I'll spend the rest of my life showing you how much."

"Show me now," she pleaded.

Groaning, I lowered my mouth to hers, my tongue immediately seeking entry. Her lips parted and I was once again able to lose myself in her. I pulled her closer, tucking her into me as I shifted so she was now under me in the large chair. Again and again, my tongue explored her sweetness, delving and tasting, desperate for her. My hands traced her curves, loving how right she felt moulded into me. Her hands were under my shirt pressing me against her, soft encouraging whimpers escaping from the back of her throat when I broke away to caress and worship her neck with my lips, wanting to rediscover all of her. I moaned as I felt her hand slip under the waistband of my pants pulling me closer to her. I could feel myself losing control and I pulled back. "Not here in a chair, Rabbit. I want to love you—I want every inch of you loved and it can't happen in a chair."

"Take me to our bed," she whispered huskily.

Our bed.

No two words had ever been sweeter.

I stood, taking her with me. Her head was buried in the crook of my neck, her lips moving on my skin in silent words of adoration, her warm breath filling my senses. Swiftly, I took her to our room and laid her on the bed. I looked down at her with her hair spilled across the pillow, her eyes gazing up at me burning with a thousand emotions. She sat up, pulling the shirt over her head. "Please, Joshua," she beseeched, her hand stretching out. "Please." I stopped at the sound of the desperation in her voice. We were too close to the edge already; our emotions taut and so close to breaking. I needed to slow both of us down.

I shook my head and knelt in front of her, wrapping my arms around her shaking form. "Hush, Rabbit," I crooned softly into her ear. "You never have to beg." I held her until I felt her body calm, pulling back to stroke her soft hair away from her face. "Let me do it my way, please?" I whispered lovingly as I trailed gentle kisses along her ear and neck. I laid her back on the pillows when I felt her body shiver in response. "That's it, Rabbit. *Feel* how much I love you." I encouraged her as I nudged at her lips with my tongue, sweetly stroking the warmth of her mouth. Slowly, I let my hands and lips show her what I was feeling. Long strokes of my tongue on her skin had her gasping, while my hands caressed and worshipped her curves.

I cherished every inch of her body with my mouth, murmuring words of adoration into her skin, branding her with my love. Finally, I slid into her welcoming warmth; a deep groan of need slipping from my mouth when I was surrounded by her pulsating heat. I moved slowly at first, getting to know her all over again and then gave into the desire raging within me. I crashed my lips to hers and I began thrusting harder and faster, our moans lost in the depths of each other's mouths as we raced towards the moment's completion. Rabbit's body arched and twisted under mine, her legs wrapped around my hips tightly and her hands in constant motion over my skin, touching, feeling, fingers digging deeper as her passion raged. And then she shattered under me, her body stilling as she came, forcefully crying out my name as she tore her lips from mine, gasping. I buried my head into her neck and continued to move within her until my own release raged through me, the power almost overwhelming. My roar echoed in the room as I panted into her warm neck before finally ceasing my motions.

Rabbit pulled my shaking form down on top of hers, refusing to let me go, and we lay silent, basking in the quiet of the early evening. Wrapping her closely to me, I rolled over, keeping her tucked into my side. One hand tangled into her soft hair, stroking her head and feeling the weight of her tresses against my palm, while the other clasped our hands together, fingers intertwined. Her head rested against my arm, her breath warm on my chest as we lay encased in momentary peace.

"There are so many things I need to tell you," she whispered after a while. "There is so much about me you don't know."

"No," I whispered back. "I *know* you. I've always known *you*, Rabbit."

I pressed a kiss into her hair. "But I want to hear anything you want to tell me. You can tell me anything, anytime … and let me get to know the rest of you that is … Lizzy."

I felt her smile against my chest.

"That sounds so strange coming from you. But I like it."

I smiled. "I like it as well. It suits you. But not as much as Rabbit."

She burrowed a little closer. "No, not as much as Rabbit."

I nuzzled her head. "We have lots of time, Rabbit." I lifted her face from my chest and made sure she understood me. "Nothing is taking you away from me again. Whenever you want to talk, you just talk. I'll listen."

"I never want to leave here again," she whispered, her hand caressing my face.

I shook my head sadly. "You have to, Rabbit." Her body stiffened and her eyes grew wild with panic. I held tighter to her hand, realizing my poor choice of words. "That's not what I mean. I left this place today. For the first time in many years. And, I plan on leaving it again. Except this time, I want you beside me. Together, we can do it, Rabbit. Okay?"

Her eyes calmed.

"Okay."

I pulled her close again and held her tightly.

So much to learn about her. So much for her to discover still about me.

So much to learn about how to be the man she needed.

I closed my eyes and prayed I was strong enough.

⇒Chapter Thirty-Four⇐

Joshua

"I don't like fish, Joshua."

I looked up from my plate, confused. I looked down again. "This isn't fish, Rabbit." I poked at my food. "Is it?"

She smiled faintly. "No, its chicken, I think."

"Ah," I nodded. "Cecilia often puts chicken in her casseroles." I looked at Rabbit; she was pushing her casserole around her plate not really eating much. She hadn't said a lot since I had insisted we needed to eat and, regretfully, pulled her out of bed, redressing her in my shirt and socks, but not before kissing every inch of her skin before I covered it up. Cecilia had left a casserole for us to eat and all we had to do was heat it, and I had assumed she would be hungry by now.

"So, you don't like any fish, Rabbit? Or a specific species?" I teased, trying to figure out the strange comment.

"To eat. I don't like fish."

"Okay. Any particular reason?"

Her voice was quiet. "It was almost all I got to eat. Sometimes chicken, but usually fish. Fish and salad. I was always so tired of fish and salad."

Instantly, I felt the anger start to build and I gripped my fork tightly. "No fish then, Rabbit. Ever. Not a problem. You don't have to eat any fucking salad either if you don't want."

She nodded, but didn't look up.

"Joshua?"

I could hear a tremor in her voice. I moved my chair closer to hers

195

and captured the hand I could see fidgeting with the hem of my shirt. "What, pretty girl?"

She looked up at me and I could see the tears forming in her eyes. I wanted to kill Brian James for what he had done to her. What he had reduced her to. However, I kept my anger inside and I squeezed her hand in encouragement.

"Would you cook me a steak tomorrow?"

"I'll cook you a whole fucking cow if that's what you want," I assured her and kissed her hand.

I was rewarded with a shaky, teary-eyed smile. "No, I think one steak will do."

I nodded. "Consider it done." I pushed her plate toward her. "Please try and eat, Rabbit, just a little, okay?"

"I'm not really hungry, Joshua. I'm sorry."

I shook my head. "Okay. You can have something later if you want."

I racked my brain, trying to figure out what to do next. I told her to tell me anything, anytime. But, I wasn't sure how to respond without showing my anger. If she knew how angry it made me to hear how she was treated, she wouldn't talk.

I sat back and looked at her. Then, grinning, I leaned forward and lifted her chin with a finger, gently ticking her skin. "So. A steak. Definitely *not* a vegetarian then, Rabbit?"

She shook her head, her lips twitching as she recalled our dinner weeks ago.

"And, the alcoholic thing? Anything you want to tell me? Confession is good for the soul they say. "

A small grin tugged on her lips. "No, I'm good."

I nodded.

"Any substances you're addicted to? Anything you just can't do without?" I smiled as I continued to chuff her under the chin.

Despite the glimmer of tears still in her eyes, a real smile broke out on her face. "One thing."

"And that is?"

"You."

Instantly, Cecilia's casserole lost all its appeal to me as well. Leaning forward, I pulled her onto my lap and crashed my mouth to hers. Her arms wound around my neck and held me tightly. I pushed my chair back and stood, lifting her, never breaking contact with her lips. I strode down the hall toward the bedroom.

Eating was far too overrated.

<hr />

I woke up with a start. The bedroom was pitch-black, the fire having burned down to small, glowing embers in the grate. I put my hand out and found only empty space in the bed beside me. I sat up abruptly, turning on the light and blinking with the sudden brightness. Rabbit wasn't in bed. In fact, it didn't look like she had even been there. I felt the bed again. Her side felt cold and smooth to my touch. I looked around, feeling disoriented. The bathroom door stood open. The hallway was dark. I listened, but the entire house was still. My heart began to beat faster and I threw the covers back and stood up, looking down in confusion. I had sleep pants on. I had made love to Rabbit before we fell asleep, wrapped around each other. How could I have pants on?

My heart was now beating so loudly it echoed in my ears. The events of the last day played out in my mind. Getting in the chopper, determined, but tense and shaking, wrapping Rabbit in my arms and taking her away from the hospital, bringing her home, making love to her last night. I shook my head trying to clear the fogginess.

I looked down again. No. I put pants on to go get her a snack. Hadn't I? My head turned to the nightstand. Why was there no plate and glass there? A strange ache began in my stomach. My eyes strayed to the chair her clothes had been on. It was empty. I sat back down heavily, as my hands began to shake.

Had I dreamed it? Had I not brought her home? Was she still there ... with him?

Still scared and alone?

Had the rescue all gone so smoothly because it wasn't real?

My breath caught in my throat and I felt moisture gathering in my eyes. Getting up, I stumbled into the hall and called her name. Nothing but silence greeted me and I stood clutching the doorway.

How was I going to make it through the day if I had to relive it?

What if I didn't get her back?

What if it didn't happen the same way as in the dream?

What if there were problems?

What if I failed and I didn't get to her this time?

I pushed off the wall and staggered toward the kitchen. I could hear my own gasping breaths echo in the quiet of the house and I stood looking around the darkness, lost. I snapped on a light and stood motionless, gazing at the emptiness. The plates from dinner were gone. The house was empty.

It hadn't been real.

My voice was rough as I spoke into the silence.

"*Rabbit.*"

A noise had me spinning around and the door to the mudroom opened, Bear barrelling in from the outside, bringing with him a swirl of cold air. And, behind him, in my parka, walked Rabbit. For a moment, my eyes drank her in as she stared at me, surprised to see me standing there.

"Joshua?"

Her voice broke my trance and I lunged forward, my chaotic emotions propelling me. Rabbit stepped back at the suddenness of my approach, but I reached out and dragged her to me. Immediately, my lips found her skin, kissing and caressing her cheeks, forehead, nose, anywhere I could reach, finally covering her mouth forcefully as my hands tore off the parka and pulled her to me. I groaned as I felt the coolness of her form against mine and I lifted her to the top of the freezer, kissing her deeply, my hands grasping at her. I could feel her hands on my back, stroking me, and I knew she was trying to understand my sudden behavior, but I couldn't stop. She gasped into my mouth as I tore away the shirt she was wearing, but I only deepened the kiss, my tongue refusing to leave her mouth. I pulled her forward, tearing away her shoes then her pants, pulling mine down. Her legs wrapped around me and I thrust forward, burying myself in her.

Powerfully, I claimed her again and again, my body surging forward in desire and relief, needing to feel her around me. Needing that emotional and physical connection. Her legs were locked around my hips urging me forward with every stroke and her hands had crept up into my hair, holding me closely as I took her until I was spent. I released her mouth and growled her name in a long low, groan as my orgasm thundered through me. I felt her own release follow as she wrapped herself tightly around me, whimpering softly. Burying my head into her neck, I breathed her in as I slowly came back to reality, holding her closely.

She was here. She was safe.

She was mine.

Rabbit shivered in my arms and my head snapped up.

What had I just done?

Taken her without so much as a warning. I hadn't spoken a word.

In the mudroom no less.

I groaned quietly.

My eyes found hers, not sure what to expect. The soft gaze of warmth that met mine eased my mind instantly.

"So, hello ..." she whispered.

I leaned forward, my forehead resting on hers.

"Feel better now?" her sweet voice murmured.

I opened my eyes back up and gazed at her. "You were gone. I thought it was a dream. I thought I was alone again." My voice was raspy and still filled with emotion.

"Oh, Joshua," she stroked my cheek. "Bear was restless and I couldn't settle either, even after you got me a snack."

I looked at her, blinking. I *had* gotten up. I had put on my pants when I'd gotten up to get her some crackers and milk. I remember watching her nibble on them as I fell asleep, secure in the knowledge she was beside me again.

I shook my head. "I did get you a snack then? I thought I did ... but I woke up and the room was cold. You weren't beside me and the house was dark and quiet ... and it felt so empty." My voice caught. "It was as if I had dreamed it all. That I hadn't gotten you back."

"You did get me a snack, Joshua. You took care of me. Like you always do. You fell asleep, sweetheart," she whispered. "You were so tired and you were so deep into sleep that I didn't want to disturb you. I got up and tidied the kitchen and then took Bear outside for some air and a run. I thought it would do us both some good. I thought I would be back before you even woke up and missed me. I'm sorry you woke up so disoriented and I wasn't there."

I looked down to where we were still joined and looked back up sheepishly. "Sorry about the ... jumping on you with no warning."

She laughed affectionately and cupped my face, kissing me sweetly. "It was quite the *impressive* greeting." Leaning forward, she nibbled my ear. "And extremely *hot*, Joshua."

Grinning, I flexed my hips and we both groaned at the sensation. "Good to know, Rabbit," I moaned huskily as I felt myself growing hard inside her again.

I looked down at her, arching an eyebrow. "Shall we go from one extreme to another?"

She looked at me, unsure.

Grinning and giddy, I kissed her and spoke lowly into her ear. "Freezer to hot tub, Rabbit? I'll warm you up *and* take my time."

She shivered and her arms wrapped around my neck.

"Hot tub," she murmured into my ear.

I held her tightly all the way downstairs.

⇒Chapter Thirty-Five⇐

Joshua

The bright light of mid-morning woke me. I lay blinking, staring at the pillow beside me and then smiled. Rabbit made sure I *knew* she was there. Even though we had been wrapped around each other in the night on my side of the large bed, she had obviously mussed up her side purposely. And, sitting on her pillow were the two tiny rabbits I had given her. I picked up one of the rabbits, feeling its softness.

"Hi."

I looked up and felt my heart stutter at the sight. Rabbit stood in the doorway, holding a mug of coffee, smiling shyly at me.

I sat up and held out my arms. She walked forward, stopping only to place the mug on the nightstand, and crawled onto the bed. I wrapped my arms around her and nuzzled into her soft hair. "Hi," I whispered back at her. "You look so pretty today."

I felt her blush against my bare chest. I pulled back and lifted her warm face. Could she be more adorable?

"I like you in pink." My fingers stroked her warm cheek. "Both clothing and skin wise." I grinned. Her blush deepened and she didn't meet my eyes.

"Why are you blushing, Rabbit? I'm sure it's not like you've never been told how pretty you are before," I teased her softly.

She shook her head. "No one has told me that since my dad died," she whispered.

I felt both a tug of sadness for her and the rekindling of my anger. Of course. That fucker withheld affectionate words from her as well.

I tilted her chin up, forcing her to meet my eyes.

"Every day, Rabbit. I promise to tell you every day how much you mean to me. I think you're the loveliest woman I have ever seen."

She blinked. Her face broke out with her sweetest smile. I smiled back and kissed her tenderly. We looked at each other quietly.

"I'm making omelettes."

I laughed. I loved her randomness. "So you were coming in to get my lazy ass out of bed?"

She shook her head, smiling. "No, my hair is in the way. I thought I remembered having a hair tie in here. I was going to look for it."

Sheepishly, I held up my wrist. "This one?"

"Joshua, why are you wearing my hair tie on your wrist?"

I pulled her forward. "Because you had touched it. Worn it in your hair. I wore it under my watch because I wanted it next to my skin," I admitted quietly into her ear as I awkwardly gathered up the heavy tresses, pulled the band off my wrist and wrapped it around the messy ponytail I had created. "You, ah, might want to fix that," I said, indicating my sloppy handiwork.

She shook her head. "No. It's perfect." She leaned up and kissed me. "Just like you." My hand flew up, holding her close, enjoying the feeling of her soft lips as they moved over my skin. When her hands began stroking teasingly across my chest, drifting slowly across my nipples, rolling and stroking before dropping down to my already straining cock, I groaned.

It didn't matter that I had made love to her twice before we slept, or claimed her in a frenzy of passion on the freezer in the middle of the night, or that we then brought each other to a shuddering release in the hot tub after that. Right now, it felt like forever since I had felt her wrapped around me, hot and wanting.

"Did you start those omelettes, Rabbit?" I asked roughly, not really caring if she had.

"No," she breathed.

"Good," I growled and flipped her on her back, covering her with my body. "Right now, the only thing I want to sink my ... *teeth* ... into ... is you."

My mouth swallowed her giggle, reveling in the sweet taste of her laughter.

"Shower with me?" I murmured into her ear, hating the thought of even getting out of our warm bed. She looked up at me blinking slowly. I frowned, and stroked her cheek. "On second thought, Rabbit, you should stay in bed. You look so tired, my girl."

She shook her head. "No, I want to make breakfast ... well lunch at this point I suppose. I'm fine, Joshua. Neither of us got a lot of sleep last night," she teased.

Her exhaustion went beyond one sleepless night, but still, I felt a pang of guilt. I stroked her soft cheek again. "I should have let you sleep. I was selfish ... and you are just too irresistible for your own good."

She smiled and stretched her body, arching like a contented cat in the sun and then burrowed back into my chest.

"You're pretty hard to resist yourself, Mr. Bennett," she whispered. "And I'd rather be tired but feel like this than ..." her voice trailed off.

"Than what?"

"Than tired, alone and scared like I have been. I couldn't sleep there, Joshua. The house was so cold, so ... forbidding. I hated it."

I tightened my grip on her.

"You never have to go back there again, Rabbit."

She looked up, the need in her eyes breaking my heart. "Promise me that, Joshua. Please."

I cupped face, staring down into her eyes. I spoke slowly and clearly. "Never, Rabbit. He will *never* take you away from me. You will *never* go back there."

She sighed shakily, but smiled. "I'll hold you to that."

I kissed her tenderly, resting my lips against hers. "You do that," I murmured against the softness.

I continued to hold her, savoring the closeness with her.

She pushed on my chest lightly. "I'm hungry. Let's shower and then you can take care of your assignment while I make the omelettes."

I let her up regretfully. "My assignment?" She smiled at me. "You promised me a steak today, Mr. Bennett. You need to forage for it, I believe."

I grinned. "I'll happily forage for you. Not only that I'll cook my offering too."

She smiled. "That's what I like to hear."

Despite saying she was hungry, Rabbit ate very little again. Even when I pulled her chair over and coaxed her, trying to feed her myself, I was only able to get a few more mouthfuls into her. "You need to eat, Rabbit," I pleaded softly.

She looked away. "I'm trying, Joshua. Please." She shook her head.

I laid down the fork. I wouldn't push her. And, I'd cook her a big dinner. "Maybe another snack later then, yes? After your nap?"

She looked at me, frowning. "We just got up. I wasn't planning on taking a nap."

I stood up and scooped her up, ignoring her protests. "*I* just got up. You've been up for a while. And, I didn't let you get much sleep last night, so I want you to rest." I placed her on the sofa and grabbed the blanket off the back, draping it over her. I leaned down and kissed her forehead. "Please."

"Where will you be?" I could hear the anxiety in her voice.

"Right here." I indicated the other end of the sofa. I picked up my laptop and sat down lifting my legs so they were stretched out beside her. Bear lay down on the floor by her head, chuffing at her to let her know he, too, was close. Her hand dropped down and stroked his head quietly. "My protectors," she mumbled sleepily, already drifting.

I squeezed her leg. "Always, Rabbit."

<hr>

She slept restlessly. I kept rubbing her leg and murmuring comforting sounds, letting her know I was close. I spent the time watching over her while on the laptop. I checked every news source I could find, looking for any leak about another disappearance of Elizabeth James. I was greatly relieved to find nothing. I contacted Cecilia and Trevor, confirming their arrival for the next day. I only referenced the other items Trevor was working on, but he did assure me things were going forward. I also spoke quietly via webcam with Daniel, who agreed to come out with them the next day and examine Rabbit after I told him of my concerns. He was horrified to find out she had not been examined properly while she had been gone and was thrilled to find out she was back with me and safe.

And, finally, I went to a website Cecilia recommended, wanting to order Rabbit a few more items of clothing. Not that I minded her wearing any of mine, but I was sure she would prefer things that actually fit her. I found the website and the vast selection highly confusing. What the hell were capri pants? And, why would someone want to wear stretchy denim? Wouldn't that be sort of … saggy?

Finally, I found a page of casual clothing. But not before I went through the business casual section and the evening casual. I shook my head. No wonder it took women forever to shop. How the hell they even knew what these terms meant was beyond me. None of it looked very casual or comfortable to me.

The first thing that caught my eye was a pair of pink, fluffy slippers. Rabbit's feet were always cold, so I added those to the cart. I grinned with the success of my first item. Then I read through the large number of shirts and colors and my confidence began to fade quickly. Clearly, I was out of my comfort zone. Apple Green and Celery? They looked the same to me. Mango? Watermelon? Candy floss pink? Did they name all their colors after food? And, the vast choices of fabric blends; I had no idea there were that many types out there or what Rabbit would prefer.

Twenty minutes later my cart was still empty other than the slippers and I was sure I had actually pulled some of my hair out. Why couldn't it all be as simple as 'fluffy' and 'pink'? Finally, I selected a few shirts that stated they were extra soft and chose colors I thought Rabbit would like. Including the candy floss pink.

I looked over at Rabbit, frowning. Her pants were black and she didn't like black. I searched and found some more of the soft leggings she liked in more of the strangely named colors. How did they match them? I knew women were big on matching things. Thundercloud Grey and Barely Taupe seemed safe. I didn't want her to ever wear black unless she wanted to. I almost shouted in happiness when I found the socks and they were simply labelled cream, white and pink. I knew all those colors! Finally!

I resisted the impulse to buy her a huge number of articles. I wanted her to pick things she wanted as well. I wanted her to make all her own decisions about *what* she liked, and be her own person. But if she had these then at least we were okay for a while. Once things were safer, we could try going into town. Cecilia always said for a small town there were some 'lovely stores' for shopping. But not yet. Not until I knew Rabbit would be safe.

Rabbit's eyes flew open and she sat up, her chest pumping rapidly in her panic. Bear jumped to his feet, growling protectively. As soon as she saw me, she relaxed and placed a comforting hand on Bear's head.

I stroked her leg in comfort, holding her panicked gaze. "I'm right here, Rabbit."

She nodded, still looking upset.

"The memories keep coming into my dreams. Sometimes, they're so real it's like I'm back in them."

I continued to stroke her leg in comfort. "Maybe it would help if you said them. Talked about them out loud. Get them out of your head."

"I've had to keep it all in. I never had anyone to tell, Joshua."

"You do now. You can tell me."

Her gaze faltered. "What if you look at me differently? What if what I tell you makes you think … less of me?"

I waited until she met my eyes again and I shook my head. "That is simply *not* possible."

I leaned forward and placed the laptop on the floor. I patted my lap silently and extended my hand, helping her across the sofa. I settled her flush against my chest and leaned back, holding her closely. I gazed down into her deep blue pools of pain.

"Will you tell me, Rabbit? Can you do that?"

She drew in a small breath and hesitated. Then she nodded but still didn't speak. I waited patiently and finally she spoke, beginning with the sudden loss of her parents.

I listened.

It was only when the room grew dark that I shifted to turn on a light, never letting go of her. I needed her to see she had my full attention and support while she spoke, releasing the poison of her memories into the air around us.

She spoke of the last two and half years as if she was telling the story of a stranger. I rarely interrupted her, not wanting to stop her from getting the words out, only interjecting the odd comment or question when she seemed to falter.

She talked of her loneliness and isolation, especially once she realized what a mistake she had made marrying Brian, and of the first of many physical assaults she would endure. I hated hearing about how she felt fearful all the time; of never being able to meet his expectations; of wondering what her next error would be that would bring his wrath down upon her. I struggled to remain calm when she told me about the physical and mental abuse she suffered at his hands. My rage grew and burned. For the first time in my life, I felt the need to actually hurt another human being. My fury was so strong as I thought of the countless, careless scars he had inflicted on her, so many of them unseen to the human eye, that I fought to remain seated. It was only witnessing *her* pain of reliving the memories, *her* hand gripping mine, *her* body shaking in my arms that kept me anchored to the sofa.

Eventually, she stopped speaking and I realized we had arrived to the day of the snowstorm.

"What sent you into the storm, Rabbit?" I asked quietly.

"It wasn't storming when I left." She shrugged, her eyes gazing past me to the dark window.

"We had a charity function, a brunch, for the library. It was for the reading program. I was meeting Brian there since I went early to help set up. When I went to change, I realized the woman I had bought the suit from had put the wrong blouse in the garment bag. It had come with a brilliant blue one I knew Brian wouldn't approve of, so I had also bought a beige one to wear with it. I'm not sure how the mix-up happened, but it did." She sighed deeply, so much pain echoing in the sad sound. "I didn't have time to send for the car and get the beige one from home and Brian was already on his way, so I wore it; the blue one. It was so pretty and coordinated well with the suit. And, since it was all about the kids I thought Brian would just let it go other than expressing his displeasure. After all, it was just a blouse. The color suited the atmosphere I was trying to create, you know? And, the kids loved it and were so sweet when they told me how pretty I looked."

She looked at me and I nodded in understanding.

"But it more than displeased him. As soon as I saw him, I knew something was wrong. He was already angry and, when he saw me, his eyes raked over me with so much disgust that I knew I would pay for wearing an inappropriate color and 'showing off.'"

"I don't understand, Rabbit," I interrupted gently. "What is wrong with blue? Or any other color?"

"Black, navy, and brown, Joshua. Real ladies with class only wear neutral colors. At least as stated in the gospel by Brian. They blend into the background and never detract from their husband. They never call attention to themselves. They never step out of line. They *never* wear bright blue." The words were recited from memory. Obviously they had been drummed into her head over and over again. She was quiet for a minute, her eyes downcast. When she looked up, I saw the tears beginning to form.

"It started before we even got home. He was so angry; cursing and hitting me in the limo. He had never done that before. The screen was up, so the driver didn't see him, and when we got back to the house he pulled me out of the car before the driver had barely stopped. I knew ... I knew I was in for something much worse once we were in the house. Alone."

I tightened my grip on her hands. "Tell me," I urged quietly, dreading what I was about to hear, but knowing I had to hear it. She *had* to get it out.

"He dragged me upstairs. It was the weekend so there were only a couple staff around and they never saw us. Once we were in my room, he ... he was like someone possessed, Joshua." She shivered and her head dropped to my chest. I held her closer, feeling my own eyes begin to burn.

"He grabbed me and shook me so hard I thought his hands would go right into my skin. I felt like he was actually crushing my bones, the pain was so intense. He screamed and cursed as he hit me, not even caring that these marks would show. I fell and he just kept going. He tore my jacket and the blouse, and then started ... using his feet as well as his hands. He hit and kicked me everywhere."

I could feel the tears now soaking my shirt. My own were running into her hair but I refused to remove my hands from around her trembling form to wipe them away.

"I truly thought I was going to die. I couldn't get him to stop no matter how much I cried and pleaded with him. It was as if he couldn't hear me. Then ... his phone rang. And, he stopped. It was like he woke up. Whatever the phone call was about made him leave ... but he said he would be back. I knew it was time and that I had to go or I wouldn't survive when he got back."

"How did you manage it, Rabbit? You were so injured." I shuddered, remembering her horrific bruises and painful-looking imprints I had seen scattered all over her body.

"Terror-induced adrenaline I think. I somehow got up and threw some new exercise clothing I had bought for the gym into a bag and added my secret journal and a few other things ... as well as my small stash of cash I had been saving for two years. I knew I had to get to my car I had left with a friend and drive. Tracy was away, but I knew the car was there. She always let me know it was there if I needed it. And, I had to go. Right then. It was my only chance. I had to get away, as far away as possible. I had no plans past that. Just getting away." She shifted a little and shrugged. "I left the house out the back way so nobody would see me, and got to a main street and got a taxi to the subway, then made my way to Oakville. I kept my face hidden, and with the storm coming, the subway and buses were fairly deserted. No one even looked at me. I didn't want to take a cab all the way there in case Brian tried to find me and figured out Tracy had my car all along and put her in any danger." She sighed and was quiet for a moment.

"And then, I just started driving. When it started to snow, I kept going. I lost track of time, I didn't even have a destination in mind. I just had to put as much distance between us as possible. When it got really bad, I didn't care. I decided I would rather die *trying* to get away from him than let him kill me. Because I knew if he caught me, he would never forgive me. So I just kept driving. My car spun out of control at one point and somehow I ended up on your road and your driveway and I hit your tree."

She looked up at me.

"And then ... you found me."

I nodded, stroking her cheek. "Thank God." I breathed, feeling the tears still streaming down my face.

Her face crumpled and the dam burst. The sobs tore out of her painfully. Her breathing consisted of agonisingly sharp gasps and painful whimpers. Her arms wound around my neck, holding me so tightly, it actually hurt. But I let her hold me and I held her back. I rocked her, telling her over and over again how much I loved her. How brave she was to have had the courage to escape. How incredibly strong and amazing she was to have persevered and survived. I knew they were just words.

There was nothing else I could say that would make this easier or better. She needed to let the pain out and I would hold her while she fell apart.

Then I would pick up the pieces and help put her back together.

⇒Chapter Thirty-Six⇐

Joshua

Eventually, Rabbit's tears ended. I gathered her close to my chest and walked down the hall to the bedroom, her body wilting and soft in my arms. Carefully, I sat her on the bed and went to get a damp cloth. When I returned, the sight of her sagging shoulders, gently rounded into her frame caused my heart to ache once again. She looked so broken. I shook my head. Not anymore.

I knelt in front of her and gently lifted her face, lightly stroking over her tear-stained skin, wiping away the remains of her painful sobbing. Her eyes remained closed, and the only sound coming from her was the shaky, stuttering breaths that came after such an emotional outburst. I stood and grabbed two fresh shirts from the top of the dresser, making sure one of them was especially soft. "Arms up, Rabbit," I said quietly.

Her eyes opened and my heart clenched at the pain that still lingered but was pleased to see her shaky arms rise. I quickly pulled the damp shirt over her head and pulled the soft shirt back down over her torso. Then I did the same to my own shirt. Leaning down, I smiled gently at her. "It's not pink, Rabbit, but it's my second favourite color on you."

She looked down at her fingers plucking at the soft material on her arm. "Grey?" she whispered, her voice raspy from crying.

I shook my head. "No, *me*. Any shirt of mine that you're wearing instantly becomes my favorite color on you," I grinned and stroked her cheek.

And, there it was. I was rewarded with her shy smile for my corniness. Although tremulous, it was still a smile. I returned it with one of my own before leaning down and placing several tiny kisses on her lips, barely touching them as I whispered 'love you' between each one. It was she that pulled me closer and held me near as she answered back. "So *much*, Joshua."

I pulled her tightly against me.

"Always, Rabbit. Always."

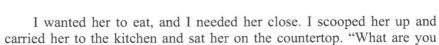

I wanted her to eat, and I needed her close. I scooped her up and carried her to the kitchen and sat her on the countertop. "What are you doing?" she asked, obviously puzzled.

"I promised I'd cook dinner, so that's what I'm going to do." I leaned forward and kissed her forehead. "And, then you're going to eat. Understand?"

She looked over at the clock. "Isn't it a bit late for dinner?"

I smiled. "We don't have to follow *any* rules here, Rabbit. If we want to eat steak at," I squinted over her shoulder looking at the clock, "9:45 p.m., then we can." I winked at her.

"Can I help, at least?"

"Can you whip up one of your pies in half an hour?" I grinned.

She shook her head. "I will tomorrow. Any kind you like."

I pretended to think. "Hmmm … hard choice, apple or blueberry … apple or blueberry … *or maybe … one of each?*" I looked at her, wide-eyed and grinning, hoping to keep her distracted and smiling.

"Done."

"Then you have the night off." I handed her a glass of wine, and turned on the indoor grill to heat up. I kept talking, telling her some amusing stories of Bear and his antics while she was gone. I desperately wanted to give her a little normalcy after her breakdown. There was so much we still had left to talk about, more painful memories she had left to share, but for tonight it was enough. I relented and let her stir-fry some vegetables to have with the steak and soon we were sitting down to eat. I purposely put only a small piece of steak on her plate but was pleased to see her eat it, although it happened very slowly. She barely touched her wine. Baby steps, I reminded myself. I had to let her get comfortable again.

After dinner, we sat on the sofa, hands clasped. I drew in a deep breath. "So Cecilia and Trevor are going to be here tomorrow. Probably just before lunch."

"Okay."

"They're bringing someone else with them," I added, unsure if she was ready for this.

She looked at me. "Oh? Frank?"

I nodded. "Yeah, Frank will be with them as well. But also an associate of Trevor's."

"An associate?"

"His name is Adam Green. He's a lawyer and a friend of Trevor's." I paused. "He practices family law, Rabbit. And, he specializes in cases that involve abuse."

I watched her intently for a reaction. At first, there was nothing and then her eyes flew to mine in panic. Her hand gripped mine tightly and I felt the instant trembling in her body.

I set down my wine glass and pulled her onto my lap. "Hey, hush. Stop, Rabbit. It's okay. He's just coming as a favor. To talk. Just to talk about your options. Please, baby, stay calm." I ran my hands over her back before encasing her in my arms, frightened that the trembles had turned into shudders.

"What's going to happen next, Joshua? What if he comes after me?" She drew back, her eyes wide and frightened. "What if he comes after *you*?" She sounded almost hysterical.

I gripped her shoulders. "Listen to me, Rabbit. No one is going to touch you. And no one, least of all Brian James, is coming after me. He's a fucking bully. But he's lost all his power, Rabbit. Can't you see that?"

She shook her head, still lost in her panic.

I tempered my voice. "Rabbit. He kept you isolated and alone. He abused you. But he didn't count on how incredibly strong and smart you were."

She looked at me puzzled. "Smart?"

"You kept evidence of the abuse, Rabbit. You got away. We have proof against him. And, we have the photos I took. He is all about image and what he sees as his rightful place in society. He *won't* want the photos to be seen."

I could feel her relaxing. The shudders had stopped, although she was still shaking.

"I'm sure he realizes your memory must have returned, Rabbit. He may not know how you got away but he knows why."

She tensed again, the tremors once again picking up.

"You're safe here, Rabbit. The tables have turned now."

"How?" she whispered.

"You were alone before. You're not anymore. You have people who will protect you. Stand up for you. Speak for you, if needed."

"You?"

"Yes. Me. Cecilia. Trevor. Daniel. Frank. And Adam, if you'll let him. We're not going to let him get to you. Ever again. We all know what he did, Rabbit. His secret isn't secret anymore."

"What do you have planned?" she asked, her voice trembling.

"I just want you to meet with Adam. Talk to him. Let him talk to you."

"Does he ... know?"

"Yes, he knows, Rabbit. He hasn't seen the pictures but he knows we have them. Trevor told him the story. He is in agreement. He thinks if he gathers everything together he can go to Brian and his lawyer, and then present the facts and your demands."

Her brow furrowed. "My demands?"

"I assume you want a divorce, Rabbit?"

She nodded.

"Well, whatever else you want. A settlement, perhaps. That's for you to decide."

"I want my books and the boxes of my parent's things in my closet."

"I'm sure we can arrange that, Rabbit. And?"

She looked at me. "Nothing. I don't want his money. I just want my life back. I'll get a job and support myself."

I felt a quiet sense of pride at her words. Of course she didn't want his money. She didn't want anything associated with him.

"Adam will talk to you about your options. He knows the right path for you to follow for that."

She shook her head. "I don't want to talk about that right now." Her voice was trembling.

"Okay," I assured her soothingly. "You can discuss all this with Adam tomorrow, Rabbit. If you don't like him, we'll find you someone you do like."

"Will you stay with me? While I talk to him?"

"Of course. Whatever you need to be comfortable." I drew in a deep breath. "I also asked Daniel to come see you tomorrow, Rabbit. I would feel better if he checked you over."

"My headaches are better, Joshua. Once I got my memory back, the other ones I had I knew were from tension. I know my appetite is off and I'm tired. It's just all from stress. Really, I'm fine."

"Please, Rabbit?" I squeezed her hands. "For me. Let me be overprotective and do this for me."

She sighed in resignation. "If it makes you feel better, then fine, Joshua, but the doctor I saw there didn't seem too concerned with anything."

I snorted. "I know you saw someone, Rabbit. I don't think you had a proper examination and I doubt he had your best interests at heart. He needs to be brought up on charges as well."

Her voice became so quiet that I had to strain to hear her. "Brian took me to the same doctor he always took me to when he got ... angry. His name is Dr. Hammond; I didn't like him, but that didn't matter, of course. He never really talked to me, just Brian. He looked me over and gave me a tetanus shot. That was all he did the last time I saw him."

I was confused. "A tetanus shot?"

She nodded. "I wasn't sure why. He muttered something about in case I had cut myself on something." She looked at me warily. "I wasn't really allowed to ask many questions. He gave me the shot before I even knew it was happening." Her hand went to the back of her neck. "It itched for days."

I kept my voice even. "Let me see, please."

She turned and pulled down the neck of the shirt. Leaning forward, I could see an indent where a needle had been inserted into her skin just below the base of her neck. I rubbed it gently, frowning at its thickness. I wasn't a doctor, but I knew that wasn't the spot for a tetanus shot. Not wanting to scare her any further, I leaned forward and nuzzled the mark with my lips.

"Sloppy job." I shrugged, after pulling the shirt back up and turning her around. My mind was racing and I knew I had to ask Daniel what they could have injected her with. Was that what was making her unwell? "Maybe Daniel can give you something for the itch. He'll check you over and he has the name for a local woman doctor at the hospital you can see from now on. But he knew I was concerned so he agreed to come see you tomorrow."

She sighed wearily. "Okay."

I looked at her. "Okay? Okay to Daniel? Okay to Adam?"

She nodded. "Okay to all of it, Joshua. It all makes me nervous, but I know it needs to happen."

"I'll be right there with you, Rabbit. If something bothers you, we stop it. Right away." I tilted her chin, looking into her tired eyes. "I promise. I know it seems fast, Rabbit, but I want to be ready."

"You think he'll come after me?"

I hesitated then nodded. "I am sure he'll search for you. Quietly this time. If possible, I would rather send our people to him so he never knows where you are."

Another tremor went through her body.

"He won't get to you, Rabbit. Ever. He will *never* touch you again. Trust me when I say that."

She looked at me and nodded. "I do trust you."

I gathered her closely. "Do you want to go to bed?"

She shook her head. "Can we sit in the hot tub first? I'm cold."

Inwardly, I grimaced. This was another sign of her exhaustion. I would feel so much better after Daniel saw her. I stood up, taking her with me. "You can have anything you want, Rabbit. Hot tub it is."

———————⟫•••◉•••⟪———————

Rabbit slept burrowed into me, her hands gripping my shirt. She whimpered a lot in her sleep but would calm when I pulled her tighter. Unable to relax, I found my fingers tracing the thickened spot on her neck repeatedly. What had the fucker done to her? I knew this wasn't a tetanus shot. A small niggling thought kept rolling through my head, but I needed Daniel's help to confirm it. If I was right, time was even more against us. Between my worry over the mysterious injection and the endless loop in my head of the memories Rabbit shared with me, I was tense and anxious.

When dawn broke and Rabbit seemed to finally slip into a more restful sleep, I slid out of bed and went downstairs to work out some of my tension. Before I left the room, I left a note telling her where I was in case she woke in a panic needing me. I left the bedroom door open, as well as the basement door, so I could hear her if she cried out. I threw myself into my workout needing to release some of the tension I was holding in. I knew today would be another rough one, especially for Rabbit, and I needed to be as calm as possible for her.

Just as I was finishing and getting into the pool, I heard her moving around. I finished up, wrapped a towel around my waist and went upstairs, heading straight to the kitchen, ignoring my dripping legs. I smiled at the sight before me. There in the kitchen was Rabbit, in my shirt, rolling out pastry at the counter. Bear was lying on the floor not far from her and I could smell the aroma of coffee brewing.

"Hey, pretty girl."

She looked up from her task and smiled indulgently at me. I could see she was still exhausted. "Making your pies," she offered sweetly, indicating the pastry.

I moved forward and kissed her. "Thank you. I'll go grab a shower. Can I scramble some eggs for breakfast? I'd hate to interrupt the pie making."

She laughed quietly and nodded. I turned around to go to the bedroom and stopped at the table. I picked up a couple of small Ziploc bags and held them up. "What's this?"

The rhythmic sound of the rolling pin stopped. I looked over at her. "Rabbit?"

She walked over and took one bag from my hand. "These are the pills he was making me take that I told you about. I thought we could have them tested? Find out what they are?"

I nodded. We would definitely be having them tested. I held up the other bag. "And this?"

She leaned forward and took the bag from my hand. She gazed down at it for a moment quietly. When she spoke, her voice was shaking. "It's the remains of the blouse I was wearing the day I ran away. I found it. I don't remember why, but I had stuffed it, or at least part of it, in between the mattresses. When I saw it all the memories started coming back. I thought ... I thought it may be something Adam could use."

"How did you get it here?"

"I had it in my pocket. There wasn't a lot of it left but I brought it with me anyway, just in case."

I took it from her, opened the package and held it up. It had been torn badly but I could see what it was. I also realized I was looking at Rabbit's dried blood on it and my stomach clenched at the thought. I quickly folded it and put it back in the bag. I pulled her to me. "That was good thinking, Rabbit. I told you how smart you are."

"He ... he was so *angry*, Joshua. He was screaming and swearing. He actually spit on me, he was so out of control. I'm sure some of that is on the blouse ..." her voice trailed off.

I looked down at her. Tangible proof. DNA. She was smarter than she realized. People had seen her wearing that blouse just hours before she was 'taken'. And, it was evidence of her blood and probably *his* saliva, not a fictional stranger's.

I kissed her head. "You did it, Rabbit. You've nailed him."

⇒Chapter Thirty-Seven⇐

Joshua

I pulled Lizzy into my side a little tighter. I was trying so hard to refer to her by her real name, especially when other people were around. Although she would always be Rabbit in private and in my head, the name now felt very intimate to me and I wanted to keep it just between us as much as possible.

We were sitting around the table, introductions having been made and coffee poured. When Rabbit had first seen Adam get out of the car, she had backed away in instant panic. I had pulled her close, whispering comforting words into her ear as I felt her shake. Even I did a double take when I saw him. Easily seven inches taller than my six foot three inches, he towered above me and I was sure he looked like a giant to Rabbit. His shoulders were huge and powerful and his stride was confident and sure as he came towards us. But when he spoke and extended his hand to Lizzy and I, his voice was gentle and his demeanor one of kindness. He shook my hand first and then tentatively offered his hand to Lizzy. "I don't bite, Lizzy. You can ask my wife. She'll vouch for me." He smiled kindly at her and then winked. "I don't suggest you listen to my kids though, they exaggerate. Really, those are just little love nips on their feet." I felt Lizzy relax and watched as his huge hand engulfed her tiny one in a brief shake. She smiled shyly up at him and asked how many children he had and their ages. The next thing I knew she was beside him, walking ahead of me into the house, his wallet out showing pictures of his five children and telling her amusing stories. I looked over at Trevor, who shrugged. "Charmer," he mouthed. Cecilia shook her head, smiling, obviously used to Adam's ways.

"Where's Frank?" Lizzy asked quietly from her chair beside me at the table.

"He's coming in a separate car with Daniel," Cecilia smiled. "This one was not ... large enough ... for everyone."

Adam laughed. "You are being too polite, Cecilia." He turned to Lizzy. "My legs took up the entire back seat sitting sideways. Happens a lot."

We all chuckled. Trevor looked over to the counter and stood up. "Are those pies? Real *homemade* pies?"

I groaned. I knew I should have hidden them. "Back off. They're mine," I growled.

Rabbit sighed and shook her head, laying a hand on my arm "Yes, Trevor, and you can have some once they cool down. Joshua is only too pleased to share with his guests, aren't you?"

I opened my mouth to disagree but thought better of it when I saw the look on Rabbit's face. "Yeah, absolutely," I said grudgingly.

"Awesome. Do you have ice cream? Gotta have ice cream with pie," Trevor enthused, not at all put off by my tone.

I shook my head. "Nope. Guess you won't want any then."

Trevor laughed and reached for his phone. "Frank had to hang around and wait for Daniel. I'll get him to pick up some."

Damn it, apparently I was sharing, no matter what.

Rabbit leaned forward and kissed my cheek warmly. "I already hid one, Joshua. And, I'll make you more."

I beamed down at her and squeezed her gently at the waist.

Adam chuckled from across the table. Then he addressed Lizzy. "I was hoping I could speak with you privately, Lizzy, about your ... situation. Trevor has filled me in somewhat, but I have other personal questions I would like to ask you, if that's all right with you. I'm sure you have questions for me. Then maybe I can advise you on your options."

Rabbit nodded. "I want Joshua to stay, please."

Adam nodded, not seemingly surprised by her request. "Whatever you want, Lizzy."

It surprised me when Rabbit spoke up again. "I don't mind if Trevor and Cecilia are here either. They know most of the story. And, without their help I wouldn't be here now."

Again, Adam nodded.

Trevor and Cecilia stood up. "We'll go take Bear for a walk. When we come back, we'll just be here if you want us, okay?"

I was grateful knowing they were trying to make Rabbit feel safe and give her some privacy.

I nodded at them, smiling in quiet gratitude. "Bear will love the walk. We'll see when you get back, Cecilia."

Adam sat back, looking at Rabbit with both sadness and admiration in his expression. For the past hour and a half he had asked questions, listened to her answers, made notes, looked at the photos, her journal and, finally, the torn blouse and the bag of pills. Trevor and Cecilia had returned and joined us about thirty minutes ago and sat quietly sipping coffee, hearing for the first time about Lizzy's flight into the storm and what happened after she returned to Brian.

"You're incredibly strong, Lizzy. You've survived so much. I'd like to take you through your options and how to move forward. Legally. You have a tremendous amount of evidence here. We can have charges filed against Brian immediately, have a restraining order issued, as well as begin divorce proceedings."

We all looked at Lizzy, who was very quiet beside me. I was shocked when she shook her head.

"No charges, Adam."

I gaped at her. "Rabbit!" came out loudly before I could stop my reaction.

"No."

Adam held up his hand, effectively silencing me. "What do you want, Lizzy? You want a divorce?"

"Yes. And, the restraining order. I don't want him to be able to come near me. Or anyone else here."

He regarded her silently. "I have to ask again. Are you certain you don't want to press charges? You are absolutely certain about this? What do you want me to do with your evidence?"

Lizzy shook her head. "No. I want a divorce. I want him out of my life. I never want to see him again." She drew in a deep breath. "Use the evidence to get the divorce on my terms."

"Rabbit," I began, wanting to change her mind. I was still shocked at her announcement of not wanting to press any charges against him. Why was she doing this? I didn't understand.

She shook her head firmly. "No, Joshua. I've thought about this. What will it get me? A lot of press and more humiliation." She paused briefly, her voice trembling. "I'll have to relive it all, talk about it, be in a courtroom with *him* staring at me, listening to his lies, making me feel like nothing again." She stood up and began pacing, her hands wringing.

"I *can't* do that, Joshua. I don't *want* to." She stopped and stared at me beseechingly. "I know you're angry with me about this. Please don't be. I *can't*, Joshua. I just … can't." Her voice dropped. "Please understand. I just want to move forward with you. Please let me do that."

I stood up instantly, and pulled her into my arms. "Rabbit, I'm *not* mad. I could never be mad at you. I just hate to see him walk away after everything he put you through. He deserves to go to jail," I implored quietly.

Rabbit looked up at me. "I don't care what he does or where he goes as long as I'm not with him." Her eyes bore into mine. "As long as I'm with you."

I searched her eyes and then nodded in defeat. She had made up her mind. As much as I hated it, I would never force her to do something she didn't want to do. I would support her, no matter what.

Adam spoke up. "Lizzy, come back and tell me what your terms are. Let me help you. Can you do that?"

She nodded wearily. I held her a little tighter and then guided her back to her chair.

Adam smiled at her. "Thank you." He paused for a drink of coffee. "I would very much like to take your case and handle this scumbag for you."

Rabbit leaned tiredly against me, exhausted from the emotional conversation. I knew she couldn't take much more today.

At one point, earlier, I couldn't take her trembling anymore and had pulled her onto my lap quietly asking Adam for a break. He had immediately stood and gone down the hall. I heard the bathroom door close and knew he was allowing us a private moment. I had looked down into Rabbit's paler than normal face. "Do we need to stop, Rabbit? Is this too much?" I whispered into her hair as I gently ran my hands up and down her arms.

She shook her head. "No. I'm okay, Joshua. It's just so … difficult." She shrugged, unable to come up with the right word.

I kissed her forehead. "You're doing so well, Rabbit. It's almost over."

We had sat quietly, her head resting on my shoulder until Adam reappeared. He stood for a minute looking at us. "We can stop if you want," he had said kindly. "But if we can get all this out, we'll be ahead of the curve. Are you up for continuing, Lizzy?"

My girl nodded and, regretfully, I had let her move back to her chair.

Now I was regarding her with worry. I wasn't sure how *much* more she could take today.

"Tell me what you want, Lizzy," Adam urged quietly.

"I want a divorce; and I want it over as quickly as possible. I want Brian to go for counseling. And, I want a five million dollar settlement to go directly to the different organizations in Toronto that deal with abused woman and children."

"Why counseling instead of jail, Lizzy?"

She shrugged. "*If* he lost the case, and even with what we have it's still an *if*, what good would possible jail time do? Make him angrier and even more inclined to hurt people? Maybe with counseling he will realize what he has done, and, never do it to another person."

I pulled her closer. She had obviously been thinking about this a lot.

Adam looked at her quietly. "What if he refuses?"

Lizzy sighed in frustration. "Then I will let you press charges." She slumped forward. "But it's not what I want, Adam."

"Joshua is correct in his observations, Lizzy. You are a very smart woman." He tapped the small pile of evidence we had assembled. "And, he's right. Brian James is a bully. Unless I'm greatly mistaken, he'll do anything not to let this leak out."

Lizzy lifted her head. "I don't feel very smart. I should have figured out what was happening before I married him."

Adam shook his head. "Men like Brian James are skilled liars and brilliant manipulators." He paused. "I did some digging. There were rumors that Douglas James had refused to hand over the reins of the company until Brian settled down. I think he decided you fit the bill, so to speak. He went out of his way to get you and mould you into what he deemed appropriate. I don't think you stood a chance once he decided you were *it*."

Lizzy shook her head, her brow furrowed in confusion. "But he still didn't give him the company. Even after we were married. He constantly dangled the company in front of Brian and how he could take it all away from him."

Adam looked at her. "Settled down and produced an heir."

Lizzy shuddered. "That wasn't likely given our ... sleeping arrangements."

I tightened my hold on her hand in silent support. She hadn't talked about that much except to say they had separate rooms, and he never came near her after the first couple weeks.

Adam shrugged. "As I said, they were just rumors my people picked up. Could be nothing."

"What do you suggest, Adam?" Trevor asked.

Adam looked at us. "I draw up the divorce papers. I'll go to James and his lawyer privately with them. I will also have this," his hand picked up the bag with the blouse, "tested for DNA evidence. And have the pills analyzed. I'll show them what we have and tell them you want a fast, quiet divorce."

"What will you cite as cause?" I asked.

"Publicly; irreconcilable differences. It's vague enough. He and his lawyer will know the truth." He turned to Lizzy, hopeful. "Unless I can convince you to let me hit hard and fast?"

She shook her head. "No. I just ... want him out of my life. I don't want to ever see him again. You can use the evidence to threaten him, but not to prosecute him. Unless it's necessary."

He sighed. "And, you want no settlement for yourself? None? You deserve one, Lizzy."

She shook her head. "No. I want nothing monetary or material from him. I want my books. And the boxes of my parent's belongings. As well as one other thing."

I looked down at her. She hadn't mentioned anything else.

"I want it in writing that he will never come after me or any of the people who helped me get away. Especially Joshua. If he ever does, or I even suspect he does, then you release the evidence." She drew in a deep breath. "If he refuses, then you go public right away. I'll go to trial to protect Joshua, to protect them, if I have to. I want *them* safe. Use what I have to stop him from ever doing this again, Adam. Let him know he will be monitored." She leaned forward, her voice earnest. "Joshua told me he no longer had the power here, Adam. Make sure he knows that. That he'll *never* have that power again; over anyone. I want that taken away for good."

Adam's smile was wide. Leaning over, he took her hand. "You have yourself a lawyer. One way or another, he is out of your life, Lizzy. I'll do my damnedest to make sure he never comes near you again."

Lizzy sighed shakily and leaned into me heavily. I spoke quietly into her ear. "I think you need a break, Rabbit. Please?" Her tired nod was all I needed.

I stood up, taking her with me. "Excuse us," I murmured and walked to the bedroom with her tucked under my arm. Instantly, Bear was up following us. I helped Rabbit onto the bed and threw a blanket over her. Immediately, Bear jumped up, wrapping himself around her curled form. I patted his head. Then I leaned down and kissed her tenderly.

"I can't just lay here, Joshua," she whispered although her eyes never opened.

"Yes, you can. Frank and Daniel are on their way. Daniel will come in and see you when he gets here. I'll look after lunch. Please, Rabbit. You did so well, but now you need to rest, sweetheart," I praised her, softly nuzzling her cheek again.

"You're not angry with me?" she asked, and I could hear the vulnerability in her voice.

I leaned down and stroked her hair.

"No." I assured her. "This is your decision. If you are sure about this, then I will support you fully." I grimaced. "I would like the chance to beat the shit out of him, though. Maybe pay him a little visit as a surprise, give him a taste of his own medicine," I mused.

Rabbit's eyes flew open and she sat up. "No, Joshua! Promise me. He could hurt you. Please," she pleaded shakily.

I stared at her, instantly regretting my flippant words.

"Violence begets violence, Joshua. *I've had enough*. Please. Promise me you won't go after him. *Promise me*!" Her voice shook in terror.

I gathered her into my arms and rocked her. "I'm sorry, Rabbit," I apologized, my voice sincere. I soothed the hair back off her head and kissed her forehead. "I didn't mean it. I was just shooting my mouth off. I won't go after him. I promise."

She sighed shakily and relaxed into my arms. "Thank you."

"Rest now," I urged quietly, laying her down and pulling the blanket back around her huddled form.

"Only until Daniel gets here."

"Sure," I readily agreed, knowing I could keep the noise down, making sure she rested a little longer.

"Don't let me sleep long," she mumbled thickly.

I stood looking at her, already being pulled under by her exhaustion. She was so strong and compassionate, especially given what she had been through. I was filled with amazement that this lovely little woman was part of my life.

My brave Rabbit.

I shook my head.

She wasn't *part* of my life.

She *was* my life now. She was everything.

⁕

Adam was pounding away on his keyboard. Frank and Trevor were sitting and talking in front of the fire. Cecilia was trying to engage me in conversation, but I was distracted. Daniel was in with Rabbit and she had insisted she was fine alone. But my eyes kept straying down the hall to the closed door.

"Joshua."

I looked at Cecilia.

"She's fine," she reassured me. "She's in good hands. Daniel is checking her over. Just like you asked."

I nodded. "She's so tired, Cecilia. And ... there's something in her neck." I said quietly.

Adam's head snapped up. Both Trevor and Frank stood up and came over. I sighed. Apparently not as quietly as I thought.

"What do you mean, Joshua?"

Just then the door opened and Daniel came out. He sat down beside me and clapped me on the shoulder. "How is she, Daniel?" I asked anxiously.

He hesitated. "She's okay, Joshua. Her blood pressure is a little low and she is clearly exhausted. She is under-nourished which could account for both. Add the intense stress she has been under, her exhaustion is not surprising. But, I would feel better running a few tests on her."

"Her neck?"

"You were correct. Definitely not a tetanus shot. I suspect you may be right about what it is. I want to take an x-ray and do some blood work as well. I'll make the arrangements at the hospital. Can you get her there tomorrow?"

I nodded and started to speak when Bear suddenly tore down the hall, growling loudly. Then he launched himself at the window, barking furiously, deep snarling growls issuing from his throat in between the loud barks. We all stood up in unison and Trevor went over to the window.

"Fuck. Frank, didn't you shut the gate when you got here? Joshua, you still have that shotgun around?"

My stomach tightened at his tone.

"Yeah."

"You might want to get it. Brian James and his henchmen are standing out front."

⇒Chapter Thirty-Eight⇐

Joshua

A gasp came from behind me. I turned and saw Rabbit standing in the hall. Her hand was covering her mouth and her body was shaking violently. I held out my hand. "Come here, Rabbit." I turned to Frank. "The gun's in the mudroom closet. Bullets are on the shelf."

As soon as she was close, I wrapped my arms around her. "You are safe. I promise you. You are surrounded by people here who will protect you. Nothing, *nothing* is going to hurt you," I said firmly. Then, I cupped her face. "Nobody is taking you away from me. Understand?" She nodded, and I carefully wiped the tears away from her skin.

"How did he find me?" Her voice trembled.

I fingered the mark on her neck. I looked at Daniel. He nodded and shrugged. "I think … I think this is a tracking device chip, Rabbit."

Her hand flew up to the back of her neck and she became impossibly paler. Then I watched in horror as she began frantically clawing at her neck.

"Get it out! Get it out!" Her voice was high and sharp as her fingernails drew blood.

"Rabbit!"

"Get it out of me!"

My hand shot up, clamping down on her wrist, trying to stop her before she could do any more damage to her skin, but she pushed my hand away.

"NO! Get it out!" She was sobbing now, tears streaming down her cheeks as her fingers scrabbled and scratched at the chip beneath her skin. I reached for her hands again, pressing them down to her sides this time and then wrapping my arms around her.

"Stop! Stop it! Rabbit!"

"Get it out of me!" She struggled against me and I held her tighter. "Let go!" she yelled.

"No!" I yelled back. "I won't let you hurt yourself, Rabbit. I won't!"

At last it seemed my voice got through to her. She stopped struggling, her sobs slowed and her body slumped against mine.

"What did he do to me?" she whimpered. I couldn't answer her, not able to trust my own voice to be calm. I didn't want her to hear the fury I could feel boiling within me. I was struggling to keep my anger at Brian under control and I didn't want Lizzy to think that anger was directed at her.

I took a slow, deep breath and made sure my tone was soft, and then reached up to cover the bleeding spot with my hand, holding her tightly. "We'll get it out, Rabbit. We will. I promise you."

"Joshua ...?" Trevor's voice was quiet. I knew he was drawing my attention to our unwelcome guests outside, but right at that moment, Rabbit was my priority. I held up my hand, letting him know I'd heard, but my eyes stayed on the distraught woman in my arms.

Pressed against me, Rabbit's breathing was calming, her sobs coming to a slow stop. I kissed the top of her head. "I promise you Rabbit, we'll get it out. As soon as we can."

She nodded against me. "Good," she whispered. "I want it gone. I want *him* gone."

"We're working on that right now, Rabbit." I smiled grimly and ran my fingers along her cheek.

"Joshua?" Trevor's voice came again and I looked toward the window, watching that bastard James, as he came closer.

"I'm going to take care of him now, Rabbit. You go back into the bedroom. Take Bear with you."

She shook her head. "No. I can't, Joshua ... don't make me go sit alone. Please. I need to be with you."

I looked down at her pleading eyes. I looked over at Adam and Daniel, who were standing close. I could hear Frank loading the gun and Trevor trying to calm Bear while watching out the window. Daniel inclined his head slightly towards me. I looked down at Lizzy. "You don't leave Daniel's side, do you understand? You. Don't. Move."

She nodded and I leaned down and kissed her softly. Cecilia handed me my parka and I wrapped it around Rabbit. I looked over at Adam.

"Ready to start earning your retainer?"

He flashed me an evil smile, his facial expression serious and stern. Suddenly, I saw the brutal lawyer that went after abusive spouses. Frank stepped out of the mudroom. "Locked and loaded," he growled.

I threw Bear's lead at Trevor and heard the click as he snapped it on his collar.

I straightened my shoulders. Today was the day Brian James was removed from Rabbit's life for good.

"Let's show that asshole who he's dealing with."

Adam and I walked out first, Frank following. My eyes narrowed and I enjoyed watching the reaction as James took in the sight of Adam, and then Frank casually holding the rifle to his side. He certainly wasn't expecting either of those imposing men. His own eyes narrowed as he took in the familiar sight of Daniel, Cecilia and Trevor. His mouth lifted in a sneer as I saw him focus on Lizzy. He had advanced forward, but the other two men remained standing by their truck. I could clearly hear Bear's low, fierce growls behind me and I hoped Trevor had a tight hold of his lead. I wouldn't mind Bear injuring *him*, but I certainly didn't want Bear hurt.

"You're trespassing. Get off my property," I snarled.

Brian laughed snidely. "Ah, you're the mystery owner. Not until I get *my* property back."

"I have nothing of *yours*."

His hand lifted and pointed to Rabbit.

"You have my wife."

"She certainly isn't your *property*. Nor is she your wife."

"I have a marriage license that says differently."

Adam stepped forward. "Not for long."

"Who the fuck are you?" Brian snapped.

"I am Lizzy's legal counsel. I suggest you get in your car and leave the property, *immediately.* Advise your lawyer to be expecting a call from me."

Brian began to walk forward again. "Get in the fucking car, Elizabeth. I'll deal with you later. I have no idea what you have been telling these people to get them to band around you. Or how the fuck you got them to come get you." His gaze turned back to us. "But let me assure all of you, she isn't stable."

Behind me I heard Rabbit's frightened whimper, and Bear's low growls turned into loud, angry snaps of his jaws.

I extended my hand behind me in a comforting gesture to both of them as I stepped forward. I didn't want to take my eyes off the scum that was currently spoiling my yard. Adam stepped forward with me and I heard the unmistakable sound of the rifle being cocked.

"Stop, right *fucking* now," Frank spoke in a low deadly tone.

I stared at Brian with all the loathing and anger I felt bubbling up inside me. "You will never *deal* with her again. You will not come near her. You will not touch her. Ever again. She is perfectly stable, no thanks to you. And, she has recovered her memory. It's over, James."

"She's lying," he denied quickly.

"If you don't know what she said then how do you know? Lying about what?"

"Everything. She is lying about everything. She's mentally unstable. She can't tell delusion from reality. She's on medication."

I shook my head. "Only the unnecessary medication you forced on her. And guess what? She choked most of them back up. And, as for her *tetanus shot*? Bad idea, James. Just another piece of evidence for her lawyer to use against you."

For a few seconds, he looked uncomfortable. But, he recovered quickly. "I had to do that. She's given to wild accusations and wandering off. This isn't the first time she's made up some crazy story. I only had that put in so I could find her and stop her from spreading malicious lies."

I heard Rabbit's horrified gasp behind me. I'd had enough. "Stop demeaning her," I roared. "She is *not* unstable, you miserable excuse for a human being. Nor is she lying! The only unstable person around here is you. Now get the fuck off my property."

"I'm calling the police. You're holding my wife against her will," he bluffed.

I laughed. "Call them. Get them out here."

I was shocked when I heard Rabbit speak up and then felt her hand slip into mine. Her voice was frightened but I could hear the determination in it.

"He isn't holding me against my will, Brian. You know that. That's what you did. I'm not coming with you. I'm staying here with Joshua."

I looked down at her, squeezing her hand for support, wanting to be angry that she had ignored my instructions, but unable to do so. I knew she needed to do this; to stand up to her abuser just once. I could feel the tremors going through her body and I knew what an effort she was making right at this moment. Her shoulders straightened. "I want a divorce."

"No."

Adam stepped forward. In his hand was a copied montage of the pictures I had taken of Rabbit's injuries. "I think you may want to change your mind about fighting this, Mr. James."

Brian stepped forward and tore the sheet out of his hand. He studied it for a minute and looked up at us. Rage was rolling off him in waves and his stance was menacing. I watched his hand crumple the paper up into a ball as he stared. Rabbit cowered into my side and, gently, I pushed her behind me, keeping my hand on her the whole time.

"It's over, Mr. James," Adam stated in a strong voice. "This is only a small piece of the evidence we have of your abuse toward your wife."

"You fucking bitch," Brian seethed.

"If you have something to say to my client, you will address her respectfully or not address her at all. Am I clear on that?" snarled Adam, stepping forward. "Get in your car. Leave. Do it. *Now*."

Brian regarded Adam for a moment. "She's not worth it," he muttered and, shrugging, he turned around.

"That's where you're wrong," I hissed.

In an instant, he turned and lunged, his greedy hands reaching out for Rabbit. I reacted, pushing her back towards Daniel and tackling James down to the ground. All around me there was movement and gasps of surprise and shock, along with Bear's angry snarls. I stared down at him, rage seeping through me as I looked into his cold eyes. I watched him briefly, struggling for air against my arm that was pinned across his throat. I leaned down, pressing harder, glaring at him. My voice was rough. "I told you. You will *never* touch her again. You will *never* see her again. Your reign of terror over her is over. Accept it, because it's not going to change." I drew in a ragged breath, struggling to keep my promise to Rabbit. "Now, get the fuck off my property … before I do something I may actually regret."

I pushed myself off him, ignoring the ripple of pain that tore through my leg. Gasping for air, he sat up. I looked around at our odd stand-off. Not once had the men with Brian moved. A glance to my right told me why, though. Frank was standing straight, the butt of the rifle firm on his shoulder and the muzzle pointed straight at them in silent warning. Adam was beside me now and Daniel just behind him, holding a visibly shaking Rabbit upright. Trevor and Cecilia were behind them desperately trying to keep Bear from breaking loose.

I looked down at Brian. "Get up. Leave. Do what Adam said and tell your lawyer to wait for his call."

I started to turn and stopped, watching him struggle to his feet. "Don't you dare destroy anything of hers. Have someone pack up her books and get the boxes of her parents' belongings out of her closet. I don't want your hands touching what belongs to her. Adam will instruct your lawyer where to send them."

Turning, I met Rabbit's eyes and the shamed and fearful look in them pierced my soul. She had done nothing to be ashamed of.

Without thinking, I spoke, my hand reaching out to her. "It's okay, Rabbit. It's over."

A biting laugh had me turn. "Rabbit? Oh, that's fucking rich. Hope you don't expect her to fuck like one, because she's the lousiest lay I ever had," Brian sneered, his voice loud and cruel.

I didn't remember moving. The first hard punch caught him in the stomach and he stumbled back toward the truck as he was gasping for air. My hand grasped his hair, pulling his face up as the next punch landed square in the middle of his face. I felt the satisfying crunch of bone under my fist and felt the warm rush of blood as it spurted from his nose. As he fell, I grabbed him, forcefully throwing him onto his back on the damp ground as I fell with him, pinning one arm behind him. I smirked grimly as I heard the bone snap at the same time my knee drove agonizingly hard into his groin. I heard his sharp inhale of agony as the pain tore through him from different angles. Behind me, I heard Rabbit's wail of horror and felt Adam's arms wrap around my waist, wresting me away from Brian as he rolled onto his side, gasping in pain.

I pulled away from Adam, panting; struggling to calm myself. As much as I wanted to continue to beat him into a bloody, senseless pulp, and didn't regret my actions, I wouldn't hit him again. I had promised her, and Rabbit was right. She had already witnessed enough violence and she didn't need to see it from me as well.

But I wasn't done with him. I could use my words.

"How does that feel, hmm, James?" I snarled. "To be on the receiving end? I hope it fucking hurts, you worthless piece of humanity. I warned you, but you wouldn't listen, would you? You will *never* disrespect her in my presence again. If I hear that you've been belittling her anywhere, I'll fucking come after you. I will destroy you, you insignificant son of a bitch."

I crouched down on my haunches and stared at him. He glared back through the haze of pain, but I could see the cracks in his armour. Bullies never take on someone their own size. I spoke slowly and without hesitation.

"You may think you're a big man in your little world, James, but in the real world—out here? You're nothing. Just another businessman. Out in this world—*my* words carry weight. Thousands and thousands of people read what I write. You so much as look towards the place where she is or say *anything* derogatory about her or act like a bigger idiot than

I already think you are and try and stop this divorce? I will use my words to let the world know what a pitiful excuse for a human being you are, Brian James."

I leaned closer, dropping my voice. "I will use every bit of my arsenal to bring you down. My celebrity status, my reputation, my money; everything. I'll bring a shit storm of press down on you like you have never seen before. And everything; every goddamn twisted act you did to that perfect little person over there will come out. Everything. Your life, your precious reputation, your business will be worthless. No one will come near you." I leaned closer, my voice venomous. "I don't think your *daddy* will be very happy about that."

I saw the shadow that crossed his face and I knew I'd hit my mark.

I stood up. "You don't deserve to breathe the same air as she does. Now, for the last fucking time, get off my property."

I turned and walked over to Daniel. I bent down and swooped Rabbit's shaking form up into my arms and walked towards the house. She burrowed her face into my chest and I dipped my head to graze her crown with my lips.

Pausing, I turned around. Brian was struggling to get to his feet, his two sidekicks helping him. Blood dripped down his face onto his shirt and his one arm hung uselessly by his side. He was unable to stand up straight and was hunched over against the pain. But his stare was intense and filled with hate. I was stunned as I surveyed how much damage I had inflicted in a short period of time, yet I couldn't find it in myself to regret my actions. He deserved it. I wasn't concerned with any backlash from what I'd done to him; he knew the consequences if he ever talked. I met his glare steadily and I sneered at him meaningfully; he didn't look so tough now. I held Rabbit tighter, knowing he would see my arms flex. Knowing he would understand I *had* her and I wasn't letting her go. He'd never get to her again. "Frank, make sure they get off the property as soon as possible. Lock the gate."

I strode toward the house, pausing in front of Trevor. Bear was calmer now that Rabbit and I were in front of him. "Give me his lead, Trevor."

He handed it to me. "Come on, boy," I urged.

I walked in the house holding the two most important things in my life.

⇒Chapter Thirty-Nine⇐

Joshua

Cecilia and Daniel followed me in. I carried Rabbit directly into the bedroom and sat her on the bed. I pulled the parka off her shaking form. Daniel appeared beside me with a damp cloth and wiped away the dried blood from her neck, examining the site. While he was doing that I went and washed the blood off my hands, not wanting Rabbit to see it. Returning to the room, I winced when I saw the scratch marks she had inflicted on herself before I had managed to pull her hands away. Her appearance was almost frightening. She was so pale, her face haunted in its expression, and her lips ragged from where she had been chewing on them the entire time. She was shaking so hard, I sat down beside her needing to comfort her. The tension in her body made it impossible for me to draw her into my arms. "Rabbit," I soothed. "It's done. He won't be back. I promise." She didn't respond or relax. Nor did she raise her eyes to look at me.

I looked at Daniel, who mouthed 'shock' at me. He turned to Cecilia. "Get me something warm and sweet. Lots of sugar, not hot, just warm. Tea, coffee; whatever is fastest. Please."

She disappeared; returning quickly and Daniel knelt down in front of Rabbit with the mug in his hand. His voice was quiet and kind when he spoke. "Lizzy? I need you to drink some of this for me, okay? It will help you feel better. Please." He helped her by holding the mug and I watched her struggle to swallow the warm liquid, her eyes shut.

After a few minutes, she spoke. "Can you take this out, Daniel?" she whispered, her voice ragged as her hand went to her neck.

"Tomorrow, Lizzy. I'll arrange it for tomorrow when you're at the hospital for the other tests."

"Not today?" Her voice was almost plaintive and I looked at Daniel with concern. Had what just happened been too much for her to handle?

He shook his head. "It's going to require stitches, Lizzy. I don't have the supplies here."

"But you'll do it?"

He nodded. "I will. I'll introduce you to Dr. Woods, as well. She will take good care of you. You'll like her. Okay?"

Rabbit nodded but still didn't look up. "May I lie down, please?"

Something in her voice broke my composure and I stood up. "Excuse us."

They moved towards the door. Cecilia murmured something about getting food for everyone and Daniel placed his hand on my shoulder. "Patience, Joshua. She's very vulnerable right now," he instructed firmly. I nodded.

I closed the door after Cecilia and Daniel left and turned back to Rabbit. She had moved and was laying on the bed as far away as she could get from my side, curled into a small ball. Her eyes were shut and I could see her chest moving in small distressed breaths. I picked up the blanket and draped it over her. Bear jumped up and lay at the end of the bed watching her anxiously. Unsure, I knelt down. "Rabbit ... open your eyes, baby. Please."

Slowly they opened and I winced at the bereft, lost expression in them.

I slowly wrapped my hands around her cold ones, stroking them gently. "I'm sorry I broke my promise, Rabbit. But, I just reacted. Frankly, he deserved it with his offensive remarks. I won't stand by and listen to anyone degrade you," I insisted. "I tried to walk away; I didn't plan it. It just happened."

She nodded silently, her eyes still glazed over in anguish. I squeezed her hands and rested my forehead against hers. I heard her soft, stuttering sigh and I pulled back and looked at her, worried.

Her eyes dropped and I gently lifted her chin. "It's over, Rabbit. Done. You're safe now." I reached up and touched her neck. "This will be gone tomorrow. There will be nothing left of him. Nothing."

She stared at me, not saying anything. Then slowly her eyes shut.

"I'm tired, Joshua," she whispered. "Can I go to sleep now?"

I felt my throat tighten. "If that's what you want, of course, Rabbit." I paused. "Do you want me to stay with you?"

I was surprisingly hurt by the small shake of her head. I stood up, unsure what to do next, "I'll, ah … I'll be down the hall if you need me." I turned to leave and felt her hand grab mine.

"I love you, Joshua. So much. I just … so awful … I just need … a little time …" the last word was broken off with a small sob.

Swiftly, I leaned down, kissing the tears that were silently sliding down her cheeks, feeling both resigned and relieved. She just needed a few minutes alone. She wasn't rejecting me. I needed to understand that she needed a little time to process what had happened.

"I love you as well, my Rabbit. I'm right here, and I'm not going anywhere." I gently pulled the blanket up around her, kissing her forehead before I left the room quickly, fighting to keep my own emotions under control.

⸻ ••◦◖◗◦•• ⸻

"I made Rabbit a sandwich." Cecilia offered me the plate.

I shook my head. "I don't think she'll eat it, Cecilia. She, ah, she wants to be alone right now." I half-heartedly lifted my own sandwich up and then put it back down. I didn't have any appetite either.

Cecilia's hand covered mine. "Today has been a very stressful day for her, Joshua. The shock alone of him showing up here would have unnerved her sufficiently. Never mind all the awful things he said."

I nodded. "She won't look at me, Cecilia. I don't understand why."

She sighed. "I have a suspicion as to why, Joshua." She stood up. "I'm going to go and take her this." I watched her pick up the sandwich and go down the hall.

Pushing my plate away, I stood up. Daniel was on the phone and I could hear him making the arrangements at the hospital for Lizzy the next day. Trevor was looking out the window. Adam was upstairs, his fingers busy on the laptop and his Bluetooth getting a workout. I heard 'restraining order' and knew he was moving full steam ahead. "Where's Frank?" I asked.

Trevor looked at me. "Having a nap."

"A nap?"

He nodded.

"We doubt he'll return, Joshua. He knows the truth is out there now. The gate is locked and you have the security cameras on, but we just want to make sure and be prepared. Frank and Adam are staying behind.

They'll take turns being awake and alert until tomorrow. One of them will stay behind when you go to the hospital with Lizzy tomorrow." He paused. "You are planning on going with her, right?"

I looked at him. It hadn't even occurred to me I wouldn't be. Beside her was exactly where I would be, no matter where it was. No matter how hard it was to do it, I was going with her. I nodded.

"How do we know he's not just pulled off somewhere down the road?" I wondered out loud. I was startled when I felt Adam's huge hand settle on my shoulder. For someone so large, he was remarkably quiet.

He chuckled. "Let's just say Brian James isn't the only one who knows about tracking devices, Joshua."

I gaped at him. "You planted something on him?"

Adam shook his head. "Tsk, Joshua. I am an officer of the court. That would be illegal. I wasn't the one who made sure he had enough strength to get in the truck and helped to hoist him up."

I looked at him, noticing the twinkle in his eye. "Frank?" I asked.

He waggled his eyebrows at me and shrugged. "I have it on good authority that the truck left the property and has yet to stop. My educated *guess* is they are heading to the airport and are planning on leaving directly from there."

His face turned serious. "How is Lizzy?"

I shook my head. "Broken."

Daniel came over. "Give her time, Joshua. Today was a massive shock and she was already struggling. Everything is set for tomorrow. I'll meet you at ten. Just let her be for today. She may act out of character or she may rebound quickly and seem okay later. But let her feel what she is feeling."

I nodded in understanding.

He moved forward and looked at me. "I suggest you get some rest yourself. You look like shit."

I couldn't help but grin. "Is that your medical opinion? Or just a friendly observation?"

He chuckled. "Both. Do you want me to look at your leg?"

I shook my head. "No, it's just strained. I'll take some painkillers and soak it in the tub."

Beside me, Adam laughed lowly. "It's not used to you using it as a weapon, Joshua? I have to say, that was a rather impressive display out there. Remind me not to get you angry with me."

I shook my head. "I shouldn't have lost my temper like that. I'm afraid I've frightened Rabbit now. He was just so fucking …" my voice trailed off as I searched for the right word.

"Vile." Adam finished for me.

I nodded.

"He deserved what he got. And then some, in my opinion. You were defending her, Joshua. She knows that. I think she is just reacting to the entire fucked-up situation here. I highly doubt she is frightened of you," Adam offered in comfort.

Daniel nodded. "I agree; her body language was that of emotional pain, not fear, Joshua. Give her some time to process what happened. Talk to her."

I smiled grimly at both of them. "I will."

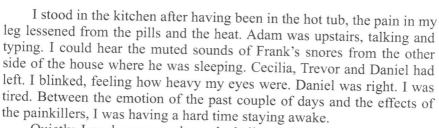

I heard Cecilia come down the hall and I turned, watching her go to the sink with an uneaten sandwich and the glass of milk she had taken to Rabbit. I grimaced, knowing she hadn't been able to get Rabbit to eat anything. I left the others discussing the plans for the rest of the day and went over to Cecilia. She looked up as I approached and I saw the glimmer of tears in her eyes.

I grabbed her arm. "What? What did she say?"

She looked at me and shook her head. "I got her to talk to me a little, Joshua. I won't break her confidence. Be patient. She'll tell you." Her voice lowered. "She's going to need some support that only you can give her."

"She'll have it, no matter what," I insisted.

Cecilia smiled. "I know that, Joshua, it's just sometimes a woman needs … reassurance, okay? What might seem insignificant to one person can be … devastating to someone else."

I was confused. But I nodded anyway.

I stood in the kitchen after having been in the hot tub, the pain in my leg lessened from the pills and the heat. Adam was upstairs, talking and typing. I could hear the muted sounds of Frank's snores from the other side of the house where he was sleeping. Cecilia, Trevor and Daniel had left. I blinked, feeling how heavy my eyes were. Daniel was right. I was tired. Between the emotion of the past couple of days and the effects of the painkillers, I was having a hard time staying awake.

Quietly, I made my way down the hall and slipped into the bedroom. Rabbit was still curled up under the blanket. The late afternoon sun was around the front of the house, leaving the bedroom bathed in a dim light. Sighing, I crawled onto the bed; desperately wanting to feel Rabbit close to me but unsure if she would want that right now. Tentatively, my hand reached out and stroked her hair that lay across the pillow, softly caressing her head and down into the thick tresses. She sighed and rolled over, fitting herself against me. I smiled in relief as one hand found its usual purchase on my shirt, anchoring herself to me. My arms wrapped around her, drawing her closer, and she burrowed into my chest and quietly breathed my name. I nuzzled my face into her fragrant smelling hair and finally allowed myself to relax. I drifted into sleep surrounded by her warmth.

The room had darkened into early twilight when my eyes opened again. I looked down and was immediately caught in the vivid gaze of Rabbit's stare. Leaning down, I grazed her lips with mine.

"Hi," I said warily.

Her answering smile was timid, her eyes troubled. Frowning, I cupped her cheek. "Tell me. Please. Did I frighten you, Rabbit?"

Her eyes widened. "No. You defended me. I know you didn't plan that, Joshua. I also know it's not in your nature to be violent with another person."

I nodded in relief. "Tell me then. What is it?"

She regarded me guardedly. "It seems to me that I'm a lot of trouble," she whispered, her voice shaking. "Are you sure … I'm worth it?"

I stared at her aghast.

Was she worth it?

Before I could answer her, she continued. "I don't have anything to offer you."

"Stop it." My voice was firm. "Rabbit, did you not hear me out there? You are *everything* to me. I will do anything for you. You don't have anything to offer? You have given me more in the short time I've known you than you realize. You have brought so much to my life. Look at what I overcame because of your love and support. Please, don't question how vital you are to me now."

"But am I … enough?"

I stared at her unable to figure out what she was saying. "Enough?" I repeated.

Her eyes looked away. "Am I enough … good enough for you … everywhere, Joshua?"

Now I was totally lost.

"Rabbit, I need you to tell me what you're thinking. What are you trying to ask me?"

She spoke so quietly I could barely hear her. "I know I don't have much experience in some areas, do I … satisfy you, Joshua?"

My eyes widened in sudden, painful understanding. Two things crashed into my brain at the same time. The sneering comments Brian made and Cecilia's quiet 'women need reassurance.' Brian had publicly degraded and humiliated her. Rabbit was questioning her ability to satisfy me sexually.

I stared down at her in disbelief. She could even question herself? After all we had shared? The passion she ignited in me? It was so ludicrous I wanted to laugh, but I could see the pain and doubt in her eyes.

I sighed sadly. Just as my words had hit the mark with Brian, his degrading ones had found a way inside her head.

I thought back, remembering our first time. Rabbit's tentativeness in returning my kisses, her hesitancy to touch me, how her hands had trembled and fumbled the first few times we had been together. But it had been endearing, her passion had been warming and she had responded so eagerly. She was a warm, giving lover.

"Rabbit," I began soothingly, leaning down close, my fingers stroking her cheek. "You are more than enough." My fingers lifted her chin. "The way you respond to me? The way you make me feel? There aren't enough words, Rabbit, to express what you do to me, body *and* mind."

She still looked unsure.

"Am I satisfied? Sexually? That's what you're asking me?"

A small tilt of her head indicated her answer. I drew in a deep breath. I was not going to let her dwell on this. "Your lovemaking more than fulfills me, but I need to be honest. No, I'm not satisfied."

Her eyes widened. Leaning down, I kissed her warmly, capturing her gaze with mine. "I will never be satisfied, Rabbit. Before we have finished making love, I want you again. When I watch you make one of your delicious pies, I want you. When you laugh or scowl at me, I want you. Fiercely. Christ, don't even get me started on how I feel when I see you curled up in the chair wearing my shirt. I can hardly fucking see straight. I'm surprised I haven't taken a header down the stairs yet. And just thinking of you sitting in the hot tub, your skin wet and glistening …" I groaned deeply and squeezed her chin lightly, my forehead resting on hers. "All the time, Rabbit. I want you all the time. And *every* time you are *more* than enough."

"He always said I was cold. Unresponsive and awkward. The few times we tried it was … awful. He said it was my fault. That I was frigid and not stimulating. And … you heard what he said earlier," she whispered. "I didn't have very much experience before him … and I had never, ah … really enjoyed myself …" her voice trailed off.

"He said a lot of really inane things out there. None of which I or *anyone else* paid any attention to, Rabbit. Don't let him do this, baby. Don't let him get to you."

I cupped her face and kissed her deeply, again and again, until she was breathless. "You are, without a doubt, the most innately sensual lover I have ever been with, Rabbit. If you didn't respond to him then the problem was *his*, not yours. I have no doubt he was a selfish bastard."

I kissed her again. "I've felt things with you I've never felt before. You've taken me places I've never been, Rabbit." Again our lips met, softly, sweetly moving together. "And I want you to take me there again."

I held her closely for a minute, giving her a chance to think about what I'd said. "It doesn't matter that you don't have a lot of experience. In fact, I'm rather grateful for that. I get to discover all of this with you. And if you're telling me I'm the first man to give you an orgasm, then I am beyond thrilled." I tapped my chest, waggling my eyebrows at her. "I'm rather possessive when it comes to you."

I was pleased to hear her soft giggle. Leaning closer, I nipped at her ear. "In fact, I'd be *thrilled* to show you again … just how unsatisfied I am when it comes to you," I whispered, pressing my growing erection against her leg.

She looked up at me, surprised.

I raised an eyebrow at her. "I told you, Rabbit. Never enough."

"But there are people here," she protested half-heartedly.

I slid my hand up her side, caressing her soft skin under her shirt. "I can be very quick and very quiet, my sexy little Rabbit. But I promise to be thorough. How about you? You wanna be *naughty* with me?" I whispered lowly, desperately wanting her to forget about everything but us for a few sweet moments. I wanted her to feel how good we were together. I wanted her to smile and feel me loving her.

And most of all, I wanted her to forget the cruel words flung her way earlier and to know that they were just empty lies told by a desperate man who wanted to inflict pain on her one last time.

Her eyes glowed in the dim light and I watched her lips curve into a smile. I smiled back before capturing her mouth with mine.

And then, quietly, thoroughly and *not* very quickly, I made her mine, happily swallowing her cries of ecstasy deep within myself, keeping them private and safe. I loved her with everything I had until she knew, without a doubt, that she was more than enough.

She was everything.

⇒Chapter Forty⇐

Joshua

My breathing was harsh and its sound filled the cabin of the truck. I looked down at my hands which were clasped so tightly on the steering wheel in front of me, that my knuckles were white. The key sat in the ignition, just waiting for me to turn it and start the engine, but I couldn't. I was desperately fighting for control, feeling confused and angry at myself.

I had done this once before. I had left the confines of my property to go and get Rabbit. I should be able to do it again.

I could feel the beginnings of a panic attack starting and I closed my eyes, trying to concentrate on slowing down my breathing. The feeling of Rabbit's arms coming around me from the back seat was a welcome comfort and I released the steering wheel, instead grabbing onto her forearms and holding her against me.

Adam's voice from the passenger side startled me. "You know, Joshua, I'm not an expert or anything but it seems to me the most important thing here is getting Lizzy to the hospital. Does it really matter if you are the one behind the wheel?"

I shook my head silently.

"Do you think that will help? If he wasn't trying to drive?" Rabbit asked, her voice close enough to my ear for her breath to tickle my earlobe.

"He did okay last time, when someone else took the responsibility of removing him from the property. Maybe it's just a matter of baby steps and this is too much all at once. Maybe if he sat in the back with you and I drive, it would work. You want to try that, Joshua?"

I forced my eyes open and looked over at Adam. His eyes regarded me with nothing but kindness and concern. I looked in the rear view mirror and was met with Rabbit's love-filled but worried eyes. Her arms tightened around me and I nodded. Adam was right. The most important thing was getting her to the hospital. As long as I was by her side, it didn't matter how we arrived. I unclipped my seatbelt and slid out of the driver's seat and into the back with Rabbit. Adam slid his seat forward, and came over to the driver's side and climbed in. Wordlessly, I moved to the other side to give him enough room to move the seat back. As he got comfortable, I pulled Rabbit into my shaking arms, burying my face in her neck. "I'm sorry," I breathed into her soft skin. She shook her head.

"No," she whispered fiercely, running her fingers through my hair. "I feel better in your arms anyway."

The truck lurched forward and I wrapped myself around Rabbit even tighter, shutting my eyes as I had done in the chopper the day we went to find her. This time, I had her sweet voice in my ear, telling me how much she loved me, how proud she was of me, to concentrate on. Her words and touch were comforting and I relaxed a little into the seat, keeping her close. I heard the sound of the gate opening in front of us and I began to tense, my breathing picking up again.

Without warning, Rabbit's words stopped and her mouth crashed onto mine. Startled, I gasped and instantly her tongue was inside my mouth softly stroking as her hands wound into my hair, holding me tight. Groaning, I gave myself up to the taste and heat of her, kissing her back with everything I had, lost in the kaleidoscope of feelings she brought out in me. Finally breaking apart, both of us gasping for air, I lifted my head. My property, my safe haven, was far behind me. And, I was surprisingly okay. In fact, I was way better than I had been a few minutes ago when I was thinking of leaving the property. Looking down, I smiled warmly into Rabbit's sweet face, my thumb tracing her swollen lips. "Nice diversion tactic, Rabbit."

Up front, Adam laughed. "I think your sidekick status just got a permanent check mark, Lizzy." Then his voice became serious. "I know this is a big thing, Joshua. I think the key may be having the actual leaving taken care of by someone else for a while. Give yourself time to adjust and work up to it. One step at a time."

I nodded, once again dropping my face into Rabbit's neck. Her arms tightened around me again and I was content to remain like that for the drive. I still had to face walking into the hospital and being in an unfamiliar environment.

"Joshua?" Rabbit's voice was a pleasant hum in my ear.

"Hmm?"

"Did you have some exercises, maybe … like some positive thoughts or something you used to do with Maggie when she was helping you to be able to leave the house the first few times?"

I nodded.

"Maybe you could try and use them again. I can help you, if you want."

I looked up at her in wonder. "You are so clever, Rabbit," I whispered. "Having you in my arms already helps more than I can tell you." Leaning back, I took her with me, pushing her head gently onto my chest. I concentrated on my breathing and reached into my memory, finding the phrases and key words I used to practice with Maggie as I took the steps to leave my front door. I began to recite them in my head, and their familiarity helped to ease the panic I was feeling. Keeping Rabbit close, I opened my eyes and watched the vista fly past; my heartbeat slowly returning to normal.

I had to do this. I could do this.

For Rabbit.

Daniel met us at the door of the hospital. Seeing him in his doctor's garb and feeling the sudden tremor that went through Rabbit reminded me of exactly why we were here. For her. Holding onto the thought of her needs, I was able to pull her off my knee and get out of the truck fairly easily. I held out my hand and helped her down, then wrapped my arm around her, keeping her close, as we followed Daniel through the maze of hallways, Adam right behind us.

Daniel led us to a small office and examination room, while Adam remained outside in the waiting area. He sat down behind the desk and indicated we should sit as well. Rabbit looked around confused.

"What is it, Lizzy?" Daniel asked kindly.

"I thought you ran a private care home, but you work here?" she asked.

He smiled. "I own it, but my wife actually runs the home. I am the primary care physician there and I maintain an office here. I'm only here three days a week and when I occasionally cover for other doctors. I've always been very interested in geriatric medicine. The home and making sure the people there get the best attention is my main focus."

Rabbit nodded in understanding.

"Okay, Lizzy, how are you feeling?"

"Better. Calmer."

"Good. Today, I am going to do a few tests, along with some blood work and we'll get that chip out of your neck. It'll be just a small incision but it'll be sore for a few days. I'll have to put one or two stitches in it that you'll need to have removed. Dr. Woods will come around and I'll introduce you to her. If you like her, she'll set you up with an appointment for a full physical. Does that sound okay?"

Rabbit nodded and I squeezed her hand gently in silent support.

"I will have a nurse in with us at all times. It's up to you if you want Joshua in the room with you as well."

I looked over at Rabbit. It was her call. I would do whatever she wanted. She smiled nervously at me. "I think I need to do this myself. But if I needed him to come back in he could?" she asked quietly.

"Without question."

I saw her deep breaths and how she seemed to steel herself, straightening her shoulders. "All right."

I smiled. My brave girl.

Daniel stood up. "Let's get started then."

<hr />

I sat beside Adam, nervously watching the door. Daniel's office was in a relatively quiet part of the hospital but there were still a fair number of people around. Before I left the office, Dr. Woods came in and introduced herself to Lizzy and me. She was an older woman, tiny in stature, but with a firm handshake and kind, knowing eyes. I had left then to give them some privacy and when the doctor came out, she stopped and shook my hand saying she would see me when Lizzy came back next time. Her eyes had widened when she took in the appearance of Adam beside me. I did a quick introduction and her eyes narrowed as she stared up at him. "You're going after the bastard who did all this?" she asked. He nodded silently. She handed him her card. "If you need something, let me know. Nail him." She looked over at me and smiled. "I'll take good care of her, Joshua." She turned and walked away quickly. Adam looked at me. "I like her. Little fireball," he chuckled. I agreed. Daniel had done well in choosing a doctor for Rabbit.

I was surprised a few minutes later to see Dave come around the corner talking with a tall woman. He headed directly for me with his hand outstretched. "Joshua!"

I stood up and shook his hand. He introduced the woman beside him as Trina, the new head of the psychiatry department in the hospital. We conversed briefly and it struck me that this part of the hospital was an unusual place for him to be. When I questioned him, he had the grace to look slightly embarrassed.

"Did Daniel ask you to 'bump' into me?" I asked, feeling both slightly annoyed yet grateful.

Dave nodded. "Joshua, I would never have thought I would see you standing here in the hospital of your own volition. It's an amazing breakthrough for you."

"It's not that easy, Dave."

He regarded me. "No, I don't imagine it is. But perhaps a great stepping stone to continuing?"

Suddenly, it was all clear. I turned to Trina. "It would seem a meeting has been orchestrated here."

She smiled, her dark eyes flashing with both humour and understanding. "I'm aware. When I heard your story, I really wanted to meet you. I asked Dave to 'arrange' an introduction." She stepped forward. "I knew Maggie O'Donnell well. She was a great doctor and a mentor to me."

I regarded her quietly for a minute and made a decision. It was time to try again. "Maybe we should sit down and talk later, get to know one another a little."

Her smile was brilliant. Her card appeared in my hand with her private contact information, and after a few more pleasantries, she and Dave walked away.

I sat down heavily. Today was turning into a long roller coaster ride of emotion and I was starting to feel overwhelmed.

Beside me, Adam spoke up. "Big day, Joshua."

I nodded silently.

"It's good to have friends that care enough about us that they are willing to risk our anger to help, isn't it?" he stated mildly.

I looked over at him. I had done the same with Rabbit; bringing him in, hoping against hope she would let him help her. And, she had.

I smiled. "Yeah, Adam. It's a very good thing."

⇒•••●❂●••⇐

Adam looked down at his phone at an incoming text message and then exploded in sudden anger.

"Motherfucker! I thought he was smarter than this. Goddamnit! What the fuck is he thinking?" His voice was low and furious as he stood up.

I looked at him in concern. "What happened?"

"Brian fucking James. That's what just happened."

243

I stood up, immediately anxious. "What?"

"Papers just arrived at the office. Divorce papers."

"Wow, that was fast."

"Charging Lizzy with adultery."

My anger was as instant as his. "Fucker," I swore. "What is he up to?"

"I have no idea. But, I'm going to find out. I need to go somewhere private. Excuse me."

I watched him walk down the hall and speak to a nurse who pointed to a door further down the hall. Adam disappeared through it, shutting the door loudly.

I sat down, my mind racing. What was he up to? Charging Lizzy with adultery? Still playing games? I shook my head. Why? To try and make himself look good?

I was distracted from my thoughts as the nurse who took Rabbit's blood earlier appeared and went into Daniel's office. A few minutes later, she came out and hurried away, reappearing shortly with some sort of machine. Not long after, I watched Dr. Woods enter the office. I stood up, growing concerned. Had there been problems with removing the chip? Was Rabbit okay? My anxiety grew to another level as I saw yet another doctor enter the office. I could feel my panic growing. Rabbit had been in there for almost an hour. Daniel had said it could be done very quickly. What was taking so long? Something had to be wrong.

I began pacing then walked over to the door, trying the handle. It was locked. I could see the swipe card box beside the door, which was how the staff was entering the room, but I had no access. I knocked, but no one came to the door. I walked down the hall, planning on asking someone to call Daniel, but the desk was now empty. Across the hall, I could hear Adam's muted voice still talking in short angry sentences. I paced a while longer, keeping my eye on Daniel's door, occasionally pulling on my hair in frustration. I had just about reached my limit and, as I stood unsure what to do next, I heard footsteps and saw Dr. Woods and the other doctor walking down the hall. I hurried towards them. "What's wrong? Is Rab ... Lizzy okay?"

Dr. Woods put a comforting hand on my arm. "She's fine, Joshua. Dr. Tate just had a few things to discuss with me and my colleague. He'll be out to collect you in a minute." Her fingers found my pulse and she frowned. "I think maybe you need to sit down, Joshua. Your pulse is racing."

"Is it out? Is the chip out?" I asked, shrugging off her concern.

"Ah, almost."

I looked at her, stunned. "What's going on?"

She took me by the arm and led me back to the waiting area which was still deserted, thankfully.

"Everything is fine, Joshua. Daniel will be out in a minute. Calm down. Lizzy is fine. I assure you."

I searched her eyes, desperately looking for a sign she was lying to me, but her gaze reflected nothing but calm assurance. I let out the breath I didn't realize I was holding in and my head sank into my hands in relief. For one awful moment I thought something had happened and I had lost Rabbit.

"You care very deeply for her, don't you?"

I lifted my head and nodded. "More than I can express."

She smiled. "That is a precious gift. Always treasure it. Ah, here is Daniel." She stood up. "Take care of her, Joshua." She went over, speaking quietly to him and then continued down the hallway. I watched Daniel approach. His face was calm but serious. Every instinct was telling me something was wrong, despite what Dr. Woods had said. Why hadn't the chip been removed yet?

"Come into my office, Joshua."

Wordlessly, I followed him, my heart in my throat. I sat down at his desk, noticing Rabbit wasn't in the room. "Daniel?"

"She's fine, Joshua. She is still in the examination room. You can go see her in a minute."

"Why isn't the chip out?"

"It is now." He leaned over and held up a small vial. "I assume her lawyer will want this."

I took the vial and placed it in my pocket. "Why the delay then?"

He leaned back. "There was a ... surprise with one of the test results. I had to do some follow-up tests to check on it."

"What sort of surprise?"

He shook his head. "That is private and up to Lizzy to share." His hand indicated the door. "Go and see her. I'll be right here." He smiled at me widely. "I'm sure you'll have ... questions."

I looked at him, confused. I needed to see for myself that Rabbit was okay.

I pushed the door open and went in. Rabbit was seated on the table, wearing a gown, her hair in a messy bun on the top of her head. I could see she had been crying and I went over, immediately wrapping her in my arms. She was trembling slightly. I could see the small bandage on the back of her neck, a bruise already forming on the area. I gritted my teeth together in anger. The fucker had caused yet another mark on her. I pulled away and kissed her. "Are you in pain?" I asked gently.

She shook her head, but the tears in her eyes were fresh. "What is it,

Rabbit?"

I looked down and saw she was clutching something in her hands. Reaching down, I tugged on the small piece of paper, but she refused to relinquish it. I couldn't tell what it was but I knew it had something to do with why she was upset. I looked in her eyes and was confused at her expression. She wasn't upset as much as almost hopeful and yet nervous looking. "Rabbit?"

Her voice was shaking. "Joshua ... I'm pregnant."

My entire body locked down. The room faded away as I struggled to remain calm.

Rabbit was pregnant.

Visions and thoughts flew through my head.

So thin. She had been so thin when I found her. She couldn't have been pregnant then. Could she?

That meant she was very newly pregnant.

My eyes shut as I realized what it meant.

Brian James had forced himself on her while she was there.

When I had sent her back to him. He had done this to her. Because of me.

I felt the bile rise in my throat and felt my hands clench at my sides. My breath was coming out in small angry gasps. I felt Rabbit's free hand cup my face and her voice pleading with me. "Joshua, please."

Instantly, I was ashamed. She needed me. I needed to be strong for her.

I opened my eyes and looked into her now frightened gaze. Everything else faded away except for one thing. Rabbit needed me. I loved her. I made a decision.

"Do you want to keep this baby?" I asked quietly.

She looked shocked. "Of course I do, Joshua! You don't understand! I need to tell you ..." her voice trailed off as I placed my fingers on her lips silencing her.

"Then I will love this child like it's my own," I vowed.

Her eyes widened and more tears fell down her cheeks. She pushed my hand away.

"Joshua, it *is* yours." As she spoke she shoved the paper in my hand.

I looked down, confused. I had no idea what I was looking at. I looked up at her, hating to dash the hope I saw in her eyes, knowing she didn't want to tell me what had transpired. I shook my head. "I can't have children, Rabbit."

She shook her head right back at me. "Then it's the second coming, Joshua. I know what you're thinking. But Brian didn't touch me while I was there. I swear he didn't. He hasn't touched me since the first couple weeks of our marriage. The only person I have been with is you."

I stared at her, unable to process what she was saying. He didn't touch her?

Her hands came up, cradling my face. "I love you so much knowing you would stand by me and love someone else's baby, Joshua. But the baby is yours."

"How?"

My thoughts were chaotic and I lifted my hands to her arms, grasping them. I didn't understand. The baby was mine? How? Was it possible?

God, I wanted it to be possible.

Rabbit's hands stayed on my cheeks, her thumbs constantly stroking in small circles of comfort. She smiled, keeping her tear-filled eyes on mine.

"Rabbit, I can't ... they *told* me I can't ..."

Her eyes were shining and her smile widened as another single tear slipped over her cheek.

"Yes, Joshua, you can."

She took my hand and I watched as she placed it over her belly, holding it there. "You *did,* Joshua."

I felt like all the breath had been knocked from my body, like I'd been hit with a wrecking ball. I couldn't form words or thoughts; all I could do was stare at my shaking fingers as they spread wide over her tiny form, rumpling the thin cotton of the hospital gown.

"How?"

I lifted my bewildered eyes to her again. Keeping my gaze, she called out calmly for Daniel. A moment later, I felt his comforting hand on my shoulder.

"Sit down before you fall down, Joshua. We've had enough surprises today."

Reluctantly, I moved my hand from Rabbit's belly and lowered myself shakily onto the examination table beside her. I looked at Daniel.

"I don't understand. They said there was too much damage after the attack. That I would probably never father a child," I recited what I had been told like it was gospel.

Daniel smiled. "The key word there is probably, Joshua. It was never conclusive. And, you never pursued it did you? Did you have any other tests done?"

I shook my head. I had been too overwhelmed with everything else that was happening at the time to pursue anything.

"When we got the blood test results, I had the OB-GYN come and do the transvaginal ultrasound immediately. Lizzy is roughly five weeks pregnant. Doing the math, I would say she was with you at that time."

I stared at him, trying to comprehend what he was saying.

Rabbit was pregnant.

With *my* child.

Our child.

I was going to be a father.

I looked at her, staring back at me with nothing but love and joy in her eyes, waiting for me to come to terms with the information I had just been given. I stared down at the photo in my hand. The little blurry blip on the paper was my child. I felt my eyes fill with tears, and ignoring the fact that Daniel was still there, pulled Rabbit into my arms, weeping with joy.

Laughing and crying, I looked up after a minute as he stood, grinning widely at us.

"Is everything okay? Are they all right?"

Daniel smiled. "All looks well, Joshua. I want Lizzy resting and eating more. Her body has been through a lot of emotional and physical trauma so we want to give her a chance to recuperate and get stronger. The OB-GYN as given her a prescription for some vitamins. They'll do another ultrasound in a few weeks and give you some more definite dates." He clapped me on the back. "This most definitely explains the exhaustion. You need to take care of her, Joshua."

I nodded, burying my head in Rabbit's neck.

"I'll take such good care of both of you, Rabbit," I promised fervently.

"I know you will. You already do," she responded.

I tightened my arms. I had so many questions. I looked up at Daniel again. He smiled in understanding.

"I'll come see you both in a couple of days, and answer all your questions. Take her home. Celebrate this miracle."

I nodded and held out my hand. Daniel shook it firmly. "Congratulations, both of you."

He left, closing the door behind him. We sat quietly for a moment.

"I would have told you," she whispered.

I pulled away and looked down at her.

"Rabbit?"

"If he had done that. I would have told you."

I stroked her cheek. "I thought you were trying to protect me."

Her voice was soft. "You would have still loved it?"

I nodded. "The baby would still have been part of you, Rabbit. How could I not?"

She smiled tenderly, turning to kiss my palm.

"The baby is a part of *us,* Joshua."

I smiled widely, still overwhelmed with the news and nodded. "Us."

I stood up. "Let's go home. You need to rest and I need to cook you some more steak."

Rabbit smiled and then her face turned serious. "I think we have things we need to talk about."

I nodded. "We do. But not today. Today is all about you, me, and this little miracle blip I'm already in love with."

Rabbit sighed and smiled, her eyes shining. "Then take *us* home, Joshua."

I smiled widely.

I needed to take my family home.

My family.

⇛Chapter Forty-One⇚

Joshua

I fumbled around, my hands shaking, trying to help Rabbit get dressed. Smiling, she pushed my incompetent fingers away. "I can get dressed on my own, Joshua. Go sit in Daniel's office."

I leaned forward, grasping her face in my hands and kissing her softly. I had no words at the moment. Her sweet smile was full of understanding as her hand reached up and stroked mine that was resting on her cheek.

"Go," she instructed quietly.

I placed one last lingering kiss on her forehead and I left her to get dressed. I sat down, legs shaking, in a chair in front of Daniel and he looked up at me smiling. "Okay there, Joshua?" he asked, but didn't seem overly concerned.

"Are you sure she's all right, Daniel? That the baby is okay? She's been through so much," I asked quietly, my fear evident in my voice.

Daniel leaned back. "She's a strong woman, Joshua. Everything looks fine. And now that we know she is pregnant, you can take extra precautions for a while; make sure she gets lots of rest, eats well and takes her vitamins. She needs to try and avoid as much stress as possible. She has certainly had enough of that."

I nodded. "What about … what about the drugs he had her on?"

Daniel shook his head. "Not a trace of them showed in her blood work. Your girl is smart and it would appear she took very few of them.

They never got a chance to build-up in her system. The bastard was trying to keep her head fuzzy. He is quite the piece of work."

I growled in anger. "Fucker."

Daniel leaned forward. "Help her avoid stress, and make sure she gets lots of rest, Joshua. That's the best advice I can give you right now. Give her and the baby a chance to catch up. Gain some weight. Catch up on sleep. Let her body recover. I suggest some fruit smoothies with protein powder." He smiled. "And, some rich ice cream added in. Easy for her to digest and full of calories."

"Anything else?"

"Limit the alcohol. An occasional glass of wine is okay. And no hot tub. The heat isn't good for the baby."

I looked at him, panicked. "We've been in the hot tub a lot."

He laughed. "And she is fine, Joshua. Going forward, either stay out or lower the temperature to bath water."

I sighed in relief. That I could do. I shifted in my seat. "What about … um … what about physical restrictions?"

He looked at me. "Physical restrictions?"

I heard a small snort behind me as Rabbit came through the door.

"Physical restrictions? Seriously, Joshua. Are you asking me if it's okay to still have sex?" Daniel asked, trying to keep a professional face.

I nodded, squirming slightly in my chair.

Was that allowed when someone was pregnant?

I had no idea.

Internally, I grinned. I had never gotten anyone pregnant before.

Daniel chuckled subtly. "Yes. That isn't an issue. I don't suggest over-strenuous positions … no acrobatics. But sex is perfectly safe." He arched an eyebrow at me. "I think it's safe to assume you can simply continue as you have been." He grinned and winked.

Behind me, Rabbit giggled quietly at my discomfort and squeezed my shoulder. My hand drifted up to hold hers, squeezing it gently in return.

I smiled at Daniel in relief. "Good to know."

<hr />

Adam was waiting for us and we quietly shared our happy news with him. He was pleased for us and understood our need to keep it private for the time being. He informed us that he needed to get back to Toronto immediately, so once we got back to the house, he would get his things and depart. I looked at him, silently beseeching him to keep the latest news of Brian quiet for the time being and his silent nod told me he understood. Wordlessly, I handed him the vial from Daniel, knowing he would take care of what had to be done. Until we knew for sure what was happening, I didn't want Rabbit stressing.

"Is Frank going back with you?" Rabbit asked as we made our way down the hall, my arm wrapped around her, holding her close.

Adam looked at her. "Does Brian wear the overcoat he had on yesterday a lot?"

Rabbit looked confused but nodded. "Usually, most days. Why?"

Adam smiled. "I think it's safe to say Mr. James is safely back in Toronto and will remain there. His overcoat will come in very handy to make sure. I spoke with Frank. He is willing to stay here if you want or come back with me to help out with some, ah, checking I want done."

"Take him back with you, I'll have the security cameras on and the gate closed. If anything comes up, I'll call the police."

Adam nodded. "I actually spoke with the local precinct already. They know there is a situation, so if you call them, they'll respond."

We stopped by the truck. Adam regarded us briefly. "Lizzy, there is a restraining order on Brian being processed now. He can't come near you. Nor can anyone associated with him." Beside me, she nodded. "Joshua, I'm sure he won't do anything. He is not going to risk bad press right now. Just be diligent, okay? And, stay in touch." He clapped me on the shoulder. "I'm on it, Joshua. I promise both of you that Brian James is history."

I lifted my eyebrow at him questioningly.

He smiled calmly at me. "Let's go. I have an important meeting with a colleague this afternoon. It's going to be *very* revealing."

I relaxed. He was meeting with the asshole's lawyer today. He was indeed on it and I smiled in understanding.

He grinned back. "You look after your family and let me handle this."

I nodded. Nothing was more important than Rabbit's safety or the wellbeing of her and my child. The gun and the phone were staying close and the gates shut.

<hr />

I looked up from the laptop, smiling. Rabbit was sound asleep again, but her toes were starting to move, indicating she would wake up soon. She looked so peaceful when she slept now, and the only sounds escaping from her mouth were tiny little snuffles that made me grin. Beside her, Bear snored away loudly on the floor. Since Adam and Frank had left three days ago, our routine had pretty much been the same.

Wherever one of us was so was the other. Rabbit was calmest when I was close and my touch soothed her. Simply having her close brought me a contentment I had never experienced before, so the intimacy was welcome. Rabbit slept a lot, with Bear a constant companion by her side. He seemed to sense something was different and had taken on an even more protective stance when it came to her, rarely leaving her side even when she slept.

Yesterday, when I had suddenly felt the need to paint, Rabbit joined me up in the studio once I had the loft warmed up with the heaters and had brought over some extra blankets. As usual, within ten minutes of her sitting down, she drifted into sleep, Bear at her feet, and I found myself sketching and shading, completely absorbed in my work. It wasn't until she stirred a few hours later that I even moved from the easel. Crouched in front of her, I was pleased to see her looking more rested. She had gotten up and gasped in pleasure over the watercolor I had been working on. "It's so full of light, Joshua," she whispered. "Can we put it in our baby's room?" My already full heart swelled and, wordlessly, I had taken her in my arms, only able to nod.

Our baby.

Our baby's room.

There just wasn't anything I could say to express the joy those small words brought me.

Her soft sigh drew me back to the present. She was waking up slowly. Her eyes opened and met mine and I smiled at her. "Hey," I said smiling, rubbing her feet that were resting in my lap.

She blinked sleepily at me. "I did it again."

I laughed. "You're following doctor's orders. Wanna smoothie?"

It was her turn to laugh. "I'm going to turn into one, Joshua, if you keep making them for me to drink."

My face turned serious and I placed my hand on her stomach gently. "They're good for you and besides, I think she likes them. You sleep very well after you have one."

"She?" Her voice was soft as she looked down and placed her hand on top of mine.

I nodded. "A little girl rabbit. My bunny girl. BG."

Her eyes filled with tears.

"What if it's a boy?"

I grinned. "My Jack Rabbit then. Either way, Rabbit, I will love our child fiercely. Just like I do their mother." I watched a tear slip down her cheek. "Don't cry, Rabbit, please."

"Happy tears, Joshua. I'm just so full of happy tears."

I smiled and wrapped my hand around hers. "That's all I want you to have, Rabbit. Happy tears. Now BG needs a smoothie." I grinned as I stood up. "When I get back I want to show you all the cool things I found online. Did you know how much stuff a baby needs? It's incredible."

Rabbit laughed. "We have lots of time, Joshua. Um, *BG* won't be here for a while yet."

I grinned. "I know. Still, we have lots to do before she arrives."

Rabbit laughed. "Okay, Joshua. Go make me another smoothie and then show me what you've found. Then I'm going to go and putter."

"Putter? You need to rest."

She groaned. "Exactly. Daniel said rest, not sit on my ass all day and sleep."

I knelt down beside her. "You're sleeping so much because you need it, Rabbit. Don't push yourself. There is nothing you have to do. Let me look after you, please."

She smiled and cupped my face. "I love how you want to take care of me, Joshua. But I feel like doing something. I was thinking of maybe making a pie for after dinner, and maybe that I'd cook tonight. Pasta?"

I wasn't going to argue with that. I stood up, holding out my hands and grinning. "Well, that activity I can fully support. I'll help after I make your snack. Come to the kitchen with me, okay?"

Rabbit laughed, placing her hands in mine. "Okay."

Adam called the next day. He thought we should know that Brian James's father had passed away of a sudden heart attack. He also let me know that the follow-up meeting he had with Brian and his lawyer would be postponed until the following week. We spoke briefly, and after I hung up, I hesitated before letting Rabbit know what Adam had said. I wasn't sure how she would take the news or if she would even care. She was quiet for a moment and then shrugged her shoulders. "I suppose I should feel bad for him; or Brian even. But nothing he did ever pleased his father. And, Douglas James never seemed to like me." She suddenly laughed bitterly. "I was never good enough for either of them. That was the one thing they seemed to have in common." She looked up at me and I was surprised to see a look of anger in her eyes. "I still don't understand why, Joshua. Why did Brian insist on staying married to me? Why did he do all those awful things to me? Why didn't he just let me go? I wasn't what he wanted—he made that very obvious!" Tears began to pour down her cheeks and I pulled her into my arms, trying to soothe her. I had no answers for her.

"I'm not sorry he is gone. He was an awful man. He knew what

Brian did to me; I know he did … but he did nothing to stop it!" Her voice was becoming hysterical and I regretted telling her. Daniel said to keep stress to a minimum. I held her tighter and felt her body shaking hard with sobs as I rocked her. "Hush, Rabbit. Please calm down. Please, sweetheart."

I pulled back and held her wet face in my hands, forcing her to look at me. "Listen to me. *He* is a fucking stupid, self-centered, narcissistic ass. I can't tell you why he did what he did and I can't understand how he could have done such terrible things. Especially to you, Rabbit." I stared at her, not allowing her to break my gaze, my thumbs drawing circles on her damp skin. "*He* is the one that is not enough. He doesn't even deserve to share this planet with you. He is a cruel, thoughtless, heartless bastard. He deserves to be alone the rest of his life. I hope his entire life is filled with regret. I hope he's alone the rest of his miserable, lonely, pathetic, unimportant existence." I drew in a breath. "I hope his company fails, his hair falls out and his dick shrivels up and drops off," I added for good measure.

Rabbit's eyes widened at the last statement. But apparently my childish outburst had stopped her building hysteria. When I stopped to take a breath, she lifted a finger to my mouth. "Are you done?"

I shrugged and kissed her finger. "He doesn't deserve to be a part of any of your thoughts," I mumbled against her skin.

She regarded me sadly. "I try not to think about him, Joshua. Sometimes it just … overwhelms me."

I observed her for a moment.

"I don't want you overwhelmed, Rabbit. Maybe … you need someone to talk to? Someone who won't go crazy at the mention of the bastard's name?"

"You mean therapy?"

I nodded and reached over to hold her hand. "To help you deal with this. Move forward."

She was quiet for a moment and then nodded. "I think I need to, Joshua. I need to put this in the past." Her hand lifted to her stomach. "I have so much to move forward for."

I leaned forward and kissed her softly. My brave girl. She was so much stronger than she gave herself credit for. I looked down at her tiny hand holding mine over our child. My gaze drifted to the window. There was a whole world out there that our child would need to be a part of; school, friends, birthday parties, appointments. I thought of memories of my own childhood: parent/teacher nights, school concerts, trips to the zoo, family vacations … I had to be able to be there for our child as well. I wouldn't be able to do so if I couldn't walk past the fucking gate. We both had to move forward.

"Then I think we both should go for some counseling, Rabbit. You need someone you can talk to about your past and I need to push forward. Our baby is going to grow up and need a world outside these gates and I want to be at their side when they walk through them."

She smiled widely. "*Oh*, Joshua. Yes. You can do this. I know you can." She wrapped her arms around my neck and held me tight. "I'm so proud of you."

"Both of us, Rabbit. We both need this. We'll talk to Trina and you can decide if you want to become her patient as well or if there is someone else you would prefer. Whatever you're comfortable with."

She nodded in agreement. "Okay, Joshua. We'll both go."

I nodded. "Okay. I'll make the call."

I pulled her back to me and held her, breathing in her soft scent deeply.

Together we would do this. For ourselves, for each other and for our family.

The change in Lizzy was obvious when Adam visited two weeks later. She was already looking healthier. The smoothies and rest were doing their job and Adam told her so as he kissed her cheek and shook my hand.

His grin was wide as he looked at the fresh pie sitting on the counter. Rabbit knew lemon was his favourite and had made sure to make one before he arrived. He insisted on going through all the legal items first so that he could sit and enjoy his 'treat' afterwards.

My brow furrowed as I looked at Adam across the table. "He dropped the adultery charge? Did he finally use his brain for once?"

He nodded. "He has agreed to a quiet divorce. And, surprisingly, the counseling as well as the donation. I have the signed agreement papers. These will go to a judge next. Since neither party is contesting it, things should move along quickly."

I looked over at Rabbit who was sitting, suddenly pale and quiet, beside me. I knew how worried she had been about the proceedings. When I had told her about the adultery charge a few days ago, I had been surprised at her reaction. She had simply shrugged and said, "Let him." When she saw my shock, she had smiled. "I don't care how he is gone from my life as long as he *is*, Joshua. If it makes him feel like a big man to blame me, let him. I have no plans on seeing any of the people he associated with ever again anyway." Then she had frowned. "Unless it would reflect badly on you? On your career? That the press would use that?" Her eyes had widened as she spoke and I hastened to alleviate her worries.

"Rabbit, I don't give a flying fuck what anyone else thinks. All I care about is you. And, I agree getting rid of that bastard is the priority here. I just hate that he gets to have the upper hand here."

"But he doesn't," she had insisted. "I don't care if people see it as him divorcing me rather than me divorcing him. In the grand scheme of things, it just doesn't matter, does it? As long as he is gone from our lives?"

I smiled and kissed her. As usual, she was right. If she was happy, safe and free from him, that was all that mattered.

Now hearing the latest development, I slipped my arm around her shoulders, drawing her close to me as I focused back on Adam. "What do you think changed his mind?"

Adam tapped the thick file beside him. "I had a meeting with his lawyer in regards to the contents of this file. I think he sat with his client and persuaded him it was in his best interest not to pursue such a stupid claim. Brian had contacted him the day he left here with instructions on the adultery claim; I think he was angry when he left your property that day and reacted to it. No doubt once his anger subsided he realized just how unwise his claim was. I imagine his lawyer had something to do with the decision once he saw this and convinced him it would be more *prudent* to take a different approach." He paused. "I'm pretty sure he also thought hard on what you had to say to him, Joshua. It was rather … direct. Only a total idiot would ignore that sort of warning."

I snorted. I was pretty sure the asshole *was* an idiot. In fact, I was certain of it. Adam grinned at me knowing exactly what I was thinking, winked and then sat back. "His lawyer was rather shocked to find out the only requests were for your few personal items, the donation, the signed letter saying no retribution would be sought, and the cost of your legal fees. The no personal settlement thing was a surprise, I think. Especially given the evidence we have of Brian's abuse."

Rabbit looked over at him, her eyebrow arched. "My legal fees, Adam?"

He grinned at her. "I'm expensive, Lizzy. I decided that rat bastard should pay for my services, not you. I also decided extra time needed to be spent on your case. I am going to cost Mr. James big time. Besides the *seven* million I put forth for the donation."

Rabbit's head tilted as she regarded him quietly. "Seven million? I requested five."

Adam shrugged with a grin. "Typo on the draft. He agreed to it.

With his father passing, the bastard can certainly afford it. And, the way it is being distributed he gets zero credit for it. None."

Rabbit smiled gratefully "Thank you, Adam."

He smiled back at her. "If the only thing I can hurt is his pocketbook, then I am gonna hurt it badly, Lizzy."

Both Rabbit and I chuckled. Adam's face turned serious. "I would prefer to go after him for a lot of money, Lizzy. For you. You deserve it. And I could get it. Easily." His fingers once again tapped the file. "I doubt there would be much pushback if I tried. You could use it as a nest egg for the future."

Rabbit shook her head. "No, Adam. I want this over. I don't want his money. Even if I needed it, I wouldn't touch it. It came at too high a price for me to ever want it. I want no tangible connection left to him. I'm fine with your fees being covered, I hadn't really thought of that."

I couldn't stay quiet. "Neither Lizzy nor my child will ever want for anything—ever. No matter what, Adam. Lizzy doesn't need his money. What's mine is hers, and once we're married, everything will have her name on it. In fact, I want to talk to you about a few legal items while you're here."

I felt her stiffen beside me and looked over but her eyes were downcast. Softly, I squeezed her shoulder and felt her relax, but I could feel that she was still tense.

Adam sighed. "I'll be honest; it just doesn't sit well with me, Lizzy, but you're the client and I'll do what you want."

"It is," she insisted. "Just move it along, Adam. Please."

Something was off in her voice and I looked back over at her, frowning. But again, she wasn't meeting my eyes.

I looked at Adam, who sent me back a questioning look before he assured her he would do exactly that.

"So how is therapy going?" he asked, changing the subject as Rabbit got up and began slicing up the pie and pouring coffee.

"It's been ... interesting," I shrugged. "Trina will be out again today, and tomorrow I'm going to drive us into the hospital for Lizzy's next ultrasound."

"Trina comes here?"

I nodded. "She has been here almost every day for the past two weeks. She feels it's important to start where I'm the most comfortable. She thinks she needs to be with me as I push myself through the act of leaving the property. We have a daily session and she sits with me as I drive, each day going further. The last few days have been good. If all goes according to plan, I will soon be able to drive myself through the gate, and once I can handle that, we'll expand my comfort zone." I shrugged rather self-consciously, still feeling the shame of my phobia weighing on me.

Rabbit's hand reached up and cupped my cheek and I looked down at her. "I'm so proud of you," she whispered lovingly, her fingers stroking my skin. Capturing her hand with mine, I kissed her palm, smiling. Always so encouraging, and always finding the right words to lift my spirits. That was my Rabbit. She smiled at my gesture, pushing my plate toward me. "Eat your pie, Joshua."

"That's great, Joshua. It's a fucking tough thing to do. Don't sell yourself short." Adam clapped me on the shoulder. "And you, Lizzy?" Adam's voice was gentle as he spoke to her. "Are you finding things better being able to talk to someone?"

She nodded. "Yes. Anna is great. She comes out with Trina a few times a week and we sit here and talk. She helps me get things out and deal with them."

Adam smiled. "That's great. You both need to be able to put the past behind you and concentrate on the future. You look so much better, Lizzy. I'm pleased to see it."

Rabbit laughed. "If by better you mean well-rested and fed, then you're correct. Joshua hardly lets me do anything unless it involves baking something, and every time I turn around, there is a smoothie or a snack waiting for me to eat. I'm gonna be as big as a house by the time the baby is born."

Both Adam and I laughed. I doubt she had gained more than five pounds, but she was healthier looking and more relaxed. She was right, though, I didn't want her doing anything strenuous and I had been a little overboard on the resting thing. She was starting to push back and that was a good sign of her strength coming back.

I leaned forward, kissing her softly, my hand finding its way to her stomach, caressing it tenderly.

"BG likes the smoothies," I reminded her.

Her smile was soft.

"Yes, Joshua, we both do. Both of us love how you look after us."

I grinned.

"Good to know, Rabbit."

⇒Chapter Forty-Two⇐

Joshua

The day was winding down. Adam had left, promising to be in touch as soon as he had more news of the divorce proceedings. The remainder of his favourite pie went with him, despite my sulking, but Rabbit had whispered she had saved me a piece so I let him go unscathed.

Trina had come and we had a good, although exhausting, session and now Rabbit and I were sitting and soaking in the hot tub. I had lowered the temperature to make it like a warm bath, knowing how much she enjoyed the relaxing bubbles. Other times, I simply turned it up and used the heat to soothe my leg, but in truth, I preferred the warmth of Rabbit beside me. Her hands were busy kneading my leg; today, Trina had decided I needed to walk off the property rather than drive and we ended up walking further than either of us had expected.

I looked over at Rabbit, watching her concentration as she stroked and kneaded the muscles. She had been quiet since our meeting with Adam and I wanted to know why. Something had upset her.

I reached my hand down and stilled hers. She looked up, startled. "Joshua?"

I moved and pulled her over onto my lap and then reached up and tucked a strand of hair behind her ear that had come loose. The whole time, her eyes watched me warily as they had done most of the day. I didn't like that. "Talk to me, Rabbit."

Immediately, her eyes darted away, focusing elsewhere. "About what?" she whispered.

I cupped her face. "No. Look at me. Something happened this morning. You've been skittish ever since. And don't tell me it was because of discussing the divorce. I know it was something else; I just don't know what."

Her eyes looked at me, and I couldn't understand the confusion and worry I saw in them. "Rabbit, please. You're killing me here. Tell me."

"You don't ... you don't *have* to marry me because I'm pregnant, Joshua. I would never take your child away from you," she whispered brokenly. "Whatever papers you had Adam draw up, I'll sign."

I stiffened in shock.

That was what she thought?

That I only wanted to marry her because she was pregnant? That I wanted to make sure she didn't take the baby away?

I felt anger trickling down my spine as I regarded her slouched shoulders. But it wasn't directed at her. The blame for this lay strictly at that bastard, James' feet. He had made her feel she wasn't enough for so long, she actually still believed it. She found it difficult to believe she could be loved just for being herself; for the amazing woman she was.

Suddenly, I saw how my statement must have sounded to her. We had never even discussed marriage. It was my own assumption she would want to be married before the baby was born, if possible. That she even *wanted* to get married again. I had just assumed she would want to marry *me*. I had never really asked her. I only knew I desperately wanted to marry her. I had just never told her before opening my mouth and saying it in front of Adam.

I groaned at my carelessness and pulled her close. "Rabbit, I'm so sorry. God, I'm such an asshole at times. I have no idea how you put up with me." I sat back and lifted her chin. "I didn't think before talking this morning."

Her brow furrowed. I gently pressed my thumb to the 'V' between her eyes. "We've never talked about this, Rabbit. I've never asked you how you feel about getting married again. If that is something you want to do."

She shrugged, her eyes still wary. "I think marriage is a wonderful thing for people who are in love."

I smiled gently. There was no doubt we had that going for us.

I took in a deep breath. "I've never asked you if you want to marry me as much as I want to marry you."

Tears filled her eyes. "You *want* to marry me?"

I smiled at her, nodding my head. "So much, Rabbit." My hand moved to her stomach. "And if there was no BG, I'd still want to marry you. I want to spend the rest of my life with you. Do you really doubt that?"

I could see her struggling with her answer. I hated seeing her unsure, even though I understood where her insecurities stemmed from. "*Rabbit.* I love you. You have brought so much to my life and I don't even want to think of trying to be without you. I want to be by your side and experience every joy this life has to offer *with* you." I gathered her hands in mine and kissed them, holding her gaze. I also now understood why she had left the room, saying she needed some fresh air, when I had started to talk to Adam. I had planned on telling her everything once Trina left and we had relaxed for a while, but I had no idea she had been thinking anything like this. If I had, I would have addressed it sooner.

"The things I was discussing with Adam? It was just regarding things I want setup for you; bank accounts and extra health care coverage for you and the baby. And how soon I *could* marry you after the divorce. I would never ask you to sign some sort of agreement about our child, Rabbit. I don't want to control you. Those days are over for you. Please believe that." My hands gripped hers tightly between us. "Life with me will be different, Rabbit. It will be good. I swear."

I watched as a tear slid down her cheek. "Do you … do *you* want to marry *me*, Rabbit?" I asked warily.

Her eyes glimmered with tears. "Yes, I do, Joshua. So much."

I pulled her to me and kissed her intensely. I pulled back, breathing deeply. "Let me do this right then. I love you. More than I can even express … and I want to spend the rest of my life with you. Will you marry me?"

"Yes," she whispered and leaned forward, pressing her lips to mine.

"Together, Rabbit. We'll make our decisions together. You are my partner. I love you," I murmured. "We'll figure out the future together."

She smiled warmly. "Together."

I hesitated. "Rabbit, I want you to do whatever makes you happy, but I really don't want you worrying or looking for a job. You don't have to, financially. I know it sounds old fashioned but I want to look after you. I want to look after our child. You have been through so much and I want you here, safe, with me. I like being able to take care of you."

She regarded me for a moment. "But, if I wanted to?"

I smiled and cupped her face. "Then I would support you. But right now, is that something you want?"

"No, not really. I like being here with you. I like helping you with your work," she admitted softly, and then sighed. "I get so tired I'm not sure I could work right now. Although the library is looking for volunteers. Maybe I could help out there a little?"

My hand ghosted over her stomach lightly. "Perfect. I know how much you love working with books. But nothing too much, okay? I don't want you overdoing it."

She nodded, smiling widely.

I shook my head in wonder. It was so easy to please her. "Good. It's settled. Just a few hours at the library and the rest here with me." I stroked her cheek. "I like you home. I love having you help me. You have such a good eye and I work well with you. Even my editor noticed how little there was to be worked on in the last few chapters."

"I enjoy it as well. I just, well, I just felt I needed to contribute to things here, Joshua. That I should find a job and at least bring some sort of offering to this relationship."

I stared at her, aghast. I gathered her hands up, clasping them to my chest. "Rabbit. Look at me." I waited until her eyes were focused on mine. "I don't ever want to hear you say that again. You *contribute* more than I can possibly express. You have given me my life back. You are carrying my *child;* something I didn't think was possible. You have enveloped my entire life with love and hope." I shook my head. "I don't care if you ever hand me a pay stub at the end of the week, because what you *contribute* to us is invaluable. It is worth more than money." I pressed on her hands. "Tell me you understand that. Please."

I watched as her eyes softened and she nodded. "Thank you," she whispered.

I shook my head and leaned forward, resting my forehead against hers. "No. Thank you. For being you. For loving me. For agreeing to marry me." Once again, my hand strayed to her stomach. "For our child." I captured her lips softly. "I love you, Rabbit."

Her arms wrapped around my neck. "I love you, Joshua. So much."

I pulled her close and kissed her, and her response had my body humming with desire. I needed to be closer to her. I needed her.

Tenderly, I ran my hands over her curves, loving the shiver I felt run through her. I pulled her closer, running my lips up her neck to her ear. "I'm *aching* again, Rabbit. Do you think you can help me with that?" I whispered as I arched up into her warmth. Her answering whimper made me smile. I looked into her eyes. "I want you, pretty girl. But not in the tub. I'm taking you upstairs with me and I'm going to love you. Until you cry out my name and feel how much love I have for you."

"Yes, show me. Please, Joshua," she whispered. "*Now,* please."

I pulled her close. I needed to take her upstairs.

"Arms, Rabbit."

The day of our next appointment, we left early for the hospital. Each step was slow and, at times, painful, but together we did it. I had to pull over a few times to catch my breath, but throughout the entire trip, Rabbit held my hand firmly over her stomach, and encouraged me. She talked about the baby, what she had planned for the nursery, and all the things we were going to do as a family, sometimes even getting me to laugh at her outlandish ideas. By the time we arrived at the hospital, I was relaxed enough for the next step: entering the building. I was grateful to see Trina at the entrance and it made it easier to leave the truck and take Rabbit into her appointment. I was excited to see the ultrasound of BG myself this time. From what I read in the books I had had purchased, we might be able to hear the heartbeat. Concentrating on the goal at hand helped me make it through the busy hallways to the maternity wing, which was quieter and had less people around.

While we were in the waiting room, Daniel came by to say hello and see how Rabbit was doing. He seemed pleased at her appearance and told us he would be in his office if we wanted to drop by afterward with the latest pictures.

Inside the room, I waited in the office until Rabbit was examined and it was time for the ultrasound. I stood beside her, feeling excited, and watched the screen as the wand slowly rolled over her stomach. The sound of blood flow was coming from the monitor, but so far, I couldn't hear a heartbeat. Our baby doctor, Dr. Sue, as she insisted on being called, was doing the ultrasound herself. She was a warm, pleasant person who seemed to connect well with Lizzy and had answered my entire list of questions patiently. She reached up and tapped the monitor.

"There's your little one," she said, smiling. I looked at the small odd-shaped blip on the screen, smiling along with her. But then I saw her pause and frown briefly before pulling the wand back and forth over Rabbit's stomach. I heard her mutter 'oh my' quietly and look at Rabbit, who was staring at the screen, her eyes wide. I looked at the monitor again, not sure what I was seeing. "Is something wrong?" I asked tensely, my hand automatically reaching for Rabbit's.

"No, Joshua. Everything looks fine," Dr. Sue assured me with a smile.

Something was off. I could tell by her voice and the way Rabbit was reacting. I began to panic. "What? What is it?"

It was as if I hadn't spoken. Like I wasn't even in the room. Dr. Sue looked at Rabbit. Rabbit's voice was full of tears when she spoke. "Really?" Dr. Sue smiled and nodded at her, and then put a finger to her lips. "Listen," she said.

A different noise filled the room and I realized I could hear the soft thump of my child's heartbeat. I listened to the strange rhythm. Should it be beating so quickly? I knew the heartbeat would be fast, I'd read about that, but was it supposed to be *this* fast? There was barely a break between beats.

"Why does it sound so fast?" I asked loudly, now in a full blown panic. Something was wrong that I wasn't seeing and nobody was telling me anything. "What's happening?"

Rabbit squeezed my hand and pointed to the screen. "Nothing's wrong. Look, Joshua. Look closely."

I stared at the screen through the tears that had sprung up in my eyes. I couldn't see anything that made any sense. Intently, I listened to the heartbeat that seemed to fill the room. My head snapped up and I met Rabbit's eyes. There was more than one. What I thought was a rapid sound was two separate beats.

My eyes widened. I stepped forward, closer to the monitor, and traced the blip. There were *two* tiny blips, moulded closely together. Turning back to Rabbit, I saw she was crying too. Dr. Sue stood up as I wordlessly stared at Rabbit. The room seemed to start pulsating around me and I struggled to focus on Rabbit's face. I could feel my body beginning to sway and I felt very strange, as if I was losing control of my limbs. I heard Dr. Sue talking, but her voice seemed distant and fuzzy.

"Congratulations. It's twins." Her voice became louder and I heard her say my name, but I wasn't able to respond.

Those were the last words I heard before everything went dark.

━━━━━➤➤•◆◆◆◆•◆◆◆◆◆◆•━━━━━

Hands were slapping my cheeks. My eyes flew open and I stared into Dr. Sue's concerned, yet amused, eyes. I struggled to sit up, raising my hand to my aching head. "What happened?"

Dr. Sue smiled. "I think you found yourself a little overwhelmed, Joshua, and you held your breath too long. You passed out. Luckily, I stopped you from hitting the ground too hard."

I stared at her. I passed out? Searching my memory, I heard her words. "Twins? Rabbit's having twins?"

Behind Dr. Sue, Rabbit spoke. *"We're* having twins, Joshua."

I pushed myself up, Dr. Sue putting a hand on my arm to keep me steady. "Easy there, Joshua." I paused to get my bearings then closed the space to Rabbit, who was sitting up on the exam table regarding me with anxious eyes. When I reached her, I wrapped my arms around her, breathing her in. *"Rabbit,"* I whispered adoringly into her hair. *"Baby."*

She laughed softly. *"Babies,* Joshua." Her hand came up, cupping my face. "Are you okay?"

I nodded, but sat down beside her. Dr. Sue came over with a cup of water and watched as I drank it. "Your head glanced off the table a little, Joshua. Have Daniel check it before you go, okay?"

I nodded, my eyes focused on the paper in her hand. Smiling, she handed me the pictures from the ultrasound. "Everything is fine, Joshua. Lizzy is healthy. The babies are healthy. Your little family is doing fine."

My hand greedily grasped the paper and I stared at the picture of our babies.

Two.

Two little rabbits.

I looked up. "Do we know what they are? Boy, girl?"

Dr. Sue shook her head. "Too soon, Joshua." She turned to Rabbit. "Get dressed and I'll meet you in the office to answer any questions and we'll set you up with your next appointment." She smiled widely. "I'll clear a little extra time, because I know you'll have questions, Joshua," she laughed teasingly.

When she left, I turned and gathered Rabbit up in my arms again. "Twins, Rabbit. Two BG's!" I whispered, excitement evident in my voice.

She pulled away and smiled; her happiness radiant. "Maybe two Jacks, or one of each, Daddy."

I looked at her grinning. "Say that again."

She cupped my face. "Daddy."

I leaned in and kissed her deeply, my voice suddenly thick with emotion. "Thank you. I never thought I would ever father a child. And, now we're having *twins*." My hand covered her stomach, softly stroking, and I raised my eyes to her in wonder.

Rabbit's fingers tenderly stroked my face. "I think that puts to rest the doctor's 'probable' theory, Joshua. I'd say your swimmers are doing just fine," she chuckled and waggled her eyebrows at me.

I laughed. "So it would seem." I rubbed my head. "The news caught me off guard though. I don't think I've ever passed out before."

Rabbit leaned up and kissed my bruised forehead lightly. "We'll go and see Daniel."

I groaned. "He is gonna laugh his ass off over this."

Rabbit chuckled and snuggled her head onto my chest. "No, he won't, Joshua. The news was a little ... shocking. I had no idea, either. It's probably a good thing I was lying down at the time." She sighed softly. "This is gonna be a huge adjustment."

I laughed. "I have never looked forward to adjusting to something as much as I am this, Rabbit." I stood up, looking at her, my mind racing. "We need to get two of everything. Good thing we hadn't ordered stuff yet. Do we need two nurseries? Do babies share a room? You need more rest. And lots of smoothies. More meat. I think babies need protein. I need to get a list of things we need to avoid from Dr. Sue. And classes, there are classes we should take. I should probably get more books. I'm sure there are special books about twins. I'll ask Dr. Sue. Should I carry you around? Maybe you shouldn't be walking ... and maybe ..." My rapid ramblings were cut short when Rabbit placed her hand over my mouth.

"Relax, Joshua. Breathe. I can't have you passing out again. One step at a time. But, most importantly, I am perfectly capable of walking. I don't need you carrying me. Okay?"

Smiling, I kissed her soft palm, and stood up. I took in a deep breath and nodded. "Okay. Let's get you dressed and go ask some questions. Then I am taking you home and making my little *bunnies* a smoothie." I grinned. "They like them. No arguing with me ... Mommy."

Rabbit's brilliant smile said so much.

"Okay, Daddy. No arguments today."

Six weeks later, I pulled back onto the road leading to the gate and home. Today had been a trying day. Another session with Trina that I drove myself to, at the same time leaving Rabbit alone. I hated leaving her alone. The first time I tried, I never made it to my appointment. I had to turn around and go get her. Finally, after several attempts, I was able to make it all the way to the hospital, but only with Rabbit's voice in my ear via the Bluetooth device I put in the truck. I was so distracted during our session; Trina gave up and sent me home. Since then, I had gotten better, but I still hated leaving Rabbit. Often she came in with me and walked around the shops in town. Eventually I was actually able to join her after and be comfortable, even to the point that we often ate a meal while we were in town, which was a huge step for me. But today, she was tired and just wanted to stay home and refused to let me cancel my appointment. I pulled up to the gates, frowning. Why were they open? Stepping on the gas, I tore up the driveway, relaxing a little when I saw the UPS truck. I pulled up and waved at Jay as he stepped back into the truck and drove away. Rabbit made her way over to my truck, smiling. "Hi," she waved. "Did you bring the ice cream?"

I laughed, holding up the bag. "Tell the bunnies Daddy got it. Go get the bowls, Rabbit. I'll go park the truck and be right there."

I pulled forward into the barn and got out, glancing over at the fully restored Escort that had arrived yesterday. I hadn't shown it to Rabbit yet, since she hadn't been feeling well and had been rather emotional. I was waiting until the right time, when she felt a little calmer, but I knew she'd love it. The car held a sentimental value to her and I wanted her to be able to keep it. I stood looking at it for a minute, smiling as I imagined her reaction when she saw it. Leaning over, I grabbed the ice cream. This was one of Rabbit's major constant cravings and I literally couldn't keep enough on hand. Last week it had been Banana Fudge. This week was Black Cherry. Just as I grabbed the bag, I heard Bear start barking. The deep, angry growls were loud and ferocious, alerting me to danger. Then I heard Rabbit's terrified cry and my blood ran cold. I dropped the bag and ran as fast as I could. I rounded the corner and stumbled at the sight before me.

A car I didn't recognize.

Bear, aggressive in his stance and growling deeply, pacing in front of an obviously pregnant, frightened Rabbit.

Two men, not moving, by the car.

One of them—Brian James.

⇒Chapter Forty-Three⇐

Joshua

What the fuck was that bastard doing here?

I ran to Rabbit's side and pulled her shaking form protectively against me. Instinctively, one hand went to her already rounded stomach. "Are you all right? Did he touch you?" I asked anxiously, my voice quiet, while keeping my eyes on the two men in front of me. "Steady, Bear, stay," I added lowly.

"No. He hasn't moved." Her voice was panicked. "Why is he here? Oh God, Joshua, don't let him … the babies …" her hand gripped the top of mine on her stomach as her voice trailed off into tears and I pulled her even closer.

"He's not getting near you, Rabbit," I promised.

"You're pregnant, Elizabeth." Brian's voice was snide. "That was fast."

"You shut your fucking mouth, James. Don't you dare talk down to her," I roared, glaring at him, not surprised to see him lower his eyes immediately.

Such a typical bully. Fucking coward.

"How the fuck did you get in here?"

"We came in as the truck was leaving."

"Then fucking find your way out in the same fashion. Get off my property."

They didn't move. I stepped in front of Rabbit protectively, but they still didn't budge. I moved forward, Bear matching my steps. "Get off my property, *now,*" I hissed. I could feel my fists clenching, and I knew it would only take the smallest provocation from either of them and I would start swinging. Happily.

Behind me, Rabbit spoke. "Joshua! Please … don't touch him. No violence. *Please,*" she begged and the fear in her voice stopped my thoughts. I backed up slightly, but let Bear stay where he was. They were both fearful of him, judging by the rapid eye movements as they glanced between him and me. They had no way of knowing he would never attack unless I commanded him to do so, and probably, the worst he would do was knock them to the ground and growl down at them. But I let them remain fearful and ordered him to stay as I returned to Rabbit's side, digging in my pocket for my cell phone.

"Are you a complete idiot, James? You're breaking your restraining order just by being here," I snarled. "I'm calling the police."

I was shocked when he simply nodded. "I expected you to. I assume it will take them ten or fifteen minutes to get here. That's enough time."

Reaching behind me, I gently pushed Rabbit backwards. I spoke calmly to her. "Go inside the house. Lock the door. Call Adam, Rabbit."

James stepped forward. "No."

I felt Rabbit push herself into my back in terror. Her shaking had increased and I could feel her hands pressing tightly against my sides. This stress wasn't good for her or the babies.

I shook my head furiously at him. "You have no say in what she does or doesn't do anymore, James. Get the fuck off my property *now.*" Bear stood, growling low in his throat, waiting for me to give the signal for him to move.

Brian raised his hands is supplication. "I'm not here to hurt Elizabeth. Or tell her what to do. All I'm asking for is a chance to talk to her."

"She doesn't want to talk to you. She doesn't want you to be here. You're not *supposed* to be here. Leave." I hit speed dial for Adam and listened as it started to ring.

The man beside Brian held up his hand. "Please. Let him speak. He isn't asking to be alone with Elizabeth. Just a chance to say something. Then we'll leave."

Adam's voicemail picked up. "Brian James is here," I hissed into the phone and hung up.

"What do you have to say that is so important that you're willing to risk going to jail for? Or are you so fucking stupid you didn't think about that, James?" I growled.

"I did. I am hoping Elizabeth won't press charges. I'm leaving the country. I wanted to apologize to her before I do."

I stared at him. "Fucking what? Pardon me?"

"Elizabeth. Please. Let me say what I need to say. And I'll leave. I'll never come near you again." He held up an envelope in his hand. "I have my copies of the divorce papers here. I signed them this morning. You're free of me."

"Thanks for the news-flash," I spat out. "Now leave."

"Why, Brian? Why did you do what you did?" Rabbit surprised me by stepping out from behind me and I wrapped my arm around her, pulling her close.

Brian shook his head. "I can't possibly explain it well enough in a short time."

"Try," she insisted.

I started to dial 9-1-1, but Rabbit lifted her hand towards me. "Stop, Joshua. I have a few things I want to say."

"Rabbit," I warned, surprised.

"I'm fine, Joshua. You're right here. I'm safe. *Please.*"

Reluctantly, I put the cell phone down. If Rabbit wanted to talk, I would let her. I knew she still wanted answers that I couldn't give her. But I kept the phone in my hand, ready to start dialing.

"You didn't love me."

"No," he said honestly. "I didn't."

"Why did you marry me?"

"I needed to get married. You were a good candidate. You seemed ... controllable. And yet you had this ... warmth about you. People looked at me differently when you were beside me. It was a good image for me." He drew in a deep breath. "I married you because I wanted my father off my back. He kept threatening to take the company away unless I settled down."

For a minute, there was silence. Rabbit waited.

"I wasn't happy, Elizabeth. I was miserable. I was caught in between a rock and a hard place. And I took it out on you. It wasn't my intention to do so ... it just happened. I was just so angry all the time. And it escalated. Every time my father criticised me, I berated you. He belittled me, I belittled you. Every time he told me how far from perfect I was and reminded me what an utter failure I was as his son ... I hurt you. You never did anything but try and please me. I know that." He shrugged his shoulders. "I know none of this means much to you. I imagine my apology is meaningless, given what I put you through. But I wanted you to try and understand my side of things, even if it doesn't excuse what I did."

Beside me, Rabbit was still.

I rolled my eyes. "That was the worst excuse for an apology I've ever heard. You said your piece, James. Now keep your promise and leave," I demanded.

He turned to the car. But Rabbit spoke up again, her voice firm. "No. Why, Brian. I want to know. What happened that day? What did I do that day that was so unforgiveable you had to hurt me like that?"

Brian turned back and stared at her. We all knew what day she was referring to.

His hands were clasping and unclasping at his sides. He shifted his weight from foot to foot. My eyes widened in instant understanding when I saw the man beside him slip his hand into Brian's and squeeze it. "Tell her. She deserves to know the truth."

"My father had been at me for weeks. He wanted a grandchild. He was threatening to sell the company if I didn't get you pregnant. I never let him know we weren't … intimate. I had managed to keep that hidden as well. He honestly thought I was trying; that we were trying. He was pushing me to get tested for infertility, to have you tested. I knew it was just a matter of time before he found out that we didn't even share a room. That *everything* I had been struggling to keep hidden would come out. But I couldn't, Elizabeth. I couldn't touch you. I was … in love with someone else."

"Randy," Rabbit said, sounding surprised. "You're gay," she gasped, in sudden understanding.

Brian nodded and sighed deeply. "That morning, Randy and I had a huge argument." He looked over at the man beside him and grimaced. "He was tired of living in secrecy. Of my father threatening me all the time. Of only being a small part of my life. He said I had to choose between him and the company. I was deranged with anger and bitterness. I was frustrated and beyond caring about anything anymore. I was so tired of living a lie, of pretending to be something, someone, I was not. If Randy was gone, nothing much really mattered. Then I saw you. So pretty and so highly thought of by so many people. Adored by all the kids in the room. All the parents beaming at you. The perfect spouse. My father stood there," he snorted, "my *father,* who never had anything good to say about you, or anyone else for that matter, looked at me and told me you were a better representative of the James family than I ever would be." His eyes looked straight at Rabbit. "I snapped."

I watched Rabbit's posture change. She stiffened and her shoulders drew back. When she spoke, her voice was almost strangled.

"You were *angry* because I was doing *exactly* what you wanted. What you *demanded* of me all the time."

He shrugged self-consciously. "I don't imagine that makes much sense to you."

"Because *you* were tired of hiding."

He nodded.

"*You* were tired of being something you weren't."

"Yes. It was so hard, Elizabeth. You have no idea."

She stared at him. Her voice shook with anger when she spoke. "*No idea?* Didn't you realize, Brian, that I was hiding? That I was being forced to be something I wasn't? That I was alone and confused? I didn't have the *luxury* of knowing why. I didn't have *someone* to turn to. You made me a prisoner and then punished me for being exactly what you wanted me to be. You took away my worth. You made me doubt myself. You *hurt* me time and time again. Did you ever think of any of that?"

He regarded her in shock. "No."

She looked at Randy. "Did you know what he did to me?"

Randy shifted uncomfortably. "Not to the extent of what I know now. I knew he was ... strict with you."

"*Strict?*" Rabbit hissed. "He beat me, repeatedly; he isolated me and broke me." She shook her head. "You're no better than he is. The two of you deserve each other."

She stepped back into my embrace. I wrapped my arm around her, holding her shaking form.

Rabbit's head tilted as she regarded him. Her head nodded slowly as a thought occurred to her. "Your father is dead. You don't have to hide anymore. Why are you leaving?"

"I sold the company. We're going to do some traveling and then we are moving somewhere new so we can start fresh."

Rabbit pushed my arm away and took another step forward, her stance now obviously livid. I laid my hands on her shoulders, offering silent support. Bear moved and stood beside her, his growls getting louder. "You *sold* the company? The same company you were so desperate to keep that you abused me again and again for months because you were pretending to be something you weren't?" Her voice was loud and heated now.

He nodded. "I finally realized it didn't make me happy. Randy did. I want to be happy. My father and I argued the night he died, Elizabeth. I told him the truth. He was so livid he threw me out of his house and I never got a chance to talk to him again. It made me realize how short life is. And that I needed to start living it. Not hiding from it."

Randy suddenly spoke up. "Brian is a good man, Elizabeth. He's trying to move forward ..."

Rabbit held up her hand, her voice tight with disbelief. "Brian is a good man? A *good* man, Randy?" She laughed bitterly. Her hand came up and squeezed mine. "Last night I knocked over my coffee and *this* man teased me about being a klutz, wiped up the mess, brought me another coffee and kissed me." Her hand moved and pointed in Brian's direction. "One evening at a dinner, I knocked over a glass of water and that *good* man dislocated my shoulder pulling me up the stairs when we got home." She stepped forward, her body visibly trembling. "Last week, I wore a shirt that was so bright it made your eyes hurt and Joshua told me I was beautiful." Her voice dropped. "One day, I wore a blouse that was not to his liking and that *good* man of yours beat me so badly I thought I was going to die. Do you want me to continue?"

Randy's voice was shaking as he tried to defend Brian. "He regrets his actions. He does. He's done so well with his counseling..." his voice trailed off as I snorted.

"His counseling?" I laughed. "He's barely even scratched the surface regarding the amount of counseling he needs. Any doctor with any sense would ..." I stopped short.

Doctor.

My eyes narrowed. "You son of a bitch. You're not leaving the country for a fresh start. You're running. You know that doctor you had hiding all Lizzy's injuries is being indicted. You're leaving before your name gets brought up. You *fucking* coward."

Brian averted his eyes, but didn't say anything.

Rabbit looked at me then stared at him for a minute. "Why did you look for me when I left?"

"My father made me. He said we had to find you. To protect our name. The reputation he had built up. He made up the cover story and bought people off. He said ..."

Rabbit shook her head as she held up her hand. "I don't understand. What if I hadn't lost my memory? What then?"

He shrugged. "He had a plan for that as well. He had all your records altered to show a trail of mental instability. It was his idea to drug you and keep your head fuzzy so you would act strangely and make people think it was true. He thought ..."

Rabbit suddenly snapped. "I'm tired of hearing about what your father thought. You're a grown man, Brian. You just don't act like it." She shook her head, sighing wearily. "In fact, I don't want to know anymore. I was nothing to you. You hurt me because I was nothing to you but a means to an end. You had no problem destroying me or my life as long as *you* were protected. No problem drugging me to make you look like the better man for putting up with a slightly crazy wife. Because it was always about the image for you. Wasn't it?"

Brian remained quiet although he was shifting uncomfortably under

Rabbit's anger.

"*Wasn't it?*" she demanded.

He looked up. "Yes."

"You want my forgiveness so you can go and be happy, is that it? You can move on?"

Brian nodded. "I did everything you asked. You have your divorce. I even donated more money than you asked. I've gone for counseling. I'm trying, Elizabeth."

Rabbit's head bowed for a minute. I began to move forward. I was done with this farce. She'd listened to enough of his bullshit excuse for an apology. But then she spoke. "Do you remember, Brian, that day when I told you I wasn't happy and that I thought we should get a divorce? If you had just been honest with me and told me what was happening, I think ... no, I *know* I would have helped you." Rabbit sighed, sounding frustrated, before continuing.

"I would have stayed married to you until you could figure out a way to fix your life. I didn't love you, Brian, but unlike you, I did care. If you had acted like a human being and talked to me instead of breaking my wrist, I would have helped you." Rabbit shook her head again, and her voice was thick with tears. "And now you want my forgiveness. Well, you can't have it, Brian. I gave you everything but this. *This*, I won't give you. Go and live your life. But I'm not sure you will ever know what it is to be really happy." She stepped back into my side and her hand slipped into mine, holding it tightly.

"But know this, Brian. I *am* happy. I'm loved and I'm cared for. I will stay that way because of the man next to me." Her hand tightened on mine. "*This* man knows what the meaning of love is, Brian. The goodness in *him* is beyond description. That's something you will never understand. Ever."

Then she looked at Randy.

"You'd better hope he is never unhappy with you, Randy. Because once you feel his foot drive into your ribs over and over again, or know how it feels when his fist slams into your skin so hard that the bruises show up before he has finished hitting you, it's going to be hard to remember that he's a *good* man." Her breath shuddered out roughly. "Because I know how that feels, how that hurts. I'm not only talking physically."

I watched Randy stiffen and his hand loosen in Brian's grip. Brian looked down, tightening his hold as his stance became uncomfortable and he turned to Randy, shaking his head.

"No, I won't. I swear."

But it was obvious Rabbit's soft words had resonated with Randy.

His hand withdrew from Brian's tight grip and he crossed his arms over his chest and leaned against the vehicle away from Brian. I could see Brian panicking at his physical extraction.

But my attention was immediately back on Rabbit. As quickly as her anger had flared, it disappeared, and beside me, I felt her sag. I scooped her up, her head falling against my chest and I felt her tears soaking into my shirt.

I looked up at Brian, eyeing him steadily. "If you have caused her or my children harm, I will hunt you down. It doesn't matter where you run, I will find you. I promise you that."

Brian's face registered surprise at my words. He shook his head. "It wasn't my intention to bring her any further harm. I swear."

I shook my head. "You don't get it, do you? Coming here was selfish. You wanted to make yourself feel better. It *wasn't* for her. It was for *you* ... it's always about you. You should have practiced your speech better, James. You're pathetic. You didn't come here to apologize, you came here for absolution. Well, you're not getting it. You're not getting your forgiveness so that you can run away and live happily ever after. The only one getting a happily ever after is her." I tightened my arms. "She will be loved and safe for the rest of her life. I hope the two of you are fucking miserable. It's exactly what you deserve." I looked down at Rabbit's pale, tear-streaked face, frowning. "You have two minutes to get in the car and go. Leave the country. Don't ever come back here."

Brian's shoulders drooped. He looked over at Randy, who shook his head and opened the door.

I watched them leave, and turning, I strode into the house, carrying Rabbit. I watched the car go through the gate from the security camera and immediately switched the gates to lock and carried her to our room.

⸺⸺•••◆••••⸺⸺

After I laid Rabbit on the bed, I grabbed my ringing phone and spoke with Adam, telling him what happened. He hung up, cursing amidst the promises to call back soon. I went to the kitchen on the pretext of getting Rabbit some juice and called Daniel, begging him to come see her. Dr. Sue was out of town and I was desperate for reassurance. Although he assured me she was probably fine, he agreed to come out. I grabbed the juice and went back to Rabbit. She was still lying curled into a ball and I quickly pulled off her shoes and sat her up to remove her jacket. I helped her sip some juice and laid her back down. Immediately, I lay down beside her and pulled her into my arms. She was still shaking and I pulled a blanket up around us. Slowly, I rocked her, one arm wrapped around her as the other hand rubbed soft circles on her gently rounded stomach, which always soothed her. I murmured soft, loving words into her ear and held her as her trembling began to ease off.

"It wasn't me," she whispered.

"Never, Rabbit. You know this," I insisted quietly.

"I always thought maybe I should have done something different, tried harder ... something," she admitted, looking up at me.

I moved my hand up to her face, cupping her cheek. "No, Rabbit. You were perfect. Nothing you did would have been right. You heard him."

"It was all him."

I nodded.

"He *is* selfish. He used me to cover up the fact that he was gay. He was willing to destroy me totally, just to hide from his father what he was. I was just a good photo op and a cover."

I nodded, sadly.

"It wasn't me."

I shook my head. "You are so much more than a photo op, Rabbit." My voice was gentle, my hand stroking her cheek. "You are everything to me. You are my entire world. He is just a self- centered, selfish asshole who isn't even worthy of your time."

"And, today was all about him, wasn't it?"

"Yes, it was. It will always be about him, Rabbit."

She looked at me. "He's gone. And he's not coming back, right?" Her voice was shaky and I could see she needed reassurance.

"Never, Rabbit. He will never come near you again. I won't let him touch you. I promise."

She burrowed her head in my chest and we stayed silent for a minute.

"I love you, Rabbit."

Her arms tightened around me. I stroked her back softly, keeping her close, letting her feel that I was right there with her and *for* her.

After a while, her shaking finally ceased. She looked up at me shyly. I caressed her cheek, wondering why she was looking at me so timidly. "I'm divorced now," she whispered.

"Yes, you are."

She hesitated, biting her lip. Then she stared at me intently. "Will you marry me, Joshua?"

I blinked at her, shocked. Then I felt the thrill of her words as they settled into my brain. I grinned at her playfully, pretending to be stunned. "Rather forward of you, Rabbit. I'll have to think about that." I pursed my lips teasingly, as my hand caressed her stomach. "Is this a package deal?"

She nodded; a small smile on her face.

I leaned forward and kissed her soundly. "Then name the date, Rabbit. I'm so ready to marry you."

I heard the intercom buzz in the kitchen. Rabbit stiffened. "Who is that?"

"Um, Daniel."

"Oh, Joshua, you didn't."

"I wanted to make sure you were all okay, Rabbit. You were so upset," I pleaded with her to understand. "I can't risk anything happening to you." I paused. "Or our babies."

She sighed. "Well, it's too late now anyway. Go let Daniel in, Joshua."

"I love you, Rabbit. We're now officially engaged. You can't back out."

She smiled. "Good to know, Joshua."

<hr />

Daniel stood up and spoke to Rabbit gently. "Okay, your pulse is rather fast and your blood pressure is slightly elevated." He held up his hand to stop me from interrupting. "But given what just occurred, it's not surprising."

"The babies?" I asked quietly.

"They are fine. Lizzy is fine, Joshua." He clapped his hand on my shoulder. "Your family is fine. Relax."

I let out a deep breath.

Daniel turned back to Rabbit. "Just rest for the day, Lizzy. Let Joshua look after you. If you need me, just call."

She nodded and I went over and tucked the blanket around her, my hand lingering on her stomach. I kissed her forehead softly. "You heard him. Rest. I'll be back soon."

"You're not leaving?" Her voice was anxious and I hastened to reassure her.

"No, Rabbit. I'll just be in the kitchen with Daniel for a bit and then I'll be back, okay?"

She nodded and I patted the end of the bed and Bear jumped up. I scratched his head. "Good boy, Bear. Looking after our girl. Good job."

He chuffed and laid his head down on her feet, watching her closely. My phone rang and I heard Adam growling and barking orders on the other end as I answered.

"Joshua. I can have the police waiting for James on this end. He'll be arrested for breaking the restraining order. His jackass assistant as well. They were already in the air when the cops got there on your end."

"He said he was leaving the country. Is that true?" I asked quietly, my hand stroking Rabbit's head as I stood there.

"Yeah. His lawyer is fucking freaking out about this stunt. He is due to leave in a couple days. His plans will be put on hold thanks to his stupidity."

"He's running, isn't he?"

"Of course he is. He's a coward. The story is that he is going on an extended tour of Europe, but he is trying to stay ahead of the investigation of Dr. Hammond We can stop him, Joshua."

I knelt down beside Rabbit. "What do you want me to do?" I asked her quietly.

She shook her head, her exhaustion evident. "I want him gone. I don't want to deal with this, Joshua. It doesn't matter. It just doesn't matter. Get him as far away as possible."

I grimaced but nodded. "Let him leave, Adam."

I held the phone away from my ear as he exploded in anger. He ranted on for a few minutes and then suddenly became silent. "Sorry, Joshua. This fucker just keeps catching all the breaks."

"I know. We need him to be gone, Adam."

He sighed heavily.

"*Rabbit* needs this, Adam."

"Then it's done."

Suddenly, he chuckled darkly. "No charges, eh? Well, nothing saying I can't go meet his plane and let him know what I think of his visit. In fact, his own lawyer is so riled up maybe the two of us will form a little welcoming committee for James and the Jackass. There is a lot I want to say to him. And, I will personally make sure he's on that plane out of the country. Maybe I can't press charges, but I can certainly stir up enough questions so I make sure his name comes up in the investigation with Dr. Hammond. Enough to ensure he will never return to this area for fear of actual charges filed. Once he is out of the country he won't try coming back."

I laughed bitterly. "I like the sound of that. Say it for all of us, Adam. Do whatever you have to do."

"Oh, I intend to, Joshua. Tell Lizzy he will never even consider coming near her again after I am done. I guarantee that. If he tries, I will happily forget I'm an officer of the court."

The image of Adam staring down at James, his dark eyes threatening and angry, made me chuckle. When livid, he was fucking terrifying. Coward that he was, James most likely would shit his pants when he stepped onto the tarmac and saw what was waiting for him.

"Have a good time, Adam," I said mildly. "I expect a full report."

I hung up and looked down at Rabbit. "Is Adam going to take care of it?" she asked sleepily.

I leaned down, kissing her again. "Most definitely."

"Joshua?"

"Yes, my pretty girl?"

"Where's my ice cream?"

Fuck.

⇒CHAPTER FORTY-FOUR⇐

Joshua

Two weeks later, the sun shone high in the late afternoon sky, its beams warming the inside of the new SUV we were sitting in. I grinned as I watched Rabbit checking out the interior of the vehicle. We both smiled at the car seats already installed in the back, just waiting for their passengers. I knew it was early to have put them in, but seeing them just helped make all this more real for me. Rabbit knew exactly what I was thinking when she first saw them and had simply kissed me with a smile on her face. "You like it, Rabbit?"

She looked at me. "Joshua, I swear this is more luxurious than most people's homes. I think you went overboard."

I shook my head. "It's the safest SUV out there. The rest is just packaging. The safety rating was what decided it for me. For the babies."

She snorted. "Uh huh. I know about boys and their toys, Joshua. I highly doubt the babies will care about a navigation system or a built-in cooler."

I laughed. "Okay … maybe a few things were not totally necessary. But really … rather cool."

She smiled. "Yes, Joshua, very cool."

We were quiet for a moment, both looking at the building in front of us.

I looked over at Rabbit, smiling. "You ready to do this?"

Her answering smile was brilliant, but she only nodded in reply. I could see her hands beginning to fidget with the material of her soft yellow dress as her nerves got to her. I got out of the SUV and went around to her side and opened the door. "It's just us, Rabbit, and the people we know. The only thing that changes today is your last name. And the fact I can happily tell the world you belong to me. Forever."

She looked at up me, with the sweetest smile as her hands adjusted my tie.

"You like that, don't you?"

I grinned. "More than I can say. Now, are you ready to come inside and marry me?"

She held out her hand. "I am."

I grinned and helped her out of the truck. I tucked her under my arm as we walked up the steps to the tiny chapel where a small group was waiting for our arrival.

"Close, Rabbit. It's 'I do.' Keep practicing. You have about ten minutes to get it down pat." I leaned down and kissed her head. "But I'll be right beside you if you need a reminder."

She laughed softly. "As long as you're beside me, Joshua, I'm good."

I squeezed her gently.

"Always, Rabbit."

An hour later, I was standing off to one side in the warm private room in Rabbit's favourite little restaurant in Huntsville. For a small town, there were several places to dine, but Rabbit liked the coziness of this place. I found it comfortable as well, and we often ate here when we were in town. I watched, smiling, as my wife moved around talking to people. The guest list for our wedding was small but meaningful.

Cecilia, Trevor, Daniel, Ellen, Adam, Heather and Frank were all in attendance. As a surprise, I had flown in Tracy, who was thrilled to be there. I felt she had played a significant part in Rabbit's life, and especially in her escape and wanted her to be there to see Rabbit happy. Rabbit was overjoyed to see her and I noticed Frank seemed rather taken with her as well. He was noticeably close to her at all times, and from the glances she kept sending his way, the attraction seemed mutual. Also in attendance were Dave and his wife, as well as Trina, Anna and Dr. Sue and their respective partners. Rabbit had insisted that our pilot, John, and his wife join us since he was so instrumental in helping her come home.

I smiled as I looked around at our friends as they talked and laughed. I was still nervous away from the house, but today was an especially good day and I was managing well. I wanted today to be special for Rabbit. She had told me how sterile her wedding day with Brian had been and I wanted today to be nothing like that. I wanted it filled with love and laughter and good memories for her; for us. I had given Cecilia strict instructions that anything Rabbit mentioned or wanted, she was to have today. The only time I had stepped in was when Cecilia told me about a dress Rabbit had seen but bypassed due to the price. I told Cecilia to buy it and Rabbit's excitement when she saw it overrode the lecture I'd been subjected to for canceling the 'perfectly acceptable one' she had decided on and ordering this much more expensive one. I smiled, remembering how her eyes had shone with tears when I told her 'perfectly acceptable' wasn't good enough for her any longer as I kissed her into agreeing to keep the dress. But seeing how beautiful she was in it more than made up for the scolding. Cecilia had outdone herself, keeping things simple just as Rabbit wanted but still evoking a sense of occasion. The candles and flowers that filled the room were perfect. A photographer wandered around snapping pictures and, as per my instructions, made sure Rabbit was in most of the shots.

Rabbit's lovely dress flowed and swirled around her, somehow managing to emphasize her baby bump, which I loved. Its soft yellow color reflected the light that shone from her eyes when she looked at me. Carrying the twins made her seem further along in her pregnancy than she actually was. Her glow was beautiful; her happiness evident. Her left hand now glittered with a bezel-set diamond eternity band. She hadn't wanted a large engagement ring, but I did want her to have something stunning and her reaction to my offering had been nothing short of effusive. My own left hand carried a heavy, wide band of gold. Looking down I smiled as it glinted in the light. The symbolic gesture of our exchanging rings was so simple, yet so meaningful that it had taken my breath away. I looked up to see Trina standing beside me.

"You are doing very well, Joshua," she commented quietly.

I nodded. "I still find it easier when Rabbit is close," I admitted.

She smiled. "It will get less stressful as time goes along. I'm proud of your determination. And your success." She paused for a moment. "Maggie would be as well."

The sudden lump in my throat made it impossible for me to answer right away. She leaned forward with a quick but warm hug. "Go and find your lovely wife. Congratulations, Joshua."

I nodded silently and sought out Rabbit, needing her close. As I slipped my arm around her waist, I sighed in quiet relief at the feeling of her nestled into my side. My free hand immediately went to her bump, caressing the surface. I loved the feeling of her soft, full curves which changed and grew fuller with each passing week, and I smiled knowing our healthy children were the cause of them. Leaning closer, I checked to make sure she was okay. "Do you need to sit, my pretty wife?" I asked quietly.

She glanced up me. "I'm fine, Joshua." Her brow furrowed slightly. "Are you okay, sweetheart?"

I nodded, leaning down to steal a soft kiss. "Just an emotional day, Rabbit. A good one," I assured her.

Her hand cupped my cheek. "A very good one. I love you, Joshua."

My lips sought hers again, the kiss deeper this time. "I love you, Rabbit."

Daniel appeared beside us. "Okay, my friends. Enough of that. Unless I'm mistaken, that is what got you in trouble in the first place."

I chuckled as I felt Rabbit's cheeks get warm. I adored her shy blushes.

"Dinner is being served. Come join your guests. We have a lot to celebrate today." He grinned at me. "What changes your life has seen in only a few months, Joshua."

I smiled.

He was so right. The beginning of the year had seen me alone and trapped in a prison of my own making with no key to be found. Then a snowstorm had brought me my salvation. Now, with the snow long gone and late spring around us, I was married to the wonderful woman nestled into my side, two babies due to be born in the fall and surrounded by love and laughter. Rabbit was my key.

"Lead the way, Daniel. I'm ready to celebrate."

And proudly, I escorted my wife toward our friends who were waiting to celebrate with us.

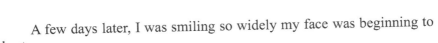

A few days later, I was smiling so widely my face was beginning to hurt.

"Really?" I looked at Dr. Sue, who was smiling back at both Rabbit and me, as she pointed to the monitor. I was seated beside Rabbit's head since Dr. Sue refused to allow me to stand during the scans since my slight mishap. "A boy *and* a girl? One of each?"

Dr. Sue laughed. "Well, I don't think there's any room for more in there, Joshua, so yes, one of each. Both are very healthy."

I leaned down and kissed Rabbit, hard. Her eyes were filled with tears. "A Jack and a Bunny girl, Rabbit." I grinned at her.

She laughed as I helped her to sit up. Dr. Sue handed us the latest pictures before she left the room and I stared down at them.

A son and a daughter.

I looked up at Rabbit's tender expression. "Now we have to pick names from our top five, Joshua."

I leaned forward. "I know which one I want for our daughter, Rabbit. You pick for our boy."

She smiled and cupped my cheek. "Jack then. Jack Anthony Bennett."

I grinned. "That's a good, strong name for our son."

Her voice was soft. "Danielle?"

I nodded. "Danielle Emily." For my mother. My voice caught. "Elly."

Rabbit smiled. "Perfect. Jack and Elly."

I swallowed the lump in my throat and wrapped my arms around Rabbit.

Jack and Elly.

Our children.

"I can't wait to meet them," I sighed eagerly. "How is it possible to love someone—two little someones—this much when you've never even seen them?" I looked down at Rabbit. "I didn't know my heart could hold so much love, Rabbit."

She smiled and cupped my face, her fingers stroking small circles on my cheeks. Her expressive eyes were filled with love and joy.

"I had no doubt, Joshua. No doubt at all."

———◆◆◆◆◆———

"No, I don't want anything, Joshua."

I sat back flummoxed. "Not even ice cream, Rabbit?" She *always* wanted ice cream.

"No." Rabbit lay on her side, looking uncomfortable and upset.

I leaned forward and stroked her brow. "Does you head ache today?" I asked softly.

Rabbit shook her head but I saw the tears that slipped out from behind her closed lids. My heart clenched at the sight. Dr. Sue wanted her calm. Relaxed. Rabbit's blood pressure had been all over the map; she had developed pre-eclampsia and was now on bed rest. Bright lights bothered her and she had a lot of headaches. She had been so brave and determinedly cheerful at first, but the past few days her emotions had been ragged.

"Rabbit ..."

She began crying in earnest. I stretched out behind her and wrapped my arms around her, my hand rubbing her tummy, as I whispered soft hushing noises into her ear. "Soon, Rabbit. Dr. Sue says just another couple weeks and she'll do a C-section. You're doing so well, sweetheart. Just hold on a little longer," I pleaded gently. "Please, Rabbit, don't cry."

"I'm sorry. I'm just so ... tired of lying here. I'm tired of the headaches and the nausea. I want to go outside. I want to go for a walk. I want to sleep on my back. I want to make love to you. I want to wake up with my head buried in your chest and your arms around me. I want to bake you a pie! I'm just so useless!" The last words came out in a high-pitched whimper.

I smiled into her hair. "I want you to bake me a pie too, Rabbit. I haven't had pie for three weeks," I whined into her ear. "And I miss your face buried in my chest as well. Nothing is sexier than feeling you drooling on me in the morning," I chuckled lowly. "And you haven't rubbed my ... *leg* ... in days," I whispered. "All you do is lie here, looking beautiful and pregnant. You get to be all glowy and eat ice cream. I have to walk Bear alone and talk to Cecilia every single day now."

"Stop it," she half sobbed, half giggled.

"Stop what?" I asked innocently as I nibbled her ear gently. "Seriously, woman, you *are* so lazy. Lying here, denying me the drooling and the rubbing and the pie ... letting the world revolve around you while you only do one little thing." My arms tightened around her. "Protect and nourish our children. I mean really, Rabbit, how utterly ... *selfish* ... of you."

"Stop trying to make me laugh."

"Oh, I'm sorry. Was I doing that?"

She sighed deeply. I felt the shudder run through her body at the same time someone started kicking. I smiled and rubbed my hand over the movement. "Someone wants Mommy to calm down," I whispered. "They don't like it when she's upset." I paused, my voice turning serious. "Neither do I."

Reaching over, I turned her face to mine, my fingers stroking her tear-stained face. "I know this is hard, Rabbit. But you're doing so well. Tell me what you need to make it easier. Tell me what you want. I'll do anything, my pretty girl. Anything. But please don't cry."

"I don't know what I want. I just feel so ..." Her shoulders shrugged. "Just ignore me, Joshua. I'll feel better in a little while. "

"No, I won't ignore you. This isn't like you, Rabbit. There has to be something I can do. You need a change of scenery or something," I insisted.

Her eyes filled up again. "I want to go outside and sit but I can't. The light hurts my eyes and the chairs are uncomfortable. I'm afraid if I got into one, I'd never get out," she sobbed.

I let her cry, rocking her. Dr. Sue had told me this might happen. Rabbit was only allowed up for a very limited amount of time every day and usually by the time she had a shower and got dressed, her time was up until later in the day. The past few days after a walk around the porch in the evening she was so tired that was all she did. I knew she missed being outside. She was used to being busy and active, so I knew the imposed resting was getting to her. I spent most of my time at the desk I had setup in the bedroom, not wanting to be away from her and leave her alone in our room for hours at a time. I had her help me with edits to distract her, played board games with her to pass the time, and when her head was aching, I sat beside her, rubbing her back and reading to her. She said the sound of my voice soothed both her and the babies. But today, there was no soothing and I knew she was reaching her limit. Even Bear and his antics hadn't made her smile the past couple of days.

I looked down and smiled sadly. She had cried herself to sleep. It didn't take much to exhaust her these days and her emotional outburst would certainly do it. My hand stroked her hair that was still damp from her shower and I leaned forward and kissed her cheek. She burrowed into her pillow, facing away from me, and I sighed. I did miss her burrowing into me. But the swell of her stomach prevented that at the moment. And, sex was off the table, which frustrated both of us. There had to be something I could do to make her happier.

An idea formed in my head and I gently disentangled myself from Rabbit and went to call Cecilia. An hour later my idea had been bought and purchased and would arrive the next day. I grinned as I hung up. Rabbit would love it.

⋙ ●●●○●○●● ⋘

"Oh, Joshua!" Rabbit's voice was filled with delight and her hands clapped with excitement when I carried her outside the next afternoon.

I grinned down at her, being gentle as I laid her down in the soft hammock. A pre-made gazebo complete with bug screens had been set up, providing shade and comfort while giving her the freshness of being outdoors. The large hammock was plush and filled with pillows and a blanket, in case she got cold. A couple of chairs and a table were close where I could sit and use the laptop while she rested in the hammock. Leaning down, I kissed her tenderly. "I should have thought of this sooner. I know you're still lying down, Rabbit, but at least it's a change of scene and the fresh air will do you good. I made sure it was all Dr. Sue approved."

She sighed and looked around her. Her hand reached up and I grasped it in mine. I let her pull me down for a sweet kiss. "Thank you," she breathed.

I smiled down at her. "Anything. Anytime. Always, Rabbit."

"It's lovely."

I nodded. "I'll have a more permanent structure built next year. It'll be good for Jack and Elly in the summer. It'll be a great place to sit in the evenings. But for now, this will let you be outside, but not in the bright light."

"You're so good to me."

I laughed and knelt beside her, my hand going to her tummy where I could see rapid movements happening through her shirt. "I think they like it out here." I looked at Rabbit, pleased to see her looking happier today than yesterday. "I like to be able to look after you, Rabbit. You mean everything to me, my pretty girl. Everything. All I want is for you to be happy."

"I am." She smiled at me. "I'm happier with you than I ever imagined I could be. I love you so much, Joshua."

I kissed her softly. "You have given me so much, Rabbit." My hand pressed tenderly on her rounded stomach. "You've made my dreams come true; ones I had long since given up ever hoping for. You complete my life. You *are* my life."

"*Oh*, Joshua." Rabbit's arms wrapped around my neck, drawing me down to her mouth. I lost myself in the sweetness of her kiss, my desire suddenly raging, and I groaned roughly when I pulled away.

"Want to join me on the hammock?" Rabbit looked at me, waggling her eyebrows.

I smiled down at her, shaking my head. "I'm not sure that's advisable at the moment. I'm rather tempted to break Dr. Sue's rule."

She looked up at me from under her lashes, smiling. "Just rather?"

I groaned, dropping my head onto her shoulder, struggling to calm my body and my breathing. "Don't, Rabbit," I pleaded quietly.

She turned her head, her mouth damp against my ear. "Let *me* be good to *you*, Joshua, please?" I felt her hand snake down under the waistband of my loose pants, wrapping around my aching erection. I groaned at the contact, thrusting myself against her palm. "I can't … but I want you to, please. Let me, Joshua … please."

The unanticipated pleasure was so great; I gave in quickly and groaned as I felt my pants fall and her hand begin to move freely. It felt like forever since she had touched me. My hands grasped at the pillows around her head and I covered her mouth with mine as I gave into the heat of her strokes. I kissed her over and over again, my tongue dancing with hers in the sweetest of rhythms as her hand worked me into a frenzy of need. Her tiny hand had never felt so powerful or flexible as it did right at that moment, and she stroked me rapidly into a mindless sense of want. My body arched into her grip as my fingers clutched and twisted the soft material beneath them. My sudden orgasm had me gasping out her name as I came hard and fast, kneeling beside her on the soft grass. My body slumped forward, my head now resting beside hers on the pile of pillows as I tried to recover from the intensity of my response. Slowly, my eyes opened and I gazed at her. "Wow. That was … unexpected."

She giggled. "I thought maybe you needed that."

I grinned at her and leaned forward, kissing her lovingly, nuzzling her lips. "Are you okay?"

She nodded. "I'm fine. Dr. Sue said touching *you* was allowed, Joshua. I asked."

I closed my eyes briefly in both embarrassment and gratitude. "I feel rather guilty about not being able to, ah, return the favor, Rabbit."

She laughed softly. "I'm good, Joshua. Right now, I don't think I'd enjoy it. I'm too achy."

I stroked her cheek and leaned forward, brushing her lips with mine. "You just took care of my *ache*, Rabbit. Rather effectively, I might add. So, I'll take care of yours." I pulled off my shirt and wiped her hand. "I'm going to go and, uh, freshen up and when I come back, I'll rub your back. Deal?"

She nodded happily.

Ten minutes later when I returned, cool drinks in hand and the iPod ready to play some soft music, I found her sound asleep in her hammock, a small smile on her face. Bear was now sitting at the end of the hammock, eyeing me with distain, no doubt at my recent activities with Rabbit. I stared back at him. "She offered," I muttered. He huffed and laid his head down on his paws. "Don't judge me," I huffed right back at him.

Damned disapproving dog.

I set the drinks down and grabbed the blanket, and tucked it around Rabbit, not wanting her to get cold.

I leaned down and kissed her cheek gently.

"My girl," I whispered. "I love you."

───────────────

A few days later, I stood outside listening to the wind blow through the trees as I replayed the phone conversation with Adam that had just ended.

"Joshua, I thought you would want to know Randy is back in Canada. He came to see me."

I had immediately stood up and gone outside. I didn't want Rabbit to wake up and hear this conversation. "Why?" I had hissed.

"He's alone."

"Where is James?"

"In jail. In Russia."

I had stopped pacing. "What? What the hell was he doing in Russia?"

Adam had sighed. "They were traveling. One night, Brian got a little drunk and high-handed with Randy. It was the first time he had ever actually seen that side of him. I guess what Lizzy said to him hit a nerve and he was very vocal with Brian who, of course, said it would never happen again."

"But it did?"

"Yeah, in a bar in Russia. He accused Randy of flirting with another man. Randy denied it and left the bar after Brian started pushing him around again. Apparently, after he left, Brian decided to keep drinking and then got into it with the guy he accused Randy of flirting with. He hurt him pretty badly, but the guy is going to recover. It turns out, though that he is the son of a bigwig in the military there. Big mistake on Brian's part."

I whistled.

"How serious is this?"

Adam laughed. "He's in Russia, in jail and is up on attempted murder charges. Randy walked out on him and his lawyer here won't even take his calls. Brian fired him that day at the airport so he is under no obligation to talk to him. He is doing jail time, no matter what. His money means nothing there. His name means nothing there. There is no way out of this for him. He finally picked on the wrong person at the right time with a bar full of witnesses. He can't come home because he'll face jail time here as well. So basically, he's fucked."

I chuckled darkly. "Couldn't happen to a better guy." I paused. "What are Randy's plans?"

"He is moving back to Alberta. He is done with Toronto and wants to go home. You don't have to worry about him bothering you or Lizzy. He came specifically to tell me that." He paused. "Are you going to tell her?"

I sighed. "I can't keep it from her, so eventually, yes. She would want me to tell her. But not now. She needs to stay calm and the babies are due soon. He isn't even a blip on the radar right now for her and I want it to stay that way. Someday, I will tell her."

Adam laughed into the phone before he hung up. "Good decision, Joshua. Never hide stuff from your wife. Somehow, they always find out."

I shook my head and went inside. I walked down the hall and stood looking at Rabbit, who was asleep, curled up with the special pregnancy pillows supporting her. I was grateful she had been napping when Adam called. As much as I rejoiced in the fact that James was finally in jail where he belonged, it wasn't something Rabbit needed to know right now. After his surprising appearance, Adam had indeed been there to meet him when his plane had touched down. What followed had been a 'no holds barred' verbal assault that ensured he would never come near Rabbit again. I suspected there was more to the story than Adam had told me, but I let it pass. It was done. And true to his word, Adam made sure he was out of the country two days later. Not long after that Dr. Hammond was indicted and a warrant was issued for Brian James, ensuring if he ever stepped foot back in the country, he would be arrested immediately.

Once we had confirmation that he was out of the country, Rabbit had become stronger and more secure. The old fear that he would suddenly show up was gone. The haunted look had left her eyes and I had to admit that just letting him go was for the best. The fact that he was far away on the other side of the world brought her peace and she was able to move forward with greater ease. Now, looking down at her, I wanted nothing that reminded her of the past or her painful memories associated with him. I only wanted her thinking ahead to her life with me. With our children. I only wanted her to feel safe and loved. Because she was.

⎯⎯⎯•••◑•••⎯⎯⎯

Two weeks later, I was at Rabbit's side while our children came into the world. What I had thought was love for them before they were born was nothing compared to the overwhelming surge of emotion I experienced when I held them in my arms and gazed down at them in wonder for the first time. My tears mingled with Rabbit's as I kissed her, my lips expressing the gratitude and love that my voice was unable to at that moment.

Nothing prepared me for the adjustments of the next few days and weeks.

I watched in amazement as Rabbit fed our children for the first time.

I marveled at the loving, instinctive way she took to motherhood.

I was awed at her patience in teaching me what seemed to come so easily to her.

The love and adoration I had for her grew tenfold. What before was beautiful, became glorious when it came to her.

The proudest moment of my life was carrying, first, my children, and then my wife into our home and feeling the sense of utter contentment and fulfillment at the sight of all three of them settled safely together on the sofa.

My eyes glazed as I stood watching my family.

Rabbit's eyes lifted and she met my gaze with a soft, tender expression.

"Hey, Daddy," she whispered softly.

My heart was full.

The afternoon sun was warm as it shone through the nursery windows. I found myself once again standing at the side of the crib gazing down on my children with complete adoration. My hand tenderly stroked the tiny forehead of my son, smiling as his nose wrinkled in his sleep. His sister was tucked against his side, an ever-present appendage. The second crib sat empty. Every time we tried separating them into their own cribs, the end result was the same. Heart-wrenching sobs from Elly and searching hands and angry little growls from Jack.

"I thought I'd find you in here." Rabbit whispered from beside me. My arm instantly wrapped around her and drew her close.

Leaning over, I kissed her forehead. "You're supposed to be resting," I admonished her gently. "They'll be awake soon and looking for dinner."

Rabbit laughed softly, her hand rubbing Elly's tummy tenderly. "I can't stay away either," she admitted. "Our little miracles."

I watched in wonder as Elly squirmed and shifted. Immediately, Jack's hand adjusted and found purchase on her again. "Did you see that?"

Rabbit hummed. "He does it all the time. Protective; just like his daddy. He hates being away from her."

"I suppose after being that close for all those months, separation would be hard," I mused. I looked at her, grinning. "This is gonna look strange on the playground, though."

I was rewarded with her smile and sweet laugh. "You know very well Dr. Sue said this was perfectly normal, Joshua. They'll grow out of it."

I sighed. "Not completely, I hope."

Rabbit nestled deeper into my side. "Like I said, he's your son, Joshua. Something tells me he'll always be protective of Elly."

I smiled.

My son.

"Jack and I will always look after the women in our lives," I whispered quietly, my lips nuzzling Rabbit's soft cheek. "Now back to bed."

"Will you lay down with me? I need some snuggles."

"Well then, you're lucky, aren't you? Rabbit snuggles are my specialty." I grinned as I guided her down the hall and helped her back into bed. I knew her incision from the C-section was still tender, and I carefully lay down beside her, letting her find a comfortable spot against me. I wrapped my arm around her gently and softly stroked her hair as she fell into a restful sleep. The days of nightmares and headaches were behind us and I loved seeing her relaxed and resting serenely.

The quiet of the afternoon was peaceful. There had been so many smiling faces here since Rabbit and the babies had come home that I swore the echoes of their joy were still permeating the rooms of our home, circling in the air.

So many good wishes and congratulations.

So many tiny outfits to look at, piles of stuffed toys to be hugged.

So much love.

All because of my Rabbit.

It all started with a snowstorm and a lost, frightened woman.

It ended here.

With my family —safe and peaceful.

Because she found me and calmed the storm.

⟫EPILOGUE⟪

Joshua

Eight months later ...

I stood, looking down at my suitcase, a shirt hanging from my hands. All I had to do was put it in the suitcase and I was done. Packed. Ready to go.

Except I wasn't.

I sat down on the bed, and lowered my head into my hands as I felt the undeniable stirrings of panic blooming in my chest.

I couldn't do this.

I wasn't ready.

I didn't *want* to do this.

I stood up to go and find Rabbit and let her know this trip wasn't happening, only to see her standing in the doorway regarding me silently.

"Hi." Her smile was gentle, and her voice low. "You okay, sweetheart?"

At a loss for words, I shook my head and sat back down.

She pushed off the door frame and came over, tugging the shirt out of my hands and folding it. I watched without a word as she placed it in the suitcase.

"Did you pack your shaving stuff?"

I nodded. "And your trunks? I brought my swimsuit. I hear the hotel has an amazing hot spring spa attached to it. That should feel great on your leg," she chatted at me.

"Rabbit ..." my voice trailed off.

She stopped fussing with the zipper on the case and moved over, standing between my legs. "We have to go, Joshua."

"I'm not ready."

Tenderly, she cupped my face, her fingers stroking my cheeks. "Yes, sweetheart, you are. You're just feeling tense at the thought. I'll be right by your side the whole time."

I looked at her, noticing her unusual pallor. "Are you ready to do this?"

She drew in a deep breath. "No. But I have to. For you. For us. For Jack and Elly. We promised Trina we'd do this."

I shook my head. "We promised we'd try."

She smiled sadly. "Deciding the night before not to go is not trying, Joshua." She looked at me knowingly and sighed. "We have to try. We have to. This interview is the perfect time to do this. For both of us."

I shook my head. "I hate it when you make sense, Rabbit."

She laughed "No, you don't." Leaning down, she grazed her lips over mine. "You love me."

Sighing in defeat, I pulled her against me and kissed her deeply. "Damn right I do."

She chuckled quietly and held out her hand. "Let's go and have supper with the munchkins and Cecilia. Trevor will be here any minute. You can spend the evening grilling him on the emergency protocols you have set up and familiarizing him with all the key points on your lists of how to care for your children properly."

I narrowed my eyes at her. "Are you making fun of my lists, Mrs. Bennett?" I growled in mock indignation.

Rabbit laughed as she leaned down and kissed me warmly. "Not in the slightest, Mr. Bennett. Your organizational skills are to be congratulated. I'm sure everything Trevor and Cecilia could want or need to know is on *one* of your lists." She turned and walked toward the door. "And, about a hundred things they have no desire or need to know, for that matter."

"Hey! I'm just covering all the bases!" I insisted as I followed her down the hall. "I just wanted to make sure Trevor had all the information he needed."

I heard Cecilia laughing from the front room. "Your lists are big enough to be your next book, Joshua. That's an awful lot of words for one night's instructions."

I sat down across from her, scooping Jack up off his blanket and tossing him in the air, smiling as he laughed in delight, Bear watching me with protective eyes. "Shut it, Cecilia. These are important care packages you are looking after. And besides, its two days plus a night. That's a long time."

She snorted. "Oh … so sorry, I stand corrected. Two days plus a night. Maybe you'd better check those lists again, Daddy. You may have missed something."

I smiled down at Jack. He gazed up at me, his blue eyes so much like Lizzy's, set in his little chubby face. My panic began to swell again. How could I really leave him or Elly for that long? I looked up at Cecilia, and she quickly became serious when she saw my expression.

"It's going to be fine, Joshua. Trevor and I will take good care of them. You'll be great in your interviews," she assured me comfortingly. "You have to do this. You need to be strong for Lizzy."

I looked up and saw Rabbit watching us anxiously from the kitchen. She was right. Rabbit was equally stressed about not only leaving the babies overnight, but being back in Toronto for the first time since I had brought her back with me well over a year ago. I smiled at her reassuringly. Her answering smile was sweet, but nervous. Cecilia was right, I had to be strong.

We could do this. As long as we were together, we could do this.

I gave up around three o'clock. I sat up and carefully eased out of bed. Rabbit had probably only been sleeping for about half an hour. And, that was only after I had held her closely, stroking her head and humming quietly until she relaxed and finally drifted into sleep.

Silently, I made my way across the hall and into the nursery. The nightlight cast a soft glow over the cribs as I stood looking down at my children. Although they finally slept in separate cribs, they were placed beside each other. Often when I came to check on them, I found them on their sides, facing each other, their little arms flung in the same direction. Tonight was no exception and as I stood looking down on them, I felt the rush of love that always engulfed me as I watched them. They were two little tiny bringers of joy. Every day was filled with laughter and new experiences. Watching them discover the world around them was magical, and it had led to the writing of a new series of books. Children's books that I had written with Rabbit's encouragement, that I also illustrated. In the beginning, I had written them only to read them to Jack and Elly, but Cecilia insisted I allow my publishers to read them. Although they had been skeptical over the huge change in genre, they had loved them. Now I was working with a whole new team in the children's division and the books would be published very soon. This led to the necessary meeting in Toronto and the interviews I had agreed to do, after much coaxing from both the publishers and Trina.

I stood over my children, watching their peaceful sleep, and I matched my breathing with Jack's steady, even breaths. Slowly, I felt myself relax as I thought back to my talk with Trina about this final hurdle.

"You want me to what?" I asked incredulously.

"I want you to plan an overnight trip away, Joshua," Trina replied calmly. "It's time."

"I'm not leaving Rabbit and the babies."

"No, just the babies. Rabbit needs to face her fears and return to Toronto as well. You can face this together and support each other."

I shook my head. Leave the children overnight and return to Toronto? "She'll never agree to it."

But she did.

"Trina is right, Joshua. You've done so well. You come and go all the time now and handle it almost effortlessly. But we've never tried to have you away longer than a few hours," she said thoughtfully when I told her that night after the twins were asleep. "Cecilia and Trevor would love to watch the twins. They've offered so often. They'll be thrilled."

"What about you, Rabbit? Do you think you could handle going back to Toronto?"

She looked at me, already unconsciously biting her bottom lip in nervousness. Leaning forward, I pulled the soft flesh away from her teeth and tapped it to demonstrate my point. "Do you really think you're ready?"

She looked at me quietly. "All that's left there are bad memories, Joshua. Brian can't hurt me anymore. The thought of going back isn't pleasant, but if you're with me, Trina is right—I need to face it and leave it in the past. Once and for all."

I nodded. Brian James hadn't lasted long in Russian prison. When Adam had let us know of his death, my tender-hearted wife had surprised me by expressing grief at his passing. She had stared at me with tears in her eyes. "No one should waste their life like that, Joshua. He had everything given to him and threw it all away. And he died alone. That wasn't living. I pity him. I mourn the waste of his entire life, not his death." I had held her in my arms and let her cry, amazed at her capacity for forgiveness.

Reaching over, I pulled her onto my lap. "My publishers want me to come there and meet with them. Do a couple interviews about the new books. I've been stalling them but I could make the arrangements ..." my voice trailed off. I refused to pressure her. This had to be her decision. And, whatever she decided, I would support her. I didn't care what anyone else thought or said. Rabbit's comfort and opinion were the only things that mattered.

"Then talk to them, Joshua," she sighed quietly. "We'll do it together."

I lifted her face and studied her expressive eyes, which always told me what she was thinking. They stared back, nervous, but resolved.

I nodded. "I'll make the arrangements, Rabbit."

She burrowed into my chest and my arms tightened around her. "Just promise me you'll stay close, Joshua."

"I won't let you out of my sight," I promised.

"Good to know," she whispered as she leaned up and kissed me.

I startled as I felt Rabbit's arms wrap around me. "Come to bed, sweetheart."

Turning, I wrapped her in my arms tightly. "I was just watching them sleep."

"And thinking about tomorrow?"

I nodded.

Her arms tightened. "They'll be fine. Cecilia and Trevor will take good care of them. We're only a couple hours away. John can have us home fast if we have to get here."

"I'm more worried I won't be able to handle this, Rabbit," I confessed sadly, thinking of the goals Trina wanted me to achieve, or at least attempt to achieve. "I feel totally overwhelmed right now at the thought of all we are going to do in the next couple days."

She tilted her head up toward me, frowning. "Then stop thinking about the whole picture, Joshua. We'll take it one goal, one new experience at a time. Together. Just one thing at a time, okay?"

Leaning down, I captured her lips with mine. "You are so smart," I whispered, as I dragged my lips up to her ear and nibbled on her soft lobe.

She chuckled quietly. "First step is coming back to bed."

"Not much point to that, really. I'm not sure I can sleep."

Her hands wound into my hair, pulling me back to her lips. "Pretty sure I can figure out a way of tiring you out, sweetheart. But you have to come back to bed first."

I smiled at her playful tone and leaning down, lifted her up into my arms. "Lead the way, Mrs. Bennett."

The sound of the helicopter approaching the next morning kicked my nerves from frayed into overdrive. Goal number one: leave the property. Although I could do it most of the time without a reaction, today was different. Travelling by helicopter meant I was farther away than I had been in a long time. Bear, who hated the sound, slunk down the hallway to the bedroom, where I knew he would hide until after we had left and the sound of the chopper had faded away. Part of me wanted to join him in his escape. My eyes flew to Rabbit, who was holding Elly as she chatted quietly with Trevor and Cecilia. My own arms tightened slightly on Jack, who slept peacefully in my arms, replete after his morning meal.

How would he and Elly react when they woke up and we weren't here? What if Cecilia couldn't get them to settle? My mind raced as I tried to remember if I had listed all the ways of distracting them when they fussed. I stood up, intent on making sure the pacifiers were on the counter, when Rabbit's voice broke through my thoughts. "Joshua."

I looked over at her. "They'll be fine. Let's go put them in their cribs and then we have to go." She regarded me quietly for a moment and came over to where I was standing. Her hand came up and caressed my cheek. "One step at a time, Joshua. Now, breathe for me. Deep, calming breaths. You can do this."

Nodding, I focused on her breathing and matched it. After a minute, I opened my eyes and smiled at her. Silently, I followed her down the hall, and together we kissed our children, tucked them safely into their beds and returned to the kitchen. I could feel her slight tremor as we walked away, and I drew her into my side tightly in silent support.

Cecilia smiled at us. "Trevor took your bags out." She handed me a folder. "This has everything in it, Joshua: your itinerary, meeting schedules and some notes I made for you. Adam is meeting you at the airport."

I looked at her surprised. "Why?"

She smiled. "We thought a friendly face would make you both feel better. You're having dinner with him, Heather, Tracy and Frank tonight, once you finish your meetings with the publisher. Your interviews are tomorrow. We are going to be fine. Daniel and Ellen are coming out later today so, between all of us, your babies are in capable hands."

Lizzy smiled. "We know that. Thanks, Cecilia."

I looked down at my wife. "Ready to do this?"

She took in a deep breath. "Right beside you, Joshua."

Leaning down, I kissed her forehead gently. "Good to know, Rabbit."

Both Rabbit and I were solemn as the chopper took off and we watched our home fading from view. Our hands were clasped tightly together and I kept my gaze on her, trying to match my breathing with hers. John wasted no time lifting off once we were onboard, and I was sure he was under strict instructions not to listen to any sudden excuses as to not leaving. I squeezed her hand gently and raised it to my mouth, kissing it lovingly; grateful she was there with me. I knew she was anxious about returning to Toronto and even more anxious about being away from the children for a long period of time. We needed each other to be strong.

Arriving at the airport, it was a relief to see Adam's large frame waiting for us, his wife, Heather, by his side. Hugs and pleasantries were exchanged and John shook my hand, promising to be ready to take off the next day by 6 p.m. "You have your phone?" I asked quietly. Smiling in understanding, he nodded. "We can take off anytime, if needed, Joshua. Just call and I'll make all the necessary arrangements."

"Thanks, John."

He grinned and waved at us before leaving to file his paperwork and I turned to Adam. "What's the plan?"

He chuckled and withdrew a sheet of paper from his pocket. "Well, according to Cecilia's itinerary, once we check you into the hotel, we have time for lunch before you need to be at the office. Cecilia, in her great wisdom, has you staying in a hotel that is walking distance from your publishers, as well as one of our favorite restaurants. So, let's start there, shall we?"

I nodded and we walked to the car, Lizzy's hand tightly clasping mine. My phone chirped with an incoming message and I grinned when I saw the pictures that came on the screen. Smiling, I handed the phone to Lizzy and watched her delight as she looked at pictures of the twins waking up from their nap and having a bottle. Cecilia was obviously taking the pictures while Daniel and Ellen fed the babies, Bear watching over them. Squeezing her hand, I leaned over and whispered to her. "They're both fine, Mommy." Her eyes were misty as she nodded at me, handing the phone back, but not speaking. Leaning over, I kissed her forehead. "I'm sure Cecilia will send pictures all day. And, you can call as often as you want, okay?"

"That's a good thing." She nodded.

Wrapping my arm around her, I drew her tightly against me in the back of the car. "It is, Rabbit."

⟫•◦•◉•◦•⟪

Adam and Heather were full of gossip and funny stories during lunch, helping both Lizzy and I relax. Cecilia had indeed picked a great hotel and the building my meetings were in was literally a ten minute walk away. It would cross another item off my list: taking a walk on the streets in Toronto, something I had not done since the attack.

"How long do you expect your meetings to be?" Adam asked as we were eating lunch.

I shrugged. "No more than a few hours. It is mostly to meet everyone, go over the illustrations and the book layouts, and make a final decision on how to package them."

Adam nodded. "And you, Lizzy?" His tone, as always, was gentle when he spoke to her. "What are your plans?"

"I was going to accompany Joshua, and just wait in the reception area until he was done. I have a book with me."

Adam and Heather exchanged a glance.

"I wanted to introduce her to some people there, but we hadn't decided on exactly what was happening after that," I hedged. The truth was, I wanted Rabbit to go back to the hotel and relax and she was insisting on staying in the building to wait for me. I didn't want her sitting alone in a waiting room for the afternoon, but she seemed to feel she needed to be there, and she felt she would be uncomfortable sitting in during my meetings, even though I assured her she was welcome.

Heather spoke up. "I thought maybe you would like to go shopping, Lizzy. I know you don't get into the big city very often and thought you would like to go to a few different stores? There is an amazing children's store here. So many wonderful things for your little ones!"

I watched a flurry of emotions go through Lizzy's expressive eyes. She looked at me, completely conflicted. I knew she would love to go and buy the children some things, yet she had already decided she needed to be where I was. I also saw her anxious reaction to the thought of being out in public, in Toronto, without me beside her. Adam leaned forward. "Tracy was hoping to spend a little time with you also, and she thought she would accompany you shopping. Frank is, ah, busy this afternoon, but she is free for the afternoon. I've always been interested in the book creation process so I had hoped Joshua might allow me to sit with him in his meetings, just as an interested observer. Then we could meet after back at the hotel."

I looked at him, instantly seeing through his causal offer. Lizzy could go shopping, enjoy herself with friends and Frank was going to be following them. She would be perfectly safe. Adam would be with me, so I wouldn't be alone. He would be introduced as my lawyer and no one at the office would think twice about him being there. Walking with him,

I would undoubtedly be safe. Closing my eyes, I took in a deep breath, part of me grateful for friends who cared so much that they went to these lengths to help us, and part of me annoyed I needed them. But when I opened my eyes and met Adam's steady gaze, the only thing I could feel was gratitude. I nodded silently at him before I turned to Lizzy, smiling. "What do you think, Rabbit? Shopping with Tracy and Heather sounds like a great deal more fun than sitting in the hotel or the reception area."

She seemed to hesitate, so I slid my chair closer and reached for her hands in comfort. "What is it?"

"I promised you I would stay with you. Are you sure you're okay with this?" she asked, her voice anxious.

"Yes, Rabbit." I nodded. "It's a great solution. I don't want you sitting in the waiting room or by yourself in the hotel, feeling anxious. You can meet everyone tomorrow before my interviews. This afternoon, go and do something fun with Heather; I'm more than good with that idea. I can concentrate on what I came here to do. You can go hog wild and buy Jack and Elly some presents. They'd love that," I encouraged her. "Maybe buy yourself some things as well?"

She smiled up at me tenderly, reaching up to caress my cheek. "So brave, Joshua. I knew you could do this."

Leaning down, I kissed her. "Because you're beside me, Rabbit. That's the reason. We will both accomplish another goal." I pulled back. "So, we ready to do this?"

Rabbit smiled and nodded.

Grinning, I wrapped my arm around her and we turned to Adam and Heather. "You have a shopping partner, Heather. Do me a favor, though?"

Heather smiled. "What's that, Joshua?"

"Make sure she spends a ton of money, okay? And not just on the babies. I want her to buy anything she wants."

Heather clapped her hands in delight as Adam shook his head in disbelief. "You have no idea what you just unleashed, Joshua."

Rabbit chuckled. "I'll see what I can do, Joshua. And, Adam? Tell Frank he doesn't have to skulk in the shadows, I am quite okay with him joining us."

Adam threw his head back in laughter. "Can't fool you for a minute can we, Lizzy?"

She shook her head. I smiled as I leaned forward, kissing her cheek, my words quiet. "It's for your safety and my peace of mind, Rabbit. Don't be upset."

She shook her head. "I'm not."

Then she smiled widely at me. "Besides, Frank can carry all the bags for us." She waggled her eyebrow. "I plan on there being many of them."

I chuckled, thrilled at how well this seemed to be going. "Good to know, Rabbit."

We all laughed as Adam picked up his phone and began typing. "I'll fill him in on his new assignment."

I sat back quietly, knowing that, thanks to good friends and their support, I could do this.

"That was very interesting, Joshua. Thanks for letting me sit in." Adam slapped me on the shoulder as I narrowed my eyes at him, trying to gauge if he was being sarcastic. But his returning gaze was steady and honest. He smiled at me. "Really. I had no idea how much work goes on behind the scenes of putting a book together. Fascinating, actually."

I nodded. "It's quite the process, especially with the illustration aspect. That's a first for me, as well. My other books, I just sort of discussed the covers and someone else put it together."

"You are very talented. Lizzy is gonna love her surprise."

I grinned as I looked at the package in my hand—the advance copies of the first three books. Today, we had finalized the next three, and I would see those soon. I hadn't known these were ready yet and I knew she would be thrilled to see them. I could hardly wait to see her reaction to my inscription, which was, of course, dedicated to her and my own little bunnies.

Adam paused. "Walk or cab?"

I hesitated. Our lunch had run so long after I had seen Rabbit safely off with Frank that we had grabbed a cab over to the office. Watching her leave had been very difficult and I wasn't able to face walking down the street at that point. Drawing in a deep breath, I made a decision. "Walk."

"Directly to the hotel?"

I shook my head. I needed to do this. "Let's go the long way, Adam."

"Pushing all your limits today, Joshua?"

I nodded.

Adam turned in the opposite direction of the hotel. "Let's go."

I was surprisingly relaxed as Adam and I walked along, discussing some of the changes I saw in the buildings and skyline. Having his large presence beside me, as well as the fact that the sun was still out, no doubt helped me stay focused. It wasn't until we stopped at a light and I looked down the street, realizing where I was, that I stopped and stiffened.

"Joshua?"

I shook my head wordlessly, my chest tight as I stared down the block. I glanced at Adam who was watching me warily and, before my determination could falter, I began walking. I knew Adam was behind me. I knew daylight lingered. I knew I was safe. Yet my heart beat rapidly and my stomach clenched as I stopped at the entrance to an alley and stood silently, my muscles coiled and tense, my breathing rapid.

"Is this where you were attacked, Joshua?" Adam's voice was low and calm.

I nodded.

"You lived around here?"

I swallowed deeply. "The complex is two blocks farther down." My voice was shaky. "I was so close to home. Five minutes either way and they probably would have been in another alley."

"Attacking someone else."

My head snapped in his direction. "I never thought of that."

He shrugged. "Makes sense. They were so high; they were going to attack someone until they got what they wanted."

"I always wondered if they would have beaten me so badly if I had more money on me. If they had gotten what they wanted."

"From the reports I read, Joshua, they were half out of their minds. I think you were in for a world of pain no matter what."

I was silent. I took in a deep breath and took a few steps forward. The alley itself was the same as any other alley I had seen. A few garbage bins against the walls, some graffiti spray painted on the concrete, a car parked farther down by the back entrance of some business. Nothing that screamed danger or warned you to be frightened. Every step forward had my breath coming out in sharper gasps and my stomach clenching, but I kept moving forward until I was there. The spot I remember being dragged to before my world exploded in a haze of pain and blood.

I stood there, utterly still as I looked around. I could feel my hands clenching in the effort to stay there. Every part of me wanted to run back out of the alley and not stop until I reached the safety of Rabbit's arms. The sudden longing to be home with the babies and her filled me and I felt a shudder run through me. This had been a bad idea. Adam's voice startled me.

"I'm amazed you're able to do this, Joshua."

I shook my head sadly. "I'm fucking terrified right now, Adam."

"Doesn't matter. You're still fucking doing it."

I looked at him wearily.

"You are. What happened here changed your life irrevocably. Not everyone would be able to stand where you are right now, Joshua. And you are. You're standing. You're living. You fucking overcame what happened and you're here. You're okay. That, in my books, is fucking amazing. You should be so proud of yourself." He shook his head. "Lizzy is going to be. At least, she will be once she finishes kicking my ass for letting you do this without her knowing."

I had to chuckle at his last statement.

"You have a great life, Joshua. Success, friends. Children. And your Rabbit."

I looked at him and nodded.

"Especially Rabbit."

He smiled. "Are you ready to go and see her now?"

I looked around the alley and sighed shakily in relief. Adam was right. I had overcome what happened here. Now I could put it in the past and move forward.

I nodded. "Yeah. I'm ready to go. I need her now."

He clapped me on the shoulder. "No doubt she is ready for you as well. Big afternoon for both of you, I'd say." He smiled. "Tonight is a night to celebrate, my friend."

I nodded and followed him out of the alley.

I didn't look back.

I walked into the hotel suite, calling Rabbit's name. I heard her muffled voice and followed it, smiling as I saw a large pile of bags in the bedroom and finding her up to her neck in bubbles in the deep bathtub in the en-suite. Greedily, my eyes drank her in as she smiled gently at me from the tub.

"I missed you," she murmured. She held out her dripping hand and I moved forward to take it, leaning down to drop a kiss on her forehead. The feeling of home flooded through me the instant I touched her and I felt immense relief at being back with her.

"It's not the hot tub, but it's pretty big. Want to join me?"

I grinned as I hastily removed my clothes. I didn't want big right now; I wanted to be as close to her as I could be. She moved forward and I slipped in behind her, pulling her tight against my chest and wrapping my arms around her. I sighed deeply and rested my chin on her shoulder; breathing in her warm scent, I felt myself relax with her closeness. The room as quiet for a few minutes as we both just rejoiced in the sweetness of being together.

"Were you okay this afternoon, Rabbit?"

"I was nervous at times, but having Frank there helped. I even managed to wander into a few stores on my own and I was okay."

I held her tighter. "That's my brave girl."

"I actually enjoyed myself. It felt good."

"Shopping was a success, I see?"

She nodded, tilting her head up to look at me. "I got so many things for the babies, Joshua. I forgot how huge a selection there can be."

I nuzzled her neck, my tongue swirling over her damp skin. "Tell me you bought some things for yourself, Lizzy."

"I did," she gasped softly as I bit down gently on her earlobe.

"Good."

"I bought you some things as well."

"Thank you. I love them," I whispered into her ear huskily, earning me another shiver.

"You haven't seen them yet."

"Doesn't matter. You picked them. I'll love them." My lips moved down her neck again.

I felt her hands tighten on mine and I pulled back. "Rabbit?"

"Was it awful, Joshua? You look so drawn," she whispered.

I sighed and shook my head, resting it back on her shoulder. "No. It was fine. Great even."

"Something happened. Tell me."

I shifted and pushed her forward, only to spin her and pull her back against me so I could see her face.

"Nice move, Joshua." She winked at me as her legs wrapped around my waist, drawing her closer.

"I still have one or two tricks up my sleeve, Rabbit."

She smiled. "I love your tricks." Then her face became serious. "Tell me, please."

Quietly, I told her about the walk I took with Adam. How it felt to be standing in that alley again. What Adam had said to me, and finally, how desperately I needed to get back to the hotel and be with her.

Tears gathered in her eyes and fell slowly down her face as I spoke. After I was silent, her arms wrapped around me, drawing my head down to her neck as she rubbed loving, gentle caresses over my head and back. I pulled her tightly against me, needing to feel her loving warmth.

"*Joshua*, Adam is right. That is amazing. I am so proud of you, sweetheart. So proud," Her sweet voice praised me. She pulled back slightly and looked down at me. "That wasn't even on your list of goals."

I shook my head. "It just happened."

She smiled. "You are the bravest man I have ever met, Joshua

Bennett. I'm so proud you're mine."

"I didn't feel so brave standing there, shaking."

"But you did it, Joshua. Even terrified, you did it. Not because you had to; you did this for you. Trina is going to be so thrilled!"

Her hands cupped my face. "I told you, sweetheart. One day you would overcome what those bastards did to you. You ended it today. *You* did."

I pulled her to me, crashing my lips against hers, dominating her mouth. I needed to taste her, to fill my head with thoughts of her, of now. "I need a new memory, Rabbit," I pleaded quietly. "Please."

Her arms wound around my head, pulling me closer as she drew my lips back to hers. "I'm here, Joshua. I'm always here."

Her sweetness burned into my brain as she kissed me, her velvet tongue stroking mine. Her hands gently stroked my back, touching me with so much love; I could feel it sinking into my skin, warming me from the inside. All other thoughts ceased to exist as I lost myself to her tender comfort. Wrapped in her embrace, I felt myself centre and loosen, everything else fell away. All that mattered was right now, this moment, this need, and my Rabbit. I groaned as I felt her ease herself up, wrapping herself around me, as I slipped into her warmth. Slowly, she built a rhythm for us, undulating over me. The warm water crashed around us and rained over the edge of the tub, but neither of us cared. My lips could not leave hers, my hands could not move away from her skin as we moved and rocked and loved. Rabbit's body tensed and stilled and she threw her head back with a low, sexy moan. Watching her, I felt her pulse around me, which triggered my own release. I sighed out her name like a prayer as I held her tightly, arching up as I spilled deep within her.

She collapsed against my chest and I held her closely, leaning back in the tub, sinking below the water, warming us both. After a few quiet moments, she glanced up, smiling shyly at me from under her hair which had come loose and fell in waves around her face. She peeked over the edge of the tub and giggled. "Nice job."

I leaned over to take a look and grinned. "Told you I had a couple tricks up my sleeve, Rabbit."

She chuckled. "And one of them was creating Lake Joshua in the bathroom?"

I laughed. "Lake Joshua. I like the sound of that." Leaning up, I grabbed one of the large towels hanging over my head and threw it on the floor. "That can start soaking it up."

She smiled gently at me. "Better now?"

I stroked her cheek. "You always make it better, Rabbit."

"Good to know." She looked around. "I don't know what time it is.

Do we have time to add some more water and just cuddle before we go to dinner?"

I reached over and turned the taps on. "We'll make time." I wrapped her tightly against me. "Stay right here, Rabbit."

We could be late for dinner.

Right now this was where we needed to be.

❖❖❖❖❖

I watched Lizzy's mood change slowly during dinner. She remained smiling and seemingly interested, answering questions and chatting with the group, but I could sense her distress growing. Cecilia sent us both pictures of the twins settled down for the night and I noticed that both times they arrived, Lizzy had excused herself. When she returned from the restroom, I saw her eyes were overly bright and her manner slightly different. No one else seemed to notice, but I knew what was wrong. She was homesick and missing her children. Tonight was *her* biggest challenge.

Internally, I shook my head. My brave wife was doing exactly what she thought she should be doing and acting accordingly, but I knew I could help. Quietly, I excused myself and went to make two important phone calls. When I returned, the group was discussing moving on to a local nightclub, but I knew that wasn't what Lizzy wanted. "If you don't mind, I think Lizzy and I will pass. I am rather weary from the day and I need to call it a night soon," I informed them as Lizzy shot me a grateful glance.

Outside, goodbyes were exchanged and the others departed. Lizzy and I were both silent on the way back to the hotel, content to simply hold hands in the cab. Once we were in the room, she moved into the bathroom and I changed into my sleep pants and sat waiting for her. When she came out, I held my hand out and pulled her into my arms. "Tell me," I said quietly.

"It's silly."

"Tell me anyway."

Her eyes were filled with tears when she looked at me. "I've never failed to be there to tuck them in. I miss them so much, Joshua."

I smiled lovingly at her. "Why is that silly, Lizzy?"

"Because its only one night. It's one of my goals to be away from them for one night … but I hate it!" And then she burst into tears.

I pulled her down onto my lap and held her.

"You've been so brave and accomplished so much and I can't even do this without getting all emotional," she sobbed.

"Hey," I lifted her chin. "Rabbit, you've been just as brave as I have. You are doing it. You may not like it but you are still doing it. What you are feeling is perfectly natural, Rabbit. You're their mother; of course you miss them. I miss them as well."

"I want to go home," she whispered, her voice shaking.

I soothed the hair away from her face and wiped the tears from her cheeks. "I do as well. So I made a call and I changed my interviews to eight o'clock. I also called John. He is making the arrangements and we'll be in the chopper by eleven. Home after lunch. We'll be there when the babies wake up from their nap instead of after they've gone to bed. You can tuck them in tomorrow night. We both will. How does that sound?"

Her arms flung around my neck, her sobs muffled as she buried her head in my shoulder. I rocked her for a minute and then pulled back.

"We both accomplished something today, Lizzy. We have both faced a fear from our past. We both got some closure. But our life, our future, is waiting for us at home. As far as I'm concerned, the trip was a success, but I am done with the goals. We'll come back, whenever you want. We'll bring the babies with us. Stay longer. But for now, we go home. It's what we both need and that is way more important than checking off another item from a list. You are more important than that."

Her hand cupped my cheek.

"I love you, Joshua. Thank you."

I kissed her gently. "Anything you need, Rabbit."

"You take such good care of me and our family," she whispered as she snuggled against my chest.

I smiled down at my sweet wife, my lips grazing her head. "Good to know, Rabbit. Good to know."

⇒THE END⇐

⇒ABOUT THE AUTHOR⇐

Melanie Moreland lives a happy and content life in a quiet area of Ontario with her husband and fur children. Nothing means more to her than her friends and family, and she cherishes every moment spent with them.

Known as the quiet one with the big laugh, Melanie works at a local university and for its football team. Her (box) office job, while demanding, is rewarding as she cheers on her team to victory.

While seriously addicted to coffee, and somewhat challenged with all things computer-related and technical, she relishes baking, cooking, and trying new recipes for people to sample. She loves to throw dinner parties and socialize, and also enjoys traveling, here and abroad, but finds coming home is always the best part of any trip.

Melanie delights in a good romance story with some bumps along the way, but is a true believer in happily ever after. When her head isn't buried in a book, it is bent over a keyboard, furiously typing away as her characters dictate their creative storylines to her even more inspired tales, for all to enjoy.

Printed in Great Britain
by Amazon

45318468R00183